Prais

'A powerful account of individual lives trapped in one of the greatest tragedies of the 20th century.' *Times*

'Exquisite... It is Zuleikha's perspective and the way in which she adapts that capture our attention... Her transformation from a passive to a powerful protagonist is one of the joys of Yakhina's work.'
Financial Times

'Guzel Yakhina's sprawling, ambitious first novel *Zuleikha* reminds us just how brutal the Soviet system was... *Zuleikha* does an admirable job of dramatizing a historical period rapidly receding into the forgotten past... Dramatic and eventful, [it] sweeps us into a distant era.' *New York Times Book Review*

'Written in a rich and highly visual prose... Zuleikha's story is one of injustice and pain, but also of a woman's emancipation and renewal.' *Associated Press*

'Guzel Yakhina's novel hits the heart. It's a powerful anthem for love and tenderness in hell.'
Ludmila Ulitskaya, author of *The Big Green Tent*

'An intimate story of human endurance.' *Calvert Journal*

'While many writers have attempted to comprehend Soviet history's darkest moment, Yakhina finds a way to make it new.'
Russia Beyond the Headlines

'[A] story of survival and eventual triumph. Winner of the 2015 Russian Booker prize, this debut novel draws heavily on the first-person account of the author's grandmother, a Gulag survivor.'
The Millions, Most Anticipated Books of 2019

'A powerful Russian saga, giving an immense overview of life under communist rule… This author is a master at painting an image of the world as it was then.' *Marjorie's World of Books*

'*Zuleikha* has an energy that is hard to resist.' *Strong Words*

'Yakhina's debut novel has shaken the Russian book world so deeply over its first three years of life that her second book topped the 2018 sales charts alongside international bestsellers by Dan Brown and Jojo Moyes… This tale of a woman who holds onto compassion while enduring atrocity also features cinematic narration and intricate plot construction.'
Meduza, 2019's Top Russia-Related Books

Zuleikha

Guzel Yakhina

*Translated from the Russian
by Lisa C. Hayden*

ONEWORLD

A Oneworld Book

First published in North America, Great Britain and Australia by Oneworld Publications, 2019
This paperback edition published 2019, Reprinted, 2020, 2023
Originally published in Russian as Зулейха открывает глаза by
AST, Redaktsia Eleny Shubinoi imprint, 2015

Published by arrangement with ELKOST Intl. Literary Agency

Copyright © Guzel Yakhina, 2015, 2019
Translation copyright © Lisa C. Hayden, 2019

The moral right of Guzel Yakhina to be identified as the Author of this work has been asserted
by her in accordance with the Copyright, Designs and Patents Act 1988

ISBN 978-1-78607-684-7
eBook ISBN 978-1-78607-350-1

Published with the support of the Institute for Literary Translation (Russia)

This book has been selected to receive financial assistance from English PEN's PEN Translates
programme, supported by Arts Council England. English PEN exists to promote literature and
our understanding of it, to uphold writers' freedoms around the world, to campaign against the
persecution and imprisonment of writers for stating their views, and to promote the friendly
co-operation of writers and the free exchange of ideas. www.englishpen.org

Typeset by Fakenham Prepress Solutions, Fakenham, Norfolk NR21 8NL
Printed and bound in Great Britain by Clays Ltd, Elcograf S.p.A.

Oneworld Publications
10 Bloomsbury Street
London WC1B 3SR
England

Stay up to date with the latest books,
special offers, and exclusive content from
Oneworld with our newsletter

Sign up on our website
oneworld-publications.com

CONTENTS

PART ONE

THE PITIFUL HEN

ONE DAY

Zuleikha opens her eyes. It's as dark as a cellar. Geese sigh sleepily behind a thin curtain. A month-old foal smacks his lips, searching for his mother's udder. A January blizzard moans, muffled, outside the window by the head of the bed. Thanks to Murtaza, though, no draft comes through the cracks. He sealed up the windows before the cold weather set in. Murtaza is a good master of the house. And a good husband. His snoring booms and rumbles in the men's quarters. Sleep soundly: the deepest sleep is just before dawn.

It's time. *All-powerful Allah, may what has been envisioned be fulfilled. May nobody awaken.*

Zuleikha noiselessly lowers one bare foot then the other to the floor, leans against the stove, and stands. The stove went out during the night, its warmth is gone, and the cold floor burns the soles of her feet. She can't put on shoes. She wouldn't be able to make her way silently in her little felt boots; some floorboard or other would surely creak. Fine, Zuleikha will manage. Holding the rough side of the stove with her hand, she feels her way out of the women's quarters. It's narrow and cramped in here but she remembers every corner, every little shelf: for half her life she's been slipping back and forth like a pendulum, carrying full, hot bowls from the big kettle to the men's quarters, then empty, cold bowls back from the men's quarters.

How many years has she been married? Fifteen of her thirty? Is that half? It's probably even more than that. She'll have to ask Murtaza when he's in a good mood – let him count it.

Don't stumble on the rug. Don't hit a bare foot on the trunk with the metal trim, to the right, by the wall. Step over the squeaky board where the stove curves. Scurry soundlessly behind the printed cotton curtain separating the women's quarters of the log house from the men's … It's not far to the door now.

Murtaza's snores are closer. *Sleep, sleep, for Allah's sake.* A wife shouldn't hide anything from her husband, but sometimes she must, there's no helping it.

The main thing now is not to wake the animals. They usually sleep in the winter shed but Murtaza orders the birds and young animals to be brought inside during cold snaps. The geese aren't stirring but the foal taps his hoof and shakes his head; he's awake, the imp. He's sharp: he'll be a good horse. Zuleikha stretches her hand through the curtain and touches his velvety muzzle: *Calm down, you know me.* His nostrils snuffle gratefully into her palm, recognizing her. Zuleikha wipes her damp fingers on her nightshirt and lightly pushes the door with her shoulder. Thick and padded with felt for the winter, the door gives way heavily, and a frosty, biting cloud flies in through the crack. She takes a big step over the high threshold so as not to jinx anything – treading on it now and disturbing the evil spirits would be all she needs – and then she's in the entrance hall. She closes the door and leans her back against it.

Glory be to Allah, part of the journey has been made.

It's as cold in the hallway as outside, nipping at Zuleikha's skin so her nightshirt doesn't warm her. Streams of icy air beat at the soles of her feet through cracks in the floor. This isn't what troubles her, though.

What troubles her is behind the door opposite.

Ubyrly Karchyk – the Vampire Hag. That's what Zuleikha calls her, to herself. She thanks the Almighty that they don't live in the same house as her mother-in-law. Murtaza's home is spacious, two houses connected by a common entrance hall. On the day forty-five-year-old Murtaza brought fifteen-year-old Zuleikha into the house, the Vampire Hag – her face a picture of martyred grief – dragged her own numerous trunks, bundles, and dishes into the guest house, and occupied the whole place. "Don't touch!" she shouted menacingly at her son when he tried to help her move. Then she didn't speak to him for two months. That same year, she quickly and hopelessly began to go blind, and then, shortly thereafter, to lose her hearing. A couple of years later, she was as blind and deaf as a rock. She now talks constantly and can't be stopped.

Nobody knows how old she really is. She herself insists she's a hundred. Murtaza sat down to count recently, and he sat for a long time before announcing: "Mama's right, she truly is around a hundred." He was a late child and is already almost an old man himself.

The Vampire Hag usually wakes up before everyone else and carries her carefully guarded treasure to the entrance hall: an elegant milky-white porcelain chamber pot with a fanciful lid and delicate blue cornflowers on the side. Murtaza brought it back from Kazan as a gift at one time or other. Zuleikha is supposed to jump at her mother-in-law's call, then empty and carefully wash out the precious vessel first thing, before she stokes the fire in the stove, makes the dough, and takes the cow out to the herd. Woe unto Zuleikha if she sleeps through the morning wake-up call. It's happened twice in fifteen years and she doesn't allow herself to recall the consequences.

For now, it's quiet behind the door. *Go on, Zuleikha, you pitiful hen, hurry up.* It was the Vampire Hag who first called her *zhebegyan tavyk* – pitiful hen. Zuleikha started calling herself this after a while, too, without even noticing.

She steals into the depths of the hallway, toward the attic staircase. She gropes at the smooth banister. The steps are steep; the frozen boards occasionally groan just enough to be heard. Scents of chilly wood, frozen dust, dried herbs, and a barely noticeable aroma of salted goose waft down from above. Zuleikha goes up: the blizzard's din is closer, and the wind pounds at the roof and howls at the corners.

She decides to go on all fours across the attic because were she to walk, the boards would creak right over the sleeping Murtaza's head. If she crawls, though, she can scurry through. She weighs so little that Murtaza can lift her with one hand, as if she were a young ram. She pulls her nightshirt to her chest so it won't get all dusty, twists it, takes the end in her teeth, and gropes her way between boxes, crates, and wooden tools, cautiously crawling over the crossbeams. Her forehead knocks into the wall. Finally.

She raises herself up a little and peers out of the small attic window. She can hardly make out the houses of her native Yulbash, all drifted in snow, through the dark, gray gloom just before morning. Murtaza once counted, reaching a total of more than a hundred and twenty homesteads. A large village, that's for sure. A village road smoothly curves and flows off toward the horizon, like a river. Windows are already lighting in some houses. *Quickly, Zuleikha.*

She stands and reaches up. Something heavy and smooth, with large bumps, settles into her hands: salted goose. Her stomach jolts, growling in demand. No, she can't take the goose. She lets go of the bird and searches further. Here! Hanging to the left of the attic window are large, heavy sheets of paste that have hardened in the cold but give off a slight fruity smell. Apple *pastila*. The confection was painstakingly cooked in the oven, neatly rolled out on wide boards, and dried with care on the roof, soaking up hot

August sun and cool September winds. You can bite off a tiny bit and dissolve it for a long time, rolling the rough, sour little piece along the roof of your mouth, or you can cram a lot in, chewing and chewing the resilient wad and spitting occasional seeds into your palm. Your mouth waters right away.

Zuleikha tears a couple of sheets of *pastila* from the string, rolls them up tightly, and sticks them under her arm. She runs a hand over the rest. There's still a lot, quite a lot, left. Murtaza shouldn't figure anything out.

And now to go back.

She kneels and crawls toward the stairs. The rolled-up *pastila* prevents her from moving quickly. She truly is a pitiful hen now: she hadn't even thought to bring any kind of bag with her. Zuleikha goes down the stairs slowly, walking on the edges of her curled-up feet because the soles are so numb she can't feel them. When she reaches the last step, the door on the Vampire Hag's side swings open noisily and a shadowy silhouette appears in the black opening. A heavy walking stick knocks at the floor.

"Anybody there?" the Vampire Hag's deep, masculine voice asks the darkness.

Zuleikha goes still. Her heart pounds and her stomach shrinks into an icy ball. She wasn't fast enough. The *pastila* is thawing, softening under her arm.

The Vampire Hag takes a step forward. In fifteen years of blindness, she has learned the house by heart, so she moves around here freely and confidently.

Zuleikha flies up a couple of stairs, her elbow squeezing the softened *pastila* to her body more firmly.

The old woman turns her chin in one direction then another. She doesn't hear or see a thing but she senses something, the old witch. Yes, a Vampire Hag. Her walking stick knocks loudly, closer and closer. Oh, she'll wake up Murtaza!

7

Zuleikha jumps a few steps higher, presses against the banister, and licks her chapped lips.

The white silhouette stops at the foot of the stairs. The old woman's sniffing is audible as she noisily draws air through her nostrils. Zuleikha brings her palms to her face. Yes, they smell of goose and apples. The Vampire Hag makes a sudden, deft lunge forward and swings, beating at the stairs with her long walking stick, as if she's hacking them in half with a sword. The end of the stick whistles somewhere very close and smashes into a board, half a toe's length from the bare sole of Zuleikha's foot. Feeling faint from fright, Zuleikha flops on the steps like dough. If the old witch strikes once more … The Vampire Hag mumbles something unintelligible and pulls the walking stick toward herself. The chamber pot clinks dully in the dark.

"Zuleikha!" The Vampire Hag's shout blares toward her son's quarters.

Mornings usually start like this in their home.

Zuleikha forces herself to swallow. Has she really escaped notice? Carefully placing her feet, Zuleikha creeps down the steps. She bides her time for a couple of moments.

"Zuleikhaaa!"

Now it's time. Her mother-in-law doesn't like to say it a third time. Zuleikha bounds over to the Vampire Hag, "Right here, right here, Mama!" and she takes from her hands a heavy pot covered with a warm, sticky moistness, just as she does every day.

"You turned up, you pitiful hen," her mother-in-law grumbles. "All you know how to do is sleep, you lazybones."

Murtaza has probably already woken up from the noise and may come out to the hallway. Zuleikha presses the rolled-up *pastila* more tightly under her arm (she can't lose it outside!), gropes with her feet at someone's felt boots on the floor, and races out. The storm beats at her chest and takes her in its solid fist, trying to knock her down. Zuleikha's nightshirt rises like a bell. The front steps have turned into a snowdrift overnight and Zuleikha walks down, feeling carefully for the steps with her feet. She trudges to the outhouse, sinking in almost to her knees. She fights the wind to open the door. She hurls the contents of the chamber pot into the icy hole. When she comes back inside, the Vampire Hag has already gone to her part of the house.

Murtaza drowsily greets Zuleikha at the threshold with a kerosene lamp in his hand. His bushy eyebrows are knitted toward the bridge of his nose, and his cheeks, still creased from sleep, have wrinkles so deep they might have been carved with a knife.

"You lost your mind, woman? Out in a blizzard, undressed?"

"I just took Mama's pot out and back."

"You want to lie around sick half the winter again? So the whole household's on me?"

"What do you mean, Murtaza? I didn't get cold at all. Look!" Zuleikha holds out her bright-red palms, firmly pressing her elbows to her waist; the *pastila* bulges under her arm. Is it visible under her shirt? The fabric got wet in the snow and is clinging to her.

But Murtaza's angry and isn't even looking at her. He spits off to the side, stroking his shaved skull and combing his splayed fingers through his scruffy beard.

"Get us some food. And be ready to leave after you clear the yard. We're going for firewood."

Zuleikha gives a low nod and scurries behind the curtain.

She did it! She really did it – yes, she, Zuleikha, yes, she, the pitiful hen! And there they are, the spoils: two crumpled, twisted, clumped-up pieces of the most delicious *pastila*. Will she be able to deliver it today? And where should she hide these riches? The Vampire Hag roots around in their things when they're out so she can't leave it in the house. She'll have to bring it with her. Of course that's dangerous. But Allah seems to be on her side today, so she should be lucky.

Zuleikha tightly rolls the *pastila* into a long band and winds it around her waist. She lowers her nightshirt over it and puts on a smock and baggy wide pants. She braids her hair and throws on a scarf.

The dense gloom outside is thinning by the head of her bed, diluted by the overcast winter morning's feeble light. Zuleikha pulls back the curtains – anything's better than working in the dark. The kerosene lamp standing on the corner of the stove casts a little slanted light on the women's quarters but the economizing Murtaza has turned the wick so low the flame is barely visible. Never mind; she could do all this blindfolded.

A new day is beginning.

By noon, the morning snowstorm has subsided and the sun is peering out of a sky that has turned bright blue. They set off for firewood.

Zuleikha is sitting at the rear of the sledge, her back to Murtaza, watching the houses of Yulbash grow distant. Green, yellow, deep blue, they're looking out from under the snowbanks like brightly colored mushrooms. Tall white candles of smoke melt away in the celestial blueness. Snow crunches loudly and deliciously under the runners. Sandugach, perky in the frosty cold, occasionally snorts and shakes her mane. The old sheepskin under Zuleikha warms her. The precious band around her belly is warm and heats her, too. If only she can manage to deliver it today.

Her arms and back ache. A lot of snow piled up during the night and Zuleikha spent a long time sinking her shovel into the snowbanks to clear broad paths in the yard, from the front steps to the large storehouse, to the small storehouse, to the privy, to the winter shed, and to the back yard. After all that work, it's nice to sit and do nothing on the rhythmically swaying sledge, to sit so comfortably, bundled up in a strong-smelling sheepskin coat, to stick her numbed hands into her sleeves, rest her chin on her chest, and close her eyes …

"Wake up, woman, we're there."

Gigantic trees surround the sledge. White pillows of snow on spruce boughs and sprawling heads of pine trees. Rime on birch branches as fine and long as a woman's hair. Powerful walls of snowdrifts. Silence for many versts around.

Murtaza binds laced snowshoes to his felt boots, jumps down from the sledge, flings his rifle on his back, and tucks a large axe into his belt. He takes his poles in his hands and doesn't look back as he confidently tramps a path into the thicket. Zuleikha is right behind him.

The forest near Yulbash is good, bountiful. In the summer it feeds the villagers with large wild strawberries and sweet-beaded raspberries; there are pungent mushrooms in autumn. There is a lot of game. The Chishme flows from the forest's depths, usually gentle, shallow, and filled with swift fish and sluggish crayfish, but it's rapid, grumbling, and swollen with meltwater and mud in the spring. During the Great Famine, it was these alone – the forest and the river – that saved people. And Allah's mercy, too, of course.

Murtaza has gone a long way today, almost to the end of the forest road. This road was built in the old days and leads through to the far border of the light part of the forest. It then extends into Last Clearing, which is surrounded by nine crooked pines, and breaks off. There is no further road. The forest ends and there begins the *urman*: dense evergreen woods, thickets broken by storms, and the abode of wild animals, forest spirits, and all kinds of evil. Centuries-old black spruce trees with sharp, spear-like tops grow so thickly in the *urman* that a horse cannot go through. And there are no pale-colored trees – red pines, speckled birch, or gray oak – whatsoever.

People say it's possible to go to the lands of the Mari people by walking through the *urman*, away from the sun for many days in a row. But what person in his right mind would decide to undertake such a journey? The villagers didn't even dare cross the border of Last Clearing during the time of the Great Famine. They nibbled at tree bark, ground acorns from the oaks, and dug up mouse burrows in search of grain, but they did not venture into the *urman*. The few who did were never seen again.

Zuleikha stops for a moment and places a large basket on the ground. She looks around anxiously – Murtaza really shouldn't have gone this far.

"Is it much further, Murtaza? I can't see Sandugach through the trees anymore."

Her husband doesn't answer; he's up to his waist on the untrodden path, forging his way ahead, pushing his long poles into snowdrifts, and trampling brittle snow with his broad snowshoes. Small clouds of frosty steam puff up over his head. He finally stops near a tall, straight birch with a magnificent growth of *chaga* and approvingly slaps its trunk: *This one.*

First they trample down the snow around the tree. Then Murtaza tosses off his sheepskin coat, grabs the curved axe handle very firmly, points the axe at the gap between trees (*we'll fell it there*), and begins chopping.

The blade glints in the sun and enters the side of the birch with a short, resonant *chakh* sound. "*Akh! Akh!*" answers the echo. The axe chops at the thick bark, intricately engraved all over with black ridges, then pierces the pale-pink woody pulp. Wood chips spatter like tears. An echo fills the forest.

It can be heard in the urman, *too*, Zuleikha thinks, uneasy. She's standing waist-deep in snow a little further away, clasping the basket, and watching Murtaza chop. He raises the axe high, pulling it back slightly, supplely bends his torso, and smoothly swings the blade into the white chip-filled crevice on the side of the tree. He's a strong man, large. And he works ably. She was given a good husband; complaining would be a sin. She herself is small, barely coming up to Murtaza's shoulder.

Soon the birch begins shuddering more and groaning louder. The axe wound in its trunk resembles a mouth wide open in a silent scream. Murtaza tosses the axe, shakes the twigs from his shoulders, and nods at Zuleikha: *Help me.* Together they press their shoulders into the rough tree trunk and push, harder and harder. There's a sharp cracking noise and the birch collapses to the ground with a loud groan of farewell, raising a cloud of snowy dust into the air.

Husband straddles the conquered tree and lops off its fat branches. Wife snaps off the thin branches and collects them in the basket, along with smaller kindling. They work silently for a long time. Zuleikha's lower back aches; exhaustion weighs on her shoulders. Her hands are freezing despite her mittens.

"Murtaza, is it true that in her youth your mother went into the *urman* for several days and came back all in one piece?" Zuleikha straightens her back and bends at the waist, resting. "The holy man's wife told me about it, and she heard it from her granny."

He doesn't answer; he's measuring the axe against a gnarled, crooked branch sticking out from the trunk.

"I'd die of fear if I ended up there. My legs would probably stop working right away. I'd be lying on the ground, my eyes shut tight, and praying nonstop, as long as my tongue would move."

Murtaza strikes hard and the branch springs off to the side, humming and quivering.

"But they say prayers don't work in the *urman*. It's all the same – you die whether you pray or not. What do you think?" Zuleikha lowers her voice. "Are there places on earth that Allah's gaze doesn't reach?"

Murtaza draws his arms far back and drives the axe deeply into a log. The sound rings in the cold air. He takes off his shaggy fur hat, wipes his reddened, blazing, bare skull with his hand, and spits on the ground, savoring it.

He sets to work again.

The basket is soon full. It can't be lifted so it can only be dragged away. The birch has been stripped of branches and chopped into several logs. Long branches lie in neat bundles in the snowdrifts around them.

They haven't noticed darkness is falling. When Zuleikha looks up at the sky, the sun is already hidden behind ragged shreds of cloud. A gust swoops in; the drifting snow whistles and swirls.

"Let's go home, Murtaza; it's getting stormy again."

Her husband doesn't answer as he continues winding rope around fat bunches of firewood. When the last bundle is ready, the storm is already starting to howl between the trees like a wolf, drawn-out and mean.

He points a fur mitten at the logs: *Let's move those first.* There are four logs with the stubs of their former branches, each longer than Zuleikha. Grunting, Murtaza heaves one end of the fattest log from the ground. Zuleikha takes the other end. She can't manage to lift it immediately and dawdles for a while, adjusting her position.

"Come on, woman!" Murtaza cries out impatiently.

Finally, she's done it. She's embracing the log with both arms, pressing her chest into the pink-tinged whiteness of fresh wood that's bristling with long, sharp chips. They're moving toward the sledge. They walk slowly. Her arms shake. *I cannot drop it, Almighty, I cannot drop it.* If it fell on her foot, she'd be a cripple for the rest of her life. It's getting hot and there are warm little streams running down her back and belly. The precious band under her breasts is soaked through – the *pastila* will taste of salt. That doesn't matter, she just needs to take it today …

Sandugach is standing obediently in the same place, lazily shifting from hoof to hoof. There aren't many wolves this winter; *Allah is perfect*, so Murtaza isn't worried about leaving the horse alone for a long time.

Once they've dragged the log onto the sledge, Zuleikha falls alongside it, tossing off her mittens and loosening the shawl around her neck. It hurts to breathe; it's as if she's run through the entire village without stopping.

Murtaza strides back to the firewood without saying a word. Zuleikha crawls down from the sledge and trails along behind him. They drag over the remaining logs. Then the bundles of fat branches. Then the thin branches.

Once the firewood has been stacked on the sledge, a heavy winter dusk is already covering the forest. Only Zuleikha's basket remains by the freshly hewn birch stump.

"Fetch the kindling," Murtaza tells her and starts securing the logs.

The wind has begun blowing in earnest, angrily whipping up clouds of snow and sweeping away the tracks they've trampled. Zuleikha clasps her mittens to her chest and rushes along the disappearing path into the forest's darkness.

By the time she reaches the familiar stump, the basket has already been covered with snow. Zuleikha snaps a branch from a bush and starts wandering around, poking at the snowdrift with the switch. She'll be in for it if she loses the basket. Murtaza will scold her and then cool down; but the Vampire Hag – she'll quarrel to her heart's content, ooze venom, and remind Zuleikha about that basket till the very day she dies.

And there it is, the dear thing, lying there! Zuleikha pulls the heavy basket out from under a layer of drifted snow and exhales, relieved. She can return. But which way? The blizzard dances fiercely around her. White streams of snow are rushing up and down in the air, cloaking Zuleikha, swaddling and entangling her. The sky sags between the sharp tops of the spruces, like a huge piece of gray cotton wool. The trees around her are merging into the darkness and now all resemble one another, like shadows.

There's no path.

"Murtaza!" shouts Zuleikha, as snow pelts her mouth. "Murtazaaa!"

The blizzard sings, peals, and whistles in response.

Her body is weakening and her legs are growing limp, as if they're made of snow, too. Zuleikha sinks to the stump with her back to the wind, holding the basket with one hand and gripping the collar of her sheepskin coat with the other. She can't leave this spot or she'll lose her way. It's best to wait here. Could Murtaza leave her in the forest? Now that would make the Vampire Hag happy. And what about the *pastila* she'd got hold of? Could that really have been for nothing?

"Murtazaaa!"

A large, dark figure in a shaggy fur hat emerges from a swirl of snow. Firmly grasping his wife by the sleeve, Murtaza pulls her through the snowstorm behind him.

He won't allow her to sit on the sledge: there's a lot of firewood and the horse won't make it. And so they walk, Murtaza up front, leading Sandugach by the bridle, and Zuleikha following, holding the back of the sledge, feebly lifting her unsteady feet. Her felt boots are crammed with snow but she doesn't have the strength to quickly shake them out. She needs to keep stride with the sledge. Plod along, left, right, left, right … *Well, come on, Zuleikha, you pathetic hen. You know you're done for if you fall behind. Murtaza won't notice. You'll freeze to death in the forest.*

Even so, what a good person he is to have come back for her. He could have left her there in the thicket. Who's to care if she lives or not? He could have said she lost her way in the forest, he couldn't find her, and a day later nobody would even remember her.

It turns out she can stride along with her eyes closed, too. That's even better because her legs are working but her eyes are resting. The main thing is to keep a firm hold of the sledge.

Snow is beating painfully at her face, getting inside her nose and mouth. Zuleikha raises her head and shakes it off. She's lying on the ground and the back of the sledge is disappearing ahead of her; the white whirling blizzard is all around. She stands, catches up to the sledge, and grasps it tightly. She decides not to close her eyes until they reach their house.

It's already dark when they arrive in the yard. They unload the firewood by the woodpile for Murtaza to split tomorrow, unharness Sandugach, and cover the sledge.

The windowpanes on the Vampire Hag's side are dark and coated with thick frost but Zuleikha knows her mother-in-law senses their arrival. She's standing by the window now, alert to the movements of the floorboards. She's waiting for their jolt when the front door slams, after which they'll tremble pliantly under the master's heavy footsteps. Murtaza will undress, wash after the trip, and go to his mother's quarters. He calls this "our little evening chat." What can you talk about with a deaf old lady? Zuleikha doesn't understand. But these chats are long, sometimes lasting for hours. Murtaza is calm and tranquil when he returns from his mother's house; he might even smile or joke a little.

His evening meeting plays into Zuleikha's hands today. As soon as her husband puts on a clean shirt and goes to see the Vampire Hag, Zuleikha throws her sheepskin coat – which hasn't even dried – on her shoulders and runs out of the house.

The blizzard is covering Yulbash with heavy, coarse snow. Zuleikha trudges down the street, bending low into the wind and leaning forward as if she's praying. Small windows of houses lit with the cozy yellow light of kerosene lamps barely peek out in the darkness.

And there's the edge of town. Here, under the fence of the last house is the home of the *basu kapka iyase:* the edge-of-town spirit. Zuleikha hasn't seen him herself but people say he's very angry, peevish. And how could he be otherwise? That's his line of work – sitting with his nose toward a field and his tail toward Yulbash, chasing evil spirits away from the village, not allowing them beyond the edge of town. He's the intermediary for helping villagers who have requests for the forest spirits. It's serious work so he has no time for merriment.

Zuleikha opens up her sheepskin coat and feels around in the folds of her smock for a long time, unwinding the damp band at her waist.

"I'm sorry to disturb you so often," she says into the blizzard. "If you could just help me once again? Please don't refuse me."

It's no easy matter to please a spirit. You have to know what each spirit likes. For example, the *bichura* living in the entrance hall isn't picky. If you set out a couple of unwashed dishes with leftover porridge or soup, she'll lick them off during the night and be satisfied. The bathhouse *bichura* is more finicky: give her nuts and seeds. The cowshed spirit loves foods made from flour, and the gate spirit prefers ground eggshell. But the edge-of-town spirit likes sweets. That's what Mama taught Zuleikha.

Zuleikha brought candy the first time she came to ask the *basu kapka iyase* for a favor, which was to request that the *zirat iyase*

Guzel Yakhina

– the cemetery spirit – look after her daughters' graves, cover them warmly with snow, and chase away evil, mischievous forest spirits. She later took nuts in honey, crumbly light pastries, and dried berries. Now, she's bringing *pastila* for the first time. Will he like it?

She pulls apart the stuck-together sheets of *pastila* and tosses each one in front of her. The wind catches them and carries them away into the field, where it will twirl and swirl them for some time, bringing them to the *basu kapka iyase*'s lair.

Not one sheet returns to Zuleikha, so the edge-of-town spirit has accepted the treat. This means he will grant her request by having a talk with the cemetery spirit and convincing him. Her daughters will lie in warmth and calm, right up till spring. Zuleikha has been rather afraid of speaking directly with the cemetery spirit. After all, she's a simple woman, not a wisewoman.

She thanks the *basu kapka iyase* – she bows low into the darkness – and quickly hurries home before Murtaza leaves the Vampire Hag's. Her husband is still at his mother's when she runs into the entrance hall. She thanks the Almighty – she fans her face with her hands – for He truly is on Zuleikha's side today.

Exhaustion immediately envelops her in the warmth. Her hands and feet are like lead and her head is like cotton. Her body demands one thing: rest. She quickly rekindles the stove, which has cooled since morning. Sets a place for Murtaza at the wide sleeping bench, tossing some food on it. Runs to the winter shed and rekindles the stove there, too. Feeds the animals, cleans up after them. Brings the foal to Sandugach for an evening feed. Milks Kyubelek, strains the milk. Takes her husband's pillows down from the high storage shelf and plumps them (Murtaza likes sleeping on high pillows). Finally, she can go to her area behind the stove.

Usually it's children who sleep on trunks; grown women are entitled to the small part of the sleeping bench that's separated from the men's quarters by a drape. But the fifteen-year-old Zuleikha was so short when she came into Murtaza's home that the Vampire Hag said on the very first day, boring into her daughter-in-law with eyes that were then still bright, yellow-tinged hazel, "This shorty won't even fall off a trunk." And so they settled Zuleikha on a large, old pressed-tin trunk covered with shiny protruding nails. She hadn't grown since then, so there'd been no need to resettle her elsewhere. And Murtaza occupied the whole sleeping bench.

Zuleikha spreads her mattress and blanket on the trunk, pulls her smock over her head, and begins unplaiting her braids. Her fingers aren't minding her and her head falls to her chest. She hears the door slam through her drowsiness; Murtaza's coming back.

"You here, woman?" he asks from the men's quarters. "Light the stove in the bathhouse. Mama wants to bathe."

Zuleikha buries her face in her hands. The bathhouse takes a long time. And bathing the Vampire Hag … Where will she find the strength? If only there were a couple more moments to sit just like this, without moving. Then the strength would come. And then she would stand. And light it.

"Got it into your head you'd sleep? You sleep in the wagon, sleep at home. Mama's right, you're a lazybones!"

Zuleikha leaps up.

Murtaza is standing in front of her trunk. He has in his hand a kerosene lamp with a flickering flame inside; his broad chin, with a deep dimple in the middle, is tense with anger. Her husband's trembling shadow covers half the stove.

"I'm running, I'm running, Murtaza," she says, her voice hoarse. And she runs.

First clear a path to the bathhouse in the snow; she hadn't cleared it in the morning because she didn't know she'd have to light the stove. Then draw water from the well, twenty buckets of it because the Vampire Hag likes to splash around. Light the stove. Strew some nuts for the *bichura* behind the bench so it doesn't play tricks, like putting out the stove, letting in fumes, or impeding the steaming. Wash the floors. Soak the bundles of birch leaves. Bring dried herbs from the attic – bur-marigold for washing female and male private places, mint for delicious steam – and brew them. Lay out a clean rug in the entrance. Bring clean underclothes for the Vampire Hag, Murtaza, and herself. Don't forget pillows and a pitcher with cold drinking water.

Murtaza put the bathhouse in the corner of the yard, behind the storehouse and shed. He built the stove according to the latest methods, fussing for a long time with designs in a magazine brought from Kazan, soundlessly moving his lips and drawing a broad fingernail over the yellowed pages. He laid bricks for several days, constantly referring to the drawings. He ordered a steel tank, to its specifications, at the Kazan factory of the Prussian manufacturer, Diese, and installed it on the exact protruding ledge that was designated, then smoothly attached it with clay. A stove like this both heated the bathhouse and warmed water quickly, you just had to add the logs in a timely manner – it's not just a stove, it's a lovely sight. The mullah himself came to have a look and then ordered the exact same thing for his own home.

As Zuleikha deals with the tasks, her exhaustion burrows somewhere deep, conceals itself – maybe in the back of her head, maybe in her spine – and rolls itself into a ball. It will crawl out soon, cover her like a dense wave, knock her from her feet, and drown her. But that will be later. For now, the bathhouse has heated up and the Vampire Hag can be called to bathe.

Murtaza can enter his mother's quarters without knocking, but Zuleikha is supposed to stamp her feet loudly on the floor in front of her door for a long time so the old woman will be ready for her arrival. If the Vampire Hag is awake, she feels the floorboards trembling and the harsh gaze of her blind eye sockets greets her daughter-in-law. If she's sleeping, Zuleikha needs to leave immediately and come back later.

"Maybe she went to sleep," Zuleikha hopes, diligently stamping by the entrance to her mother-in-law's house. She pushes the door and sticks her head through the crack.

Three large kerosene lamps in decorative metal holders brightly illuminate the spacious room – the Vampire Hag always lights them before Murtaza's evening arrival. The floors have been scraped with a thin blade and rubbed with river sand so they shine like honey (Zuleikha wore all the skin off her fingers shining it during the summer); snow-white lace on the windows is starched so crisply it could cut you; and hanging on the walls are smart, long, red and green embroidered towels and an oval mirror so huge that Zuleikha can see her full reflection in it, from head to toe. A tall grandfather clock gleams with amber varnish, its brass pendulum slowly and relentlessly ticking away the time. A yellow flame crackles in a tall stove covered with glazed tiles. Murtaza has stoked it himself; Zuleikha isn't allowed to touch it. A cobweb-thin silk valance on the beams under the ceiling borders the room like an expensive frame.

The old woman sits enthroned in the corner of honor, the *tur*, drowning in heaps of plumped pillows on a mighty bed with an ornate cast-iron headboard. Her feet rest on the floor in soft milk-colored felt boots embroidered with colorful braiding. Her head – which is wrapped in a long white scarf all the way to her shaggy eyebrows – stands straight and steady on her droopy neck. Her narrow eye openings are set atop high, broad cheekbones and look triangular, thanks to eyelids that sag crookedly on each side.

"A person could die waiting for you to heat the bathhouse," her mother-in-law calmly says.

Her mouth is sunken and wrinkled, like an old goose rump; she has almost no teeth but speaks distinctly and intelligibly.

As if you'll die, thinks Zuleikha, creeping into the room. *You'll even be saying nasty things about me at my funeral.*

"But don't get your hopes up: I'm planning to live a long time," the old woman continues. She sets aside her jasper prayer beads and gropes around for a walking stick darkened with age. "Murtaza and I will outlive you all. We have strong roots and grow from a good tree."

"Now she'll talk about my rotten root," sighs Zuleikha, doomed, as she brings the old woman a fur cap, felt boots, and a long, robe-like dog-hair coat.

"Not like you, so thin-blooded." The old woman extends a bony foot in front of her; Zuleikha carefully removes the soft, almost downy felt boot and puts on a tall, rigid felt boot. "You didn't end up with either height or a face. Of course maybe there was honey smeared between your legs in your youth but then again that spot didn't exactly flourish, now, did it? You only brought girls into the world and not one of them survived."

Zuleikha pulls too hard at the second boot and the old woman cries out from pain.

"Easy there, little girl! I speak the truth and you know it yourself. Your family line is ending, wasting away, you thin-boned thing. And that's how it should be: a rotten root should rot and a healthy one should live."

The Vampire Hag leans on her walking stick, rises from the bed, and immediately stands an entire head taller than Zuleikha. She cranes her broad chin, which resembles a hoof, and directs the gaze of her white eyes at the ceiling:

"The Almighty sent me a dream about that just now."

Zuleikha throws the robe-like coat on the Vampire Hag's shoulders, puts on the fur cap, and wraps her neck with a soft shawl.

All-powerful Allah, another dream! Her mother-in-law rarely dreamt, but the dreams that came to her turned out to be prophetic. They were strange and sometimes ghastly visions filled with hints and innuendo, where what was to come was reflected indistinctly, distorted as if by a hazy, warped mirror. Even the Vampire Hag herself was not always able to interpret their meaning. A couple of weeks or months later, the mystery would come to light, when something would happen, usually bad and rarely good, but always important, repeating with twisted precision a picture from a dream that was already half-forgotten.

The old witch was never wrong. In 1915, right after her son's wedding, Murtaza appeared to her, trudging among red flowers. They were unable to unravel the dream but there was soon a fire in the household; the storehouse and old bathhouse burned to the ground and so the answer to the riddle was found. One night a couple of months later, the old woman saw a mountain of yellow skulls with large horns and predicted an epidemic of foot-and-mouth disease that would go on to mow down all the cattle in Yulbash. The dreams came for the next ten years, all sorrowful and frightening: children's shirts desolately floating along the river, cradles split in half, chickens drowning in blood … During that time, Zuleikha gave birth to and immediately buried four daughters. A vision of the Great Famine in 1921 was scary, too. Air as black as soot appeared to her mother-in-law and people were swimming in it as if it were water, slowly dissolving, gradually losing their arms, legs, and heads.

"Are we going to sweat here much longer?" The old woman impatiently knocks her walking stick and is first to head for the door. "You want to make me sweat before going outside so I catch cold?"

Zuleikha hurriedly turns down the wicks on the kerosene lamps and rushes after her.

The Vampire Hag stops on the front steps; she doesn't go outside alone. Zuleikha catches her mother-in-law by the elbow – the Vampire Hag jabs her long, gnarled fingers painfully into Zuleikha's arm – and leads her to the bathhouse. They walk slowly, carefully placing their feet in the loose snow: the blizzard hasn't subsided and the path is partially covered again.

"It must have been you that cleared the snow in the yard, wasn't it?" the Vampire Hag smirks with half her mouth, standing in the entryway, allowing her snow-covered coat to be taken off. "It shows."

She shakes her head, throws her cap on the floor (Zuleikha quickly dips to pick it up), fumbles for the door, and goes into the changing room by herself.

It smells of steamed birch leaves, bur-marigold, and fresh damp wood. The Vampire Hag sits down on the wide, long bench by the wall and freezes in silence: she's permitting herself to be undressed. Zuleikha first takes off her white headscarf embroidered with large, heavy beads. Then a roomy velvet vest with a patterned clasp on the stomach. Beads: a coral strand, pearl strand, glass strand, and a hefty necklace that has darkened over time. A thick outer smock. A thin inner smock. Felt boots. Baggy wide pants; one pair, a second. Downy socks. Woolen socks. Cotton socks. Zuleikha wants to pull the heavy crescent earrings from her mother-in-law's fat, creased earlobes but she screams, "Don't touch! You might lose something … Or say you lost it …" Zuleikha decides not to touch the rings of dulled yellow metal on the old woman's misshapen, wrinkled fingers.

When her clothing is neatly laid out in a strict, set order, taking up the entire bench from wall to wall, Zuleikha's mother-in-law carefully feels all the objects, pursing her lips in dissatisfaction, straightening and smoothing out some items. Zuleikha quickly throws her own things in the laundry basket by the entrance and leads the old woman into the steam room.

As soon as they open the door they're enveloped in hot air and the aromas of white-hot stones and steamed bast fiber. Moisture begins streaming down their faces and backs.

"You were too lazy to heat it properly, it's barely warm," the old woman says through her teeth, scratching her sides. She climbs up on the highest steaming shelf, lies with her face toward the ceiling, and closes her eyes – so she'll be soaking wet.

Zuleikha takes a seat by the basins she prepared and begins kneading at the dampened bundles of birch leaves.

"You're kneading them badly," says the Vampire Hag, continuing to grumble. "I might not see, but I know it's bad. You're running them back and forth in the basin like you're stirring soup with a spoon, but you have to knead it like it's dough. What made Murtaza pick you anyway? So careless of him. Honey between the legs isn't going to satisfy a man his whole life."

Zuleikha gets onto her knees to work the leaves. Her body starts feeling hot right away, and her face and chest grow wet.

"That's better," a raspy voice carries from above. "You wanted to hit me with unsoftened bundles of leaves, you good-for-nothing. But I won't allow you to disrespect me. Or my Murtaza, either. I won't allow it. Allah granted me this long life to defend him from you. Who else but me will stand up for my little boy? You don't love him, don't honor him, you only pretend. You're a cold, soulless faker, that's who you are. I feel it, oh, how I feel it."

Not a word more about the dream, though. The mean old woman will wear her down all evening. She knows Zuleikha is desperate to hear about it. She's torturing Zuleikha.

Zuleikha takes two bundles of leaves trickling with greenish

26

water and goes up to the Vampire Hag on the steaming shelf. Her head enters a dense layer of baking air under the ceiling and begins to throb. Her vision blurs as grains of color flash and float before her eyes.

There she is up close, the Vampire Hag, stretched out from wall to wall, almost like a landscape where odd hillocks of hundred-year-old flesh and thick landslides of skin seem to have been dropped between protruding bones. Meandering streams of glistening sweat flow along that entire uneven valley, where indented gullies and magnificent rises alternate.

The Vampire Hag needs to be beaten with leaf bundles in both hands, beginning at the belly. First Zuleikha carefully draws a bundle of leaves along her skin as preparation, then begins thrashing the Vampire Hag with each bundle in turn. Red spots appear immediately on the old woman's body; black birch leaves fly off everywhere.

"And you don't know how to beat me, either. How many years have I been teaching you?" The Vampire Hag raises her voice to outshout the long, lashing swats. "Harder! Go on, go on, you pitiful hen! Warm my old bones! Hit meaner, you good-for-nothing! Get your thin blood moving, so it thickens! How do you love your husband at night if you're that weak, huh? Murtaza will leave, leave for another woman who will beat and love him harder! Even I can strike harder. Beat me better or I'll hit you! Grab you by the hair and show you how to do it! I'm not Murtaza, I won't let you off! Where's your strength, you hen? You're not dead yet! Or are you?" The old woman is shouting at the top of her lungs by now and her face lifts toward the ceiling, distorted by fury.

Zuleikha swings with all her might, striking with the bundles of leaves as if they were an axe, at a body that glimmers in the wafting steam. The birch switches shriek as they split the air and the old woman shudders heavily; broad crimson streaks run across her belly and chest, where blood is swelling into dark grains.

"Finally," the Vampire Hag exhales hoarsely, throwing her head back on the bench.

Zuleikha's vision darkens and she climbs down the steps from the steaming shelf to the slippery, cool floor. Her breathing is rapid and her hands are shaking.

"Make it steam more and then get to my back," the Vampire Hag commands calmly.

Glory be to Allah, the old woman likes to wash on the lower level. She sits in a huge wooden basin filled to the brim with water, carefully lowers the long, flat bags of breasts that hang to her bellybutton into the basin, and begins graciously extending her arms and legs one at a time to Zuleikha, who rubs them with a steamed bast scrubber, washing balls of grime to the floor.

Now it's time for the hair. Her wispy gray braids, which fall down to her hips, need to be unplaited, lathered, and rinsed out without grazing the large, hanging crescent earrings or spilling water into unseeing eyes.

After rinsing in several pails of cold water, the Vampire Hag is ready. Zuleikha leads her out to the changing room and begins wiping her dry with towels, wondering if the old woman will reveal the mysterious dream to her. Zuleikha has no doubt she already told her son everything today.

But then the Vampire Hag extends a gnarled finger and pokes Zuleikha hard in the side. Zuleikha yelps and steps away. The old woman pokes again. And then a third time and a fourth. What's wrong with her? Did she steam too long? Zuleikha jumps aside, toward the wall.

Her mother-in-law calms down a few moments later. She holds out a demanding hand in a habitual gesture, impatiently motioning with her fingers, into which Zuleikha places a pitcher of drinking water she readied in advance. The old woman takes greedy mouthfuls and the drops run down the deep folds at the corners of her mouth to her chin. Then she swings and forcefully hurls the pitcher into the wall. The pottery clangs loudly, smashing to pieces, and a dark water spot creeps down the logs.

Zuleikha's lips move in a brief, soundless prayer. *All-powerful Allah, what's happened to the Vampire Hag today? She's so worked up. Could she be going soft in the head due to her age?* Zuleikha waits a bit. Then she cautiously approaches and continues dressing her mother-in-law.

"You're silent," the old woman utters in condemnation, allowing herself to be dressed in a clean undershirt and baggy wide pants. "You're always silent, mute. If I had to live with someone who was silent all the time, I'd kill them."

Zuleikha stops.

"You could never do anything like that," she continues. "You can't hit or kill or learn to love. Your fury's sleeping deep inside and won't ever wake up now, and what's life without fury? No, you'll never really live. In short, you're a hen and your life is hennish." The Vampire Hag leans back toward the wall with a blissful sigh. "My life, though, has been real. I'm already both blind and deaf but I'm still living, and I like that. But you're not living. That's why I don't pity you."

Zuleikha stands and listens, pressing the old woman's felt boots to her chest.

"You'll die soon: it was in my dream. Murtaza and I will stay in the house, but three fiery angels will fly here for you and bring you straight to Hell. I saw everything as it is: how they pick you up and how they hurl you into a carriage and how they carry you over the precipice. I'm standing on the front steps, watching. And you're silent even then, just mooing like Kyubelek, your green eyes wide open, gawking at me like an insane woman. The angels roar with laughter, holding you firmly under the arms. Thwack of a whip and the earth opens wide, smoke and sparks coming up through the crack. Thwack and you've all flown off, disappearing into the smoke ..."

Zuleikha's legs are weakening and her hands release the felt boots. She leans against the wall, slowly sinking down onto a thin rug that gives little protection from the cold floor.

"Maybe that won't come true soon," says the Vampire Hag, yawning broadly and deliciously. "You know yourself that some dreams are fulfilled quickly, others months later so that I'm already starting to forget them ..."

Zuleikha seems to have lost control over her hands, but she somehow dresses the old woman. The Vampire Hag notices her fumbling and smirks unkindly. Then she sits on the bench and leans resolutely into her walking stick.

"I'm not leaving the bathhouse with you today. Maybe you don't have your wits about you after what you've heard. Who knows what will come into your head. And I still have a long time left to live. So call Murtaza; let him lead me home and put me to bed."

After wrapping her sheepskin coat more firmly around her sweaty, bare body, Zuleikha trudges to the house and leads her husband back. He runs into the changing room without his hat, not shaking off the snow stuck to his felt boots.

"What happened, *Eni?*" He runs up to his mother and grasps her hands.

"I can't ..." The Vampire Hag's weakened voice suddenly stirs and she drops her head to her son's chest. "I can't ... no more ..."

"What? What is it?" Murtaza drops to his knees and begins feeling her head, neck, and shoulders.

Her hands shaking, the old woman somehow unfastens the

ties on the front of her smock and pulls at the collar opening. A crimson spot with large black grains of clotted blood is darkening on a light triangle of skin in the gap. A bruise stretches from the opening in her undershirt down toward her belly.

"Why … ?" The Vampire Hag curves her mouth as if it were a sharply angled yoke for carrying pails and two large, glistening tears roll from her eyes before disappearing somewhere in the finely quivering wrinkles on her cheeks. She presses herself against her son, shaking soundlessly. "I didn't do anything to her …"

This brings Murtaza to his feet.

"You!" He growls indistinctly, drilling his eyes into Zuleikha and groping at the wall next to him.

There are bunches of dried herbs and bundles of bast scrubbers under his hand – he pulls them off and flings them away. A heavy broom handle finally settles in his palm. He grasps it firmly and raises it threateningly.

"I didn't beat her!" says Zuleikha in a stifled whisper, jumping away toward the window. "I never, not once, laid a finger on her! She asked me herself –"

"Murtaza, *ulym*, don't beat her, have pity," sounds the Vampire Hag's trembling voice in the corner. "She didn't pity me, but for her, please –"

Murtaza hurls the broom. The handle strikes Zuleikha on the shoulder, hurting; her sheepskin coat falls to the floor. She drops the felt boots herself and darts into the steam room. The door shuts behind her with a bang and the bolt clatters; her husband is locking her inside.

Pressing her hot face to the small steamed-up window, Zuleikha peers through a dancing shroud of snow as her husband and mother-in-law float to the house like two tall shadows. As the windows on the Vampire Hag's side light up and then go dark. As Murtaza strides heavily back to the bathhouse.

31

Zuleikha grabs a large dipper and scoops water from the basin on the stove; fluffy puffs of steam rise from the basin.

The bolt clatters again and Murtaza is standing in the doorway in just his underclothes; he's holding the same broom in his hand. He takes a step forward and closes the door behind him.

Hurl boiling water at him! Right now, don't wait!

Zuleikha is breathing rapidly and holding the dipper in front of herself in outstretched hands as she steps away and presses her back to the wall; her shoulder blades sense a sharp bulge in the logs.

Murtaza takes another step and knocks the dipper from Zuleikha's hands with the broom handle. He lurches toward her, throwing her to the lower steaming shelf. Zuleikha's knees strike it hard and she sprawls on the shelf.

"Lie still, woman," he says.

And he begins beating her.

A broom on the back isn't painful. It's almost like a bundle of birch leaves. Zuleikha lies still, as her husband ordered, but she shudders and scratches the shelf with her nails at each strike so he doesn't beat her long. He cools off quickly. She was given a good husband after all.

Then she steams and washes him. When Murtaza goes out into the changing room to cool off, she washes all the laundry. She no longer has the strength to wash herself – her exhaustion has returned, filled her eyelids with heaviness, and clouded her head – but somehow she draws the scrubber along her sides and rinses her hair. All that's left is to wash the bathhouse floors and then sleep, sleep.

As a child, she was taught to wash floors on her hands and knees. "Only a lazybones works bending from the waist or crouching," her mother taught her. Zuleikha doesn't consider herself a lazybones and now she's wiping the slippery dark boards, sliding along them like a lizard on her elbows and knees. Her belly and breasts hover right over the floor, her leaden head is bent low and her rear end is raised high. She's feeling unsteady.

The steam room is soon washed clean and Zuleikha moves on to the changing room: she hangs the damp rugs on the storage racks that line the wall under the ceiling – let them dry out – gathers the shards of the pottery pitcher and sets to scrubbing the floor.

Murtaza is still lying on the bench, undressed, wrapped in a white sheet, and resting. Her husband's gaze always forces Zuleikha to work harder, more diligently, and faster: let him see she's not a bad wife even if she isn't tall. And so now she's gathered the remains of her strength and – sprawled on the floor – is drawing the rag along the already clean boards in a frenzy: back and forth, back and forth, her mussed, wet hair bouncing in time with her uncovered breasts creeping along the floorboards.

"Zuleikha," utters Murtaza in a low tone, gazing at his naked wife.

She straightens up, still kneeling and holding on to the rag, but doesn't have time to raise her sleepy eyes. Her husband clasps her from behind and throws her, stomach down, onto the bench, brings all the weight of his body upon her, breathing heavily and wheezing as he begins to rub against her, pressing her into the hard boards. He wants to make love to his wife, but his body doesn't want to; it has forgotten how to obey his desires. Finally, Murtaza stands and begins dressing. "Even my flesh doesn't want you," he tells her without looking, and leaves the bathhouse.

Zuleikha slowly rises from the bench, the same rag still in her hand. She finishes washing the floor. Hangs up the wet sheets and towels. Dresses and trudges home. She lacks the strength to be upset about what happened with Murtaza. The Vampire Hag's scary prophecy – that's what she'll think about, but only tomorrow, tomorrow. When she wakes up.

The light is already off inside the house. Murtaza isn't sleeping yet; he's breathing loudly in his part of the house; the boards of the sleeping bench creak under him.

Zuleikha gropes her way to her corner, her hand guiding her along the warm, rough side of the stove, then she falls on the trunk without undressing.

"Zuleikha," Murtaza calls out to her; this voice is satisfied and affectionate.

She wants to stand but cannot. Her body spreads on the trunk like a thin pudding.

"Zuleikha!"

She crawls down to the floor and kneels in front of the trunk, but can't tear her head from it.

"Zuleikha, hurry up, you pathetic hen!"

She rises slowly and drags herself to her husband's call, reeling. She crawls onto the sleeping bench.

Murtaza's impatient hands pull down her baggy pants (he grunts peevishly: *Now that's a lazybones, hasn't even undressed yet*), lays her on her back, and lifts her smock. His uneven breathing grows closer. Zuleikha senses her husband's beard, long and still smelling of the bathhouse and frost, covering her face; the recent beating on her back aches under his weight. Murtaza's body has finally responded to his desires and he hurries to fulfill them, greedily, powerfully, at length, and triumphantly.

When she's fulfilling her wifely duty, Zuleikha usually pictures herself as a butter churn inside which a housewife's strong arms beat butter using a fat, hard pestle. Today, though, there are none of those thoughts, only a heavy blanket of exhaustion. She is distantly aware of her husband's stifled snorting through a shroud of sleep. The unceasing jolts of his body lull her, like a rhythmically rocking cart ...

Murtaza climbs off his wife, wiping the damp back of his head with his palm and calming his labored breathing; he's breathing wearily, with satisfaction.

"Go to your own place, woman," he says and pushes her unmoving body.

He doesn't like her to sleep next to him on the bench.

Without opening her eyes, Zuleikha's feet slap off to her trunk, and she doesn't even notice she's already sleeping soundly.

A KNOCK AT THE WINDOW

Will I die?

A deep-blue storm drones outside the window. Zuleikha is kneeling and cleaning Murtaza's kaftan with a bristle brush. The kaftan is the main decoration in the house: quilted felt, covered in velvet, smelling of a strong male, and as huge as its owner. It hangs on a fat copper nail, its magnificent sleeves shimmering, and it graciously allows the frail Zuleikha to grovel at its feet and clean drops of mud from its hem.

Will I die soon?

The mud in Kazan is rich and of high quality. Zuleikha hasn't been there; she's never once left Yulbash, except to go to the forest or cemetery. She'd like to, though. Murtaza once promised to take her with him some day. She is afraid to remind him, so all she can do is watch silently whenever he is preparing to leave. He'll tighten the harness on Sandugach, pound the loosened wheels with a heel, and pretend not to notice her.

So if I die, then I won't see Kazan?

Zuleikha narrows her eyes at Murtaza. Now, he's sitting on the sleeping bench and fixing the horse collar. Fingers with brown nails as hard and strong as the trunks of young oaks nimbly thread a slippery leather strap into the wooden base. He's just returned from the city but he went to work immediately. A good husband – what can you say.

Will he marry someone else quickly if I die?

Murtaza grunts with satisfaction: *It's ready!* He puts the collar on his own powerful neck, testing the strength of his handiwork, his thick tendons swelling under the steep wooden curve. Yes, a man like this would marry, and very quickly.

And what if the Vampire Hag was wrong?

Zuleikha's brush swishes. *Whoosh-whoosh. Whoosh-whoosh. Shamsia-Firuza. Khalida-Sabida.* First and second daughters. Third and fourth. She often runs through those names as if they were prayer beads. The Vampire Hag foretold all four deaths: Zuleikha had simultaneously found out from her mother-in-law about each pregnancy and each newborn's impending death. Four times she had carried to term both the fruit in her womb and a hope in her heart that this time the Vampire Hag would be wrong. But the old woman turned out to be right every time. Could she really be right now, too?

Work, Zuleikha, work. What was it Mama used to say? Work drives away sorrow. Oh, Mama, my sorrow doesn't obey your sayings …

There's a knock, the signaling knock, at the window: three quick knocks, two slow. She shudders. Did she imagine it? Then again: three quick knocks, two slow. No, she didn't imagine it, this can't be a mistake; it's the same knock. The brush falls from her hands and rolls along the floor. Zuleikha looks up and meets her husband's heavy gaze. *May Allah protect us, Murtaza, not again?*

He slowly removes the collar from his neck, throws his sheepskin coat on his shoulders, and shoves his feet into his felt boots. The door slams behind him.

Zuleikha rushes to the window, melts the jagged patterns in the frost on the glass with her fingers, and presses her eye to the little hole. There's Murtaza opening the gate, fighting the beginnings of the snowstorm. A dark horse thrusts its muzzle out of swirling white flakes and a rider powdered with snow leans from his saddle toward Murtaza, whispers something in his ear, and dissolves into the blizzard again a moment later, as if he'd never been there. Murtaza returns.

Zuleikha falls to the floor, fumbles for the brush that rolled away, and sticks her nose into the hem of the kaftan. A woman shouldn't display excessive curiosity, even at a moment like this. The door lets out a long squeak as fresh, frosty air comes in. Her husband's lumbering steps slowly float past behind her back. They're not good steps; they're slow and tired, somehow doomed.

Her chest is pressed to the cold floor, her face to the soft kaftan. She's breathing shallowly and soundlessly. She hears how loudly the fire is crackling in the stove. She pauses, then turns her head slightly. Murtaza is sitting on the sleeping bench in his sheepskin coat and snow-covered, shaggy fur hat; the bushes of his eyebrows have come together at the bridge of his nose, the sparkle of large white snowflakes in them slowly dimming. A wrinkle furrows his brow and his eyes are expressionless, lifeless. And Zuleikha understands: *yes*, again.

And Allah, what will happen this time? She squeezes her eyes shut and lowers her forehead, which has instantly broken out in a sweat, to the cold floorboard. She feels moisture there. Snow is melting from Murtaza's felt boots and streaming across the floor.

Zuleikha grabs a rag and crawls on her knees, mopping up the water. The top of her head bumps into her husband's toes, which are as hard as iron. She slaps the rag at the melted snow around his feet, not daring to lift her head. A large, prickly felt boot comes down on her right hand. Zuleikha wants to tear her hand away but the boot presses down on her fingers like a rock. She looks up. Murtaza's yellow eyes are right next to her. Reflected light from the fire dances in pupils as huge as cherries.

"I'm not giving it up," he whispers quietly. "I won't give up anything this time."

Sour breath burns at her face. Zuleikha moves aside. And she feels the other felt boot fall on her left hand. Just so long as he doesn't crush her fingers; how would she work without fingers?

"What's going to happen, Murtaza?" she babbles plaintively. "Did they say? Grain has to be turned in now? Or cattle?"

"What business is it of yours, woman?" he hisses in response.

He takes her braids and winds them around his fists. Zuleikha's eyes are next to his hot mouth. Gobs of spittle glisten in the deep, brown crevices between his teeth.

"Maybe the new authorities don't have enough women? They've already taken grain and cattle, too. If they want land, they'll take it away. But women, now that's a problem." Murtaza's spittle is spraying Zuleikha's face. "The Red commissars don't have anybody to mate with."

His knees are squeezing her head. Oh, how strong her husband's legs are, even though he's gone all gray.

"They ordered all the women be rounded up and turned in to the chairman of the rural council. Whoever disobeys will be assigned to that collective farm place. Forever."

Zuleikha finally realizes that her husband's joking. She just doesn't know if she should smile in response. She understands from his sharp, heavy breathing that she shouldn't.

Murtaza releases Zuleikha's head. Removes his felt boots from her fingers. Stands and wraps his sheepskin jacket tighter.

"Hide the food, like always," he quickly tells her. "We'll go to the secret storage place in the morning."

He takes the horse collar from the sleeping bench and goes out.

Zuleikha pulls a ring of keys from a nail, grabs a kerosene lamp, and runs into the yard.

There hasn't been a warning for a long time now and many people have begun storing their food in the old ways, in cellars and storehouses, instead of hiding it. That turned out not to be a good idea.

The storehouse is locked and a slippery ball of snow is stuck to the big, paunchy lock. Zuleikha gropes at the keyhole with the key, turns once, twice, and the lock gives unwillingly, opening its mouth.

The meager kerosene light illuminates the wall's smooth yellow logs and high ceiling, where a black square gapes – the trapdoor to the hayloft – but it doesn't reach the darkening corners in the distance. The storehouse is spacious, solid, and built to last, like everything in Murtaza's household. The walls are hung with tools: vicious sickles and scythes, toothy saws and rakes, heavy planes, axes, and chisels, blunt-faced wooden hammers, sharp pitchforks, and crowbars. There's also horse tack and harnesses: old and new collars, leather bridles, stirrups that are rusted or gleaming with fresh oil, and horseshoes. Several wooden wheels, a hollowed-out trough, and a copper basin with shiny curves (*thank you, Murtaza, for bringing it from the city a couple of years ago*). A cracked cradle hangs from the ceiling. There's a smell of grain hardened by frost, and cold, spicy meat.

Zuleikha remembers the times when dense, plump-cheeked sacks of grain towered to the ceiling here. Murtaza would walk between them, satisfied, smiling serenely, and tirelessly re-counting them, placing a palm on each sack with a tremble, as if it were a magnificent female body. It's not like that now.

She places the kerosene lamp on the floor. There are fewer sacks than fingers on her hands. And each is thin, with flabby, drooping sides. Back in 1919, they'd learned to pour grain from one sack into several, as soon as the food confiscation detachments neared Yulbash. Everything had been unfathomable then and those raiding parties became more and more like wanton spirits with every year that passed: scarier than a demonic *alabasty* woman, as gluttonous as a giant evil *dev*, and insatiable, like Zhalmavyz, the huge cannibal woman. It was difficult to hide a tightly stuffed sack, and besides, then all the grain was gone immediately if it was found. It's a different story if there are several skinny ones: they're easier to store (each one in a different place) and not so awful to part with. What's more, Zuleikha could drag the thin sacks around, one at a time, without Murtaza's help, hiding them herself while he went around to the neighbors to figure out what was happening.

If not for the snowstorm, many villagers would have made their way into the forest this evening. Each prudent homeowner had a hiding place under the protective cover of fir boughs and crackling fallen branches. Murtaza had one, too. But where could you go in a blizzard? The only hope was for mercy from the heavens. *Allah grant that nobody arrive before morning.*

Zuleikha starts hiding the grain and food.

She buries a couple of sacks right there, in the storehouse; the cellar in the earthen floor by the wall has served them loyally for the last ten years. She's afraid to store them in the hayloft because many people hide theirs in lofts. She places several precious sacks of seed grain marked with white paint in the false bottom of the steel water tank in the bathhouse.

Now it's the horsemeat's turn. Long horse intestines resembling wrinkly fingers, tightly stuffed with dark red spiced meat, hang in bunches from the ceiling. Oh and do they smell! Zuleikha's nostrils draw in the sharp, salty aroma of *kyzylyk*. It's best to hide this sausage in a place where the smell can't be picked up. In the summer, it would have been possible to climb up on the roof and lay it in even rows on the little brick ledges inside the chimney; that wouldn't have done anything to the meat except make it smell more delicious from the smoke. But the roof is covered in ice now so she can't climb up there without Murtaza. She'll have to put it in the house, under a floorboard, securely sealed in thick iron boxes, to keep out rats.

Nuts are next. Hard little hazelnut balls roll and knock inside their shells like a thousand wooden rattles as she lugs the long, narrow sacks from the storehouse into the winter shed and places them in the bottom of the manger then sprinkles them with hay. The cow and horse watch the fuss around their feeders with indifference. The foal peers out from under Sandugach's belly, squinting curiously at his mistress.

Zuleikha places the salt, peas, and carrot flour from the cellar on a wide shelf under the outhouse roof and covers it with boards.

She brings honey in large wooden frames wrapped with thin, sugared rags up to the attic. It is there, under some boards, that she also hides the salted goose and heaps of *pastila* stiffened from the hard frost.

The last thing left to hide is five dozen large eggs, shining with gentle whiteness in the depths of a birch bark container, where they're lying in soft straw.

Maybe they won't come after all?

These were wicked guests who made themselves at home in any household, not asking permission to seize the owner's last food supplies or painstakingly selected seed grain that had been carefully stored for next spring's planting and was thus even more valuable. And they were also ready to strike, jab with a bayonet, or shoot anyone standing in their way, without a second's hesitation.

In her fourteen uneasy years of hiding from these uninvited guests in the house's women's quarters, Zuleikha has observed many faces through the curtain's folds: unshaven and groomed, blackened from the sun and aristocratically pale, with iron-toothed smiles and strict, prim expressions, briskly speaking in Tatar, Russian, and Ukrainian, or keeping sullenly silent about the dreadful truths that were inscribed, in even square letters, on thin sheets of paper worn at the creases that they kept trying to stick under Murtaza's nose.

Those faces had many names, each more incomprehensible and frightening than the next: grain monopoly, food confiscation, requisition, tax on foodstuffs, Bolsheviks, food appropriation detachments, Red Army, Soviet power, regional secret police, Komsomol, State Political Administration, communists, authorized this and that ...

Mostly long Russian words with meanings Zuleikha didn't understand ... so to herself she called those people the Red Horde. Her father had told her a lot about the Golden Horde, whose harsh, narrow-eyed emissaries collected tribute for several centuries in this part of the world and took it to their merciless leader Genghis Khan, his children, grandchildren, and great-grandchildren. The Red Hordesmen collected tribute, too, but Zuleikha didn't know who received it.

At first they collected only grain. Then potatoes and meat. And during the Great Famine, in 1921, they began making a clean sweep of everything edible. Poultry. Cattle. And everything they could find in the house. It was back then that Zuleikha learned to divide the grain between several sacks.

They hadn't made an appearance in a long time now; Yulbash had calmed. During that period that had the peculiar name "New Economic Policy," peasants were allowed to cultivate the land without worry and were even permitted to hire wage laborers. After listing so scarily, it seemed that life was leveling out again. Then last year Soviet power unexpectedly took on an appearance that was familiar to all the villagers and so wasn't frightening: former wage laborer Mansur Shigabutdinov became the head of the rural council. He wasn't born locally – he dragged his aging mother and the bachelor living with her after him, from the next canton, long ago. Malicious gossips joke that he hasn't ever in his life had the honor of saving up bride-money for a good fiancée. They call him Mansurka-Burdock behind his back.

Mansurka persuaded several people to join his own Party cell and meets with them in the evenings to discuss things. He organizes gatherings and enthusiastically summons villagers into an association with the scarily named kolkhoz, but hardly anyone listens to him on that collective farm: only those as needy as he is go to the gatherings.

But now it has happened again, the signaling knock at night, like the nervous beating of an unhealthy heart. Zuleikha looks out the window. Lights are burning in the neighboring houses, so Yulbash isn't sleeping; it's preparing for the arrival of uninvited guests.

So where should she hide those eggs? They'll crack in the cold, so she can't put them in the attic, the hallway, or the bathhouse. They need to be concealed in warmth. They can't go in the men's quarters because the Red Hordesmen will turn everything upside down there; that had already happened more than once. In the women's quarters? Those tyrants won't be shy; they'll search everything there, too. Maybe with the Vampire Hag? The unbidden guests had often faltered under the old woman's stern, unseeing gaze, so searches in her mother-in-law's house were usually short and rushed.

Zuleikha carefully grasps the bulky birch container and darts out to the hallway. There's no time to mill around by the door asking permission to enter so she opens it and glances in. The Vampire Hag is sleeping, snoring loudly, her cleft chin directed at the ceiling, where light is cast in blossoms of whimsical flowers: the kerosene lamps are burning in case Murtaza gets the urge to look in on his mother this evening. Zuleikha steps over a fat log at the threshold and scampers into the area behind the stove.

And what a nice stove it is! It's as huge as a house, covered in smooth, almost glassy, decorative tiles (even on the women's side) with two deep kettles that are never used: one's for preparing food, the other's for boiling water. If only Zuleikha had kettles like this. She's been struggling along her whole life with just one. She places the container on a ledge and removes the lid from a kettle. Now she'll pile the eggs inside, sprinkle them with straw, and bolt back to her own house. Nobody will even notice …

The door opens with a squeak as Zuleikha piles on the last egg. Someone's stepping heavily over the threshold; the floorboards groan from the strain. Murtaza! Her hand cramps from the unexpectedness, the shell crunches very quietly, and the cold, slippery liquid slowly oozes through her fingers. Her heart turns into the same kind of thick goo as the egg that burst in her hand and it's flowing along her ribs, to somewhere below, toward the chill in her belly.

Should she leave now? And admit she intruded into her mother-in-law's quarters without permission? Confess to the broken egg?

"*Eni*." She can hear Murtaza's low voice.

The old woman's snore is stifled and stops right away. The bedsprings make an extended moan – the Vampire Hag is raising her large body as if she's heard her son's call.

"My darling," she says quietly, in a hoarse, half-awake voice. "Is that you?"

Hanging in the long silence are the sounds of the old woman's body cumbersomely settling and Murtaza's heavy sigh.

Without breathing, Zuleikha carefully uses the rim of the kettle to wipe the slippery egg from her hand. Hugging the stove and pausing after every movement, she takes several soundless steps to the side, leaning her cheek against the warm tiles and pulling back the folds of the curtain with her index finger. Now she sees them, mother and son, through the gap in the curtain. The Vampire Hag is sitting very straight on the bed as always, with her feet on the floor, but Murtaza is kneeling and his gleaming head is pressed into his mother's belly, arms firmly clasping her large body. Zuleikha has never seen Murtaza genuflecting. He would not forgive her if she were to come out now.

"*Ulym*," says the Vampire Hag, breaking the silence, "I sense something's happened."

"Yes, *Eni*. Something's happened," says Murtaza, not tearing his face from his mother's belly, muffling his voice. "And it's been going on for a long time. If you only knew what's been happening here ..."

"Tell your old mother everything, Murtaza, my boy. Even if I can't hear or see, I feel everything and can console you." The Vampire Hag is patting her son's back, just as people stroke overexcited stallions after races to calm them.

"How are we supposed to live, *Eni*? To live!" Murtaza rubs his forehead against his mother's knees, as if burying it deeper. "They keep robbing, robbing, robbing. They're seizing everything. When you've nothing left, and the only thing to do is to join the forefathers, they let you catch your breath. And when things begin to recover and you lift your head a little, they're robbing you again. My strength is gone and my heart has no patience!"

"Life is a complex road, *ulym*. Complex and long. Sometimes you want to sit down at the side of the road and stretch your legs, just let everything roll on past even if it's to the netherworld itself; but sit down and stretch, that's allowed! It's why you came to me. Sit with me for a while, rest, take a breath." The old woman is speaking slowly, drawing out her words, as if she's singing or reading a prayer to the beat of the pendulum in the grandfather clock. "You'll find the strength to stand later and get on your way. For now, though, I sense that you're tired, sweetheart, you're very tired."

46

"There were whispers today that something's afoot again. I don't know if I can even face getting out of bed tomorrow. People are thinking that they're either going to start taking away land or cattle or both at the same time. The seed grain's hidden but what's the use if they take the land? Where would I sow it, the potato patch? I'll die first. I'll sink my teeth in and fight and I won't give it up! Let them register us as kulaks, I won't give it up! It's mine!" He pounds his fist on the bed frame, and its high metallic voice sings plaintively in response.

"I know you'll think of something. You'll sit now, talk with me, and think of something. You're strong, Murtaza, my boy. Strong and smart, like I was." The old woman's voice is warming, sounding younger. "Oooh, I was something … When your father caught sight of me, he drooled all the way to his belt and forgot to wipe it up, that's how much he wanted to mount me. Men like you, *real* men, are like rams. When you see someone who's a little stronger than yourselves, you immediately want to start butting heads, trampling, and winning. What fools!"

She smiles and the web of wrinkles on her face trembles, playing in the gentle kerosene light. Murtaza is breathing more evenly, more calmly.

"I used to say to him: 'You need to watch yourself biting into this apple, you skinny-legged thing. You'll break off your teeth!' And he says to me, 'I have lots of teeth.' And I tell him, 'Life's long, you might not have enough, be careful!' Not a chance, I only excited the stud …" The Vampire Hag's laugh is muffled, as if she's coughing.

"That summer when we were playing *kyz-kuu*, and all the boys were chasing after the girls, Shakirzyan only came after me, like a dog after a bitch in heat. I had the most beautiful pinafore in Yulbash for *kyz-kuu*: black velvet with beaded flowers that I embroidered all winter! And on my bosom" – the old woman presses a lumpy, long-fingered hand to her hollow chest – "a two-strand necklace. My father had given me his own three-year-old Argamak horse. I jump in the saddle and the necklace starts jingling, gently and invitingly – the fellows only see me. Oh, my, my … Shakirzyan keeps galloping and galloping, and it's making his horse lather, and he's red himself from fury but he can't catch me.

"And as soon as I see the grove of nut trees in the distance, I hold the Argamak back a little, as if I'm giving way. And your father's glad because he's been chasing like a madman, so he thinks he's about to catch up. And right at the grove, away I go, I bring my heels together and the Argamak is off like an arrow, and Shakirzyan just gets dust in his face. He's sneezing but I've already turned around in the grove and taken a whip out of my boot. It's my turn now! The whip is strong and braided and I've purposely tied a knot at the end to make it hurt more. So I'll catch up to him, as usually happens, and give him a thorough lashing: *You couldn't reach the girl, so you'll pay for it, here you go!* I had a good laugh, a good yell – after all, he didn't catch me once, not one single time!"

The Vampire Hag wipes little teardrops away from the corners of her eyes with the back of her hand.

"Oh and I let him have it that summer! He reminded me of that for the rest of his life: he'd beat me hard, a lot, and with a whip, too. He'd tie a knot on it about the size of a fist and whack with it like it was a club while I'm laughing in his face: 'What,' I say, 'you're copying me? Think up something of your own. Don't you have the brains?' He's madder, whipping harder, even panting and holding his heart, but he couldn't ever break me like that. Well, and where is he now? Feeding the worms for half a century. And I've lived two of his lives and begun a third. Strength comes from above."

The Vampire Hag covers her white eye sockets.

"You're like me, *ulym*, my heart. You have my blood in your veins. My bones under your flesh." She's stroking the gray stubble on her son's shaven head. "And the strength in you is mine: mean and undefeatable."

"*Eni, Eni* ..." Murtaza is squeezing his mother's body tightly, grasping, as a wrestler embraces an opponent or a lover embraces the body of a woman he desires.

"Even the first time I looked at you – your little red body, wrinkled fingers, eyes still blind – I understood immediately that you were mine. Nobody else's, just mine. I birthed ten for my husband but the last one for myself. There's a reason the umbilical cord was as thick as an arm. Your grandmother could barely saw it with a knife. 'Your little son,' she said, 'doesn't want to be torn away from you.' And you really didn't want that: you stuck yourself to my breast, you grabbed at it like a tick. And you didn't tear yourself away: you drank me for three years, like a calf. All that's left of my breasts is sacks. And you slept with me. You were already huge and heavy, and you'd sprawl out on the sleeping bench like a star and your little hand went to my breast so it wouldn't get away from you. You didn't even let Shakirzyan near me – you screamed bloody murder. And he'd curse something awful, he was so jealous. But what would he have fed you during the famine if I hadn't had milk in my breast then?"

"*Eni, Eni* ..." Murtaza repeats, muffled.

"It was a scary time. You're already three, you want to eat like an adult. You suck a breast dry – how much of that liquid milk is there? Not nearly enough food for you! And you're kneading at it like mad, tearing with your teeth, *I want more, more*. But it's already empty. Give me some bread, you ask. What do you mean, bread? By the end of the summer, we'd eaten all the straw off the roof, all the locusts in the area had been caught, and that weed, orache, was a real delicacy. Anyway, where could you find it – orache? People went crazy, reeling around the woods like forest spirits, ripping bark off trees with their teeth. Shakirzyan went to the city

49

to earn money in the spring and I was alone with you four. At least you got the breast – the older ones got nothing …"

Murtaza mumbles something unintelligible, pressing himself to his mother. The Vampire Hag takes his head in her hands, lifts it, and her unseeing eyes look sternly into her son's face.

"Don't you dare even think about that, do you hear? I've told you a thousand times and I'll tell you the thousand and first: I didn't kill them. They died on their own. From hunger."

He's silent, just breathing loudly, with a whistle.

"It's true I didn't give them milk. I saved everything in me, to the last drop, for you. At first they tried to fight: they wanted to take the breast away from you by force. They were stronger than you. But I was stronger than them. And I wouldn't let them harm you. Then their strength was gone and you grew stronger. And they died. All of them. There was nothing else."

The Vampire Hag presses a hand against her chin, scrunching up the wrinkles on her face; her other hand, shaking slightly, covers her eyes. Reflections of the kerosene lamps flash dimly among her gold rings.

"And do you hear, *ulym*? We did not eat them. We buried them. Ourselves, without the mullah, at night. You were just small and forgot everything. No, they don't have graves – my tongue's tired from explaining to you that everybody was buried that summer without graves. Cannibals went around to the cemeteries in herds and as soon as they'd see a fresh grave, they'd dig it up and eat the deceased. So believe me – finally believe me – half a century later. The people who spread those foul rumors about you and me already became earth long ago themselves. But you and I are alive. There's obviously a reason Allah sends us mercy like this, isn't there?"

"*Eni, Eni.*" Murtaza grasps her raised hand and begins kissing it.

"So there you go." The Vampire Hag leans toward her son, hovering over him. Two skinny white braids fall on top of Murtaza's back, reaching to the floor. "You're the strongest, Murtaza. Nobody can defeat or break you. And you yourself know that's what yesterday's dream was about. If anyone's fated to leave this house or this world, it's not you. Your small-toothed wife couldn't bear you a son and will soon disappear into the netherworld. But you're so young you could continue your family line. You'll have a son yet. Don't be afraid of anything. You and I will stay in this house, sweetheart, and we'll live a long time yet. You because you're young. And me because I can't leave you on your own."

The slow, unrelenting beat of the squeaky mechanical heart in the huge grandfather clock is becoming distinctly audible.

"Thank you, *Eni*." Murtaza rises heavily from his knees. "I'm going."

He strokes his mother's face and hair. He helps her into bed, plumps the pillows, and covers her with a blanket. He kisses both arms on the wrist, then the elbow. He turns down the wick and it darkens. The door slams behind him.

The old woman soon starts wheezing drowsily, sailing back off to an illusory dreamland on a luxuriant bed of airy feather mattresses and blankets.

Zuleikha presses her eggshell-covered hand to her chest, soundlessly steals toward the door, and slips outside.

Murtaza is crouched by the stove, gloomily splitting kindling. The flame's yellow reflections dart along the axe blade, up and down, up and down. Waddling like a duck, Zuleikha walks back and forth over the floorboards concealing their secret food supplies – do they squeak too much?

"Stop." Her husband's voice is hoarse, as if it's snapped.

Frightened, Zuleikha leans against the trunks stacked up by the window, hastily straightening the lace *kaplau* with her hand (only guests and her husband, of course, are allowed to sit on these coverlets). Oh, but he's mean today, irritable; it's as if he's been possessed by a demon. He went to see his mother but didn't calm down. He's waiting for the Red Horde. He's afraid.

"After fourteen years they'll have learned all our hiding places by heart." Murtaza's axe cuts easily through the wood. "They'll take the whole house apart if they want, one log at a time, and find what they need."

The mountain of white slivers is growing around Murtaza. Why does he need so much kindling? They wouldn't use that much in a week.

"All we can do is guess: will they take the cow or the horse?" Murtaza finally swings and drives the axe into a chunk of wood with all his might.

"It'll be time to plow soon," Zuleikha sighs meekly. "It would be better if they took the cow."

"The cow?" Murtaza lurches back immediately, as if he's burned himself.

His breathing is rough and rapid, and it whistles. Like a bull before it rushes a rival.

Without rising from his knees, Murtaza flings himself toward Zuleikha. She recoils in fear. *May Allah protect us ...* Murtaza's powerful shoulder easily moves the trunks aside. He picks up the groaning floorboard with his fingernails. He plunges his arm into a black hole that's breathing damp cold and removes a flat metal box. The lid, chilled from the frosty air, clinks dully. Murtaza hurriedly stuffs a long squiggle of horsemeat sausage into his mouth and chews, frenzied.

"I won't give it up," he murmurs, his mouth full. "I'm not giving up anything this time. I'm strong."

The aroma of horsemeat floats through the room. Zuleikha feels her mouth swell with sweet spittle. She hasn't eaten *kyzylyk* since last year. She takes a fresh round loaf of bread from the stove ledge and extends it to Murtaza: *Eat it with bread.* He shakes his head. His jaws are working quickly and powerfully, like millstones. She can hear the tough horse sinews scraping under his sturdy teeth. Glistening strands of spittle fall from Murtaza's open lips to the collar of his shirt.

Without taking the sausage from his mouth, Murtaza's hand fumbles around in the corners of the box. He pulls out a loaf of sugar that gleams a soft white in the duskiness then hits it with all his might using the butt of the axe – a large piece splits off and gleams, sparkling with blue where it broke – then he sticks his hand in one of the trunks and finds a faceted glass vial: it's rat poison he brought from Kazan last year. He pours liquid from the vial on the piece of sugar.

"Understand, woman?" He laughs loudly.

Zuleikha backs toward the wall, frightened. Murtaza places the oozing sugar on the windowsill and wipes his wet hands on his belly. He admires it and throws his head back, laughing, with the *kyzylyk* sticking out of his mouth.

"If they come for the livestock and I'm not here, give it to the cow and horse. Understand?"

Zuleikha gives the barest of nods, pressing her back against the wall's bulging logs.

"*Understand?*" Murtaza hasn't heard a response, so grasps her by the braids and jabs her face at the windowsill, where the sugar is drying in a bitter-smelling puddle and looks a lot like a large piece of ice melting slightly in the warmth.

"Yes, Murtaza! Yes!"

He lets her go, laughing with satisfaction. Sitting on the floor, he chops off pieces of the *kyzylyk* with the axe and stuffs them in his mouth.

"Nothing ..." he mutters through his even chomping. "I won't give it up ... I'm strong ... Nobody can defeat or break me ..."

So, Allah, this is what fear does to my husband. Zuleikha looks around warily and moves the faceted vial of liquid death as far away as possible. She replaces the floorboard and pushes the trunks over it. As she's adjusting the folds of the patterned *kaplau* over the trunks, neatly arranging everything back in its usual place, window glass explodes into smithereens. Something small and heavy flies in from outside, thudding against the floor.

Zuleikha turns around. The large hole in the window looms like a black star with many points, and slow, shaggy snowflakes float into the room. Small pieces of glass are still dropping off, jangling gently as they land.

Murtaza is sitting on the floor, his mouth stuffed. Between his spread legs is a stone wrapped in thick white paper. Murtaza unwraps it and continues to chew, stunned. It's a poster: a gigantic black tractor's large treads are crushing horrid little people who are scattering in every direction like cockroaches. One of them looks a lot like Murtaza; he's standing, frightened, and aiming a crooked wooden pitchfork at the tractor's steel bulk. Heavy, square letters are falling from above: "We'll destroy the kulak as a class!" Zuleikha can't read, especially in Russian. She understands, though, that the black tractor is about to run over the tiny Murtaza and his ridiculous pitchfork.

Murtaza spits a scrap of sausage on the sleeping bench. He wipes his hands and mouth thoroughly with the crumpled poster and flings it into the stove. The tractor and the horrid little people writhe in tongues of orange flame, turning to ash in an instant, then Murtaza grabs the axe and dashes out.

Almighty, all is at Your will! Zuleikha leans toward the window – it's webbed in long cracks. Murtaza bursts outside with his tunic open at the chest and his head uncovered. He looks around, using his axe to threaten a blizzard that's running wild. There's nobody there – *glory be to Allah* – otherwise Murtaza might have hacked them down, brought sin upon his soul.

Zuleikha perches on the sleeping bench and positions her flushed face toward gusts of wind from the broken window. This is no doubt the dirty work of Mansurka-Burdock and his lowlifes from the Party cell. They've walked from household to household more than once, agitating people to join the collective farm and arguing with them. They've covered Yulbash with posters. They had not yet dared break windows. But now things had come to that. It's obvious they know something's afoot. May a devil take them. They'll have to go to the next village for new glass. Such expenses. And the house will cool down overnight …

Murtaza still isn't back. *May he not catch cold.* Out in a blizzard without his sheepskin coat – it really is as if a demon has possessed him …

Zuleikha leaps up suddenly. She runs headlong from the house into the hallway. She throws open the door.

Murtaza and Kyubelek are standing in the middle of the yard, forehead-to-forehead. Murtaza is tenderly stroking the cow's furry face, which is trustingly nestled against his own. Then he takes the axe from behind his back and slams its butt between Kyubelek's large, moist eyes framed with long lashes. The cow collapses to the ground with a quiet, deep sigh, and a thick snowy cloud rises around her.

Zuleikha screams loudly and races down the front steps toward Murtaza. He jabs his fist in her direction without looking. She falls on her back and the steps hit her in the ribs.

The axe whistles. Something hot spatters Zuleikha's face. Blood. Murtaza is working quickly and powerfully with the axe, not stopping. The blade enters the warm flesh with an even groan. Air hisses as it leaves Kyubelek's lungs. Blood gushes out of the vessels with a rumbling gurgle. Solid pink steam cloaks the motionless beef carcass, which Murtaza is quickly breaking into pieces.

"There's your requisitions in 1916!" Murtaza chops through the bones as easily as if they were branches. "The food armies in 1918! 1919! 1920! There's your taking grain for resale! There's your food tax! There's your grain surplus! Take! That! If! You! Can!"

Sandugach is rearing by the door to the cowshed, neighing harrowingly, beating the air with her heavy hooves, and showing the whites of her crazed eyes. The foal is darting around under his mother's legs.

Murtaza turns toward the horse. His tunic is red and his chest is steaming heavily in its wide-open collar; the axe in his hand is black with blood. Zuleikha rises up a little on her elbows, pain searing from her ribs. Murtaza steps over the cow's muzzle, its teeth bared and sharp, its inky-blue tongue hanging out, and heads toward Sandugach.

"Plow? How are we going to plow?" Zuleikha throws herself on Murtaza's back. "It'll be spring soon! We'll die of hunger!"

He tries to shake her off, swinging his arms; the axe he clutches in his right hand whistles. Zuleikha sinks her teeth into her husband's shoulder. He cries out and flings her off, over his shoulder. She flies, the earth and sky changing places again and again. Then something large and hard, with prominent sharp corners, is pushing at her back – is it the front steps? She rolls onto her stomach, half-slides, half-scrambles up the icy steps, and scampers into the house. Her husband stomps after her. Doors slam sharply, like a shepherd's whip, hitting once, twice.

Zuleikha runs through the room. Broken window glass clinks under her feet and she leaps on the sleeping bench, squeezes herself into the corner, and covers herself with a pillow. Murtaza is already beside her. Sweat drips from his beard and his eyes bulge. His arm swings. The axe cuts through the pillowcase and pillow cover in an explosion of white feathers. The feathers fill the room, hanging in the air like a cloud.

Murtaza lets out an extended whoop and tosses the axe to the side, away from Zuleikha. The blade flashes through the air and plunges into the carved window frame.

Feathers fall from above in a slow, warm blizzard. Breathing heavily, Murtaza wipes off something white that's stuck to his bald skull. Without looking at Zuleikha, he pulls the axe out of the window frame and walks out. Glass crunches loudly under his heavy steps, like ice-crusted February snow.

Snowflakes float into the house through the broken window, blending with the floating down. The white swirl inside the house is elegant and festive. Carefully, trying not to cut herself, Zuleikha plugs the hole in the window with the chopped pillow. She sees the scrap of *kyzylyk* on the sleeping bench and eats it. It's delicious. *Praise be to Allah.* Who knows when she'll be able to eat *kyzylyk* again? She licks her fatty, salty fingers. She goes outside.

All the snow by the front steps is the color of juicy wild strawberries mashed with sugar.

Murtaza is chopping meat in a distant corner, on the wooden block by the bathhouse. She can't see Sandugach and the foal.

Zuleikha goes into the cowshed. And there they both are, in their pen. Sandugach is licking her foal with her long, rough tongue. They're alive! *Glory be to Allah.* Zuleikha strokes the horse's warm, velvety muzzle and scratches the foal on its ticklish withers.

And in the yard, thousands of snowy flakes settle on the red snow, covering it and turning it white once more.

AN ENCOUNTER

Murtaza's secret storage place is in a secure spot. Everything he has thought up and built with his own hands is good and sound enough to last for two lives.

Today they rise before dawn. They eat a cold breakfast and leave a yard still lit by a translucent moon and the last pre-dawn stars. They reach the place before daybreak. The sky has already turned from black to bright blue; trees covered in white are filled with light and touched by a diamond brilliance.

There's a morning quiet in the forest and the crisp snow crunches especially loudly under Murtaza's felt boots, like the fresh cabbage Zuleikha chops with a hatchet in a wooden vat. Husband and wife make their way through deep, dense snowdrifts higher than their knees. They're carrying precious cargo on two wooden spades, like stretchers: sacks of grain for planting, carefully wound with rope to the spade shafts. They carry it cautiously, protecting it from sharp branches and rotten stumps. Zuleikha will be in trouble if the burlap tears. In his exhaustion from waiting for the Red Horde, Murtaza has become a complete madman – he would hack her to death, like Kyubelek yesterday, without blinking an eye.

Up ahead, a clearing is already turning blue between spruce trees touched with rime. The birch trees part, tiny icicles jingling on their cottony branches, and they reveal a broad clearing adorned with a thick cover of snow. There's the crooked linden tree with the long crevice-like hollow, too, alongside a chilly rowan bush. They've arrived.

There's a small bird on a linden branch. Its dark blue breast is like a shard of sky and its eyes are like black beads. It looks closely at Zuleikha, chirruping and unafraid.

"Shamsia!" Zuleikha smiles and stretches a hand wearing a thick fur mitten toward the bird.

"Stop chattering, woman!" Murtaza flings a handful of snow and the bird darts away. "We came to work."

Frightened, Zuleikha grabs a spade.

They begin shoveling away the deep snow under the linden tree and soon the outline of a small, dark mound begins to show through. Zuleikha tosses off her mittens and quickly clears it, smoothing with hands that redden in the icy air. Under the cold snow is the coldness of stone. Her fingernails scrape snowy crumbs out of the rounded Arabic script, her fingers melting the ice in the shallow dimples of the *tashkil* over the long wave of letters. Though unable to read, Zuleikha knows what's carved here: "Shamsia, daughter of Murtaza Valiev." And the date: "1917."

While Murtaza is clearing their eldest daughter's grave, Zuleikha takes a step to the side, drops to her knees, and gropes under the drifts for yet another gravestone, throwing the snow around with her elbows. Her numbed fingers find the stone themselves, slipping along the iced-up letters: "Firuza, daughter of Murtaza Valiev. 1920."

The next gravestone: Sabida. 1924.

The next: Khalida. 1926.

"You shirking?" Murtaza has already cleared off the first grave and stands, leaning on the shaft of the spade, his eyes boring into Zuleikha. His irises are yellow and cold, and the whites of his eyes are dark, a clouded ruby color. The wrinkle in the middle of his forehead is moving as if it were alive.

"I'm saying hello to everyone," says Zuleikha, looking down guiltily.

The four slightly tilting gray stones stand in a row, looking at her silently. They're low, the height of a year-old child.

"It'd be better to help!" Murtaza grunts and plunges the spade into the frozen earth with all his might.

"Oh, but wait!" Zuleikha throws herself on Shamsia's grave-stone and presses her forearms to it.

Murtaza's breathing is loud and displeased but he's set the spade aside; he's waiting.

"Forgive us, *zirat iyase*, spirit of the cemetery. We didn't want to bother you before spring but we had to," Zuleikha whispers at the rounded patterns of letters. "And forgive us, daughter. I know you aren't angry. You yourself are glad to help your parents."

Zuleikha rises from her knees and nods: *Now we can continue.* Murtaza gouges at the earth by the grave, attempting to place the spade in a frozen crevice that's scarcely visible. Zuleikha digs at the ice with a stick. The crevice broadens gradually, growing and giving way, then finally opening up with an extended crack and uncovering a long wooden box, from which there wafts the smell of frozen earth. The sunny yellow grain makes a whooshing sound as Murtaza carefully pours it into the box, and Zuleikha places her hands under its heavy, flowing stream.

Grain.

It will sleep here over winter, between Shamsia and Firuza, in a deep wooden coffin. And when the air has begun to smell of spring and the meadows have already been warmed, it will lie down in the earth again, so it can sprout and develop as green shoots on tilled soil.

It was Murtaza who thought of digging out the secret place in the village cemetery. Zuleikha was initially frightened: isn't it a sin to disturb the dead? Wouldn't it be best to ask the mullah's permission? And wouldn't the spirit of the cemetery be angry? But she later agreed – let their daughters help with the chores. And their daughters helped meticulously. This was not the first year they had watched over their parents' supplies until spring.

The box's lid bangs shut. Murtaza strews snow on the disturbed grave. Then he winds the empty sacks around the spade handles, tosses them over his shoulder, and heads into the forest.

Zuleikha sprinkles more snow on the dug-up gravestones, as if she were covering them with a blanket at night. *Goodbye, girls. We'll see you in the spring if the Vampire Hag's prediction doesn't come true before then.*

"Murtaza," Zuleikha calls quietly to him. "If anything happens, put me here, with the girls. To Khalida's right, that place is free. I don't need a lot of space, you know that."

Her husband doesn't stop; his tall figure flashes between the birches. Zuleikha quietly murmurs something to the stones in parting and pulls her mittens on her stiff hands.

There's chirping again on the linden branch: the nimble, blue-breasted little bird has returned to its place. Zuleikha waves joyfully to it – *Shamsia, I knew that was you!* – and dashes after her husband.

The sledge rides along the forest road, not hurrying. Sandugach snorts, urging the foal to keep up. The foal gallops joyfully beside her, sometimes sinking thin legs into snowdrifts on the roadside or poking a hook-nosed muzzle at his mother's side. The foal has tagged along with them today. And rightly so: let him get used to trips to the forest.

The sun hasn't yet reached midday but their work is already done. Glory be to Allah, nobody noticed them. A snowstorm will sweep away their tracks at the cemetery any day and it will be as if nothing happened.

As always, Zuleikha sits on the sledge facing away from Murtaza. The back of her head senses heavy, gloomy thoughts stirring in his mind. She had hoped her husband would calm down a little after hiding the grain and that the large wrinkle on his forehead, the one that looks as if it was hacked by an axe, would smooth. But no, the wrinkle hasn't gone away; it's even deeper now.

"I'm going into the forest tonight," he says, speaking to something in front of him, addressing either the collar on Sandugach's neck or the horse's tail.

"What are you talking about?" Zuleikha turns and fixes her mournful gaze on her husband's stern back. "It's January ..."

"There'll be a lot of us. We won't freeze."

Murtaza has never gone into the forest. Other men had, in 1920 and 1924. They huddled in groups, hiding from the new authorities. They either slaughtered livestock or brought it with them. Their wives and children stayed at home to wait and hope their husbands would return. Sometimes they did, though more often they didn't. The Red Horde shot some; others went missing.

"Don't expect me before spring," Murtaza goes on. "Look after my mother."

Zuleikha is watching the rough, spongy sheepskin tightly stretched between her husband's powerful shoulder blades.

"I'll take the horse." Murtaza makes a kissing noise and Sandugach obediently quickens her pace. "You can eat the foal."

The young one hurries after his mother, amusingly throwing his legs forward, then backward, frolicking.

"She won't survive," Zuleikha says to Murtaza's back. "Your mother won't survive, I'm telling you."

His back is gloomily silent. Sandugach's hooves thump into the snow. Magpies mockingly jabber somewhere in the forest. Murtaza takes the shaggy fur hat from his head and rubs his glistening, bumpy scalp; barely visible steam rises from his smooth pink skin.

The conversation is over. Zuleikha turns. She has never in her life been left on her own. Who will tell her what to do and what not to do? Scold her for poor work? Protect her from the Red Horde? Feed her, too? And what about the Vampire Hag? Did she make a mistake? Will the old woman stay in a house without her beloved son but with her despised daughter-in-law? And *Allah, what is this all for?*

The singing overtakes them as suddenly as a gust of wind, replacing the sad squeaking sound of sledge runners with a confident male voice. There it is, beautiful and deep, somewhere far in the woods. The words are Russian, the melody unfamiliar. Zuleikha wants to listen but for some reason Murtaza's bustling along, urging on Sandugach.

> We won't rely on other powers,
> No god, no swell, no tsar.
> We'll claim the freedom that is ours,
> They'll know whose hands these are.

Zuleikha's Russian isn't bad. She understands that the words in the song are good, about freedom and salvation.

"Hide the spades," Murtaza tells her through his teeth.

Zuleikha hastily wraps the spades in sacks, covering them with her skirts.

Sandugach is trotting quickly but still not fast enough – she's been adjusting to the foal's uneven run. And the voice is coming closer, overtaking them.

We'll fight the tyrant and dethrone him,
These hands of ours must do.
We'll break the manacles we owe him
While the iron's hot and true.

The song of a working person, Zuleikha decides, a blacksmith or
smelter. It's already clear this person is riding behind them along
the forest road and will soon catch up to them, out from the trees.
How old is he? Probably young: there's a lot of strength, a lot of
hope, in his voice.

For this will be the war to settle,
Our fate for good and all;
It's time for humankind's last battle
And the Internationale.

In the distance, dark silhouettes are flickering swiftly between the
trees. Now a small cavalry detachment appears on the road, too.
At the front is a man with an easy, straight posture, and it's clear
from afar that he's neither a blacksmith nor a smelter but a warrior.
When he rides closer, the broad green stripes on his gray military
overcoat become visible; on his head there's a pointed, coarse hat
with a reddish-brown star. A Red Hordesman. He's the one singing.

It's up to us, the laboring masses
Of the world to rise and fight;
The rule of landlords surely passes
And we'll seize what's ours by right.

Allah endowed Zuleikha with excellent vision. In the bright
sunlight, she discerns the Red Hordesman's face, which is uncom-
monly smooth for a man: it's really like a girl's, with neither

mustache nor beard. His eyes seem dark under the brim, and his even white teeth look like they're made of sugar.

And once that mighty lightning flashes
To strike the proud and cruel,
The sun will blaze down on their ashes
When the proletariat rule.

The Red Hordesman is already very close. When he squints from the sun, crows' feet at the corners of his eyes run under the long, coarse fabric earflaps of his pointy hat. He's shameless, openly smiling at Zuleikha. She lowers her eyes as a married woman should and buries her chin deeper in her shawl.

"Hey, boss, is it far to Yulbash?" the Red Hordesman asks, riding right up to the sledge and not taking his eyes off Zuleikha. She senses the hot, salty smell of his horse.

Murtaza doesn't turn; he keeps urging on Sandugach.

"Gone deaf or something?" The rider presses his horse's sides lightly with his heels and overtakes the sledge in two bounds.

Murtaza suddenly slaps Sandugach's back with the reins. She leaps abruptly forward, knocking her chest into the soldier's horse, so that it neighs with alarm, stumbles off the road, catches its back legs in a snowdrift on the roadside, and flounders in the snow.

"Or gone blind?" The Red Hordesman's voice is ringing with rage.

"The little man's scared. He's hurrying home to hide under Mama's skirts." The cavalry detachment has caught up to the sledge, and a swarthy little man, whose upper lip is raised in amusement, revealing a bright gold tooth, brashly eyes the sledge. "They're a nervous bunch!"

How many of them are there, anyway? No more than you could count on all your fingers. The men are solid, sturdy. Some are in military overcoats, some just in sheepskin coats pulled in at the waist with a broad reddish belt. Each has a rifle on his back. The bayonets glisten in the sun; it's dazzling.

And one's a woman. Lips like bilberries, cheeks like apples. She sits squarely in the saddle, head raised high, bosom pushed forward, allowing herself to be admired. Even under the sheepskin it's obvious that chest would be enough for three. A picture of wholesomeness.

The horse that was forced off the road finally makes its way back and its rider grabs Sandugach by the bridle. The sledge stops and Murtaza tosses aside the reins. He hides his sullen expression and doesn't look at the cavalrymen.

"Well?" the soldier asks, threatening.

"Oh, they don't speak a word of Russian here, comrade Ignatov," calls out an elderly soldier with a long scar across half his face. The scar is white and very even, like a stretched rope. From a saber, Zuleikha guesses.

"Not a word. So then ..." Ignatov attentively examines the horse, the colt hiding under her belly, and Murtaza himself.

Murtaza is silent. His shaggy fur hat is pulled over his forehead, screening his eyes. Curly little clouds of dense steam float out of his whitened nostrils, covering his mustache with a raggedy frost.

"Well, you are a gloomy one, brother," utters Ignatov, pensive.

"His wife gave him a talking-to!" The swarthy soldier with the gleaming gold tooth winks at Zuleikha, first with one eye, then the other. The whites of his eyes are as murky as the liquid in oatmeal and his pupils are small nuggets. The members of the detachment laugh. "Tatar women, oh, but they are harsh! You won't get away with anything! Isn't that right, Green Eyes?"

Her father called her Green Eyes when she was a child. That was a long time ago. Zuleikha no longer thinks about the color of her eyes.

The detachment laughs louder. Ten pairs of audacious and mocking eyes scrutinize her intently. She uses the edge of her shawl to cover her cheeks, which are burning.

"They're harsh but not especially pretty," the busty cavalry-woman adds lazily, turning away.

"How could they compare to you, Nastasya!" whoop the Red Hordesmen.

Zuleikha hears how hoarse and labored her husband's breathing is behind her back.

"As you were!" Ignatov resumes scrutinizing Murtaza. "So where'd you go so bright and early, boss? And with your wife, too. I see you weren't chopping up any wood. What'd you lose in the forest? Come on, don't look away. I see you understand everything."

The horses stamp their hooves and snort loudly in the quiet. Zuleikha senses but doesn't see that the furrow on Murtaza's forehead is deepening, cutting into his skull, and the dimple in his chin is trembling, like a bobber over a fish caught on a hook.

"They were digging mushrooms out from under the snow," says the soldier with the gold tooth, lifting Zuleikha's skirt a little with his bayonet; the spades' blades peer out from under sacks. "But they didn't gather much!" He picks up one of the sacks with the point of his bayonet and shakes it in the air.

The brigade's snickering swells into waves of laughter. A few large yellow grains fall from the sack to Zuleikha's skirt and the laughter ends abruptly, as if it had been cut by a knife.

Looking down at her hem, Zuleikha takes off a mitten and hurriedly collects the grains in her fist. The cavalrymen circle the sledge, silently surrounding it. Murtaza slowly moves his hand toward the axe tucked in his sash.

Ignatov tosses his reins to a cavalryman who's ridden over, and jumps to the ground. He walks up to Zuleikha, takes her fist in both hands, and forces it open. Up close, it's obvious his eyes aren't dark at all but bright gray, like river water. Beautiful eyes. And his fingers are dry and unexpectedly hot. And very strong. Zuleikha's fist yields, unclenching. On her palm are long, smooth grains that gleam in the sun like honey. Quality wheat seed.

"Mushrooms, then," Ignatov says softly. "So maybe, you kulak louse, you were out digging in the forest for some other reason?"

After sitting like a statue, Murtaza suddenly turns sharply toward the sledge and looks Ignatov in the eye with hatred. His stifled breathing gurgles in his gullet, and his chin shakes. Ignatov unfastens the holster on his belt, reaches for a black revolver with a long, hungry barrel, points it at Murtaza, and cocks it.

"I won't give it up!" Murtaza wheezes. "I won't give up anything this time!"

He swings the axe. Rifles click all at once. Ignatov presses the trigger. A shot blasts and the echo spreads through the forest. Sandugach neighs with fright. Magpies drop from the spruce trees and hurry off into a thicket, screeching loudly. Murtaza's body collapses onto the sledge, his feet toward the horse, face down. The sledge shudders heavily.

The rifles stare at Zuleikha, the black barrels gleaming under the needles of their bayonets. A blue puff of smoke rises from the revolver. There's a bitter smell of gunpowder.

Ignatov, stunned, is looking at the body prone on the sledge. He wipes his upper lip with the hand that's holding the revolver and stows the weapon in his holster. He takes the axe that fell from its owner's hand and swings, plunging it into the back of the sledge, just a finger's length from Murtaza's head. Then he leaps into his saddle, digs his heels into the horse, and speeds off down the road, full tilt, without looking back. Snow sprays out from under the horse's hooves like dust.

"Comrade Ignatov," the soldier with the gold tooth shouts after him. "What about the woman?"

Ignatov only waves: *Leave her!*

"So much for the mushroom picking, Green Eyes," the soldier says, pushing out a broad lip in conclusion.

The cavalrymen hurry off behind their commander. The detachment flows around the sledge like waves around an island. Sheepskin coats with fleecy collars, shaggy fur hats, gray overcoats, and the red stripes on their trousers float past, speeding after the horseman in the pointy-topped cavalry hat. The clatter of hooves soon fades in the distance. Zuleikha is left by herself, in the middle of the forest's stillness.

She sits motionless with her arms folded on her knees and her small fist squeezing the wheat grains. Murtaza's powerful body is sprawled out on the sledge, freely stretching his arms and legs, head comfortably turned on its side, long beard spread out along the boards. He's sleeping, just as he always does on his bench, taking up the entire space. There's not even enough room for small Zuleikha to fit alongside him.

The wind plucks at the treetops. Pine trees creak somewhere in the forest. A couple of hours later, the foal is hungry and finds his mother's teat with his lips and suckles milk. Sandugach inclines her head, contented.

An unhurried sun drifts along the horizon then slowly sinks into large snow clouds wafting in from the east. Evening is falling. Snow pelts down from the sky.

Without receiving her master's usual shout and slap on the rump with the reins, Sandugach takes a timid step forward. Then a second and a third. The sledge begins to move, creaking loudly. The horse strides along the road to Yulbash, and the happy, sated foal skips alongside. The reins lie on the empty driver's spot. Zuleikha is sitting on the sledge, her back to the horse, her unseeing gaze looking at the forest that remains behind.

On the road, where the sledge stood all day, is a deep-red spot about the size of a small round loaf of bread. Snow falls on the spot, quickly covering it.

Later, no matter how hard she tries, Zuleikha cannot remember how she got home. How she left the horse in the yard, still harnessed, and grasped Murtaza under the arms and dragged him inside the house. How heavy her husband's huge, unwieldy body was, how loudly his heels knocked against the front steps.

She fluffed his pillow nice and high, just how he loves it, undressed him, and laid him on the sleeping bench. Lay down alongside him herself. They lay like that a long time, all night. The wood Murtaza had thrown in the stove that morning had burned down long ago and the logs of the cooling house crackled resonantly from the cold. The window that was broken yesterday had already burst and shattered with a flat, glassy jangle, and a mean wind mixed with prickly grains of snow whipped through the square window's bare frame. And still they lay there, shoulder to shoulder, their wide-open eyes looking at the ceiling, which was first dark, then thickly flooded with white moonlight, then dark again. For the first time, Murtaza didn't send her off to the women's quarters. That was utterly surprising. A feeling of immense surprise would be the only thing from that night that remained in Zuleikha's memory.

After the edge of the sky has turned alarmingly scarlet, foretelling a chilly dawn, there's a knock at the gate. The knock is loud, angry, and insistent. A tired master of the house knocks meanly and relentlessly like that when returning home and discovering someone has locked his house from the inside.

Zuleikha hears the noise – it's far away and indistinct, as if it's coming through the feather mattress. But she doesn't have the strength to stop staring at the ceiling. Let Murtaza get up and open it. It's not a woman's job to open doors at night.

The bolt on the gate clanks, letting in uninvited guests. The yard fills with voices and the neighing of horses. Several tall silhouettes float through a yard that's still dark. The door in the entrance hall – the door into the house – bangs.

"Well, now, this is cold! Did everybody here die or something?"

"Get the stove going! We'll freeze, damn it."

The clatter of hobnail boots on frozen boards. Floorboards squeaking loudly, alarmingly. The clang of the stove damper. The scratch of a match and the sharp smell of sulfur. The crackle of a fire flaring in the stove.

"Where are the people who live here?"

"We'll find them, don't fret. Have a look around for now."

The wick in the lamp flickers as it flares up: crooked black shadows dance along the walls and a soft, warm light is already beginning to fill the house. A broad-nosed face ruined by large pockmarks leans over Zuleikha. It's Mansurka-Burdock, chairman of the rural council. He's holding a kerosene lamp right next to his face, making the round pox scars seem as deep as if they'd been hollowed out by a spoon. He's looking purposefully at Zuleikha. He shifts his gaze to Murtaza's thinned face, scrutinizes the black clotted hole on his chest, perplexed, and whistles, at a loss.

"Zuleikha, we came to see your husband ..."

An ornate little frozen cloud blossoms by Mansurka's mouth. He speaks Russian with a heavy accent but briskly, coherently. Better than Zuleikha. Mansurka's become adept at chatting with the Red Hordesmen.

"Get up, we need to talk."

Zuleikha doesn't know if this is real or a dream. If it's a dream, why does the light hurt her eyes so much? If it's real, why are the sounds and smells carrying from so far away, as if from the basement?

"Zuleikha!" Mansurka is shaking her by the shoulder, first lightly, then harder. "Get up, woman!" he shouts loudly and angrily, finally in Tatar.

Her body responds to the familiar words like a horse to a slap of the reins. Zuleikha slowly lowers her feet to the floor and sits up on the sleeping bench.

"There you go." Mansurka switches back to Russian, satisfied. "Ready, comrade representative!"

Ignatov is standing in the center of the house, his hands tucked into his belt and boots placed far apart. Without glancing at Zuleikha, he takes a wrinkled sheet of paper and a pencil from his rigid leather map case. He looks around, annoyed.

"What is this anyway? How many houses have I seen without a table or bench? How am I supposed to write a report?"

The chairman hurriedly thuds his palm on the lid of the top trunk by the window:

"You can do it here."

Ignatov somehow settles in on the trunk; the linen *kaplau* wrinkles up under his large body and slips to the floor. He breathes on his hands to warm them, licks the pencil's point, and scratches it along the paper.

"They haven't yet cultivated socialist life," Mansurka mutters in an apologetic tone, holding on to the trunks, which are attempting to slide in various directions. "Heathens, what can you expect from them?"

There's a sudden crash of smashing pots and the ringing of copper basins falling in the women's quarters. The hens are clucking in a frenzy. Someone's tangled in the folds of the curtain, swearing loudly and colorfully. The soldier with the gold tooth springs out from behind the curtains in a cloud of feathers and down. He has one hen under each arm, loudly squawking in alarm.

"Well, how about that! Green Eyes!" he says joyfully when he sees Zuleikha. "May I?" Without stopping or releasing the fluttering chickens from his armpits, he neatly pulls the lacy web of *kaplau* out from under Ignatov's feet with a magician's quick motion. "I'll take these trunks a little later." He finally backs toward the door under Ignatov's angry gaze and disappears, leaving a swirl of feathers behind him.

Ignatov finishes writing and places the pencil on the completed report with a thud:

"She can sign it."

The sheet of paper on the trunk is white, like a folded, embroidered towel.

"What is this?" Zuleikha slowly shifts her gaze to Mansurka. "What's it for?"

"How many times have I said that you have to call me comrade chairman! Is that clear?" Mansurka menacingly raises his chin, which shows through his reddish beard. "You teach them a new life, but they just don't … Look, we're evicting you." He glances around, dissatisfied, at the bed where Murtaza's powerful body lies, dark. "Just you. As a kulak element of the first category. Active counterrevolutionary. The Party meeting ratified it." Mansurka's short finger pokes at the paper on the trunk. "And we're requisitioning your property to use for the rural council."

"Don't confuse me with newfangled words. Just tell me, comrade Mansurka, what's going on?"

"That's for you to tell me! Why isn't your Murtaza's property collectivized yet? Are you going against state power, as individual peasant farmers? I've tried convincing you so much my tongue's going to fall out. Why isn't your cow at the collective farm?"

"There is no cow."

"What about the horse?" Mansurka nods at the window: Sandugach is outside, still harnessed and standing in the yard with the foal circling her legs. "Two horses."

"But they're ours."

"*Ours*," he mimics her. "And the flour mill?"

"How can you have a household without one? Remember how many times you yourself borrowed ours?"

"That's just the thing." His already-narrow eyes squint. "Leasing equipment used for labor. A sure sign of the dyed-in-the-wool, deep-rooted, irredeemable kulak!" He squeezes his small hand into a mean, wiry fist.

"Pardon me, excuse me ..." says the soldier with the gold tooth, who's returned and is now pulling a stack of pillows in embroidered cases out from under Murtaza's head, which thuds against the bench. He strips curtains from the windows and embroidered towels from the walls and carries a huge heap of linens, pillows, and quilts out of the house in his outstretched arms. Unable to see anything in front of him, he kicks open the creaking front door.

"Careful, Prokopenko, you're not in your own house!" Mansurka snaps after him. He tenderly strokes the wall of bulging logs and the carved patterns on the window frame, where he fingers the deep notch from the axe and clicks his tongue in distress. "Sign it, Zuleikha; don't drag it out," he sighs amiably and sincerely, unable to tear his loving gaze from the smooth, fat logs generously caulked with stringy, high-quality oakum.

Prokopenko's head pokes through the doorway again, his eyes gleaming with excitement:

"Comrade Ignatov, the cow, there's ... only the meat's left. Should we take it?"

"Add it to the inventory," Ignatov says gloomily and rises

from the trunk. "Are we going to be here a long time working on political education?"

"What's with you, Zuleikha?" Mansurka arches his thin eyebrows reproachfully toward the bridge of his nose. "These comrades came all the way from Kazan to get you. And you're delaying them."

"I won't sign it." She utters this to the floor. "I'm not going anywhere."

Ignatov walks over to the window, raps his knuckles on the glass, and nods to someone outside. The floorboards groan under his boots, squeaking for a long time. *He's standing on the sausage and doesn't know it*, thinks Zuleikha.

A soldier bursts into the house. Zuleikha recognizes him: his face is dark red and his scar is completely white after standing in the cold for so long.

"Five minutes for her to gather her things, Slavutsky." Ignatov motions his chin at Zuleikha.

The indefatigable Prokopenko is examining the bare, seemingly unlived-in house one last time, as if he's searching for some unnoticed loot. Finally he catches the blade of his bayonet on a tapestry embroidered with a saying from the Koran that hangs high over the entrance – he tries to take it down. The ornate interlacing of Arabic letters pulls and wrinkles under the steel blade.

"That's what they have instead of icons," Slavutsky tells Prokopenko quietly in passing.

"Planning to pray?" Ignatov looks intently at Prokopenko, his nostrils quivering in disgust, and then goes out.

"There you go. And you were saying they're heathens." Prokopenko sniffs at Mansurka and hurries after the commander.

The tattered tapestry remains hanging in its place. The mullah once explained the meaning of it, saying to Zuleikha: "No soul can ever die except by Allah's leave and at a time appointed."

"You'll leave anyway, even if you don't sign it," Mansurka-Burdock tells Zuleikha.

And he points significantly at Slavutsky, the soldier with the scar. He's strolling through the house, examining and prodding the exposed beams of the storage shelves under the ceiling with his bayonet.

Zuleikha falls to her knees next to the sleeping bench, pressing her forehead to Murtaza's cold, hard hand. *My husband – given by the Almighty, to direct, feed, and protect me – what should I do?*

"We'll bury Murtaza properly, according to Soviet custom," the chairman soothes her, lovingly stroking the rough, carefully whitened sides of the stove. "Despite everything, he was a good master of the house ..."

A steel blade touches Zuleikha: Prokopenko has come up behind her and is lightly tapping her shoulder with his bayonet. She shakes her head: *I'm not going.* Strong hands suddenly scoop her up and lift her in the air. Zuleikha jerks her arms and legs like a fussy baby in an adult's arms, her baggy pants flashing under her skirts, but Slavutsky holds her firmly, until it hurts.

"Don't touch me!" Zuleikha screams out from under the ceiling. "It's a sin!"

"Are you going on your own? Or do we have to carry you out?" Mansurka's concerned voice asks from somewhere below.

"On my own."

Slavutsky cautiously releases Zuleikha. Her feet land on the floor.

"Allah will punish you," she tells Mansurka. "He'll punish all of you."

And she begins gathering her things.

"Dress warmly," Mansurka advises her, tossing wood in the stove and stoking the fire with the poker, as if he owned it. "So as not to catch cold."

Her things are soon tied in a bundle. Zuleikha winds a shawl snugly around her head and draws her sheepskin coat tightly closed. From a stove shelf she takes the remainder of a loaf of bread wrapped in a rag, and puts it in one pocket. In the other she places the poisoned sugar from the windowsill. A tiny dead carcass remains lying by the window; a little mouse had a treat during the night.

She's ready for the journey.

She stops near the door and casts a glance at the ravaged house. Bare walls, uncovered windows, a couple of trampled embroidered towels on the dirty floor. Murtaza is lying on the sleeping bench, his pointy beard thrust toward the ceiling. He's not looking at Zuleikha. *My husband, forgive me. I am not leaving you of my own will.*

There's a loud sound of fabric ripping – Mansurka is tearing down the curtain dividing the men's quarters from the women's, then he brushes off his hands, satisfied. The smashed pots, gutted trunks, and remainders of kitchen goods brazenly reveal themselves to the gaze of anyone entering. So disgraceful.

Blushing from the unbearable shame, Zuleikha looks down and runs out to the hallway.

Dawn glows in the sky.

A huge pile of household goods towers in the middle of the yard: trunks, baskets, dishes, tools … Panting from exertion, Prokopenko drags a heavy, hollowed-out cradle from the storehouse.

"Comrade Ignatov! Have a look, should we take this?"

"You fool."

"I thought it should be entered on the inventory …" says Prokopenko, offended, and then he hurls the cradle on the very top of the pile anyway since he's made up his mind. "Sweet mother of mine, do they have a lot of stuff!"

"Even so, everything belongs to the kolkhoz now." Mansurka picks up a basket that fell off the pile and neatly places it back.

"Uh-huh. Ours. The people's." Prokopenko smiles broadly and secretly stuffs a small linen *kaplau* in his pocket.

Zuleikha walks down the front steps and sits on the sledge, her back to the horse, out of habit. Sandugach, who stood too long during the night, tosses back her head.

"Zuleikhaaa!" A low, hoarse voice suddenly sounds from inside the house.

Everyone turns toward the door.

"The deceased has come to life," Prokopenko whispers loudly in the silence and surreptitiously crosses himself, as he backs toward the storehouse.

"Zuleikhaaa!" carries again from the house.

Ignatov raises his revolver. The cradle tumbles from the pile and crashes to the ground, splitting into pieces with a crack. The door flings open with an extended scrape and the Vampire Hag stands in the opening. Her long nightgown flutters and her lips quiver angrily. Her round, white eye sockets dig into the guests; her walking stick is in one hand, her chamber pot in the other.

"Where the devil are you, you pathetic hen?"

"Damn it," says Prokopenko, catching his breath. "I almost went gray."

"Look, she's alive, the old witch." Mansurka wipes perspiration from his forehead with his hand.

"And who might that be?" Ignatov stuffs the revolver back in the holster.

"His mother." Mansurka scrutinizes the old woman and whistles in admiration. "She's at least a hundred."

"How come she's not on the list?"

"Who could have known that she's still –"

"Zuleikhaaa! You'll get it in the end, Murtaza will show you!" The Vampire Hag jerks her chin up furiously and shakes her walking stick. She hurls the contents of the chamber pot in front of her with a sweeping motion. The little cornflowers on the milky porcelain flash. The cloudy liquid flies like a precise gob of spit and a large dark spot creeps along Ignatov's overcoat.

Slavutsky swings his rifle up but Ignatov flaps his arm: *As you were!* Mansurka hurriedly opens the gate and Ignatov, his expression souring, jumps on his horse and rides out of the yard.

"Should we take her?" Prokopenko shouts after Ignatov.

"All we need in the caravan of sledges is the living dead," he says, already in the road.

"Why are you sitting there?" Prokopenko leaps onto his horse and looks impatiently at Zuleikha. "Let's go!"

Puzzled, Zuleikha looks around, moves into the driver's place, and takes the heavy reins in her hands. She turns to her mother-in-law.

"My Murtaza will have your hide!" the Vampire Hag croaks from the front steps, the wind fluttering the wispy strands of her white braids. "Zuleikhaaa!"

Sandugach sets off, the foal following. Zuleikha drives out of the yard.

Prokopenko rides out last. He raises his head and sees ice-covered yellow skulls on a section of the gate: a horse bares long, sparse teeth; a bull's black eye sockets stare stubbornly; and a sheep bends his wavy horns as if they're snakes.

"No, they're heathens after all," he decides and hurries after the others.

"My Murtaza will kill you! Kill you! Zuleikhaaa!" carries after them.

Mansurka-Burdock smirks. He closes the gate from the outside, gently patting the sturdy, solid sections with his hand (*hmm, those latches will need to be stronger!*) and hurries home to get some sleep. Fifteen households in just one night is no joke. He doesn't yet know that two men are waiting to ambush him by his house.

They'll push him against the fence, breathe hotly in his face, and disappear, and he'll remain a motionless little sack hanging on the boards, pierced by two crooked sickles, his dumbfounded glassy eyes agog at the morning sky.

Zuleikha's sledge merges into a long caravan of others being dekulakized. Their procession flows along Yulbash's main street, toward the edge of town. There are cavalry soldiers with rifles lining the road. Among them is the busty Nastasya, with the magnificent cheeks, the one Zuleikha saw in the forest that morning.

"So, comrade Ignatov," she shouts teasingly, glancing at Zuleikha, "is it easier to dekulakize women or something?"

Ignatov pays no attention and nudges his horse forward at a trot.

The gate of her husband's house is growing distant, shrinking, and dissolving into the darkness of the street. Zuleikha cranes her neck and looks, looks at it, unable to turn away.

"Zuleikhaaa!" carries from the gate.

In windows along both sides of the street are the ashen faces of neighbors, their eyes wide open.

And there's the edge of town.

They've left Yulbash.

"Zuleikhaaa!" rings out a barely audible voice.

The convoy of sledges rides up a hill. The smattering of Yulbash houses darkens in the distance.

"Zuleikhaaa!" the wind howls in her ears. "Zuleikhaaa!"

She turns her head to face forward. From the top of the hill, the plain that sprawls below seems like a giant white tablecloth along which the hand of the Almighty has scattered trees like beads and roads like ribbons. Their caravan is a thin silk thread stretching beyond the horizon, over which a scarlet sun is solemnly rising.

PART TWO

WHERE TO?

Taking the Road

She's a good-looking woman.

Ignatov is riding at the head of the caravan. At times he stops to let the detachment pass by, looking intently at everyone: the gloomy kulaks on sledges as well as his own fine troops, all reddened from the cold. Then he overtakes them again because he likes to be the first to forge ahead, with only a broad, inviting open space and the wind in front of him.

He's trying not to watch that woman, so she won't think he's up to something. But how could you not watch when her curves just gallop right into your eyes like that? She's sitting there like she's on a throne, not a horse. She rocks in the saddle with each stride, her lower back arching sharply and her chest thrust forward, tightly covered in a white sheepskin coat, as if she's nodding and repeating to him: *Yes, comrade Ignatov, yes, Vanya, yes, yes …*

He rises partway in his stirrups, meticulously examining the caravan flowing past him from under the visor of his hand, as if he's protecting his eyes from the sun. In reality, he's screening his gaze, which keeps disobediently attaching itself to Nastasya.

The sledges sail on, creaking loudly along the snow. Horses snort from time to time and little clouds of steam rise like intricate flowers above their frost-covered snouts.

A man with a mussed black beard and a ferocious appearance is nervously and angrily driving a mare. Behind him are his wife – wrapped in a shawl to the brows and with a sack of an infant in each arm – and a motley little flock of children. "I'll kill you," he'd shouted when they came to his house; he'd rushed at Ignatov with a pitchfork. He thought better of things and cooled down after they'd aimed their rifles at his wife and children. No, you can't take on Ignatov with a pitchfork.

An elderly mullah ineptly holds the reins, his woolen gloves turned inside out. It's evident he's never taken anything heavier than a book in his hands in his whole life. The springy curls of his expensive karakul fur coat shine in the sun. *You won't keep a fur like that the whole way*, thinks Ignatov indifferently. It'll be taken away, either at a distribution point or somewhere else along the road. *There's no reason to dress up anyway. You're not going to a wedding …* The mullah's wife is sitting in the back, in a bulky, despondent heap. In her arms is an elegant cage wrapped in a horse blanket. She brought her beloved cat with her. A fool.

It's disconcerting for Ignatov to look at the next sledge. It would appear that, well, he'd killed a man, leaving his wife without a husband. That had happened more than once already. It was the man's own fault: he'd rushed at Ignatov with an axe, like a madman. All they'd wanted in the beginning was to ask the way. But a repugnant sort of feeling gnaws at Ignatov's guts; it won't leave him alone. Pity? That woman is painfully small and thin. And her face is pale and delicate, as if it were paper. It's clear she won't survive the road. She might have made it with her husband, but like this … Ignatov has as good as killed her as well as her husband.

He's begun pitying kulaks. That's what he's come to.

The small woman looks up as she rides past. And, oh, mother of mine, are those eyes of hers green! His horse is pawing at the ground, dancing in place. Ignatov turns in his saddle to have a better look but the sledge has already gone by. There's a black welt on its back, left yesterday when Ignatov hacked it hard with an axe.

As he looks at that mark, the back of his head is already sensing the approach of a large, shaggy chestnut horse and Nastasya's magnificent bust, bending toward its mane, breaking out of her clothes, and shouting to the whole plain with each motion: *Yes, Vanya, yes, yes, yes …*

Nastasya first caught his eye back during training.

The new recruits usually gathered in the morning in the courtyard right under his window. For two days they listened to rousing political speeches and practiced with rifles; then on the third day a certificate was shoved at them and off they went on a job, special assignments under the command of a State Political Administration colleague. There would already be a new batch in the yard the next morning. Lots of volunteers came – they all wanted to be involved in a just cause. Women turned up, too, though for some reason more women signed up for the militia. And rightly so – the State Political Administration was man's work, serious.

Take Nastasya, for example. All the training in the courtyard had come to a standstill when she arrived. The recruits' eyes bugged out at the sight of her, their necks twisted like dead chickens', and they only half-listened to the instructors. Even the instructor wore himself out, sweating all over as he explained the structure of a rifle to her – Ignatov had seen all this from his office. Somehow they trained the detachment, sent them to work, and breathed a sigh of relief. But the memory of the beautiful woman had remained in his belly like a sweet chill.

Ignatov hadn't gone to see Ilona that evening. She was a sassy kind of girl, she wasn't too young (not broken by life yet, not proud), nor too old (still pleasant to look at), and her body had turned out well (there was something to hold on to), plus she hung on his every word, couldn't gaze at him enough, and her room in the communal apartment was large, twelve square meters. This was basically too much of a good thing. She'd even told him, "Ivan, come live with me, it's a good idea!" But it turned out to be too much.

Tossing and turning on his hard dormitory bed, he heard his roommates snoring and reflected on life. Wasn't it caddish to lust over a new girl while the old one was still hoping, most likely plumping the pillows as she waited for him? No, he decided, it wasn't caddish. People experience a burning for something: that's what feelings are about. And if those feelings are gone, what's the point in clinging to the embers?

Ignatov had never been a womanizer. He was an impressive, strapping man driven by political ideology and it was usually the women who looked at him, trying to catch his fancy. But he was in no hurry to get to know them better and feel an attachment, too. This was embarrassing to admit, but he could count the number of those women in his life on the fingers of one hand. Somehow, he'd had other things to do. He'd enlisted in the Red Army in 1918 and that got him started: first there was the Civil War, then hacking at the Basmachi in Central Asia. He'd probably still be swinging a sword in the mountains if not for Bakiev. Bakiev had already become someone important in Kazan by that time: he'd transformed from lanky, redheaded Mishka into staid Tokhtamysh Muradovich with a respectable shaved head and a gold pince-nez in his breast pocket. It was he who'd returned Ignatov to his native Tataria. "Come back, Vanya," he'd said, "I desperately need my own people and can't do it without you." He knew, the sneak, how to get you. Ignatov bought into it and came rushing home to help out a friend.

That's how he started working at the Kazan State Political Administration. It didn't exactly turn out to be interesting (paperwork, meetings, etc.) but there was no use sighing over that now. He soon met a typist from the office on Bolshaya Prolomnaya Street. She had plump, sloping shoulders and the doleful name Ilona. Only now, at a full thirty years of age, had he learned for the first time about the joy of long-term contact with one person; he'd been dropping in on Ilona for four whole months. It wasn't that he was in love with her, no. It was nice to be with her, tranquil – there was that. But as for *love* …

Ignatov didn't understand how it was possible to love a woman. One could love great things: revolution, party, one's country. But a woman? Anyway, how could the very same word express one's relationship with such different entities, as if you were placing the Revolution and some woman on two pans of a scale. It ends up being silly. Even Nastasya – as alluring and winsome as she was – was still a woman. He could be with her for a night or two, half a year at most, to amuse the man in him, and that would be it, enough. What kind of love was that? Only feelings, a bonfire of emotions. It's nice while it burns but when it dies down, you blow away the ash and live on. And so Ignatov didn't use the word *love* when he spoke; he didn't want to defile it.

Bakiev summoned Ignatov abruptly one morning. "Vanya, my friend," he said, "the real assignment you've been waiting for is here. You're going to a village to fight enemies of the Revolution – there are still a lot left there." Ignatov's heart went still from joy: on a horse again, in battle again! They gave him a couple of Red Army men as subordinates and a detachment of recruits. And she – she, the adored one, in a white sheepskin coat and on a chestnut horse – was among them. Fate, for certain, was bringing them together.

He dropped in on Ilona before leaving, parting with her coolly. She immediately burst into tears when she saw the coldness in his eyes: "You don't love me, Ivan?" He got so angry his teeth even clenched. "Loving is for mothers and children!" he said and left immediately. "I'll wait for you, Ivan, do you hear? I'll wait!" she called after him, as he went. In short, she put on a show.

Nastasya's another matter. This one wouldn't wring her hands and sigh. This one knows why men need women and women need men.

There she is, riding by: smiling broadly, unashamed, looking him straight in the eye. Her sharp little teeth pull a mitten off her plump hand and she ruffles the horse's mane with her tender fingers, running her hand through the strands. Patting him.

Ignatov feels sudden hot shivers running from the back of his head, past the nape of his neck, and flowing down his spine. He averts his gaze, frowning; it's not fitting for a Red Army man to think about women on the job. She's not going anywhere. And he spurs his horse, galloping to the front of the caravan.

They've been riding for a long time. Along boundless hills that were once Kazan Governate and are now Red Tataria, they see the tail ends of other caravans stretching just as slowly and inexorably toward the capital – white-stoned Kazan. The rear of their own caravan is probably looming in front of someone else, but Ignatov doesn't know because he doesn't like looking back. Every now and then they ride through villages where the people bring bread from their houses, thrusting it into the hands of the dekulakized, sitting dejectedly on sledges. Ignatov doesn't forbid this: let them. They'll eat up less state-issued chow in Kazan.

Yet another hill has been left behind but Ignatov has already quit counting them; he's lost track. And then, in the monotonous scrape of sledge runners, he hears Prokopenko's sudden loud shout, "Comrade Ignatov, come here!"

Ignatov turns. The caravan's even ribbon is torn in the middle. The forward part continues moving slowly ahead but the rear part is standing still. The dark figures of cavalrymen bustle around at the gap, waving their arms, their horses prancing nervously.

Ignatov rides closer. There it is, the reason: the sledge with the tiny woman with the big green eyes. The harnessed horse is standing, head down, and the foal has settled in by her belly, hurriedly sucking on a maternal udder, groaning from time to time; it had gotten hungry. The road is only wide enough for one sledge, so those behind can't ride past.

"The mare's on strike," complains Prokopenko, at a loss, his black brows knitted. "I've already tried all kinds of things with her ..."

He earnestly tugs the horse by the bridle but she shakes her mane and snorts – she doesn't want to go on.

"We have to wait until she's done feeding," the woman in the sledge quietly says.

The reins lie on her knees.

"Women wait for their husbands to come home," Ignatov snaps. "We have to move."

He jumps to the ground. From his overcoat pocket he takes bread crusts sprinkled with pebbles of coarse gray salt that he'd saved for his own horse. He thrusts them at the stubborn beast, who smacks her glistening black lips and eats. *There now, watch it* ... He strokes her long muzzle, which is prickly with stiff gray hairs.

"A caress works on a horse, too," says Nastasya, who's ridden up and is smiling broadly, gathering the semicircles of her cheeks into dimples.

Ignatov tugs at the bridle: *Come on, sweetie.* The horse finishes chewing the last crust and obstinately lowers her head to the ground: *I'm not moving.*

"You won't budge her," chimes in the taciturn Slavutsky, pensively rubbing the long thread of the scar on his face. "She won't go till she's ready."

"She won't go. That means ..." Ignatov tugs harder, then sharply jerks the bridle.

The horse neighs plaintively, showing her crooked yellow teeth and pawing at the ground. The foal hurriedly sucks at the udder, looking sideways at Ignatov with eyes like dark plums. Ignatov swings his arm and beats the mare's flank with the back of his hand: *Move it!* The horse neighs louder, shakes her head, and stands. To the flank, again. *Move it, I'm telling you! Move it! To hell with you, you damned demon!* The horses standing nearby are agitated, adding their wary voices and rearing.

"She won't go," Slavutsky stubbornly repeats. "Even if you beat her to death. She's a mother, that's all there is to it."

He's harping on it, that officer ass. He came over to the Red Army ten years ago and his way of thinking still isn't theirs, isn't Soviet.

"We'll have to give in to the mare, won't we, comrade Ignatov?" Nastasya raises her brow, stroking her horse's neck, calming him.

Ignatov grabs the foal's flank from behind and tugs, attempting to tear him from the udder. The foal's legs twitch like locusts and he slips under his mother's belly, to the other side. Ignatov topples backward into a snowbank; the foal continues feeding. Nastasya laughs melodiously, her breasts pressing against her horse's shaggy mane. Slavutsky turns away, flustered.

Cursing, Ignatov rises to his feet and brushes the snow from his hat, overcoat, and breeches. He flaps his arm at the sledges that have gone ahead:

"Stop! Stop!"

And now the cavalrymen are galloping to catch up with the front of the detachment: *Stop! Rest until further command!*

Ignatov takes off his pointy hat, wipes his reddened face, and casts angry glances at Zuleikha.

"Even your mares are counterrevolutionaries!"

The caravan rests, waiting for the month-and-a-half-old foal to drink enough of his mother's milk.

After a lush, dark blue evening has fallen on the fields, there's still a half-day of travel left to Kazan. They have to spend the night in a neighboring canton.

Denisov, the local chairman of the rural council, a stocky guy with the sturdy gait of an experienced sailor, welcomes them cordially, even warmly.

"We'll arrange a hotel for you, highest class! The Astoria! Well, no, all right, we'll do better, the Angleterre!" he promises, his smile generously baring large teeth.

Sheep are bleating deafeningly now, pushing, jumping on each other, shaking their floppy ears, and kicking their thin black legs. With his arms spread wide, Denisov drives them all into a pen behind a long cotton curtain that divides the enormous room into two halves. The last nimble little lamb is still racing around, drumming its little hooves sharply on the wooden floor. The chairman finally grabs it by its curly scruff and flings it in with the others; satisfied, he looks around, kicks smelly sheep pellets with his boot, and hospitably throws his arms open so the stripes of a sailor's jersey flash in the gap at his collar:

"So, what was I telling you about this hotel?"

Ignatov cranes his neck and looks around. Bright light from a kerosene lamp illuminates a high wooden ceiling. Long narrow windows circle the round cupola. There are shallow waves of half-erased Arabic inscriptions on dark, pitch-covered walls. Inside cavernous niches gleam bright squares, the vestiges of recently removed tapestries with quotations from the Koran.

At first Ignatov doesn't want to spend the night in a former mosque – blast it, this hotbed of obscurantism. But then he gets to thinking – actually, why not? Denisov's a smart fellow. He's got things figured out. Why let the building stand idle for no reason?

"There's room for everyone," the chairman continues boastfully, drawing the colorful curtain across. "Sheep in the women's half, people in the men's. It's a relic, of course. But it's convenient, that's a fact! At first we wanted to take out the curtain but then decided to leave it. You can count on us having guests here each and every night."

The mosque was recently transferred to the collective farm. Even the sharp smell of sheep manure can't stifle its distinct aroma, maybe of old rugs, maybe of dusty books still remaining in the corners.

The shivering deportees are bunched by the entrance, scared and gawking at the curtain, behind which the sheep continue to bellow and push.

"Find a place to settle in, dekulakized citizens," says Denisov as he opens the stove door and throws in a few logs. "In the beginning, my collective farm women were afraid of going into the men's side, too," he whispers conspiratorially to Ignatov. "A sin, they said. But then it was fine – they got used to it."

The mullah in the karakul coat is the first to enter the mosque. He walks up to the high prayer niche and kneels. Several men follow him. As before, the women crowd at the threshold.

"Lady citizens," the chairman shouts cheerfully from the stove, the fire's golden sparkles gleaming in his dark pupils. "Those sheep, they're not afraid. Follow their example."

Raucous bleating carries from behind the curtain in response.

The mullah rises from his knees. He turns toward the exiles and signals welcomingly with his hands. People enter timidly, scattering along the walls.

Prokopenko, who's crouched by a heap of junk in the corner, has unearthed a book and is picking at its pretty fabric cover decorated with metallic patterns – he's drawn to learning.

"I ask you not to take the books," says the chairman. "They're awfully good for starting fires."

"We won't touch anything," says Ignatov, looking sternly at Prokopenko, who tosses the book back on the pile, shrugging his shoulder indifferently. He doesn't want it so terribly much anyway.

"Now listen, comrade representative," Denisov says, turning to Ignatov. "Your little soldiers won't be stealing a lamb for dinner, will they? I have a shortfall in the morning whenever there's a dekulakized caravan. We've lost half the flock already, just in January! That's a fact."

"Collective farm goods? How could we!"

"Well, fine ..." Denisov smiles and jokingly threatens Ignatov with a strong, gnarled finger covered in black calloused spots. "Because you can't keep an eye on it all the time ..."

Ignatov slaps Denisov on the shoulder to calm him: *Simmer down, comrade!* How about that: a former Petersburg sailor (Baltic fleet!) and Leningrad laborer (a shock worker!), he's now one of the twenty-five thousand who's followed the Party's call to improve the Soviet countryside (a romantic!). In short, by all accounts Denisov's one of us, Ignatov thinks, and yet he still regards his own pretty poorly.

Nastasya is walking through the mosque with a leisurely, lazy stride, scrutinizing the deportees huddled in the corners. She pulls her shaggy fur hat from her head and her heavy, wheaten braid cascades down her back toward her feet. The women gasp (in a mosque, in front of men, in front of a live mullah, with her head uncovered!) and press their hands to the children's eyes. Nastasya approaches the heated stove and throws her sheepskin coat on it. The pleats on her uniform tunic are like tight musical strings that pull away from her high-set bosom under a wide belt that's so tightly caught at her waist that it seems it will burst with a twang at any minute.

"We'll put the children here," says Ignatov, not looking at her. *Am I showing pity again?* he thinks meanly. Then he reassures himself – they're still children even if they're kulak children.

"Fine, I'll freeze," Nastasya cheerfully sighs and picks up her coat.

"Let me arrange some straw for you, you gorgeous thing." Denisov winks at her.

Jostling, and with stifled shouts, the youngsters somehow settle around the wide stove, some on top of it, others beside it. The mothers lie down on the floor around it in a broad, solid ring. The rest seek out spots for themselves along the walls, on the rags lying in the corner, and on the debris of bookshelves and benches.

Zuleikha finds a half-burned scrap of rug and settles on it, leaning her back against the wall. The thoughts in her head are still as heavy and unwieldy as bread dough. Her eyes see but as if through a screen. Her ears hear but as if from afar. Her body moves and breathes but as if it's not her own.

She's been thinking all day about how the Vampire Hag's prediction has come true. But in such a scary way! Three fiery angels – the three Red Horsemen – had taken her away from her husband's household in a carriage but the old woman stayed in the house with her adored son. What the Vampire Hag had been so joyful about and wanted so much had come about. Would Mansurka figure out to bury Murtaza alongside his daughters? And the Vampire Hag? Zuleikha had no doubt the old woman wouldn't last long after her son's death. *All-powerful Allah, everything is at your will.*

She's sitting in a mosque for the first time in her life and in the main half at that – the men's half – not far from the prayer niche. It's obvious that the Almighty's will is in this, too.

Husbands allowed women into the mosque reluctantly, only for big holidays, at Eid al-Fitr and Eid al-Adha. Murtaza would steam himself thoroughly in the bathhouse every Friday and hurry off

– ruddy, with his beard carefully combed – to Yulbash's mosque for Friday prayers, after placing a green velvet embroidered skullcap on his head, which he'd shaved to a rosy sheen. The women's part of the mosque, which was in the corner behind a thick curtain, was usually empty on Fridays. The mullah instructed the husbands to convey the content of the Friday conversations to their wives, who'd stayed to look after their households, so they'd become stronger in the true faith and not lose their bearings. Murtaza obediently fulfilled the instruction. After coming home and settling in on the sleeping bench, he would wait until the low rumbling of the flour mill or the clinking of dishes quieted in the women's quarters, then he'd say his usual "I was at the mosque. I saw the mullah," through the curtain. Zuleikha waited for Murtaza to say that every Friday because it meant far more than the individual words. It meant that everything in this world has its routine and the way of things is unshakable.

Tomorrow is Friday. Murtaza will not go to the mosque tomorrow.

Zuleikha looks around for the mullah. He's continuing to pray, sitting facing the prayer niche.

"Officers on duty to their posts," commands Ignatov. "Others to sleep."

"And if someone doesn't feel like sleeping, comrade Ignatov?" The full-bosomed woman who shamelessly bared her head in the house of worship has found herself an armload of straw and is standing, embracing it.

"Wake-up will be at dawn," Ignatov responds curtly and Zuleikha is somehow pleased that the commander is so strict with the shameless woman.

Nastasya sighs loudly and tosses the armload of straw on the floor near Zuleikha.

The officers on duty arrange themselves on an overturned

bookcase by the entrance, their rifles gleaming brightly in the half-darkness. "*Rise at dawn, awake till dawn, a sailor's guard is never down!*" The chairman salutes them in parting, wishing the sheep and travelers a good night. Ignatov gives a sign and the kerosene lamp's little orange flame shrinks so only the very end of the wick smolders, barely noticeable in the dark.

Zuleikha gropes in her pocket for bread, breaks off a piece, and chews.

"Where are you taking us, commissar?" the mullah's deep-toned, singsong voice rings out in the dark.

"Where the Party's sending you, that's where I'm taking you," Ignatov responds just as loudly.

"So where is your Party sending us?"

"Ask the all-knowing Allah, let him whisper it in your ear."

"Not everyone will last the journey. You're taking us to our death, commissar."

"Well then, you must try to survive. Or ask Allah for a quick death, so you don't suffer."

The anxious deportees whisper among themselves:

"Where? Where?"

"It couldn't be Siberia?"

"But where else would it be? Exile is always there."

"Is that far?"

"The mullah said we might not last the journey."

"Allah! If only we can make it!"

"Yes. If we make it, we might survive –"

Rifles clank, reverberating, as the officers on duty load them before bed. Murmuring voices go quiet. The stove's warmth creeps through the mosque; eyelids fill with sleepiness and shut. As Zuleikha is drifting off, she sees that the mullah's wife has let her beloved gray cat out of the cage and is feeding it from her hand, shedding large tears on its soft, striped back.

"Zuleikhaaa!" The Vampire Hag's voice can be heard from far away, as if it's coming from underground. "Zuleikhaaa!"

I'm hurrying, Mama, I'm hurrying …

Zuleikha opens her eyes. The exiles are sleeping all around her, in a thick duskiness weakly diluted by the flickering kerosene light. The fire crackles in the stove; the sheep in their nook bleat briefly, sleepily, from time to time. The officers on duty are dozing sweetly, leaning against the wall, their heads hanging on their slumping shoulders.

Ugh, it was only a dream.

And then there's a sudden loud rustling, very close by. Intermittent whispering – male or female? – heated, quick, muddled, and mixed with loud rapid breaths. The darkness is quivering, turbulent, and breathing in the same place the shameless woman settled in on the armload of straw. It's moving, at first slowly, then faster, sharper, and more energetically. This is no longer darkness: it's two bodies, swathed in shadow. Something is shuddering, wheezing, and exhaling, deeply and for a long time. And then a muffled female laugh. "Hold on, you madman, I'm completely exhausted." The voice is familiar – it's her, the harlot with the magnificent cheeks. Zuleikha thinks she sees yellow hair scattering in the darkness like a heavy sheaf. The woman is breathing with her mouth wide open, with relief, and loudly, as if she's not afraid of being heard. She bends her head on someone's chest and they both go still and quiet.

Zuleikha strains to see, attempting to view the man's face. And she discerns two eyes gazing out of the darkness: he's been looking at her long and hard. It's Ignatov.

"Salakhatdin!" A heartrending shriek suddenly rings out in the depths of the mosque. "My husband!"

The kerosene lamp flares abruptly. People leap up and look around, a half-awake child cries, and the cat mews under someone's inadvertent boot.

"Salakhatdin!" the mullah's wife keeps shouting.

Cursing, Ignatov frees himself from the net of Nastasya's mermaid-like hair, hastily fastens his belt, and pulls on his boots as he walks. He runs to where the exiles are already densely bunched.

People let him through. The mullah is lying on the floor with his gray head directed toward the prayer niche and his long legs stretched out from under his curly fur coat. His enormous wife is kneeling alongside him and sobbing, her forehead on the floor. The mullah's open eyes are frozen and looking upward; his skin is stretched over his cheekbones and the wrinkles running from his nose to his chin have formed his lips into a pale, dry smile. Ignatov looks up. There's a fluid blue light in the narrow windows. Morning.

"Everybody get ready," he says to the frozen faces around him. "We're leaving."

And he walks toward the door.

Nastasya's gaze follows him. She's sitting on the armload of straw and plaiting her loose hair into a thick wheaten braid.

They get ready quickly. It is decided to leave the mullah's body in the canton for burial. At Ignatov's insistence, the mullah's wife, puffy with tears, tosses the fur coat on herself. Children help catch the cat, which has hidden behind the stove from fear, and put it back in its cage.

Outside, Zuleikha is already sitting in her driver's place, holding the reins at the ready – they're waiting for a command to leave – when Prokopenko looks around, runs over, and quickly throws something heavy, white, and shaggy onto the sledge. A lamb. He covers it with burlap and presses a crooked finger to his lips: *Shh* …

"Let's go!" rings out loudly over the whole yard. The horses snort, the escorts shout to one another, and the sledges pull out of the yard like a school of large, slow fish.

Chairman Denisov stands by the gate, smiling and seeing them off.

"Well," Ignatov says to him amiably, firmly shaking a hand as hard as the sole of a shoe, "stand firm, brother!"

"Listen, Ignatov," says the flustered Denisov, lowering his voice and furrowing his brows a little. "What would you think about raising the red flag over the mosque?"

Ignatov scrutinizes the minaret's tall tower. Its sharp top is nestled into the sky, with a dark tin squiggle of a crescent on it.

"It would be visible from far away," he replies approvingly. "Beautiful!"

"All the same, it's a cult building. It could look like some sort of … mishmash."

"There's a mishmash inside your head," says Ignatov, slapping his impatient prancing horse on the neck. "This is a genuine shed for the kolkhoz. Understand that, shock worker?"

Denisov smiles and waves his hand – how could he not understand!

Ignatov lets the last sledge go ahead of him, casts a glance over the emptied yard and gallops after the caravan, spraying crisp morning snow out from under his horse's hooves.

When the village is far behind them, Zuleikha turns around. A red flag is already waving like a small, hot flame over the slender candle of the mosque.

Rural council chairman Denisov will work another half-year in the village. By spring, he will have organized the kolkhoz and, through earnest work, greatly raised the rate of collectivization in the settlement entrusted to him.

He will battle religion with all his soul, in the Baltic fleet manner. During the holy month of Ramadan, he will organize agitational processions around the mosque, personally speak as an opponent to three clergymen in the public debate "Is religiosity needed in Soviet society?" and gather up all village Korans for burning.

The crowning achievement of his career in the small town will be obtaining a Kommunar tractor for his kolkhoz. It will be the envy of all the canton's neighboring villages, which, as yet, lack vehicles. The tractor will be the most valued and most guarded object in Denisov's enterprise.

He will propose innovative initiatives and rename the pagan holiday Sabantuy — "Holiday of the Plow" — which is celebrated in small Tatar towns during late spring, to "Traktortuy." The initiative will receive support from the center and a delegation from the Central Executive Committee in Kazan will come to the celebration, along with a landing force of newspaper correspondents. The holiday, however, will be ruined by the disrepair of the tractor itself. It will later become clear that an old local woman, the wife of a holy man, decided from good intentions to win over the tractor's spirit and secretly fed the motor an uncertain quantity of eggs and bread, causing the breakdown. The correspondents and the dissatisfied comrades from the Central Executive Committee will leave for Kazan with nothing and Denisov's career will begin a rapid decline.

He will be recalled from the village and sent home. Upon returning to Leningrad, he will find that his room in a communal apartment has been occupied by multiplying neighbors. During a desperate and drawn-out struggle with the building managers for living space, he will take to the bottle and be evicted from a dormitory a couple of years later, for drunkenness. During passportization in 1933, Denisov will be exiled from Leningrad as a person lacking an official residence permit and simply as a binging drunkard, sent first beyond the hundred-and-first kilometer, then to Ust'-Tsil'ma, and then, finally, to somewhere near Dushkachan, where his trail will be lost forever amid the rounded hills of the Baikal region.

COFFEE

Who doesn't love coffee in little china cups?

Volf Karlovich Leibe hides his face under a blanket and continues to feel the warm touch of a sunbeam on his forehead. He'll have to get up in a few moments. His work won't wait.

Soon Grunya will burst noisily into his office carrying a tray with a tiny steaming cup in her dutifully extended hands. First thing in the morning, it's just coffee and a small piece of chocolate, no food, which causes heavy thoughts and limbs. He himself will get up and throw open the drapes with a broad motion, allowing sunlight to flood the room. Grunya will cast a fastidious gaze at the dark blue dress uniform hanging at the ready and carefully remove a nonexistent dust speck from a sleeve – her bashful worship of his uniformed professorial vestments is growing all the stronger with the years. And a new day will unfurl: lectures, examinations, thousands of excited student faces …

Volf Karlovich sends the blanket to the floor with an energetic sweep, his toes fumbling at the smooth, cool leather of his slippers. The drapes fly off to the side with a swish, revealing a view familiar since childhood. This oriel window with three tall panes is like a huge living triptych where for so many years bushy old linden trees have been turning green, blossoming, dropping leaves, and after a covering of frost, blooming again, reflected in the mirror of Black Lake.

The panes are now covered with a delicate frosty mural. His German-born father would cast a majestic morning gaze through the window, as if saying an amiable hello to the winter month he called "*Januar.*"

This used to be his father's office and little Volf wasn't allowed in here. He used to steal in, though, hide out behind the curtains, flatten his nose against the cold glass, and admire the lake.

Now he himself works here. He even prefers sleeping right here, on the firm sofa by his father's ancient writing desk. A quill pen and paper are ready on the desk – good thoughts have a habit of soaring at night. He has already forgotten when he last slept in the bedroom. That was probably back before the renovations began.

Grunya's supervising the renovations, just as she has supervised everything that's taken place in the old professorial apartment. Large, noisy, with a braid that winds around her head and is as thick as an arm (her arms are as thick as a leg, too), Grunya's heavy soldier's tread entered this home for duty twenty years ago and Volf Karlovich instantly capitulated, handing over the reins of his paltry household with a submissive joy so he could plunge headfirst into the intoxicating world of the mysteries of the human body.

Volf Karlovich Leibe was a surgeon and a third-generation professor at Kazan University. His practice was extensive and people waited months for operations. Each time he raised the scalpel over a patient's soft, pale body, he sensed a cool trepidation in the very pit of his stomach: *Do I have the right?* The knife touched the skin and that chill changed to a warmth that spread to his limbs: *I do not have the right not to attempt.* And he attempted, conducting a mental dialogue with the cutaneous covering, muscle, and connective tissue through which he made his way to his goal, greeting the internal organs respectfully and whispering to blood vessels. He conversed with his patients' bodies using a scalpel. And bodies responded to him. He told nobody about his dialogues: from an outsider's perspective, this might appear to resemble mental illness.

Volf Karlovich had a second secret, too, which was that the mysteries of human birth excited him to an extreme, making his fingertips itch.

In his naive youth, intoxicated by the lectures of legendary Professor Phenomenov, he even wanted to stay and work in the department of obstetrics and female diseases. His father talked him out of it: "Deliver babies for peasant women your whole life?" Young Volf resigned himself to his father's opinion and went into the noble department of surgery.

After becoming a surgeon and dissecting in the anatomical theater the unclaimed bodies of paupers and prostitutes that had been delivered from the police station as cadavers, he would sometimes discover a small fetus in a female womb. Each of these findings brought him to a state of vague excitement. A ridiculous thought would flash: *What if this tiny little beast with the wrinkly face and caricature-like small extremities is actually alive?*

"*Hic locus est ubi mors gaudet succurrere vitae,*" said the inscription over the round building housing the university's anatomical theater: "This place is where death delights in helping life." And so it was. Unborn babies in the bellies of young women knifed from jealousy or accidentally murdered in bandits' gunfights thirsted to reveal their little secrets to Volf Karlovich: their thin voices constantly swarmed in his head, whispering, muttering, and sometimes shouting.

And he surrendered. He performed his first hysterotomy at the age of twenty-five, in 1900, the turn of the century. He already had several dozen incisions of the womb to his credit by that time, and this new operation – the cesarean section – was not especially complex for him. There was a special feeling afterward, though, since it was one thing to cut a slippery bloody slab from a tumor in the patient's womb and fling it in a basin, and something completely different to remove a live, quivering baby.

The operation went brilliantly. Then another and another. The renown of the young surgeon, "a natural," took wing in the Kazan province. And that was how he lived, working in clinical surgery for his father and in gynecology (a bit embarrassed about that and not advertising it) for himself.

When, by the way, did he last operate? Volf Karlovich begins pondering. It seems as if it wasn't long ago at all, but it's challenging to remember the exact date or reason for the operation. Teaching takes so much time and energy that some events fade from memory. He'll have to ask Grunya.

Volf Karlovich takes a watering can from the windowsill and waters his palm plant. This is the only thing Grunya isn't allowed to do in the home. Watering is a special ritual because it soothes the professor. The huge tree with glossy, fleshy leaves standing in a wooden tub on the floor is his exact contemporary. On the day he was born, fifty-five years ago, his father planted a pip in the tub and forgot it. A month later he was amazed to discover a stubborn, stubby sprout. The palm grew and gradually transformed into a tall, powerful tree, though it's true it has never once bloomed. The day it blossoms will be a holiday for Volf Karlovich.

The door opens wide with a cracking sound and Grunya bursts into the room as noisily and relentlessly as a locomotive flying along the rails. "Good morning," utter her plump lips, touched with bright lipstick. That means the morning truly is good. Just like the day ahead.

The smell of buckwheat groats with onion fills the room.

Grunya places a silver tray with a small china cup at the edge of the table.

"Please ask the workmen to begin this bedlam of theirs a little later," Volf Karlovich says with an imploring smile, standing next to the palm. "I want to work in quiet for a while."

Grunya nods silently, her head piled high with thick, interwoven braids like a ship's ropes.

"And when ..." Volf Karlovich attentively fingers the smooth, cool leaves, "... when will this endless renovation end?"

"Soon," mutters Grunya in a low voice, heading for the door. "There's not much longer to wait."

"And also, Grunya ..."

She stops by the door and turns.

"Can you recall? When did I last operate? Somehow it's slipped my mind."

Grunya furrows her low brow.

"Why do you need to know?"

Volf Karlovich shrinks under her threatening gaze.

"I feel uncomfortable when I can't remember such a simple fact of my biography."

"I'll go remember it," says Grunya dryly, nodding decisively, as if she were butting the air in front of herself, and leaves.

Clinking dishes, excited female voices, and children's crying carry through the slightly open door.

"But I asked for quiet!" says Volf Karlovich, placing his hand to his forehead like a martyr.

Grunya goes to the kitchen to fetch breakfast for herself and Stepan.

Three huge windows without curtains. Clothes lines divide the space into two uneven triangles. Six tables that seem to dance along the walls. Six kerosene cookers on the tables. Six large-bellied cabinets. All told, there are seven rooms in the apartment but Volf Karlovich doesn't have his own table. Meaning he doesn't have a kerosene cooker, either.

Women who've been passionately discussing something go quiet and disperse to their own corners when they see Grunya. The sizzling of someone's eggs in a frying pan becomes distinctly audible. Grunya's hand grabs at the clothes line and carefully shifts the hanging sheets, pushing them back into an accordion.

"I've told you not to take up my half," she says to the ceiling.

"But you don't do laundry today," says one of the women, hands on hips, sleeves rolled up.

Grunya silently unties the apron around her waist and hangs it on the freed-up clothes line: *Now there's laundry!* Then she opens the sideboard, takes out bread, and locks it again with a key. She picks up a pan of porridge from her kerosene cooker and heads for the door. The women gaze after her. Water bubbles in a basin with boiling laundry. Milk sizzles as it boils over.

It's dark in the hallway; the gas lamps haven't been working for ten years now. Cabinets and trunks block a once-wide hallway so you can't get through. There it is, communal life: darkness, overcrowding, and the smell of fried onions. Things were very different before.

Grunya pushes a door with her mighty rear end and enters her room.

"What took so long?" Stepan is at the table in just an undershirt, using a screwdriver to tinker with a large padlock. Spots of shiny black oil cover his hands.

"He's trying to recall when he last operated." Grunya places the pan on the table and pensively scrutinizes the tablecloth's pattern.

Stepan sets down the screwdriver and picks up the lock. *Click!* The shackle greedily latches shut. He takes the key lying beside it, inserts it, rotates it with a smooth mechanical sound, and the lock opens obediently.

"It's ready." His smile bares smoke-stained teeth dancing crookedly in his mouth.

"He wants to recall when he last operated," Grunya repeats, louder. "But what if he wants to recall something else?"

"You think it's that simple? He wants to recall something and then he does? He hasn't remembered for ten years, and then he wants to, so there you go?" Stepan wipes his hands on his under-shirt, breaks off some bread, and starts chewing.

"How should I know?" Grunya takes a ladle and hurls a gob of thick, steaming porridge on a dish.

"When did you send the letter?" Stepan eats the steaming buckwheat with a large spoon, not burning himself.

"It's been about a month already."

"That means they'll come soon. There's not much longer to wait. They're just regular people working there; they need time to look into things." Stepan reaches his little finger into the depths of his upper jaw for a grain that's stuck, then wipes his finger on the tablecloth. "It's our job not to miss them. And there you go!" He stands, shakes the heavy lock in the air, and hangs it on a nail by the door. "They'll shut the room off and you'll scoot right over to put a lock over the little paper seal they stick on the door. If anybody asks, say the building manager ordered it."

Sitting on a stool, Grunya moves her head a little, in agreement.

"The building manager, he won't change his mind?" She's looking out from under her brow, watching as Stepan sits back down at the table and resumes working his spoon; his muscles are rolling along his shoulders like mounds.

"Don't you be worrying." Stepan smiles broadly and there are dark spots of buckwheat in the grooves between his teeth. "Don't you be worrying 'bout nothing – I'll take care of it! Soon you'll be drinking your coffee in mister professor's room from mister professor's cups."

Her fleshy lips tremble in a flustered smile, then open up a little again, alarmed:

"Even so, I feel sorry for him. He was quite a person ..."

Stepan licks his spoon thoroughly. He walks up behind Grunya and places his sinewy hands on her round shoulders. Her marvelous bosom quivers under thin, faded cotton and slowly rises in a deep breath, like yeast dough on a stove.

"What's to feel sorry about?" Stepan mouths this, whispering in Grunya's ear. "He was, then he ended."

There's a strong male odor coming from Stepan, blended with the smell of buckwheat and machine oil. Grunya tightens her fingers on her knees, creasing the fabric of her dress.

"You earned it. Over twenty years, you deserve it. Here you are, still fetching him his food, his drinks, doing his washing. For free, mind you. So what if you used to work for him for real. And so what if he was a big fish. Your professor, he'd've died a long time ago if it wasn't for you. So he should be thanking you he's still alive."

Stepan's hands grip Grunya's shoulders. The clock on the wall ticks audibly.

"But you and me, maybe we'll be expanding later, too. Even when he's gone, what're we going to do – spend our lives huddled in two measly rooms?"

She closes her eyes and presses her ear to his rough, hairy hand. His fingers move toward the base of her neck, then further, toward the opening in her dress.

"Now then, Grushenka," he whispers quietly, "now then, my little apple ..."

The bell by the front door squawks shrilly. One ring is for the professor. The last time anyone came to see him was five or six years ago, some skinny old man passing through from Moscow to Siberia who invited the professor to teach in Tomsk, though Leibe turned him down.

Grunya leaps up. Her eyes meet Stepan's tense gaze and she presses a hand to her mouth: *Could it be* them? Stepan motions angrily with his chin: *Open it up. What are you standing there for?* She runs into the hallway, putting the unfastened buttons on her dress collar back through their holes along the way. She feels Stepan's heavy gaze behind her, beating at the back of her head from the doorway. She rattles the locks and chains for a long time, then her fingers finally cope with her nervousness. Grunya exhales with a gasp and reaches to open the heavy front door.

Ilona's standing, shifting from one little heel to another and lowering her hat brim slightly over her eyes. *Shameful, my God, how shameful …*

A mountain of a woman opens the door. She's breathing deeply and menacingly, like a dragon. She's silent and her beady eyes are looking at Ilona.

"I'm here to see Professor Leibe," Ilona says, exhaling feebly.

The mountain of a woman jabs her chin at the air, indicating a white door in the dimly lit hallway behind her. She doesn't move from her place, though: she stands, blocking the way. Ilona presses a flat little purse to her chest like a shield and edges into the apartment, feeling faint from the thick smell of onions and porridge issuing from this woman. She wants to duck behind the white door but the menacing keeper of the threshold cuts off her passage with an arm. "I'll announce you," her deep voice says with loathing before she goes into the room. Ilona is left by herself in the stuffy brown dusk of the hallway.

A bright rectangle – the entrance to the kitchen – is somewhere far ahead and from it carry the smells of laundry and lunch and the sounds of the hum of female voices, children's laughter, and a jingling bicycle bell. Along the hallway, barely discernible in the darkness, are tall doors to rooms; their white paint has partially flaked off, like fish scales. Ilona thinks someone's hiding behind them and observing. She darts off with grateful relief when the professor's door finally swings open and the portly woman's deep voice invites her to enter.

Volf Karlovich Leibe, prof. med. in gyn., luminary!: that's the note Ilona discovered in her mother's diary when she went through her things after the funeral. The word "luminary" was underlined twice. Blushing from speculation about why her mother required a "prof. med. in gyn.," she put away the notebook, which had disintegrated into sheets, in an upper storage cabinet. She only remembered it several years later when she was tossing and turning in bed, sleepless as usual. The bed was cooling after Ivan had left and she was agonizing over guesses as to why, after reaching the age of twenty-five, she had never once ... And how could she find the right words to say that while maintaining decorum?

Her girlfriends were living the full lives of Young Communist League members by falling in love, acquiring suitors – Komsomol or Party members, or shock workers at the very least – finding new ones, marrying and divorcing, and losing count of abortions. Some had even given birth to tiny pink children who screeched in horrendous voices.

Ilona had observed all those maelstroms and tangles of female fates from the sidelines, during breaks from pounding on the keyboard of a good old-fashioned Underwood, behind whose cumbersome bulk she cleverly and unobtrusively hid from life in a small office.

She'd had few suitors and nobody had asked her to marry them. No, it wasn't really "few." Of course there were suitors.

And they gave her womanly happiness, in the ways and amounts they could. She thirstily drank every drop of that happiness. But she hadn't become pregnant (what a scary word!). Her womb was a bottomless vessel that accepted everything that fell into it but lacked the power to give anything back to this world. Policeman Fedorchuk, a charming, brawny fellow, was swarthy, curly-haired, dark-eyed, and irrevocably married; bookkeeper Zeldovich was prematurely bald and gray, and loved to sleep nestled into her chest; the chemistry student with the funny surname Obida had traces of eternal hypochondria on his face … They had all floated through her iron bed with the shiny knobs on the headboard – and through her life, too – without leaving a trace. And that hadn't concerned her a bit.

Then, suddenly, there was Ivan. Vanya.

What errant wind had blown that tall, broad-shouldered looker with the arrogant gaze and upright posture into her dusty life, so reliably protected by a typewriter? Ilona latched on to him tenaciously, with all the strength of her pale fingers worn out from constant battles with the keyboard. She laughed loudly at the cinema with her head thrown back high; she blazed with shame when she put on her mother's chiffon blouse, transparent in the bright light, for an evening stroll; she tried to be passionate and tireless at night; she sewed two buttons on his uniform tunic; and she even mastered her grandmother's recipe for preparing thick Sunday pancakes.

In the heat of a recent argument, he'd thrown some enigmatic words about love for children in her face, as if he'd lashed her cheek. Could this stern military man with the cold gray eyes really want familial coziness and children?

Her mother's photograph on the bureau looked at her implacably: *Don't give in!* Ilona searched for the castoff notebook in the dusty abyss of the upper storage cabinet and after her trembling fingers found the sought-after address in the folds of its yellowed pages, she headed for "prof. med. in gyn." Vanya wants children; she'll bear them for him. If she can, of course.

The luminary could have closed his practice, changed his address, or, yes, simply grown old and died in the years that had passed. But – what enormous, improbable luck! – he still lived here, guarded by that chained-up dog, the mountain-like woman with the gaze of a hungry she-bear.

And so now Ilona is standing in the middle of the room, timidly looking downward, and the rather eccentric professor is hurrying to greet her. The hems of his quilted satin robe are fluttering and his shaggy curls form a semicircle – a halo, it occurs to her! – around a high, shining forehead that flows to the back of a head that's just as smooth. His lips press her hand, which flushes instantly with heat, since nobody has ever kissed Ilona's fingers, not even the extraordinarily affectionate policeman Fedorchuk, and this is so unceremonious, in the presence of others.

"Thank you, Grunya," the professor says in a singsong voice.

The disappointed she-bear woman releases air from her voluminous chest, slowly turns around, and carries her bulky body out of the room.

The professor courteously points a withered hand at a chair with curved wooden legs and varnished armrests that are reminiscent of éclairs at the Gorzin bakery. Ilona, who still hasn't dared raise eyelashes heavy with mascara, perches herself on the edge of a seat upholstered in flowered satin. Something small and sharp pierces the very top of her leg. A nail? She decides to tolerate it and not let on.

"Forgive my shabby appearance," Leibe's voice babbles. "I usually receive patients after lunch. But since you're already here – which I am glad about, sincerely glad! – let us speak now about your, *ahem*, question."

Shameful, oh God, how shameful … Ilona swallows a gob of saliva and looks up. The luminary is settling in comfortably behind a large desk, placing his arms on the desktop's light-gray velvet.

"I am listening with the utmost attention."

The professor's delicate-blue eyes are kindly. A hollow on his chest, with slender ribs radiating from it like sunbeams, shows out from under his wide-open robe. Ilona looks down. A luminary is permitted a lot, even possessing oddities and receiving patients while looking this outlandish.

"Hmm?" Leibe encourages her.

"I need to have a child," she exhales. "No matter what it takes."

The professor takes a silver spoon from a tray that's standing on the desk and pensively rattles it a bit in an elegant coffee cup of thin, milk-white porcelain with smoothly curving sides and a flirty little handle. The jingling comes out sounding unexpectedly muted and cheap: *dzin-dzin … dzin-dzin …*

"How long have you wanted this?"

"I haven't wanted it for so long … But I could have long ago … I mean, purely theoretically … or, rather, practically, too …" Ilona is thoroughly muddled and rests her chin against the ironed ruches on her collar. "Seven years."

"And so over the course of seven years you have had relations with men but have not once been pregnant. Is that what you wanted to say?"

Ilona sinks her head deeper into her shoulders: *Yes, exactly that.* The upholstery nail on the chair is puncturing her leg hard, persistently. Ilona's afraid to fidget: what if her dress tears?

"Well, for starters, you'll need to be examined and fill out a medical questionnaire. After that it will be clear if I can help you. Or at least attempt to help."

"I'm ready for an examination," Ilona whispers to the ruches on her collar.

"But I'm not ready, my dear girl!" laughs the professor. "Where do you wish for me to receive you, on this desk? Yes, I run my practice at home but my apartment is undergoing renovations now. Horrible, never-ending renovations! The dining room, living room, bedroom, library, examination room, and waiting room are all occupied by unbearable workmen who ceaselessly make noise for days on end. They impede my thought, work, and life, after all. All I can do is steal some calm hours at night, when they stop their endless bothersomeness. I'm forced to work by lamplight, in my own home. Like a mouse!" He nods at a sheet of paper lying in front of him. "Fortunately, this nightmare will end soon. Grunya promised there's not much longer at all to wait."

"Grunya?" Ilona simply cannot grasp what's happening. Is the luminary refusing to help?

The nail is stuck impossibly deep in her body. It's as if she's threaded on a skewer.

"Grunya knows everything," the professor says, taking his cup from the table, drawing it to his mouth, and smacking his lips in anticipation. "She's my guardian angel, I'd be lost without her. Ask her when this bedlam will end – maybe in a week or in a month – and come then."

Ilona looks up, completely worn out from shame and incomprehension.

"I can't wait, professor."

"Then" – he waves his cup in the air, dismayed – "come see me at the clinic. I receive patients there on Thursdays … or maybe Fridays … Clarify that with Grunya."

Ilona leaps up from the chair (from the nail, really) and falls to her knees in front of the professor's desk.

"Don't refuse me, professor! Help me! You're my last hope!"

"No, no," Leibe abruptly shouts, in an unexpectedly high-pitched voice. "I don't know anything! Grunya knows! Go see Grunya!"

"Only you can save me! You're a genius! A luminary!"

Ilona crawls up to the table on her knees and drops her arched hands on the desktop. A light-gray swirl rises out from under her hands and it's becoming obvious that the covering under the layer of dust has a rich green color. Dust blankets everything: the desktop, inkstand, open ink bottle with a dried pool of ink at its depths, a virginally white sheet of paper, and a pen with a broken nib that's lying on it.

Recoiling from fear, the professor places his coffee cup in front of himself as if for protection. The cup has a wide crack and is absolutely empty.

"Forgive me, in the name of God," says Ilona, slowly crawling away.

The sun is beating through dirty splotches on the three-paned window, filling the fluffy, curly halo around the professor's bald spot with a vivid golden hue. He places his cup on the tray and slows his rapid breathing. Then he makes his way out from behind the desk, all the while glancing warily at Ilona from time to time, and picks up a large tin watering can. Streams of water pour from its holey spout into a large wooden tub from which there protrudes a dry, gnarled stick bristling with the debris of dried-out branches. It's the skeleton of a long-dead tree.

"Forgive me, for God's sake, forgive me," Ilona whispers, standing and brushing off her dress. "Forgive me, forgive me …"

"Nice, isn't it?" The flustered professor smiles and draws a finger with a long, broken nail along the tree's wrinkly trunk. He leans back, admiring. His flat hands caress nonexistent leaves.

"Good day," says Ilona, backing toward the door.

"I'll be expecting you at the clinic." Leibe nods in parting, not shifting his gaze from the palm tree.

The door opens a second before Ilona pushes it. Grunya's gigantic body is in the opening, offering coat and hat. Ilona realizes she's been eavesdropping.

"Is it true that Professor Leibe receives patients at the clinic on Thursdays?" she asks in the dark hallway.

"Volf Karlovich hasn't left his room for ten years now," answers Grunya.

A genius.

Volf Karlovich shakes his head. It's embarrassing for him whenever he hears rapturous epithets like that from patients and students.

A luminary.

Come now! A little boy standing at the ocean's shore, that's how he perceives his relationship to science. And he's not ashamed to admit that from a rostrum, gazing into his students' wide-open eyes.

Only you can save me.

Alas, that's not true, either. The patient's body saves itself on its own. The doctor only helps, directing the body's strengths to take the proper course, sometimes removing something extra, unnecessary, and obsolete. The doctor and patient travel the road to recovery hand in hand, but the primary part – which is always the deciding factor – is played by the patient, with his will for life and the strengths of his body. Advanced students who've already become familiar with the secrets of pharmaceuticals and have a couple of elementary surgical operations behind them sometimes dare argue with him about that. Sweet fledglings standing on their own two feet …

Isn't it time to go to the university? The ecstatic damsel's visit disrupted the routine of his usual life and Volf Karlovich feels lost and confused. What time is his first lecture today? That depends on what day of the week it is.

What day is it, anyway?

Leibe looks at the clock but the hands are frozen, motionless, on its face.

He takes his professorial dress uniform from the back of his chair and realizes it's his father's old robe. So where's the dress uniform? The one with dense fabric of deep blue and a row of buttons, each with a stern two-headed eagle spreading its wings? The same one with the narrow snow-white enamel insignia shining on the chest, the badge of a Kazan University professor? The same one Grunya blows the dust motes from every morning? That's right, she took it out for cleaning.

Volf Karlovich takes a step toward the door. The smooth handle falls complacently into his palm. He tugs at it for a long time, as if he's amiably shaking the door's brass hand, then he pulls down sharply and strides into the black abyss that's opened up in the hallway.

Grunya is assiduously rubbing the side of a pot with a soapy rag and the white suds bubble in the thick kerosene soot, blackening. After Stepan's arrival, a desire has awakened in her to scour the kitchen utensils to an unbearable, mirror-like cleanliness, so in her powerful hands the professor's basins and skillets have begun sparkling with a hitherto unprecedented gleam that hurts the eye.

Her back senses the neighboring women's unfriendly gazes nestling between her shoulder blades. Let them look, the wretches. They dislike her so much in the communal apartment because she conducts herself as if she were the apartment's proprietress. But why shouldn't she? She *is* the proprietress. Every wall here, every floorboard, every baseboard, every flourish on the white carved wooden doors knows her hands, which have swept, cleaned, washed, and polished them hundreds of times.

When more residents were assigned housing in the professor's apartment back in 1921, she'd staunchly held the line, carefully selected the most valuable items, and moved them into her own room (lunch and tea services, silver cutlery, heavy candleholders, velvet drapes – what, was she supposed to leave them for these half-literate bumpkins?). She occupied the best table in the kitchen and the largest cabinet in the hallway, in addition to an upper storage cabinet, too. And then one dark autumn evening she took a dully gleaming silver ink set as huge as a pillow, as hefty as a rock, and bearing the personalized inscription "To V.K. Leibe, professor of medical sciences, with the deepest respect of G.F. Dormidontov, rector, Imperial Kazan University," to the building manager, with no regrets since it was obvious to any fool that you had to be friendly with building managers.

And she began waiting.

By this time, the professor was already shattered by the changes that had taken place in the country. He'd had a rough time during the war between the Bolsheviks and the Czechs fighting for the White Army, he'd fallen out of favor with the new rectors at the university (they changed fairly often during the first years of the Civil War), and his practice at the clinic had been closed. Then one morning Volf Karlovich didn't leave his room. Nobody noticed his absence. Only Grunya – when bringing a cup of the herbal slop that the professor had become accustomed to drinking for breakfast in the mornings instead of his usual coffee – quietly gasped when she looked into joyful blue eyes unclouded by further earthly sorrows. At first she was scared. Then she realized what had happened – there it was, she'd waited it out. She would be the apartment's proprietress.

She tolerated the residents, as if they were bedbugs. She simply didn't know how to poison them. Stepan, who had come into her life a couple of months ago, knew. He decided to begin with the easiest: the professor.

Grunya didn't question his plans for long. She was already sick to death of taking care of the half-crazed former proprietor. And she was desperate to be Stepan's little pussycat, lamb, or bunny, and occasionally (*forgive me, O Lord, I do sin, I repent ...*) even his little vixen.

And so the letter was written and dropped in the postbox. Grunya sweated profusely, like a horse, during Stepan's dictation, tracing out long and tricky words whose meanings she didn't understand: was bourgeois written with *ou* or *oo*? Was German written with *e* or *i*? Did spy end in *y* or *i*? Is there one *r* or two in counterrevolution? Is it one word or two? If Stepan is right, they will arrive soon to free up the professorial office with its trio of lovely windows looking out on an ancient park, floors smelling of wax, and heavy walnut furniture. Free it up for Grunya, who's already been awaiting her turn for happiness for ten long years. And even then – what was it Stepan said that morning? – they weren't going to spend the rest of their lives huddled in the two little rooms.

Grunya rinses the pot in a basin. It's suddenly become very quiet in the kitchen. The other women don't usually converse in her presence; they only exchange glances. But now the silence behind Grunya's back is thick and unusually heavy. Someone's soup gurgles, as if it's choking from agony.

Grunya turns around.

Professor Leibe is standing in the communal kitchen.

A little neighbor girl, who's always getting underfoot on her ailing tricycle, thrums the bell from fear – *ding!* – and asks, in the quiet, "Mama, who's that?"

The women have gone still: one with a ladle, another with an iron, yet another with a rag in her hands. Wide eyes stare at Leibe. But he's looking only at Grunya.

"Where's my professorial dress uniform?" he asks in a voice high-pitched with agitation.

Her hand squeezes the rag and soapsuds trickle between her fingers, dripping resonantly into the basin.

"Where's my professorial uniform? I'm asking you, Grunya."

"Let's go have a look in your room, professor," she says in a voice that suddenly sounds strained. "Let's go to your room."

"I've already looked there," Leibe persists. "Give me my uniform at once. I'm late."

The neighbor women's eyes, huge from curiosity, probe the professor's frail figure and shift their gaze to Grunya, then back.

Can it really be that he forgot for ten years, until now? Right now, when *they* should arrive any day? So Grunya will not be drinking coffee from the professor's cups, after all – oh no, she will not. And will Stepan want her like this, with one teeny little room in a communal anthill? Grunya's fat fingers, covered with white suds bursting in the air, turn cold.

"So are you going to give me my uniform?"

In the crosshairs of the neighbors' attentive eyes, she climbs on a stool and pulls a huge plywood suitcase from the overhead storage cabinet. She rummages around in it and removes from the bottom a wrinkled uniform that's lace-like from moth holes and white from dust in places.

Leibe laughs joyously and puts it on, stroking it affectionately. The stitching on the sleeve crackles, coming undone and baring zigzags of threads. A blackened button tears off and bounces along the floor, jingling into a corner somewhere.

"I just knew you'd taken it to be cleaned," the professor says, smiling with satisfaction as he straightens the worn insignia on his chest and turns around.

"Where are you going?" The presentiment of catastrophe dumbfounds Grunya.

"To the university, for a lecture," he says. He shrugs his shoulders with surprise and leaves, his backless slippers thudding.

"He could have put on shoes," says one of the neighbor women, finally regaining the ability to speak. "He'll catch cold."

Fortunately, Volf Karlovich doesn't have the chance to catch cold. They take him exactly one minute later, right there, outside the building, as half the apartment's residents stare out the windows at their strange neighbor's entrance into the world. He's just beginning to run down the steps – his feet flying on their own, lightly, as if he were a young man – when other feet, wearing polished black boots, are already running up those very same steps to greet him.

"Volf Karlovich Leibe?" they ask.

"Yes!" he answers, delighted. "You're here for me? From the university?"

"We are," they reassure him. "Let's go to the car."

"Since when did they start sending such luxurious automobiles for professors?" gushes Volf Karlovich as he settles into the back seat and feels the car's silky leather interior with childlike curiosity.

People in uniform sit on each side of him, pressing their firm shoulders against him. Leibe smiles and keeps going out of his way to shake hands. The door of the black Ford slams shut and the professor jauntily and cheerily waves a hand to the chauffeur: *Let's go!*

The Black Maria carrying away Volf Karlovich has hardly disappeared around a bend in the road, spraying snow out from under its wheels in parting, when a big, heavy padlock clasps its jaws on the door of the professor's former office. Shoving into his pocket a round, dark bottle that has long been at the ready, Stepan heads off to see the building manager. With a tsarina's gaze, Grunya surveys the neighbors crowded by the closed door – they want

to profit from the professor's furniture, the jackals! – and Grunya
goes to her room without saying a thing.

*They won't take Professor Leibe far, just straight to the State Political
Administration's regional headquarters. For a couple of weeks, investigator
Butylkin will work on cracking the German spy who's posing so successfully as a half-wit, but he'll give up in the end, deciding to send Leibe to
the psychiatric clinic at Arsk Field: they can figure out for themselves if he's
reaping anything or truly just a nut. They'll be too late, though.*

*In the middle of February 1930, the Central Executive Committee
and the Council of People's Commissars of the Tatar Autonomous Soviet
Socialist Republic will approve the decree "On the liquidation of kulaks as a
class in Tataria." A week later, it will be determined during an operational
meeting at the CEC that the pace for collectivization and dekulakization in
the republic is horrifyingly low.*

*And somehow, of its own accord, without the knowledge of the Party
leaders and upper ranks of the State Political Administration, it will work
out that certain guests of the regional State Political Administration who
aren't especially necessary for investigative purposes will be turned into
kulaks. Their cases will be misplaced, gather dust on shelves and safes,
and burn in fires. And they themselves will be transferred from solitary
confinement and pretrial detention to dungeons in a transit prison crowded
with the dekulakized. By mid-March, Red Tataria will already be in third
place in the country for its pace of collectivization.*

*Volf Karlovich Leibe will land in the legendary transit prison building,
too. He won't be the slightest bit surprised; he'll likely even be glad since he'd
started to miss people during his ten years of seclusion. Only one question
will trouble him slightly: is all well with Grunya?*

*Grunya's life will take a favorable turn. She'll drink coffee from the
professor's cups in the mornings. True, the cups themselves will turn out
to be extraordinarily inconvenient: they're small and fragile, just trouble.*

A year later, Stepan will free up another room for them, and two years later, the regional arm of the Joint State Political Administration will move to Black Lake, into the building next door. Stepan will think a little and then he'll start work there. His career will come together and very soon they won't need to free up the next room using their well-established means because they're allocated luxurious living space of their very own on Pochtamtskaya Street.

Grunya will grow bored after becoming the rightful proprietress of a large and empty new apartment, since there's nobody to battle and Stepan works day and night. And so when, at the age of forty-six, she discovers her pregnancy, Grunya will decide to carry the child to term. She will pass away during labor and the doctors from the university clinic will just throw up their hands in distress. It was too tough a case.

KAZAN

A shaggy snout bares its yellowed teeth and wails, shaking its inside-out lips. Zuleikha squeezes the reins tighter. *May Allah protect me, what is this hellish monster?*

"A camel!" cries someone behind her. "A real one!"

The outlandish beast swings its master, who's sitting between the humps and wearing a colorful quilted robe, side to side as it floats past. A sharp smell of spices trails after them.

The sledges are traveling along a central street. The caravan has formed and straightened out so the vehicles are riding close together past buildings of brick and stone, painted light blue, pink, and white, like huge carved jewel boxes. Lots of little turrets tower over the roofs; there are weathervanes blossoming with tin flowers and roof tiles glistening like colorful fish scales under spots of snow. Decorative flourishes creep along pediments and tickle the heels of half-naked men and women (*what shame this is, Allah!*) who bear heavy cornices on their muscular shoulders. Railings curl like iron lace.

Kazan.

Young ladies in little boots with heels (*how do they not fall off those!*), servicemen in mouse-colored military overcoats like Ignatov's, public servants chilled to the bone in patched coats, middle-aged women wearing huge felt boots and selling little pies (*the smell, the wonderful smell …*), portly nannies with children swathed in shawls on wooden sledges … In their hands are folders, briefcases, tubes, reticules, bouquets, and cakes …

The wind tears a pile of sheet music from the hands of a skinny young man wearing glasses, hurling it into the sorrowful face of a cow that a frail peasant is leading past on a rope.

The hulk of a tractor for agitational propaganda rolls along, its heavy wheels rumbling as it tows a large, cracked bell, around which winds a snake-like red cotton banner: "We will reforge church bells into tractors!"

Dirty slush on the road explodes into a crooked fountain under the hooves of a cavalry detachment rushing past, and under the wheels of shiny black automobiles tearing along toward it, driving in the opposite direction.

A fiery red tram flies along with a deafening clang; its brass handles blaze and there are faces clustered in its glassless windows. A small pack of waifs flit away from a gateway and hang on the handrail with frenzied shrieks. The furious conductor curses and waves his fists; a policeman is already running, cutting across the road, and blowing his whistle.

Zuleikha squints. A lot of buildings, a lot of people. All loud, vivid, fast, and strong-smelling. This is understandable since it's the capital. Kazan is generously throwing its treasures into the stunned exiles' eyes before they've had a chance to recover.

The red-and-white spire of the Church of Saint Varvara is solemn, the aperture of its bell tower window forlornly empty, and there's an inscription painted in yellow above the entrance: "Greetings to the workers of the First Tram Depot!" There's the governor-general's former home, as well decorated as a torte and now housing the tuberculosis hospital. The ice on Black Lake rings with children's laughter. The columns of Kazan University, each as thick as a century-old oak, are a delicate white.

The city's kremlin has sharp little towers like heads of sugar.

Instead of a clock, there's a large, stern face – with wise, narrowed eyes under falconine brows and a mustache like a broad wave – gazing out at Zuleikha from a round opening on Spassky Tower. Who is it? He doesn't resemble the Christian god, whom Zuleikha once saw in a picture that the mullah had shown her.

Then there's an unexpected shout: "We've arrived!" How could that be? Where had they arrived? Zuleikha looks around, confused. In front of her is a squat, dirty white building with tiny squares of windows that form a chain along one side and a tall stone wall around it, three times her height.

"Down you go, Green Eyes!" says Prokopenko, puckering his cheeks in a smile and winking, his gaze probing for the lamb under the burlap in the sledge: *Is it in one piece?*

Zuleikha squeezes her bundle tightly and jumps to the ground. Bayonets already bristle to greet her; a live corridor of young junior soldiers leads to a small open metal door. In there, then.

Prokopenko takes Sandugach by the bridle and the horse neighs shrilly, jerking under an unknown hand. Zuleikha drops her bundle and rushes to the horse, pressing her face into her dear muzzle.

"Not allowed!" is the anxious cry behind her and something sharp, a bayonet blade, presses at her back.

"Come on, now," says Prokopenko's smiling voice. "Let her say goodbye. Why begrudge that?"

"I'll count to three!" utters the stern, anxious voice. "One!"

Sandugach smells of healthy sweat, hay, the shed, and milk – of home. She exhales joyfully as she nestles against her mistress and the warm dampness of her delicate nostrils settles on Zuleikha's cheek. Zuleikha sticks her hand in her pocket and removes the poisoned sugar. The large, heavy lump weighs on her palm like a stone. Murtaza used foresight on everything: he's already headed off to his forefathers, but his thoughts are still directing his loyal wife.

"Two!"

Zuleikha opens her sweaty palm and raises it to Sandugach's face. The horse nods gratefully and joyfully. The foal jumps out from under her legs. Pushing its mother away and greedily stretching its long neck, it snuffles and smacks its outstretched lips, hurrying to take the treat.

"Three!" The bayonet is driving in, painfully, between her shoulder blades.

Zuleikha clenches her fingers and lowers her hand with the sugar into her pocket. She takes the broken-off chunk of bread from her other pocket and sticks it instead into the trusting outstretched lips of Sandugach and the foal.

Forgive me, Murtaza, for not fulfilling your order. I couldn't. I disobeyed you for the first time in my life.

Ignatov's dissatisfied voice is already behind her. "What's going on? Why the delay?"

Zuleikha takes her bundle from the ground and ducks through the open door.

For a long time, she takes small steps through a bare, ice-coated courtyard, then along a narrow corridor, following an ungainly young soldier who's striding forward, his soot-blackened kerosene lamp illuminating lumpy stone walls trickling with moisture. Another's hobnail boots thud behind her. Zuleikha draws her shoulders together from the chill. Even the cold here is particular – it's frigid, damp, and clinging. Voices carry from behind heavy doors that have tiny windows with crosses in their gratings: Russian, Tatar, Mari, and Chuvash speech; songs, cursing, a child's crying ...

"Could use some water, boss! Need to drink ..."

"... I must ask you – no, I *demand* an attorney! A Soviet court should ..."

"I want a woman, commander. Bring that one to me, huh?"

"... I beg you, the telephone number is 2-35. Just say you're calling on behalf of Pavlusha Semyonych ..."

"I've remembered! I've remembered everything! Send for Investigator Ivashov! And tell him Sidorchuk will sign the confession ..."

"... and you will burn in the fires of Gehenna until the end of time ..."

"... I'm begging you! Aspirin! The child has a fever ..."

"*On Deribasovskaya Street they've opened a new bar. It's loud with beer, and there, my dear, is where the jailbirds are ...*"

"... Let me go, sons of bitches! Bastards! Scum! Ahhhh!"

A door creaks heavily and swings open. The young soldier nods: *In here.* Zuleikha steps into an inky darkness that breathes with the smell of bodies long unwashed; the cold metal door nudges her forward. A lock clicks outside. She listens to many mouths breathing as she waits for her eyes to grow accustomed to the dark. A dull light trickles from a window with bars and Zuleikha begins to discern silhouettes.

Two tiers of bunks are crowded with people. Others sit on crates, on heaps of old clothes, and on the floor. There are so many people that there's nowhere to move to. There's the sound of loud scratching, of snoring, and low voices. A mother whispers a fairytale to her child. In one corner, they're murmuring, "Lord Jesus, have mercy on us sinners," while another voice pleads to Allah for refuge from the devil.

Nobody pays attention to Zuleikha. She makes her way inside, trying not to step on anyone's arms or legs. After reaching the bunks, she stands, not knowing where to settle because there are backs, stomachs, and heads positioned so close together here it's as if they're in several layers. Suddenly someone moves aside (it's impossible to figure out right away if it's a man or a woman), freeing up a hand-sized part of the bunk. Zuleikha perches, whispering a grateful thank you into the dark. A person turns a face – there are light curls around a high forehead, and a small, sharp nose – and announces protectively:

"I'll see you're issued clean linens and a change of footwear."

Zuleikha nods readily, agreeing. She can hear from the voice that the person is already advanced in years, respectable. Who knows what sort of ways they have here.

"You don't know where they're taking us, do you?" she asks deferentially.

"Come to me tomorrow for an initial exam," the other continues. "On an empty stomach."

Zuleikha doesn't know what an initial exam is but she nods again, just in case. There's an unpleasant nagging in her stomach as she hasn't eaten since yesterday. She takes the remainder of the bread from her pocket. Her strange neighbor noisily draws air into his nostrils and turns his head, his eyes boring into the bread. Zuleikha breaks the piece in two and extends half. Her neighbor thrusts his share into his mouth in a flash and swallows, almost without chewing.

"Strictly on an empty stomach!" he mumbles menacingly, his fingers holding back crumbs that threaten to fall from his mouth.

And with those remnants of stale bread, the foundations for an unusual friendship are laid. Zuleikha and Volf Karlovich Leibe will become conversation partners, if peculiar ones. In moments when his flickering consciousness flashes, he will occasionally speak, throwing in unconnected medical terms, recalling and clarifying diagnoses of former patients, and asking professional questions that demand no answers. She will listen gratefully, not understanding even the slightest bit of this blend of arcane Russian and Latin words but feeling an important meaning concealed behind them and rejoicing at her interaction with such a learned man. They keep silent most of the time but that silence doesn't tire either of them.

Zuleikha's fellow townspeople from Yulbash are soon settled into the cell, too: the mullah's wife with the ever-present cat cage in her lap and the morose, black-bearded peasant with his numerous descendants. Convicts from Voronezh who worm their way in with the exiles take away the cat a week later and eat it, and one of the prison officials appropriates the karakul fur coat, forcing the mullah's wife to affix her signature on a corresponding protocol regarding the surrender of property. She hardly notices the loss: she sobs for days on end, maybe about her husband, maybe about her cat.

Death is everywhere. Zuleikha grasped that back in her childhood. Tremblingly soft chicks covered in the downiest sunny yellow fluff, curly-haired lambs scented with hay and warm milk, the first spring moths, and rosy apples filled with heavy sugary juice – all of them carried within themselves the germ of future dying. All it took was for something to happen – sometimes this was obvious, though sometimes it was accidental, fleeting, and not at all noticeable to the eye – and then the beating of life would stop within the living, ceding its place to disintegration and decay. Chicks struck down by a poultry disease dropped like lifeless lumps of flesh into bright green grass in a yard; lambs skinned during Qurbani displayed their pale red innards; one-day moths poured from the sky, strewing themselves as if they were fresh snow on apples that had already fallen to the ground, their sides spotted with purplish abrasions.

The fate of her own children was confirmation of that, too. Four babies born only to die. Each time Zuleikha brought the little wrinkled face of a daughter to her lips for a kiss after birth, she would peer with hope into half-blind eyes still covered with slightly swollen lids, into tiny nose holes, into the fold of doll-like lips, into barely distinguishable pores on skin still a gentle red, and at sparse shoots of fluff on a small head. She thought she was seeing life. It would later turn out she was seeing death.

She had grown accustomed to that thought, just as an ox grows accustomed to a yoke and a horse to its master's voice. Some people, like her daughters, were allotted a pinch of life and some got handfuls; others, like her mother-in-law, received immeasurably generous entire sacks and granaries. Death awaits everyone, though, hiding in actual people or walking alongside them, snuggling up to their feet like a cat, settling on clothing like dust, or penetrating the lungs like air. Death is ubiquitous and it is slyer, smarter, and more powerful than a silly life that will always lose a skirmish.

It arrived and took away the powerful Murtaza, who had seemed born to live a hundred years. It will obviously take the proud Vampire Hag away soon, too. Even the grain that she and her husband buried between their daughters' graves – with the hope of saving it for their new crop – will rot in spring and become death's quarry, shut away in a cramped wooden crate.

It seems as if Zuleikha's time has also come. She was prepared to accept death on that memorable night, lying on the sleeping bench alongside the already dead Murtaza, so she is surprised to still be alive. She waited as the Red Hordesmen barged into the house and destroyed her home and hearth. And she waited when they brought her along the snow-covered expanses of her native land, too. And while spending the night in the desecrated mosque, to the sleepy bleating of sheep and the yellow-haired harlot's shameless shrieks. And now she is waiting again, in a damp and cold stone cell, passing the hours with lengthy reflections like this for the first time in her life.

Will her death take the shape of a young soldier with a long, sharp bayonet? Of some thief who's been moved into their cell, with a faintly predatory smile, a homemade knife hidden in his boot, and a hankering for her warm sheepskin coat? Or will death come from within, turning into disease, cooling the lungs, appearing on her forehead as hot and sticky sweat, filling her throat with heavy green phlegm, and, finally, squeezing her heart in its icy fist, forbidding it to beat? Zuleikha doesn't know.

That lack of knowledge is distressing and the long wait excruciating. Sometimes it seems she is already dead. The people around her are emaciated, pale, and spend entire days whispering and quietly weeping: so who are they if not the dead? This place – frigid and crowded, the stone walls wet from damp, deep under the ground, without a single ray of sun – what is it if not a burial vault? Only when Zuleikha makes her way to the latrine, a large, echoing tin bucket in the corner of the cell, and feels her cheeks warm with shame is she convinced that, no, she is still alive. The dead do not know shame.

The Kazan transit prison is a legendary, distinguished place through which numerous bright minds and dark souls have passed. There's good reason it's located near Kazan's kremlin, right up close. From their cells, the luckiest of the arrested can admire the dark blue onion domes of the Blagoveshchensk church, covered in golden stars, and the Storozhev tower's brownish-green spire inside the trading quarter. The transit prison has been running continuously for a good century and a half, pumping the large country's blood from west to east like a beautifully healthy heart that knows no fatigue.

In this same cell where Zuleikha is now listening to Professor Leibe's half-crazed monologue and furtively scraping the first louse out of her armpit, there sat, exactly forty-three years ago, a young student from Imperial Kazan University. The locks of hair on the top of his head were still youthfully disobedient and lush, and his gaze was serious and morose. He had been imprisoned for organizing student gatherings against the government. After ending up in the cell, he initially pounded his angry little fists at a frost-covered door, shouting something daring and foolish. His disobedient blue lips sang "the Marseillaise". He diligently did gymnastic exercises to try to warm up. Then he would sit on the floor, placing his rolled-up student uniform overcoat – irrevocably ruined by thick prison grime – underneath himself, clasp his knees with arms numbed from the cold, and cry hot, angry tears. The student's name was Vladimir Ulyanov, later better known as Lenin.

Nothing has changed here since then. First, emperors succeeded one another, then revolutionary leaders, and the transit prison served the authorities with unwavering faithfulness, as good old prisons should. Here they held exiles before sending them for hard labor in Siberia and the Far East, and, later, Kazakhstan. Criminal and political prisoners were usually housed separately, as a precaution against spreading criminal ideas. Customs established over the centuries had begun breaking down in recent times, though.

At the end of 1928, a thin stream of dekulakized people stretched to the capital from the far reaches of what was once Kazan Governate. These deportees needed to be gathered together, loaded into railroad cars, and sent on to destinations according to instructions. It was decided to hold that seemingly not very criminal contingent – which nevertheless still needed to be guarded – here in the transit prison, particularly since dekulakized people were sent along the very same age-old routes as convicts (Kolyma, Yenisei, Zabaikalye, Sakhalin …), often even in neighboring railroad cars on the same trains.

The stream gradually swelled, strengthened, and grew. By the winter of 1930, it had turned into a powerful river that flooded not only the prison itself but all the cellars near the train station, administrative buildings, and nonresidential premises, too. Hungry, furious, and uncomprehending peasants were now everywhere, taking shelter and waiting for their destiny, both hoping for it and simultaneously fearing its rapid onset. This river swept up everything in its path as centuries-old prison traditions broke down (the dekulakized were housed along with criminals and later with political prisoners, too); entire crates of documents (meaning whole villages and cantons) were lost and mixed up, making any sort of registry of those contingents – or, later, determinations of identity – impossible; and officials of various ranks from the regional and transport divisions of the State Political Administration lost their posts.

Zuleikha and those who arrived with her will end up spending an entire month in the transit prison, until the first day of spring, 1930. By that time, the cells were so densely stuffed that the prison chief had a stroke due to his desperate attempts to free himself of the specialized contingent of peasants foisted on him. Through sheer luck, they sent Zuleikha and her traveling companions on their way just before an epidemic of typhus broke out, mowing down more than half the detainees and freeing up the premises in a natural way – to the utmost relief of the boss, who was on his way to recovery at the Shamov Hospital.

February 1930 had yielded a good crop: Ignatov brought four batches of dekulakized peasants to Kazan. He sighed with relief and quiet inner joy each time he watched the kulaks disappear behind the transit prison's sturdy gates. One more useful thing had been accomplished, one more grain of sand had been tossed on the scales of history. This is how a people shapes its country's future, one grain at a time, one after another. A future that will certainly become a world victory, an unavoidable triumph of revolution both personally for him, Ignatov, and for millions of his Soviet brothers, people like the imperturbable Denisov, one of the romantic twenty-five thousanders, or the cultured, clever Bakiev.

Constant travels had saved Ignatov from the necessity of having a talk with Ilona. He'd popped in once, briefly ("Work, work ..."), and she should be grateful for that. He hadn't stayed the night. She'd figured out what was what. Anyway, what kind of personal life could you have when there's so much to do just waiting right around the corner!

Hundreds, thousands of families were floating in endless caravans of sledges along the vast expanses of Red Tataria. A long journey awaited them. Neither they nor their escort guards knew where it led. One thing was clear: it was distant.

Ignatov wasn't pondering the upcoming fate of those in his charge. His job was simply to deliver them. He'd cut Ilona off when she inquired about where they'd send those tormented bearded peasant men whose sledges had been stretching through the streets of Kazan for days on end. They'll go where oppressors and exploiters can finally atone for their dark past with honest labor, working themselves into the ground and earning – earning! – the right to a bright future. Period.

Nastasya would never have asked such a thing, though. Nastasya ... She was a ripe berry, seeping juice. All of February was as hot as May for Ignatov; just the thought of her warmed him. He wanted to believe, too, that the expeditions to the villages for "dekulakizing" – those trips through quiet, snow-covered forests with songs and jokes, those heated evening arguments with local Party activists at the rural councils with a crackling fire and a couple glasses of home brew, and those overnight stays in old mosques and barns, filled with the heat of Nastasya's body – would always happen.

And then it comes suddenly, like a saber to the top of the head: "You're going to accompany a special train."

What's that? Why me? What did I do wrong? "I'll obey, of course, comrade leader, but explain to me, Bakiev, my friend: I'm battling kulakdom here, I'm hardly ever out of the saddle. They – the enemy – don't know it's peacetime now. They have pitchforks, axes, and rifles. It's a genuine warfront! I'm needed here! And you're sending me off just to sit around on a train ..."

Bakiev's gaze through the gold rings of his pince-nez is unusually severe. "We need reliable people like you, Ignatov, for this job. What makes you think it's going to be easy? It's twenty train cars chock-full of human lives. And each is a dyed-in-the-wool kulak, harboring a sense of hurt the size of a pig, if not a cow, toward the authorities. Just you try bringing them halfway across the country and delivering them to their destination without them fighting among themselves and scattering along the way. And then there's the question – can you do it?"

"What do you mean, can I do it, Bakiev? You know me, don't you? It's not a complex matter. You put the meanest guards and the strongest locks on the railroad cars. It's a bayonet in the eye if someone moves their eyebrows the wrong way."

"Is that so?" Bakiev squints and now it's obvious how very much he's aged in this last half-year. So that's what a warm office, with its oak desk and sweet tea in lace-like tea-glass holders, does to comrades-in-arms. But Bakiev, like Ignatov, is still only thirty years old.

"They'll get there, there's no way out. I know what I'm talking about. Believe me, I've seen so many of them in this last year, those oppressors. Just reconsider, Bakiev, my friend. And tell me truly, is it not possible to send someone else? Being a nanny for a train is embarrassing ..."

"A nanny? A commandant for a special train is just a nanny in your opinion? And a thousand human heads are just trifles? When will you grow up, Ivan? All you want is to ride a steed with your saber unsheathed, and for the wind to whistle loudly in your ears! And it doesn't matter where you gallop off to or why!" And (here's the calm Bakiev for you, too): *whack!* A fist to the desk.

Ignatov whacks his fist in response. "Now, now! What do you mean, it doesn't matter? I gallop off wherever the Party orders!"

"And the Party's ordering you to set the showboating aside, too! To accept, today, the assignment on special train K-2437. Departure's tomorrow!"

"Yes, sir."

They catch their breath. Go silent. Light cigarettes.

"Please understand, Bakiev, my friend, that my heart is for the Party. It doesn't just ache for the Party, it burns for it. Everybody's heart should burn like that. Because what does our country need us for, anyway, if there's only a candle stub instead of a heart or the gaze loses its fire?"

"I do understand you, Vanya. Please try to understand me, too. Maybe you'll grasp this later and thank me – because it's for you, you damned fool, so you …" Bakiev falls silent and vigorously wipes the lenses of his pince-nez with a handkerchief as if he wants to push them out. The glass is creaking. He's strange today.

"So where are we taking this special train of yours?" Ignatov blows a stream of smoke at the floor.

"To Sverdlovsk for now. You'll stay in a holding area there and wait for orders. That's how we send everybody now, until further notice."

"Yes, sir." Ignatov's wondering if he'll have time before tomorrow to say goodbye to both women. First, certainly, to Nastasya. And later, if there's enough time, to Ilona, to be done with her for good, to end things.

They shake hands. For some reason, Bakiev suddenly spreads his arms wide and clasps Ignatov to his chest. He certainly is strange today.

"I'll drop by tomorrow to say goodbye before I leave."

"There's no need, Vanya. Consider it said."

Bakiev attaches the pince-nez to his nose and continues sorting through documents in folders. The papers cover his desk like drifted snow.

Ignatov gets up to leave and turns when he reaches the door. Bakiev is sitting motionless, up to his neck in a paper snowbank. His eyes, magnified by the pince-nez's bulging lenses, are wearily closed.

Of course he doesn't make it to Ilona's. *To hell with her. She'll assume I left on an urgent assignment.* He's gone missing before for a week or two without warning. This time he'll be away for a month, a month and a half … Exactly how long will he be racing around on the railroad, anyway? Fine, he was ordered to be a commandant, he'll be a commandant. He'll eat government-issue chow and get enough sleep; it's a long trip. He'll cart away that damned special train if that's what Bakiev needs so desperately. And then he'll say, "That's it, my friend, return me to real work. My soul's weary. It's asking for a real task …"

Ignatov's running to the train station early on the morning of the first day of spring in 1930, gulping the biting, frosty air. The trams aren't operating yet and it would be a shame to spend an entire five-kopek coin on a cab. It's a long way from the women's dormitory where Nastasya lives, so he had to get up early, before the factory whistles.

A mug rumbles in his suitcase, hitting against its plywood sides. His boots crunch on the hard-packed path along the banks of the Bulak, which is long and pierces Kazan like an arrow.

The slumbering city is lighting its first lamps and releasing occasional sleepy pedestrians onto the streets. The hoarse voices of half-awake dogs yelp; the first tram pulses somewhere in the distance.

Candle-like minarets – the Yunusov, Apanaev, and Galeev mosques – float, dissolving into the dark-blue morning mist. Denisov did well to come up with that idea back then, raising the red banner like a revolutionary at the former village mosque. Why hadn't they reached that point yet here in the capital? The Kazan minarets stick out like useless shafts poking meaningless holes at the sky.

Ignatov turns toward the bazaar. The kremlin's paper-white teeth flare up on the hill. Five-pointed stars shine on the triangular towers like little golden beams. Now that's genuine beauty, correct beauty – ours.

The station building is like an embossed gingerbread cookie: chocolaty-red, adorned with pilasters and windows, festooned with emblems and decorative urns, strewn with spangles of tiling, and studded with spires and weathervanes. Ignatov winces: the Kazan train station is Russia's gateway to Siberia, but it looks like a cultural center or some kind of museum. In a word, *ugh*.

The square in front of the station is already chaotic with people, the crush of carts, and the porters' brisk cursing. Ignatov slows from a run to a walk and calms his breathing; it's not fitting for the commandant of a special train to puff like a steam engine himself. He sternly inspects the cursing porters along the way and they grow quiet, too, when they cast sideways glances at his gray military overcoat with the red insignia on his left sleeve. Well, that's better now.

Ignatov pushes a station door that's as tall and heavy as a wardrobe. The air is thick with the smell of human sweat, bread, polished weaponry, gunpowder, sheepskin, unwashed hair, machine oil, soldiers' boots, homeless dogs, turpentine, wood, and medications. It resounds with shouting, barking, neighing, clanging, bleating, and crashing. A steam engine whistles piercingly outside, drowning out all other sounds for a moment. It's not morning here. There's no time of day here. It's perpetual bedlam. Ignatov wedges his way into the crowd, elbowing and stretching his neck in search of the right office.

"Behind me! Don't spread out! Stay together! Together, damnit!" A group of recruits in civilian clothing, wearing red armbands and with rifles at the ready, is leading a dozen scared, narrow-eyed peasants dressed in summer clothes – colorful robes and embroidered skullcaps – who are looking all around. The detachment's leader is shouting himself hoarse, yelling out commands, then he quietly hisses through his teeth, "You are trouble, you Uzbek sheep …"

"In your places! Everybody stay in your places! I'll shoot anyone who tries to escape on the spot!" bellows a slim soldier on the other side, waving his revolver around and attempting to stop several peasant women on his own. It seems they'd been sitting submissively on their bundles but had suddenly jumped up one after the other and started wailing and jabbering away, maybe in Mari, maybe in Chuvash, when they caught sight of other peasants.

"Step aside!" yell the porters, ramming the stirring crowd with unwieldy carts loaded with rocking mountains of crates containing sharp-smelling oranges and roasted beef. "Provisions for express number two! Step aside!"

Ignatov looks around with the advantage of his imposing height – seeing over the tops of shaggy fur caps, headscarves, fur hats with earflaps, embroidered skullcaps, brimmed hats, and pea coats – to find the door he needs: the office of the head of the Kazan transportation hub. The door slams loudly and incessantly, letting streams of people in and out. The train station's heart is beating. Swearing and excusing himself, stepping on people's feet and suitcases, Ignatov makes his way inside and grasps a tall, rickety wooden desk with his hands. Petitioners just like Ignatov push at him from both sides.

Ignatov takes documents from his suitcase: he has a brand-new gray folder that still crackles deliciously at its folds and carries the austere inscription "Case" and the painstakingly formed figures "K-2437." Inside there are a couple of thin sheets with the names of the dekulakized typed in small print, a little over eight hundred people in total. He holds it out to a small man with infinitely tired red eyes, who doesn't notice the folder in the midst of the constant shouting and trilling from a telephone.

"Yes, yes!" the little man yells hoarsely into the receiver. "Dispatch the Taishet train! There's congestion on number seventeen already! Dispatch Chita, too, to the same hounds of hell!"

"Is number ten to Orenburg?" The question carries over heads, from somewhere outside.

"You still here? What do you mean, Orenburg? It's to Tashkent, to the goddamned hounds of hell, you son of a bitch," the official barks in response.

Ignatov leans across the desk and jabs the folder like a sword, right at the green uniform. Barely glancing at it, the official detaches a wrinkled sheet of paper from a heap of documents on the desk, with the slanted inscription "Leningrad – remainders" written in purple ink, and shoves it at Ignatov.

"Take these people, too. Sign."

"But where –" Ignatov doesn't manage to finish as the telephone explodes in another shrill ring and the official grabs the receiver as if he wants to chew it up.

"What do you mean, a railroad car isn't expandable?" He's spitting saliva into the holes of the receiver. "It was stated: 'Load sixty per car'! The bunks are wide, people will move over a little!"

Ignatov grabs the official by the lapels:

"But where am I going to put more people? What 'Leningrad remainders'? My train's already at breaking point."

"At breaking point?" The official is losing his temper and his voice is becoming surprisingly similar to the telephone's trill. "You call fifty heads per train car breaking point? So you don't want sixty like the Samarkand train? Or seventy like the Chita train? And soon it'll be ninety per car! They'll ride standing, like horses! Now that's really the breaking point!" He grabs a stack of disintegrating fat folders from the table and hurls them back down. "There are eight thousand just dekulakized! And they all need to be sent within the week! How about that? And there are new ones every day, every damn day. Soon we'll be putting them on the rails. And you don't want to take an extra dozen mouths to feed?"

"Fine." Ignatov gives in, gloomily scrawling on the transfer slip with a pencil. "Give me your ... Leningrad remainders."

"Don't you worry," the official suddenly says quietly, blowing feverishly on the bottom of a large official stamp before imprinting "Kazan Hub" in bold blue ink on the folder. "They'll be scattered to the goddamned hounds of hell in a few weeks. You'll be traveling light."

And he enters the date: "1 March 1930."

Ignatov decides to drop in on Bakiev before his departure, anyway. He senses anxiety when he enters the building on Vozdvizhenskaya Street. Everything appears to be business as usual: a thorough young soldier is checking passes at the entrance, office doors are slamming, secretaries are clattering up and down marble stairs. But there's *something* in the air.

What?

Ignatov slows his pace. There it is, in the young lady from their division who's running past with eyes as frightened and red as a rabbit's under thick mascara-coated lashes. There it is, in several unknown soldiers straining hard as they drag heavy boxes with documents. And it's there in someone's cautious sidelong glance from behind a column.

Has something happened? Bakiev probably knows.

Without stopping at his own office, Ignatov hurries to Bakiev's office on the third floor. A long, thin corridor leads there, lined with narrow rectangular doors where the flourishes of brass handles glimmer dimly. It's usually crowded and smoke-filled here. Now all the doors are tightly closed, as if they're locked.

Something has definitely happened.

Ignatov strides along parquet that's come loose and turned dark gray over time; the marred boards squeak shrilly under his boots. He notices one of the door handles slowly dip down and noiselessly go still, then return to its position again, as if someone inside wanted to go out but thought better of it.

What the hell … ?

The door to Bakiev's office is wide open. Standing beside it are two unfamiliar soldiers with rifles. They look closely at Ignatov, unblinking.

Was it really something to do with Bakiev?

That can't be.

It can't be, but something has happened.

Ignatov lowers his gaze. *Don't stop.* His feet carry him past the office. The soldiers step back reluctantly, letting him pass. Out of the corner of his eye he notices, in the depths of the office, several overturned chairs on a floor littered with papers, the wide-open mouth of a safe, and a dark gray silhouette by the window, absorbed in reading documents.

Don't look. Don't speed up. There's an exit to the back stairs at the end of the corridor. Use that to go down and get out of here. To the train station! Ignatov strides along the corridor.

"Hey!" rings out a shout behind him.

He stops and turns around. The dark gray silhouette has come out of the office and is watching Ignatov.

"You here to see Bakiev?"

"No, sir."

"What department are you from?"

"The fifth." Ignatov doesn't know why he lies.

Would he really run if he had to? From his own? After all, they'd shoot him like a dog. Why run if you're not guilty of anything? They'd sort it out and let him go. But what if they didn't? So should he run anyway?

The silhouette silently goes back into the office. The soldiers turn away. Ignatov opens the door to the back stairs and slips down the steps to the first floor. He leaves the building without looking at anyone. He strides to the train station with his head uncovered but not feeling the cold.

Shame rolls over Ignatov like a hot wave, melting his ears. *What were you afraid of, you fool? Your own comrades, doing their job honestly?* It's a mistake about Bakiev, he tells himself. Definitely a horrendous, unbelievable, ludicrous mistake. Possibly because of someone's slander. Or maybe just a misprint, an absurd mishap. It happens, surnames get mixed up and they take the wrong person. Out of negligence.

Then why are you running away like a coward, like the lowest rat? Why don't you go back to the ransacked office and shout in the dark gray man's face: "Bakiev isn't guilty of anything! I'll vouch for him!"?

Ignatov stops and squeezes his pointy cavalry hat in his hand. And leave the special train without a commandant? It departs in an hour. They can slap you with desertion for failure to appear at the site of service. And that's summary execution. He knows because he himself has enforced sentences like this. He pulls his hat down on his head and hurries to the train station.

Everybody knows Mishka Bakiev is a clever person, a Party member, and a revolutionary. *He's our man, to his last drop of blood, to his last breath*, Ignatov thinks. *They'll sort this out and let him go for sure.* It just can't be that they wouldn't release him. Let him go and apologize in front of the entire collective. And punish those to blame.

For sure.

Until Further Notice

"Zuleikha Valieva!"

"I'm here!"

In Zuleikha's whole life, she's never uttered the word "I" as many times as she has during this month in prison. Modesty is a virtue so it doesn't befit a decent woman to say "I" a lot without reason. The Tatar language is even constructed so you could live your whole life without once saying "I." No matter what tense you use to speak about yourself, the verb will go into the necessary form and the ending will change, making the use of that vain little word superfluous. It's not like that in Russian, where everybody goes out of their way to put in "I" and "me" and then "I" again.

A soldier by the entrance yells out surnames loudly, painstakingly. Zuleikha's seeing him for the first time. Is he new?

"Volf Lee … ? Lei … ? Lei-be?"

"How many times have I asked for medical personnel to call me by my first name and patronymic!"

Volf Karlovich has repeated this phrase, word for word, every day at roll call. The other escort guards have already learned it by heart but this one peers into the darkness with surprise. And then, suddenly:

"To the exit! With your things!"

Zuleikha jolts as if she's been struck by a whip. She presses her little bundle to her chest.

The human mass around her stirs, surges, gapes, and extends hands. "Where? Where are they being sent? And us? Where are we going?"

"The rest are to remain in place!"

Volf Karlovich rises with dignity, brushes himself off, and lets Zuleikha go first. They make their way to the exit, stepping over bodies, heads, sacks, suitcases, arms, parcels, and swaddled infants. The unfamiliar soldier also calls the mullah's widow and the morose peasant's family, with the innumerable children, and leads them out of the cell.

After so many days of darkness, light from a kerosene lamp seems as bright as a sliver of sun. After the cell's stuffy air, the cold air in the corridor intoxicates. Legs tired from constant sitting have slackened and plod falteringly along, but the body is glad to be moving. How long had they stayed in the dungeons? Neighbors confirmed it was several weeks; they'd kept track with the daily roll calls.

They walk along the corridor with escort guards to the front and back. The guards sometimes stop and call for more people from other cells. When they leave the prison, there are already so many they can't be counted. Villagers, Zuleikha understands as she walks and examines the faces and clothes of her traveling companions. Some of them have fresh, even rosy, faces and were brought in recently. Others, though – like the people from her town – can barely stand. The mullah's widow has aged and grayed but she's stubbornly pulling the cat's empty cage behind her. The peasant's wife has withered to yellowness and is, as before, clasping two swaddled babies to herself like bundles.

"Finally!" Leibe's joyful whisper quivers right by her ear. "They're transferring the infirmary to the rearguard!"

Zuleikha nods. To the rearguard, fine, to the rearguard. She's seeing Leibe in the light for the first time. His facial features are as graceful as a youth's, his curly gray hair is bright and silvery, and even his wrinkles are delicate and intelligent. Long, weeks-old stubble covers his cheeks, lending him an air of nobility, and he's not nearly as old as it seemed in the beginning, probably younger than Murtaza. He's just dressed oddly, like a pauper, in an ancient, very shabby and moth-eaten blue dress uniform that's torn in many places, and he's wearing house slippers without backs on his rag-wrapped feet.

"Bunch closer together! Forward, at a jogtrot – march!" commands the soldier out in front, throwing open the door to the outside.

Daylight hits the face like a shovel. Eyes explode with redness and instantly squint to blink. Zuleikha grabs at a wobbling wall and leans against it. The wall wants to throw Zuleikha off and she finds herself sinking to the floor. She is roused by a shout:

"Stand up! Everybody stand, you bastards! You want to go back to the cell?"

She's lying on a dirty stone floor by the dungeon exit. Outside the crooked open doorway is a painfully deep-blue March sky and the large, flat dish of the prison yard covered in mirror-like blotches of puddles. Several people are lying there beside her, groaning and pressing their hands to their eyes. Some are leaning against the wall, others are crouching, kneeling, and mumbling ...

"I said forward! At a jogtrot! March!"

One by one, with their eyes narrowed like moles, people find their way outside. Reeling from the fresh air and holding on to one another, they crowd into a loose, limping bunch that keeps falling apart along the way as they lurch along Tashayak Street toward the train station at an uneven jogtrot. Brisk escort guards surround them on all sides. Their rifles are horizontal in their hands, in complete accordance with paragraph seven, instruction 122 *bis* four (dated February 17, 1930) on "The procedure for escorting former kulaks, criminals, and other anti-Soviet elements."

Their eyes quickly grow accustomed to the daylight and Zuleikha looks around. There are trains like giant snakes, with dozens of railroad cars, to her left and right. Underfoot are endless ribbons of train track and rib-like ties, along which stride the hurrying exiles' worn shoes, felt boots soaked from clinging snow, and mud-smeared boots. There's a strong smell of fuel oil. A whistle sounds ahead; it's a train drawing closer. "Let it through!" is the command from up ahead.

The escort guards stop and point their bayonets: *Get off the tracks.* A huge steam engine breathing hot raggedy fumes is already hurtling toward them, cutting through the air with its fire-red fender. The flywheels are like millstones gone mad. There's crashing and clanging; it's frightening. Zuleikha is seeing a train for the first time in her life. Daubs of white paint on the side flash "Forward to happiness!" in uneven letters, heavy air whips at their faces; and then the steam engine speeds away, pulling behind it a long chain of rumbling railroad cars.

A lanky lad of around twelve – one of the sons of the peasant man with many children – unexpectedly takes off. He jumps, catches a handrail, dangles like a kitten on a string, and rides away with the train. An escort guard shoulders his rifle. The crash of the shot merges with the whistle of the engine and a cloud of thick, patchy steam shrouds the train. The din of the train recedes just as quickly as it had arrived. The steam disperses and a small body is left lying on the tracks, lost in a sheepskin coat of the wrong size.

The mother can only silently open her mouth before her arms droop like rope. The bundles of her babies nearly fall to the ground. Zuleikha grabs one, the peasant man grabs the other. The older children huddle against their father's legs in fright.

"We're moving along. We're not loitering!"

Steel fingers of bayonets point at the track. One of them touches the woman on the shoulder: *You were ordered to move forward!* The peasant man takes his wife by the shoulders. She doesn't resist and her head is twisted back like a dead hen's, her gaze fixed on her son's small body sprawled between the rails. Still not closing her mouth, she obediently walks away with everyone, placing her feet on the ties. She walks for a long time.

Then she lets out a guttural scream and thrashes in her husband's firm grasp, swinging her arms and legs to no avail; she wants to go back. But another train is already flying toward them, roaring, and her scream is drowned out by a powerful iron chorus of flywheels, pistons, hammers, railroad cars, rails, wheels.

Zuleikha hugs the soft, warm bundle in her arms. This baby that doesn't belong to her is pink like a doll, with chubby cheeks, a tiny button nose, and delicate fluff instead of eyebrows. Snuffling in its sleep. Only two months since it was born, no more. Not one of Zuleikha's daughters lived to this age.

The exiles flow along the tracks in a long, wide stream. Another stream, smaller and made up of cold people under-dressed for the weather, is running toward them from the train station. And diagonally across the rails there rapidly strides a lone figure wearing a sharp-pointed hat and carrying a gray folder in his hand. They all gather by a large railroad car that was knocked together from crooked, poorly planed boards painted reddish orange.

"Stop!" the man with the folder quietly says.

Zuleikha recognizes him. It's Red Hordesman Ignatov, Murtaza's killer.

The convoy's leader is already hurrying toward him, whispering something in his ear, and pointing at the peasant's wife, who continues to wail. Ignatov listens, nodding from time to time and gloomily looking around at the crowd that's clustered before him. His gaze meets Zuleikha's. Does he recognize her? Or does it only seem so?

"Listen to me carefully!" he finally says. "I'm your commandant ..."

She doesn't know what a commandant is. And he said "your." Does this mean they'll be together a long time?

"... and I'm taking you, dekulakized citizens, and you, former people citizens, to a new life ..."

Former people? Zuleikha doesn't understand: former people are dead people. She looks around at the handful of people who've just joined them. Pale, tired faces. They're shivering, huddling close to one another and dressed for autumn, wearing frivolous woolen coats and silly thin shoes. A cracked pince-nez's frame gleams gold and an absurd ladies' hat with a veil shines like a bright emerald spot so it's immediately obvious that they're city people. But not dead, no.

"... a life that may be difficult and filled with deprivations and ordeals but also with honest labor that benefits our fervently beloved motherland –"

"But where to? Where are you taking us, commander?" someone from the crowd insolently interrupts.

Ignatov shoots glances at their faces, seeking out the obnoxious one. He doesn't find him.

"You'll find out when you get there," he says over their heads, with authority. "Well, then ..."

"And if I don't get there?" a daring voice rings out again, challenging.

Ignatov takes a breath. Then he pulls a pencil stub out of his shirt and thoroughly wets it with saliva.

"What's the surname of the one killed while escaping?" he asks loudly.

After hearing the answer, he opens the folder and crosses one name off the list.

"Already, one won't get there." He raises the folder and waves it around in the air. "Does everybody see?"

A bold, crooked line on a sheet tattered by a typewriter floats over the crowd.

Ignatov clears his throat.

"You drank the blood of the laboring peasantry for a long while. The moment has come to atone for your guilt and prove your right to a life in this complex present time of ours as well as in a wonderful bright future that will come about very, very soon, no doubt about it ..."

He uses words that are difficult and unfamiliar to Zuleikha. She understands little, other than Ignatov's promise that everything will end well.

"My task is to transport you – unharmed and in one piece – to that new life. Your task is to help me with that. Any questions?"

"Yes!" one of the bunch of "formers" hurries to say, in an apologetic tone. He's a stooped man with sorrowful eyes; the skin underneath them sags like sacks, like melted wax, and Zuleikha realizes he's a drunk. "If you please. Will food be provided during the travel? You must understand that for so many weeks we've already –"

"And so, food ..." utters Ignatov forebodingly, walking right up to the stooped man, whose trembling nostrils instantly turn ashen. "Be thankful that you haven't been shot! That the Soviet authorities continue thinking about you, taking care of you! That you'll go in heated railroad cars with your loved ones!"

"Thank you," the frightened man babbles to the green patches on Ignatov's chest. "Thank you."

"You're going there to be liberated from the fetters of the old world, toward new freedom, one might say!" Ignatov continues thundering, striding along the ragged line of people, whose heads are shrinking into their shoulders. "And all you're thinking about is how to stuff your belly! You'll have ... hazel grouse in champagne sauce and chocolate-covered fruit!"

He waves abruptly to the escort guard by the railroad car: *Let's go!* The other guard draws open the door, which squeals as it slides to the side so the car reveals its rectangular black maw.

"Welcome to the Grand Hotel!" smirks the guard.

"With the greatest pleasure, citizen chief!" A nimble little man with dog-like mannerisms and a persistent gaze is the first to leap up into the railroad car, throwing a foot full force into the high opening – and revealing the fraying edges of his baggy trousers – and then disappearing inside.

A dangerous person, from prison, guesses Zuleikha. *You need to stay far away from him.*

And now it's the exiles elbowing one another as they climb into the carriage to find places. The peasant men grunt, take a bounding run-up, and their feet push off, springing up. The peasant women groan, lifting their felt boots into masses of skirts, somehow clambering up, and pulling small, squealing children after them.

"And what about those who aren't able to do this like monkeys? Will you carry them in your arms?" a calm voice asks amid the clamor.

It's a stately lady with a high hairdo – a twisted tower of half-gray hair – and that bright-green hat with the veil. She's standing with her mighty arms raised, as if she's inviting someone to take her in their arms. A woman like that can't be lifted, decides Zuleikha. She's too heavy.

Ignatov stares right at the lady, who doesn't avert her gaze and just lifts a thin eyebrow: *And so?* The old man with the cracked pince-nez tugs at her shoulder, frightened, but she obstinately brushes off his hand. Ignatov motions with his chin and a guard drags a thick board out of the clamps on the railroad car door and places it like a gangway from the railroad car to the ground. The lady heads into the car, graciously nodding her hat in Ignatov's direction. Her large feet in laced shoes tread decisively and relentlessly; the board bends and shakes.

"*Votre Grand Hôtel m'impressionne, mon ami,*" she tells the guard, and he freezes, bewildered at hearing unfamiliar speech.

Zuleikha cautiously follows, carrying the bundle of her things in one arm and a sleeping child in the other. And how could this be, Allah, to contradict a man, a military man at that, and the chief at that. An old woman but brave. Or maybe she's brave because she's old? But going up on the board truly is easier.

The door squeals as it slides along its runners behind her. It's dark again, like in the cell. The heavy clang of one bolt, then a second. And that's it: one heated cattle car, numbered KO 310048 – freight capacity twenty tons, designed for up to forty humans or ten horses – is fully loaded with fifty-two deportees and ready for departure. Exceeding the planned load by twelve heads can be considered insignificant because, as the head of the transport hub in Kazan wisely noted that morning, soon they'll be going with ninety per car, standing like horses.

By the time Zuleikha has helped the unfortunate peasant and his wife, who's numb from grief, to settle in by putting the bundles with the infants to bed on the bunks as comfortably as possible – she was very sorry to tear herself away from that warm parcel, with its sweet baby smell – and found space for the restless older children, all the places have been taken and there's no squeezing in because everyone's packed the two-tiered bunks so closely. As before, Leibe helps out. He leans over from somewhere and pulls her up toward the ceiling by the hand, into the thick darkness of the second tier.

"I must ask you to observe your assigned place in the ward," he grumbles.

Zuleikha gratefully agrees as she feels her way to squeeze in between the professor and a wall that's cold as a rock. She bows her head slightly so she doesn't hit it on the frost-covered ceiling.

She pulls the shawl from her head and lays it between her leg and Leibe's bony hip; it's sinful to sit so close to an unrelated man. It's even shameful for the forefathers three generations away, as her mother would have reproachfully said. *Yes, Mama, I know. But your rules were only good for the old life. And we have – what was it Ignatov said? – a new life. Oh, what a life we have now.*

The prison man with dog-like mannerisms pulls out a match that's hidden deep in an inconspicuous crevice in the wall. He strikes it on the sole of his shoe and bends over a pot-bellied iron stove. It clatters with coal and then there's a hot fire in it, crackling, flaring up, and flooding the car with a warm, quivering light.

Zuleikha looks around and sees plank walls, plank floor, and plank ceiling. In the center of the car – like a warm heart – is the crooked little stove, part of it rusted in patterns. Along the sides are bunks darkened with time and worn to a dull brownish shine by hundreds of arms and legs.

"Why so glum, you lot?" rasps the prison man, flashing his big, gray teeth. "Take it easy, I'll be your minder. I won't let anyone harm you: I'm an honest vagabond. Everybody knows Gorelov."

Gorelov's hair is long and shaggy, like a woman's. Heavy, greasy locks keep falling over his face, turning his gaze wild and brutish. He walks along the bunks with a loose gait that's almost like a dance, and he peers into gloomy faces.

"It'd be curtains for you without a minder here, my dear people. It's a long way to ride." And then he's singing loudly, drawing out syllables: "*Hush dogs, there's no jumping trains! The screws will beat you for our pains ...*"

"How would you know, anyway?" The stooped drunk with the sorrowful eyes ("Ikonnikov, Ilya Petrovich, artist," as he would later introduce himself to his neighbors) has sat down next to the little cast-iron stove, which is already white-hot, to warm his cold hands. "Maybe they'll give us a lift as far as the Urals and throw us off."

Gorelov walks up to the little stove. He tosses an assessing glance at Ikonnikov's hunched figure, wearing a coat like a sack and scarf around his neck like a noose. Gorelov takes off a dirty shoe that's falling apart at the seams and extends it: *Hold this*. He unwinds his foot wrap for a long time then finally takes out a cigarette butt hidden between his toes. He places it in his mouth, lovingly twists the foot wrap back on, and puts on his shoe. He lights the cigarette butt from the stove and exhales smoke in Ikonnikov's face.

"How I know," he says, continuing the conversation as if nothing happened, "is that I'm an old hand. I've done two hitches, pal. I've done Sakhalin time and been pounded into Solovki grime."

Ikonnikov coughs and turns away from the smoke. Gorelov stands and scowls threateningly all around the silenced railroad car, challenging anyone to doubt him.

"This isn't freedom of the free. Procedures need to be observed," he says didactically. "But I'll be looking after you so nobody does anything foolish."

Gorelov catches a louse behind his ear with an abrupt twitch, crushes it on his fingernail, and flings it into the stove.

"*The bulls have got you by the horn,*" he sings, taking up a new tune, his broad grin revealing a large, gleaming gold crown. "*You've had it boys, now take your turn. You'll soon be sorry you were born. You're going where there's no return ...*" He's standing in the center of the car, hands in his pockets, his shoulders thrust back like wings. "Or is there someone here who can't wait and is just burning for the eternal 'no return'?"

Wary faces watch silently from the bunks. Gorelov takes a step behind the stove and knocks a wooden lid aside with his foot. Looking around belligerently, he unfastens his pants and releases a loud, taut stream into an open hole in the floor. Several women gasp, and stare at the long arc glistening in the firelight, entranced and unblinking. Their husbands tug at their sleeves and they look down, covering their children's eyes.

Zuleikha comes to her senses and turns away, too. The sound of it rings in her ears, making her face warm in shame. So that's the latrine? And what are women to do? In the cell, they went to a pail when necessary, though it was dark there. But here …

Gorelov smiles victoriously, flicking off the drops and in no hurry to tuck his manhood back into his pants.

"*Herpes genitales*, if I'm not mistaken," says Leibe. The professor's voice rings out beside Zuleikha as he looks pensively at Gorelov's bared flesh. "Three parts essential oil of lavender, one part sulfur. Rub it on three times a day. And no sexual contact until full recovery." He nods decisively, in firm agreement with himself, and then turns away indifferently.

Gorelov's face shifts and he hastily crams his wrinkled member back in his pants and leaps over to Leibe, scrambling up to the second tier like a monkey.

"Take care of that mug of yours, buster," he hisses into the vacant face, rubbing his fingertips on Leibe's dress uniform as if it were a napkin. "And thank your lucky stars that I'm the minder here. Otherwise you might get your bell rung –" Gorelov lets out a yell: he's stabbed his finger on the small badge crookedly pinned to the lapel of Leibe's uniform.

The railroad car abruptly begins moving, with a rumble.

"We're on our way! We're on our way!" The bunks boil over with excited whispers.

The hardened criminal casts a malevolent glance at Leibe and returns to his place.

Beside Zuleikha – right under the roof – there's a small window, the size of the one on the stove, and it's lined with even metal bars coated with velvety gray frost. On the other side of the grating she sees the central railway platform and the huge red station building with the lacy letters "Kazan" solemnly floating by. People are hurrying somewhere, surrounded by gleaming bayonet blades. A pair of horses neigh under militiamen. Women selling food bellow about snacks.

"We're headed for Siberia, not Moscow," someone notes.

"And where did you want them to send us? The Black Sea?"

The steam engine whistles long and loud, hurting the ears. A thick cloud of milky steam shrouds everything, creeping into eyes and mouths. When it dissipates, black skeletons of trees are already flying outside the window, silhouetted against white fields.

Zuleikha presses a finger to the grating: the frost on it is melting. The frost on the ceiling is beginning to drip, too, warmed by the stove and human breath.

They make themselves at home quickly. It doesn't involve much since they have few things and very little space. The peasants are bunched at one end of the railroad car, the Leningrad "formers" at the other. Zuleikha and the professor have ended up in the "city" half.

They introduce themselves. The tall lady in the green hat bears a name befitting her stature: Izabella. She has a long patronymic, too, and a puzzling double surname that Zuleikha doesn't remember. Izabella arranges her gray hair into a tall style each morning. Sometimes she recites poems that are intelligent, incomprehensible, and very beautiful, in Russian and occasionally, surprisingly, in French, which rumbles like the train wheels. She never recites the same poem twice. The railroad car listens. Zuleikha doesn't understand how so many varied, complex, and very long lines can fit inside one head, and a female one besides. Izabella's face remains calm and majestic, even when she's catching lice under her arms or parading toward the latrine, which they've screened off with a piece of fabric.

Her husband, Konstantin Arnoldovich Sumlinsky, is a withered old man with a sparse, triangular gray beard; he mostly stays silent. He wakes early in the morning and takes up his place by the crack in the door to wait for the first rays of sunlight, under which he places his only book, open, to read. He smiles at some pages with an approving nod, wags a finger at others as he shakes his small head in distress, and even argues with others. When he reaches the last page, he slams the book shut, pensively looks at the cover, with its picture of a small, gray grain of wheat, and opens it up again. Sometimes he and his wife speak at length in a whisper, but Zuleikha doesn't understand a single phrase, even though the conversation is in Russian, since they use such difficult words. He's a strange person and Zuleikha is rather afraid of him.

She takes a disliking to the stooped Ikonnikov. Everything about him – the wrinkled blue-gray bags under his eyes, the fine trembling of his long fingers, his small fidgeting motions, and even how he loudly and lengthily swallows with his large, sharp Adam's apple – indicates he's a drunkard. Mama always said a drunk person was worse than a beast.

Zuleikha likes Gorelov least of all, though. Nobody likes him. The car's minder holds everyone firmly by the throat. He always divides up the food himself, measuring out slimy porridge and herring soup with his own chipped mug, cutting bread with a coarse, stretched string, and mercilessly thrashing people's outstretched fingers with a spoon: *Don't get ahead of the minder.* He even pours out the drinking water from a half-rusty bucket covered with a crust of ice. He takes double portions for himself, for his labor. The peasant men look at him askance, keeping quiet. Gorelov is the first to leap from the bunks when the door opens for the daily inspection and the imperturbable Ignatov, his gaze severe and arrogant, enters the car surrounded by soldiers. The minder stands at attention in front of the commandant, poking a tense hand at his own forehead and loudly and diligently reporting that no incidents have taken place. Ignatov listens reluctantly, his body half-turned, and for some reason Zuleikha likes that he twitches his thin nostrils ever so slightly as he does. Sometimes Gorelov is summoned to the commandant's car; he returns quiet, mysterious, and even dreamy – maybe they fed him there.

They always want to eat. The belly groans, demanding. It clenches like a fist, then straightens and swells. Food is meager on their journey and it inflames rather than consoles the innards. Zuleikha remembers her mother's tales of the insatiable mythical giantess, Zhalmavyz, who eats everything that comes her way. And Zuleikha herself has become just the same. She's voraciously hungry all the time. She hadn't even known such a longing for food could exist. Her vision darkens from it; that's how bad things are. The bolt on the railroad car only needs to jingle a bit and her stomach immediately starts growling and churning: *Are they bringing something to eat?* Most often it turns out that no, it's just another inspection or a head count or a train station doctor undertaking a hurried, embarrassing examination.

Things are easier when they're moving. Zuleikha watches another life fly by in the tiny rectangular grated window – sparse little forests, small villages sliding from knolls, wrinkled ribbons of brooks, steppes resembling tablecloths, and the brush-like forest – and forgets about hunger. But she remembers it again during stops.

Sometimes she catches her neighbor's attentive gaze upon her. Leibe watches – intently, for a long time, and unblinking – as she painstakingly licks her shallow bowl squeaky clean. And then he'll suddenly give her his half-eaten chunk of bread or the remaining porridge in his dish. Zuleikha refused at first, but then she stopped. Now she just thanks him and accepts, and listens, listens to his endless muddled speeches that might be stories of medical practice or scraps of diagnoses. She soon notices that the book lover, the sullen Konstantin Arnoldovich, seems to want to join in their strange discussions, too. He needn't bother, she thinks possessively. The professor isn't about to start sharing his food with that bookworm, too!

She hasn't been able to discover if this train car has its own *iyase*, its own house spirit. It ought to; how could it not, since people are living here? Then again, how would it feed itself? There aren't even dead lice here – some people eat them themselves, others burn them in the stove – never mind breadcrumbs. She listens for it at night: the sounds of clattering or creaking under a house spirit's shaggy paws. No, there's nothing, it's quiet. The train car is soulless, dead.

It's very cold in the railroad car and they're given little coal. Candles are issued occasionally for two cloudy-glassed lamps and then it's bright for a short while.

Vestiges of their predecessors are scattered all around the train car, like greetings from the past. While investigating all the crevices and knotholes in the planks, Gorelov discovered an entire cigarette during the first half-hour of their journey. They wiped a layer of rusty dirt off the stove and read an impassioned inscription scratched with a nail that said, "Burn the scum!" The bunks are mottled with messages containing the names of loved ones, dates, oaths promising to *not* forget and *not* forgive, poems, dedications, threats, prayers, raunchy profanity, a delicate female profile, quotes from the Bible, Arabic squiggles ... The children from the large peasant family found a small cream-colored shoe while playing under the bunks, set on an elegant heel with a thin leather sole; it was for a girl of around five or six. Gorelov wanted to pull out the silk laces (anything could come in handy) but was too late because Ikonnikov, who was usually reserved, abruptly flung the shoe into the stove. A horrible smell of singed leather lingered in the car for a long while after.

Their route is long. It seems unending. The names of cities, settlements, and stations string together, one after another, like beads on a thread.

Kenderi, Vysokaya Gora, Biryuli, Arsk …

Sometimes their train races swiftly along the railroad through wind and blizzards, sometimes it lazily drags its way along sidings and branch lines, searching for a holding area, and sometimes it stands motionless in that same holding area for weeks, covered with drifted snow, its wheels freezing to the rails.

Shemordan, Kukmor, Kizner …

Sometimes at small stations a second special train running close by will flash in the crevices of the railroad car door.

"Laish!" shout the peasants, who are usually quiet. "Mamadysh! Sviyazhsk, Shupashkar!"

"We're from Lipetsk!" flies out in response.

"Voronezh! Taganrog! Shakhty!"

"From near Arzamas!"

"From Syzran!"

"We're from Vologda!"

Sarkuz, Mozhga, Pychaz …

One time after standing in a holding area yet again, the train unexpectedly sets off in the opposite direction: Pychaz, Mozhga, Sarkuz … The peasants laugh from joy, praying incessantly: "We're going home, heaven be praised, home!" They ride for almost a day. Then they come to their senses as they begin heading east again to Sarkuz, Mozhga, Pychaz …

"Nobody needs us," Ikonnikov says then. "They're knocking us around like …"

He falls silent.

"Yes, yes," says Izabella, cheering him. "You're absolutely right, like shit on a shoe. Just like it!"

And they roll on.

Agryz, Bugrysh, Sarapul …

The children begin dying first. All the children of the unfortunate peasant who had so many ran off to the other side, one after another, as if they were playing tag – first the babies (both at once, on the same day) then the older ones. His wife went after that; by then, she wasn't distinguishing the boundary between this world and the other very clearly. The peasant man pounded his head against the carriage wall that day; he wanted to crack open his skull. They dragged him away, tied him up, and held him until he calmed down.

Yanaul, Rabak, Turun …

They bury the dead along the tracks in one common pit. They dig it themselves using wooden shovels, with the escort guards' rifles aimed at them. Sometimes they don't have enough time to finish digging graves or cover the corpses properly with crushed stone before the order "To the train!" booms. The bodies are left to lie in the open, with the hope that kind people will turn up on the next special train and scatter something over them. They themselves always scatter something when their train stands by open graves like that.

Bisert, Chebota, Revda …

Ignatov never gets used to the tea-glass holder. He drinks hot water from a good old aluminum mug and lets that *thing* – fat around the middle, with even steel lacework gleaming on its gut and a daringly smooth handle – just stand on the table. The faceted glass in the holder trembles invitingly when they're in motion, sometimes bouncing: it's reminding him of its existence. But it seems silly, shameful, and simply impossible to drink from such a ridiculous object. After Sarapul, Ignatov gives it to the escort guards in the next compartment so they can amuse themselves with it. He wants to give them a disgustingly soft striped mattress with an unusually smooth cover (was it silk or something?) but then thinks better of it; they'd ruin the goods, the clods. He rolls it up and somehow stuffs it on the high shelf under the ceiling. He sleeps better on a wooden bench; it's what he's used to.

There's a lot he doesn't like in the commandant's compartment. There's the lackey-like, soundless, and subservient sliding of the door (*right-left, right-left* ...) and the foppish scalloped curtains with thin, barely noticeable stripes (let's assume bare windows are no good, but why the frills?) and the flawlessly clean, large mirror over the voluminous funnel-like tank that holds water for hand washing (he only looks when necessary, in the morning, while shaving). There's so much happening all around him! But there are lacy things and tea-glass holders here ...

Serving as the train's leader is not the easy job he thought it would be. They've already been traveling for two months. Which would be fine if they were actually moving, but more often they're just waiting. They're constantly on edge, like people in an asylum, because they're either urgently pressing ahead ("You out of your mind or what, commandant? Look, everything's backed up! Hand over your papers and push off, push off now and free up track five for me!") or holding their horses, waiting in a siding again for a week ("There weren't any orders with your name on them, comrade. You've been told to wait, so wait. And don't come see me every hour! We'll find you ourselves if anything comes up ...").

He loves those moments when the train gathers speed with a deep, ferocious rumble, rattling along the rails as if it were quivering with anticipation. He wants very much to yank the window down, stick his head outside, and put his face into the wind. He has difficulty enduring long days of painful anticipation at small stations in out-of-the-way places denoted on the map in italics.

Like now, gazing through a cloudy pane of glass covered in thick dust. Immobile black fields with small white spots (remnants of snow) spread outside. Ignatov testily taps his fingers on the varnished tabletop.

There were fifteen deaths during one eight-day stretch of idle time.

He'd noticed long ago that people die during the waits. Either the loud knocking of the wheels urges on tired hearts or the swaying of a railroad car calms them. But fact is fact: there's hardly an idle time when a couple of surnames aren't crossed out in the gray "Case" folder.

Eleven old people, four children.

When you're carrying nearly a thousand souls, there's nothing surprising in a few dying, right? The elderly from old age, some from illnesses. But children, too? Yes, that's right, from weakness. It can't be helped; it's the road.

"Comrade commandant?" Polipyev, the supply manager, puts his head inside the door with a coy knock. "So, lunch? Shall I bring it?"

And then the aroma of thoroughly cooked barley flavored with a touch of salted pork fat floats into the compartment. Crystals of salt sparkle on the long, pearly grains. There's a thick slice of spongy bread on the side.

Ignatov takes the plate from the tray. Polipyev stands meekly, arms at his sides. He used to attempt to help the commandant by spreading a linen napkin evenly on the table and placing the plate nicely in the center, setting the silverware properly (spoon with knife, to the right; fork to the left) and then the salt and pepper … But this isn't a commandant, he's a beast: "If I see those knick-knacks one more time …" *Well, be my guest if you want to chow without etiquette. Gulp your porridge down with just a spoon.*

"Comrade Ignatov," says Polipyev, lifting the empty tray in

front of his chest like a shield, "what're we going to do with the lamb?"

Ignatov looks up with a heavy, silent gaze.

"April's almost here, I'm afraid it won't keep. The ice box is good, of course, but you can't reason with the weather." Polipyev lowers his voice conspiratorially. "Maybe we should use it all? I could make any number of things out of it – country cabbage soup and navy-style macaroni. Even consommé with profiteroles ... So, soup, main course, and jellied meat from the bones: we'll eat for a week. Why have we just been eating barley since we set out from Kazan? Your fighters are looking at me with daggers in their eyes. They've promised to eat *me* if I don't give them meat."

"They won't eat you without an order." Ignatov bites off some bread and takes the spoon in his hand, chewing menacingly. "If the lamb spoils, though, then absolutely I'll see to it that they eat you."

Polipyev displays a vague smirk that could be a smile or an acknowledgement of understanding, plus submissive agreement.

"And you!" Ignatov pokes his spoon at Polipyev's chest. "Can you tell me how much longer we'll be traveling? A week? A month? Half a year? What am I going to feed you – you personally! – if we eat everything up now?"

"Well, what of it. Let it stay in the ice box, then," sighs Polipyev and disappears outside the door.

Ignatov throws his spoon.

Lamb!

Canned meat and condensed milk and butter. The refrigerator in the commandant's railroad car is stuffed with provisions. All these riches are intended for staff: escort personnel, the two stokers, and the engine driver. Well, and the commandant himself, of course. According to the plan, the deportees were to be fed at stations. And this was written in black and white in the special instruction for agencies of the transport division of the State Political Administration: "Throughout the special train's itinerary, provide uninterrupted supply of hot water to those evicted and organize feeding sites at stations serving hot food at least once every two days." Well, where are they, those feeding sites?

Ignatov realized at the very first station that this was going to be a problem. Special trains with dekulakized people stretched all along the railway, one after the other, and some were stuck for a long time on the track between stations, awaiting instructions. "Where will I find you all those provisions?" the station chief gently asked Ignatov. "Be grateful I'm giving you hot water." Ignatov expressed gratitude that hot water was offered so meticulously.

But there's not enough food for the deportees. Ignatov is glad when he manages to scare up porridge: wheat, oat, barley, occasionally spelt or broken grain. It's porridge when it can't be thinned very much. They thin soups mercilessly, for example, several times, sometimes even with icy water. Ignatov has tried arguing with the station officials about this, but it's no use – they even make accusations. "What, do you pity them or something?" they'll ask. "I'm responsible for them!" he'll snap. "Who am I going to hand over at our destination point?" "And where is your destination point?" they say, waving him off.

And truly, where is it? He doesn't know. Apparently nobody knows. At yet another station, after waiting a week or even two in a holding yard, Ignatov would receive the invariable instruction: "Proceed to point such and such, and wait until further notice." He proceeds. Arrives. Hurries to the station chief to report. And again waits until further notice.

He calms himself because he isn't the only one. He's met other, more experienced commandants at stations and they've spoken a little. Yes, they say, we're also going along until further notice. Yes, people are dying in the railroad cars. Yes, a lot. There's always this sort of natural attrition, and nobody will question that. The main thing is for you to guard them strictly, so there are no emergencies.

And it would have all been all right if not for the daily rounds … He suddenly realized he was beginning to recognize faces. Each time he sat in his compartment, plunging his spoon into hot, fluffy porridge, he would remember someone, either the emaciated, white-headed adolescent albino with the trusting pink eyes from the third car, or the fat, freckled woman from the sixth with the large scarlet birthmark on her cheek ("Boss man, share at least something, I'm wasting away, I am …"), or the small woman with the pale face and the green eyes half the size of her face from the eighth.

That same thought comes right now: all these people had hot water for lunch today. They're not people, he corrects himself. Enemies. The enemies had hot water for lunch and this makes the porridge seem flavorless.

He recalls being a three-year-old lad, sitting on the windowsill of their basement window in the evenings, watching for his mother's square shoes among the feet running along the street. His mother came home after dark. Averting her eyes, she would give him plain hot water to drink and put him to bed.

Fool. Weakling. Crybaby. Bakiev would have ridiculed him, and rightfully so.

He stands and carries his untouched dish off to the kitchen compartment, to Polipyev. Let him choke down his own barley.

That same evening, faint with a disagreeable premonition, Polipyev gives all the lamb from the icebox in the commandant's railroad car to the deputy chief of the local train station. Dark red with the finest white marbling, the meat disappears into a voluminous wicker basket and floats out of Polipyev's life forever, just as five or more kilos of butter and a dozen cans of the nicest condensed milk departed the refrigerator earlier. The handover takes place late in the evening, in darkness, on the verbal instruction of the special train's commandant but without delivery documents and receipts, throwing the cautious Polipyev into a state of vague alarm.

A half-hour later, a vat of millet porridge is brought to the train for the deportees. This is completely unexpected and so serendipitous (people hadn't been fed for two days now) that it couldn't be a simple coincidence.

"So that's how it is," Polipyev reflects spitefully, observing from his compartment window as large yellow pieces of clumped porridge are tossed into buckets (one bucket per car) with a measuring ladle. "Our menacing beast of a commandant's turned out to be just another run-of-the-mill briber."

That thought fills the supply manager with a calm satisfaction that's all the greater because he's nevertheless managed to conceal a couple of pieces of wonderful lamb. Polipyev decides to add them to the monotonous barley the next day without the commandant's knowledge. Ignatov has been eating poorly of late and is unlikely to identify the taste of meat in porridge that has already come to be hated.

On their last day standing near Sverdlovsk, there's a small incident in the eighth carriage. The special train has been kept there for nearly a week. There's a dark valley, marked in places by remnants of slushy snow but already touched with fresh green shoots, that's visible through an opening in the door about the width of the palm of a hand. (On the move and during stops, the door is permitted to be opened a little, but when entering populated areas it is supposed to be locked with two bolts.) The green is intensifying with each passing day, growing brighter, and filling the horizon.

Fooled by the train's prolonged standstill, a small red-breasted bird has decided to build its nest under the railroad car's roof, not far from Zuleikha's little window. Businesslike, it has fetched twigs and fluff, tirelessly stuffing them under the roof and chirping with excitement.

"If we stand here this long again, she'll have a chance to lay her eggs," Konstantin Arnoldovich says, without tearing himself away from his book.

"What eggs? We'll scoff it down right now!" Gorelov swallows and makes his way closer to the window, wiggling his fingers in a predatory manner and mulling over how best to bag his prey.

"Let's admire it a little longer," says Ikonnikov, drawing his squinting eyes closer to the window.

A sudden crashing blow, and dust, sand, and sawdust shower down. The little bird cheeps with fright and darts into the sky. It's Zuleikha who struck the railroad car's ceiling with a long, sturdy board she pulled out of the iron clamps on the door. She gazes after the little bird, returns the board to its place, and brushes off her hands.

Gorelov falls on the bunks with a disappointed wail – "What the hell are you doing, you fool Tatar woman!" That's it, lunch is gone. It flew away. Ikonnikov looks at Zuleikha with interest for what seems to be the first time during the journey.

"If she loses her nest, she won't lay eggs," she says curtly. "She'll be looking for her lost nest all summer."

She climbs back up on the bunk. She notices that a board on the ceiling has come detached from the blow and a narrow crevice has formed, revealing a streak of sky. And that's very nice because she can't look out the window all the time.

The train will begin moving in the evening. It will cross the Ural mountain range that night. Zuleikha will watch the stars twinkling through the crevice in the ceiling and think, *So, Allah, is there still long to ride?*

Where-where? the wheels will clatter. *Where-where? Where-where?*
And they'll answer themselves: *There-there. There-there. There-there.*

ESCAPE

"Sons of bitches! Everybody –" says a crazed, half-strangled voice from somewhere below.

Zuleikha is hanging out of the bunk, peering into the darkness. What's down there? Through the loud, rhythmical noise of the wheels come sounds of struggle, stifled grunting, and fisticuffs, which are alternately muffled, as if striking something soft, and resonant, as if striking something hard. In a narrow, slanting slice of moonlight shining through the window there are several bodies swarming by the cast-iron stove.

"I'll let you stinking bitches have it!" another stifled shout changes to grunting.

It sounds like their minder's voice. And yes, there he is, Gorelov, lying on the floor, hands tied behind his back, mouth bound by a rag, and wriggling like a little worm. Above him a couple of strapping peasants are pummeling him ferociously and enjoying it. He jerks violently, bending like a yoke, and throws them both off, but then he hits his head on a corner of the stove and goes quiet.

The railroad car isn't sleeping. The peasant men and women are matter-of-factly exchanging remarks and meaningful glances on the bunks, nodding that he had it coming. Some help tie the motionless minder more firmly, others bustle around, gathering their things.

The man who once had many children but is now a solitary peasant pulls the fat heavy board out of the iron clamps on the door. He approaches Zuleikha's bunk, gets into position, and strikes the end of the board on the same spot she hit that morning, scaring away the red-breasted bird.

"What are you doing, brother?" says Zuleikha, scared.

Not responding, he hits the ceiling again and again. He strikes in time with the clacking of the wheels so it can't be heard. The crevice widens overhead, gaping, and now there's a broad starry tongue of sky visible through the hole, rather than a narrow strip. The peasant extends the board to Zuleikha – *here, hold this!* – and leaps up on the bunk. He kneels and thrusts his wiry shoulders into the ceiling, which is already yielding. Something cracks and creaks, and a fresh breeze bursts through the gap, hitting Zuleikha in the face. The peasant pulls himself up with his arms and disappears above.

"Garrrmmmph!" Gorelov has come to and writhes on the floor, his eyes boring into Zuleikha.

The peasant man's face hangs over the star-strewn hole in the ceiling. He's smiling for the first time in several months.

"Well?" he says to those crowded below. And he extends a long, bony arm.

One after the other, the exiles grasp that hand, leap on Zuleikha's bunk, and push their way through the hole in the ceiling. Peasant men, women, and adolescents disappear above, quickly and nimbly. One fat woman gets stuck in the narrow opening, but the people below are in a hurry and those awaiting their turn press and push, and she somehow climbs through, tearing her dress and body, leaving threads and pieces of fabric on the sharp, rough wood.

Gorelov grunts and growls frightfully, his body beating against the iron stove.

"And you, sister?" The voice is just above her ear. The peasant is looking through the hole at Zuleikha, raising his brow in encouragement.

Escape? Leave the carriage where she's already spent so many long weeks? And a bunk that's heated from her warmth and smells of her body? Leave the sweet, good-natured professor and the kind Izabella? Disobey the strict Ignatov, the stern soldiers with rifles, and the angry station bosses? Disobey her own fate?

She shakes her head. *No, I won't go, may Allah protect me.*

"But you're strong, you can do it!" The peasant man extends an insistent hand.

Doubtful, she looks for a long time at the broad hand with dark, bumpy calluses. She finally lowers her head for no.

"Well, suit yourself."

Muffled footsteps knock on the ceiling. Outside the little window they can see long shadows quickly falling from the roof, flying down below the railroad embankment, and floating into the forest in a black flock. And that's that.

Zuleikha looks around and sees the railroad car has emptied out. Nearly all the peasants left, other than a few lone women and a couple of feeble old people, who having given their parting son or grandson a long and tight embrace, now sit on the bunk, their unmoving, sunken eyes looking at the hole in the ceiling where they recently disappeared.

The majority of the Leningrad "formers" have stayed; only a couple of young female students flitted off. Izabella is sitting on the bunk, firmly squeezing her husband's hand. A smiling Ikonnikov is dreamily looking at the sparkling stars in the ceiling's torn opening, for some reason whispering, "Thank you, thank you." Professor Leibe, who's been sitting alongside Zuleikha the whole time, leans back, sighing with relief.

"Freedom is similar to happiness," he purrs under his breath, "harmful for some, useful for others."

"Goethe?" Konstantin Arnoldovich comes to life on the neighboring bunk.

"Novalis," says Ikonnikov, joining in.

"No, forgive me, but I'm certain it's Goethe!"

"I won't forgive you. It's definitely Novalis."

Gorelov wriggles on the floor, groaning. Nobody has thought to untie him yet.

Zuleikha suddenly realizes she's still holding the board in her hands; she tosses it to the floor. A golden scattering of stars quivers in the splintered gap in the ceiling.

The country where Zuleikha lives is very large. Very large and red, like bull's blood. Zuleikha is standing in front of a huge map that covers an entire wall, where a giant scarlet blot resembling a pregnant slug has sprawled – it's the Soviet Union. She has already seen this slug once before, on an agitational propaganda poster in Yulbash. Mansurka-Burdock had also explained: "Here it is," he'd said. "Our motherland is immense. It stretches from ocean to ocean." Zuleikha hadn't understood then where those "oceans" were, but she remembered the slug, which was awfully funny, with a beard and a hilarious hook-like paw out front. And now, on this high wall, it truly seems immense because even two people, let alone one Zuleikha, couldn't stretch their arms across it. Along its bilberry-red body there wriggle dark blue veins of rivers (is her dear Chishme among them?), and cities and villages are black dots, like beauty marks (who could show her where Yulbash is?). Zuleikha reaches her fingers toward the shiny surface of the map but doesn't have time to touch. Ignatov's stern voice lashes like a whip:

"Is it true you helped them escape?"

Zuleikha jerks her finger away from the map. Ignatov is standing by a window wide open to the night, looking out, and smoking.

Yellow light from a kerosene lamp on the table illuminates the fabric of his uniform tunic, which is stretched taut between his shoulders under the cross of his tight belts.

"Don't deny it," he goes on. "People saw."

The night is warm and velvety outside the window. She keeps silent.

"Why did you stay?"

It would seem that Gorelov, that malicious soul, had gone out of his way to report the matter, venting his fury. Nobody had untied him, after all, and he'd lain about, wrapped up like a sacrificial lamb all night, until they reached Pyshma. Everything was discovered in the afternoon, during the stop in Pyshma. Ignatov came into their car for inspection and his face twitched and blanched when he saw the hole in the ceiling, then everyone started running in and shouting, their feet stamping. Gorelov was taken – under guard! – in one direction and the others were taken – under guard! – in the other. The hole in the ceiling was quickly boarded up but the escapees … well, just go and find them. And of course they weren't fed today because there was too much going on. In the evening they took Leibe from the railroad car first, then Izabella, Konstantin Arnoldovich, and somebody else. They were taken away and then brought back. Interrogation, said Ikonnikov. And Izabella asked him: "My dear Ilya Petrovich, is that really called interrogation?" And she was laughing very cheerfully.

It was during the night that they shook Zuleikha awake and brought her here. It's a large room where the skeleton of a once-beautiful chandelier is suspended like a huge bronze spider from a ceiling that rises into dark heights; where walls that were once covered with tinted whitewash have now been reduced to dark-brownish bricks; where a couple of mismatched black chairs have cracked varnish on their sharply bent backs; where a large, carved table in the center is burned on one side and has a stack of books in place of one leg; and where, over an austere cube of a safe in the corner, there hangs a portrait of the same wise, mustached man Zuleikha saw on the clock tower of the Kazan kremlin. Zuleikha is glad to see him – his squinting eyes look at her in a warm, fatherly way, as though they're calming and protecting her from Ignatov, who's angry in the extreme.

Ignatov turns to Zuleikha. His eyes are blacker than black, and it's as if the skin is pulled tightly over each bone of his face.

"So what's the meaning of this silence? We have an escape, about four dozen souls bolted from the train, and you're playing dumb?"

A tiny reddish flame – a hand-rolled cigarette – breathes in his fingers. He approaches the table and forcefully stubs it out in a small wooden dish filled with cigarette butts. The bowl clunks, tumbles, and falls to the floor; cigarette butts fly everywhere. "Damn it," Ignatov grumbles and starts gathering them up. Zuleikha hurries and crouches beside him. It's unheard of that a man would pick trash off the floor in a woman's presence while she watches!

The cigarette butts are cold and small, like worms. They're crumbling with ash and there's a smell of stale smoke. And Ignatov smells of warmth.

"You could be facing the camps, you fool," he says, his voice right beside her. "Or the ultimate punishment. Do you know what the ultimate punishment is?"

Zuleikha looks up. It's completely dark here under the table and Ignatov's pupils are as black as coal in the whites of his eyes.

"I don't understand Russian well," she finally says.

Harsh, hot fingers clench her chin.

"You're lying!" hisses Ignatov. "You understand everything, you just don't want to say anything. Well, talk! Did they make an arrangement to run away together? Where did they want to go? Talk!"

Her chin hurts.

"I don't know anything. I saw the same as the others saw. I heard the same as the others heard."

Ignatov's face, with its black holes for eyes, comes right up to her ear and his breath is on her cheek.

"Oh, what a stubborn Tatar woman. Zuleikha, that's your name, isn't it?"

She turns her face toward him.

"It's too bad I didn't go with them. Now I'm sorry I didn't."

The door creaks open.

"Guard!" calls out the rattled voice of the chief of security operations at Pyshma. "Where did they get to?"

The thudding of the guard's feet is hurried and frightened, like the sound of potatoes scattering from a pail. Ignatov's fingers release her chin and her skin burns as if it's been scorched. He rises from under the table and straightens his uniform:

"Yes, we're here, don't fret."

Zuleikha rises after him, placing the dish with the cigarette butts on the table. Her hands are as black as if she's been rubbing coal.

A young, pimply escort guard holding his rifle horizontally sighs with relief. He looks at Zuleikha and bursts out laughing: there are long dark streaks extending along her cheeks and chin. Ash. He wipes the grin off his face when he meets the Pyshma chief's stern gaze, then he backs toward the exit and closes the door behind him. Ignatov turns to Zuleikha and starts cackling, too, flustered.

"So, did you interrogate her?" asks the chief.

He's short and sturdy. His hands are as big as shovels, though, as if he'd stolen them from someone else. Ignatov is silent; he wipes the ash from his hands.

"I see you interrogated her," smiles the chief, glancing mockingly at Zuleikha's streaked face.

He takes a white sheet of paper from the table and scrutinizes both blank sides.

"And wrote up a report," he continues good-naturedly, crumpling the paper in his hands. "I told you, Ignatov, that interrogation is not a simple thing. An art, one might say. Experience is needed here. Mastery! Sure, he says, I know a thing or two about this!"

Either the paper happens to be very crisp or the chief's hands are firm because the sheet crunches loudly and lushly in his hands, like fresh snow.

"How about this." He rolls the paper into a firm little ball. "Leave her with me and I'll have a talk with her. You do the paperwork transferring her over to us for investigation."

Ignatov takes his officer's cap from the edge of the table, puts it on, and slowly walks toward the door. Zuleikha's gaze follows him, puzzled: *What is this? Why?*

The chief swings wide and hurls the paper pellet into a wire wastebasket by the door. He sits down at the desk and opens the top drawer. Without looking, he goes through the familiar motion of taking out a stack of paper, pens, and an ink well. Whistling something cheery, he clasps his hands together and stretches his long, strong fingers with a crack.

Ignatov stops at the door and looks at the ball of paper bouncing at the bottom of the wastebasket. He turns.

"She doesn't know where they went," he says.

"Is that what she whispered to you here under the table?" The chief shoots a glance at Ignatov across the room.

"She won't help you, comrade. She has nothing to say." Ignatov comes back into the room.

The chief leans back and the chair creaks long and strained, as if it's about to collapse, and he scrutinizes Zuleikha and Ignatov closely, as if he's seeing them for the first time. He continues stretching his fingers.

"Well, I never! You think that's very clever! You're offending me, Ignatov. Everybody talks to me. Even the mute."

"I'm taking her back."

"How about that!" The chief finally unclasps his hands and slaps them loudly on the table. "He lets an entire train car slip, comes to his senses half a day later, and I'm supposed to look into it? Find them in the taiga, catch them? They went in all directions long ago, to villages and small stations. And I'm supposed to run like hell, panting and sweating, and then file a report about why I didn't catch them! Then he even takes away my first witness, too. That's how it is, is it?"

"My job is to transport people. Yours is to catch them."

"So why are you transporting them so badly, Ignatov? You killed half of them along the way. You closed your eyes to an organized escape. And now you don't want to help the investigation and are taking away an abettor. You think you'll come out of this with clean hands?"

"I'll answer for my mistakes myself if they ask. Just not to you."

Ignatov nods to Zuleikha: *Let's go!* She shifts her gaze to the reddened chief.

"They'll ask, Ignatov, they'll ask!" he's already shouting. "And very soon! I won't even begin to cover for you. I'll tell them how you were protecting a kulak broad!"

Ignatov adjusts his peaked cap, turns on his heels, and goes out of the room. Zuleikha takes frightened little steps behind him. She casts a final glance into the room as she's leaving. The huge red slug is crawling imperturbably along the wall and the wise, mustached man is smiling tenderly after them.

Ignatov strides quickly along the tracks, holding a dim lantern with a candle in his extended hand. The small Tatar woman from car eight is running behind him, stepping lightly, almost silently. A guard is last, clattering along the ties.

Ignatov is well aware that they'll make him answer for this. What had they said to him that morning in the office? "We'll figure it out upon your return." It's clear they want him to finish his job first so they can tear him apart later. Well, go ahead, figure it out. But he won't hold back. He'll tell them everything, how they starve people along the way and how people reel, wandering and lost, at small stations. They've been underway three months and have barely crawled across the Urals. That's simply unheard of. They would have gotten there faster on foot. Attrition during that time was about fifty heads. It's too bad, even though they're kulaks: they're manpower after all – they could do honest work felling trees or building something. A whole lot more use than rotting away along the railroad tracks. And another fifty people today, whoosh ...

No, he'll answer for the escape – that was his fault, he's not denying it. Didn't keep his eyes peeled. Even the minder in that railroad car, someone so hardened ("Do not worry, citizen chief, the people in this car are a quiet, dense-headed lot and rotten intelligentsia – what would happen to them?"), had been duped. Even so, if you reasoned things out, if they'd been brought to their destination earlier, there wouldn't have been any escape at all. *Don't think for a second I'm absolving myself of any guilt*, he imagines telling them, *but I do ask that you consider the reasons for what occurred. During three months of traveling, anyone at all will have nasty thoughts and time will be found to realize those thoughts. So there it is, brothers.*

And if they ask why he removed a witness from the investigation? That small woman with the vibrant name, Zuleikha? *What can I say?* Something like a tin can is in Ignatov's path and it's satisfying to take a run-up and kick it. The can flies ahead, clinking and echoing along the rails.

They're already in the holding yard. It's not easy to find their train in the dark among so many other trains and rectangular carcasses of freight cars, the long reddish boxes of the cattle cars from which there's sometimes either quiet talking or singing. Ignatov keeps raising his dim lantern, reading the numbers on the cars. Three long, dancing shadows keep growing, soaring up the sides of the train cars and then falling to the ground, spreading along the rails.

Behind him the frightened guard shouts, "Hey, what're you doing?" Ignatov turns around. The small Tatar woman is standing sideways holding her belly, her body twisted, her head tilted back. And then she begins slowly sinking to the ground. The guard pokes his rifle uselessly in her direction: "Stop! Stop, I'm telling you!" She falls, collapsing as effortlessly and neatly as if she's folded herself in half.

Ignatov crouches beside her. Her hands are ice-cold. Her eyes are closed and the shadows from her lashes cover half her face. The guard is still standing, uselessly aiming his rifle at her.

"Put the rifle away, you oaf, and keep quiet," says Ignatov.

The guard flings the weapon over his shoulder.

"Starvation or something?" he asks.

"Pick her up," Ignatov orders the guard. "No matter what this is, there's no use guarding her until she comes to."

The guard attempts to lift her a little but he grasps her awkwardly and her head falls back on a tie with a thud. Ignatov curses – *what a clod!* – and picks her up himself.

"Toss her arm around my neck," he orders.

They walk further. The guard is now running up ahead, lighting the way. Ignatov carries her small body. She's so light! How is it possible … ? Zuleikha comes to little by little, clasping him around the neck so he feels her cold fingers on his cheek.

They send for a doctor right away (Ignatov doesn't want to wait until morning), rousting him out of bed and driving him to the station. Groaning, he climbs into the train car, clumsily hoisting up his stout legs; he's still young, only a little older than Ignatov. Zuleikha has fully come to and he examines her in the light of a kerosene lamp, wearily chewing at his sagging lower lip and tugging at a long lock of sparse hair that's been combed over early baldness.

"Heart's fine," he says indifferently. "Lungs, too. Skin healthy."

"And so ... ?" Ignatov is standing right there, in the railroad car, leaning his back against the closed door and smoking.

Ten pairs of eyes – the ten exiles remaining after the escape – are looking down at him from their bunks; nobody else has yet been assigned to car number eight because other things have been happening.

"You can calm down, comrade," the doctor yawns sleepily and he places his rudimentary instruments in his gaunt doctor's bag. "It's not typhus. Not scabies. Not dysentery. We're not going to put the whole train in quarantine."

Ignatov nods with relief and flings his cigarette butt into the cold stove. They'd stopped issuing coal for heating at the end of April after deciding it was enough; this isn't a sanatorium, and it's warm anyway.

"The cause of fainting could be anything at all," the doctor drones on, as if he's talking to himself while he heads toward the door. "Oxygen starvation, malnutrition – among other things. Or simply bad blood vessels."

"Or pregnancy," rings out loudly and distinctly from the depths of the bunks.

The puzzled doctor turns around and raises the kerosene lamp a little. Several gloomy faces overgrown with dirty beards are gazing at him, the whites of their eyes gleaming. So many of them have passed through his hands in recent months, they've all blended into one tired, dark image. One of the faces in the car, though, seems to remind him of someone or even be vaguely familiar. So familiar that the doctor raises the lamp to it. Closer, even closer. The nose is a sharp beak, the teasing eyes are like pieces of ice, there's a steep arc of a massive, high forehead with a tangled coil of glistening silver hair around it. No, it can't be. What is this?

"Professor!" says the doctor, exhaling. "Is that you?"

"She won't allow you to check the tension of the mammary glands and the Montgomery tubercles," Leibe utters in the clear, authoritative voice of a lecturer in a large auditorium. "Be so good as to at least investigate the condition of the salivary glands and facial pigmentation."

The doctor is staring at the professor; he just can't look away.

"Professor Leibe! How did you ... ?"

"Try a deep palpation of the abdomen, too," continues Leibe. "My diagnosis would be eighteen weeks."

When he's done speaking, Leibe bores a long, unblinking gaze into the doctor, who wipes his damp upper lip and sits back down on the bunk next to the frightened Zuleikha. He feels her lower jaw.

"Exhale," he quietly orders.

She shakes her head, breathing loudly and rapidly, without stopping.

"Zuleikha, my dear," says Izabella, sitting down alongside Zuleikha and taking her hand. "The doctor's asking."

"I said exhale," the doctor repeats angrily.

Zuleikha exhales and holds her breath. The doctor swallows and lays his palms on her belly. He looks significantly at the professor.

"I'm palpating an enlargement of the uterus."

Leibe laughs loudly and triumphantly, his teeth flashing in the darkness:

"I'll grade you unsatisfactory, Chernov. And I did warn you in the first year that you would not be a good diagnostician!"

Zuleikha mumbles, uncomprehending, not knowing what she's supposed to do now.

"Tell the patient to breathe," says Leibe. Content and still chuckling, he reclines on the bunk.

Zuleikha inhales convulsively.

"Professor, how did you … ?" In an attempt to find Leibe's face, the doctor thrusts the lamp into the dark bunk, where Leibe is hiding.

"You may receive your grade book at the dean's office, Chernov," answers Leibe, wrapping himself up cocoon-like in someone's sheepskin jacket and rolling closer and closer to the wall. "I have no time for consultations right now."

"Volf Karlovich," insists the doctor, sweeping the lamp's light around the bunk, "after all, we've … After all you did for –"

"I don't have time, Chernov." The voice only just carries from the depths. "I don't have time."

The doctor's lamp illuminates a rustling mountain of rags by the far wall. The mountain soon stops moving.

Zuleikha whimpers quietly, like a dog, biting the edge of her headscarf and gazing upward, staring. Izabella sits next to her and strokes Zuleikha's hands, which are clasped in fists and lying lengthways alongside her body.

Chernov shakes his head slightly as if he's shedding a hallucination, clasps his doctor's bag to his chest, and leaves the railroad car. He jumps down to the ground, leaning against Ignatov's proffered arm, and notices Ignatov's eyes are stern and tense.

"I assure you again, comrade commandant, this is nothing bad," utters the slightly annoyed doctor. *What tender commandants there are now!* "What do we have here?"

He takes a handkerchief from his pocket and wipes Ignatov's cheek. On it are four long, dark streaks that look like marks made by a small hand.

*

Pregnant? Yes, she wanted to eat all the time but of course they weren't fed. Yes, her belly had gotten a little heavier recently but she'd thought it was from aging. And the red days had stopped coming, though she thought that was from worry. But that she was pregnant? Oh, that Murtaza, he's cheated death. He's been in the grave a long time but his seed is alive, growing in her belly. It's already halfway grown.

Another girl? Of course, what else could it be? What was it the Vampire Hag said? *You only bring girls into the world.* No, that's not what she said. *You only bring girls into the world and they don't survive.*

And will this one really die, too? … Well, of course. This one will leave her as well, after having barely been born. Her bright infant's redness won't even have a chance to leave her tender skin, her tiny little eyes won't have a chance to fill with meaning, and her mouth won't have a chance to smile for the first time.

Zuleikha looks at the black ceiling. Thoughts flow as the wheels knock. A warm May night is rushing past on the other side of the plank wall. The light, half-empty railroad car rocks wildly, like a cradle. Everybody's already asleep, including the kind Izabella, who'd stroked her hand half the night, and the eccentric professor, whose bright, joyful eyes had looked at her for so long. If only she could fall asleep, too.

Was it permissible for her to request Allah to allow her child to at least stand on its own two feet? That the child at least take its first steps before leaving this world? Or was that too great an impudence? There's nobody with her to ask for advice: not Murtaza, not the mullah. *Almighty, give me some hints yourself: am I allowed to ask this of You? I won't ask for anything else, I wouldn't dare. Only this.*

And there's this thought, out of nowhere: *What if the All-powerful hears and permits your child to take its first step? What would it be to lose the child then? Might it be better for it to be right away, before getting used to the child and taking a liking to it?* She remembers how she grieved over her first daughter, who was granted one whole month of life. And then less for the second, who departed after a couple of weeks. And even less for the third, who didn't survive seven days. The fourth, who departed right away, at birth, was seen off with dry eyes.

Shamsia-Firuza, the wheels clack. *Khalida-Sabida*. And again: *Shamsia-Firuza, Khalida-Sabida*.

So wouldn't that be better? Right away? Her mama would have said that thoughts like that were sinful. That everything is Allah's will, and it's not for us to judge what and when is better … *Oh well, it's not as if I'm going to chop off my head* – which goes on thinking and thinking, filling with thoughts, like a net fills with fish.

But maybe no baby will be born. That happens, the women at the well used to whisper. The child will live a while in the belly, grow a little, and then tear itself out of its set place before its time and flow from the womb so all that's left is a clump of blood on the pants.

And the Vampire Hag isn't with her, so there's nobody to predict the outcome. Is it even good to know beforehand, anyway? But then the expectation is agonizing. And what about not knowing? That's agonizing, too, the way she's feeling now, not knowing.

She's tired, tired of agonizing. Tired of agonizing because of hunger, tired of persuading and exhorting her insatiable insides. Of her stomach in agony from bad food. Of cold at night. Of aching in her bones in the morning, of lice, of frequent queasiness. Tired of the pain and deaths around her. Of fear that it will grow even worse. And – scariest of all – of perpetual shame.

There is constant shame when she feels the heavy smell of an unwashed body coming from herself, when the soldiers indifferently slide their eyes along her uncovered head and braids during their daily inspections, when she squats behind the latrine's cloth divider for all to see, when she presses against the sleeping professor at night to try and warm up. She nearly burned up with shame when the unfamiliar doctor's puffy, indifferent fingers touched her last night. And she'd begun wailing when he announced her pregnancy for all to hear. This was so shameful, shameful, shameful. She would have to bear the disgrace in front of everybody. For the first time in her life, she cannot conceal her secret behind the tall fence of her husband's house. In her relentlessly displayed belly she will nurture a child who will leave her as soon as it is born.

And Allah, when will my journey end? Could You break it with a supreme gesture? Zuleikha presses her face into her short fur coat, which she has placed under her head instead of a pillow. Her forehead comes up against something hard and sharp. She turns the pocket inside out and finds a small, almost rock-hard lump. The sugar. The sugar Murtaza gave her. She'd already managed to forget about it but there it is, it hasn't gone anywhere and the large white crystals shine, their edges sparkling, giving off a complex aroma that's just as strong as it was last winter. Zuleikha has been carrying a longed-for death in her pocket for many weeks, likely so she could discover it at this bitter moment. What is this if not the answer to her ardent prayer?

Zuleikha brings the sugar to her face. Should she bite it a little at a time or attempt to dissolve the whole piece at once? Would the poison take effect instantly or after a short while? Would she suffer? Does it even matter?

"Sugar? *Mein Gott*, where is it from?"

The professor's joyful, surprised eyes are right beside her. He's woken up and is propped on his elbow, looking at Zuleikha. His halo of curls seems silvery in the moonlight. Zuleikha doesn't answer; she squeezes the sugar in her fist and its hard, sharp edges dig into her palm.

"Eat it, certainly eat it!" Leibe whispers, excited. "Just don't think of showing anybody, especially Gorelov – he'd take it away." He places a finger to his lips. "And I, well … I wanted, you know … to inquire …" The professor looks sideways at her belly, squints, and hesitates, finally daring to ask, "How is he feeling?"

"Who?"

"The child, naturally."

"It's a she, a girl. My line is ending. I can only give birth to girls."

"Who told you that?" The indignant Leibe sits up abruptly and nearly hits the top of his head against the ceiling. He hems and haws loudly, intently considering Zuleikha's belly: at first he's displeased, then he's uncertain, and, finally, he's delighted. "Don't believe it!" he cries, satisfied, his laughter trilling and hand waving. "Don't believe it!"

The wheels are clattering loudly, muting the conversation. *Shamsia-Firuza, Khalida-Sabida.*

"Do you think the heart's already beating?"

"What a question!" The professor chokes with indignation. "It has been for two months now."

Groaning like an old man, he awkwardly turns around on the bunk. He bends, bringing his ear toward her belly, as if he wants to hear the ardent heartbeat hidden inside, but he doesn't allow himself to touch it with his cheek. Zuleikha places her palm on his silver curls and presses the professor's head to her belly. And the shame retreats. An unfamiliar man is touching her body with his face, and sensing her smell, but she doesn't feel shame. She wants only to know what's in there, inside her.

Leibe listens attentively for a long time with his eyes closed. Then he lifts his head: his face is soft and dreamy, and he silently nods to her that everything is good.

"Eat the sugar," he reminds her, settling into his spot. "Eat it right now."

He soon falls asleep, his hands placed under his head and his smiling face raised to the ceiling as if he's admiring the stars.

Zuleikha puts the sugar back in her coat pocket. She's much calmer now that her own death – which is sweet, smells complex, and has taken on the familiar appearance of a lump of ordinary sugar – has been found and is lying next to her. She can take it at any time, whenever she wishes, and she gives thanks to Allah, who heard and answered her prayers.

The train crosses a river dappled by moonlight and spanned by a long, lace-like iron bridge that amplifies the clatter of wheels: *here it is, here it is, here it is* …

They still have a long way to go and won't reach the place until early August.

Yelan, Yushala, Tugulym …

From Tyumen, the train is sent east, toward Tobolsk. Then they rethink, turn the train around, and begin driving south.

Vagai, Karasul, Ishim …

New passengers will be settled into the eighth car. Gorelov will remain the minder and will nag and chasten everyone more than before, both fearing another escape and to win back his wavering authority.

Mangut, Omsk …

Zuleikha's belly will swell quickly. The child will begin to stir near Mangut and soon after Omsk, Zuleikha will feel a tiny little foot with a round, bulging heel under her tautly pulled skin for the first time.

Kalachinsk, Barabinsk, Kargat …

In July, the food situation will improve since not many trains come this far into Siberia, so it will be easier for Ignatov to scare up provisions. And bread will appear once again in the exiles' rations.

Chulym, Novosibirsk …

But people will die even more frequently as malnutrition and sheer exhaustion from the long trip manifest themselves. Typhus will break out in half the cars, taking away around fifty lives.

Yurga, Anzhero-Sudzhensk, Mariinsk …

In total, during the six months of travel, attrition will amount to three hundred and ninety-eight heads. Not counting escapees, of course.

Tisul, Kashtan, Bogotol, Achinsk …

As they approach Krasnoyarsk, Ignatov will use a pencil stub to cross out yet more names in the gray "Case" folder. He will realize that he sees faces rather than lines and letters when he glances at the surnames typed closely together.

Nobody knows it's their last day riding on the train. The wheels thunder and a wicked August sun is heating up the car through the window. Ikonnikov is entertaining Izabella. This is one of those rare moments when something pierces his usual gloominess, something fresh, some sort of boyish mischief, and he becomes quick, lively, even playful. Zuleikha almost likes him in this mood. She doesn't understand even a fraction of the jokes that make Izabella laugh so heartily and the reticent Konstantin Arnoldovich snort a little bit, but she tries not to miss those moments because it's nice to be among cheerful, smiling people. She's quiet and reserved, and the "formers" don't avoid her.

Lying on Ikonnikov's open palm is a thin piece of bread he stashed away that morning.

"More!" he says, impatiently wiggling his fingers.

His eyes are tightly blindfolded with someone's shirt; he's like a child playing hide-and-seek. Izabella places another piece on the artist's palm.

"More!" he demands. "Come now, don't stint on art!"

Konstantin Arnoldovich gives up his piece. Ikonnikov mumbles with satisfaction and begins mashing the bread in his long fingers.

Zuleikha watches with disapproval and sorrow. She wouldn't give up her piece for anything. It would be different if there were a purpose, but this is just an indulgence. And the crumbs are scattering on the floor so they can't be picked up.

The bread is softening in Ikonnikov's flexible fingers. He's kneading it into a pliant gray mass, mashing, mashing, and – there you go – gradually turning it into ... a toy? Someone's head! Izabella and Konstantin Arnoldovich don't look away, observing as bushy, arched eyebrows take shape under a mane of hair, an aquiline profile develops, a luxuriant mustache turns up, and a bulging chin swells ...

"*Mon Dieu*," Izabella says solemnly.

"Unbelievable," whispers Konstantin Arnoldovich. "It's simply unbelievable ..."

"Well?" Ikonnikov cries victoriously and tears the blindfold from his eyes.

In his hand is a small, absolutely living head: its gaze is penetrating and intent, and there's a wise half-smile on its lips.

"I received the Order of the Red Banner of Labor not long ago," sighs Ikonnikov. "Nineteen heads in bronze. Seven in marble. Two in malachite."

"And one in bread," adds Konstantin Arnoldovich.

Zuleikha stares at the bready bust and knows she's seen this intelligent face before somewhere, with its stern yet kind, fatherly gaze. A good person, and the artist molded it skillfully. It's a pity about the bread, though.

Ikonnikov holds the bust out to her.

"You're always giving me all your bread," she says, shaking her head.

"Not you, dear," says Izabella, her eyes indicating Zuleikha's protruding belly. "Him."

"Her," Zuleikha corrects her. "It's a girl."

She takes the bready head and hungrily bites off half, right at the mustache. Konstantin Arnoldovich breaks into a sudden, shrill whistle and turns around. Behind him, Gorelov's eyes are flashing with curiosity and his nostrils are anxiously twitching. He's obviously desperate to listen in on the conversation – he's been completely brutal since the memorable escape, sniffing out, unearthing, and searching everything, so he can report to Ignatov – but he's missed this.

"Gorelov, you ignorant soul!" Konstantin Arnoldovich's sharp, narrow little shoulders screen Zuleikha, who's still chewing. "Are you aware that our Ilya Petrovich created the scenery for the Mariinsky Theater's ballet *The Bolshevik*?"

"We don't go wagging our tails around at the ballet. And you're not very likely to now, either."

Gorelov's hand angrily snatches at Konstantin Arnoldovich's frail arm, pushing him aside: *Here, let's have a look*. It turns out there's nothing to see, though, just a pregnant peasant woman chewing with a stuffed mouth and picking crumbs out of her palm with her lips. But there was something here, there was, his gut feels it … Disappointed, Gorelov exhales through his nostrils and casts a glance out the window. Floating past are the tall, gray buildings of yet another station with large letters on their brick face.

"Krasnoyarsk," someone reads aloud.

Apparently they'll stand for another couple of weeks, no less. It really truly is as if they're riding to the edge of the earth. The din of the wheels fades. Outside is the overwrought barking of dogs. What is this for? The railroad car door slides open with a drawn-out wail and a loud, sharp voice shouts a command over the barking: "Exit!"

"What?"

"How ... ?"

"Is that for us?"

"We're already there?"

"It can't be ..."

"It can, Bella, it can ..."

"Gather your things, your things! Faster, Ilya Petrovich – what are you doing, anyway?"

"Professor, help Zuleikha ..."

"I've never been to Krasnoyarsk ..."

"What do you think, will they leave us here or take us further?"

"Where did my book go?"

"Maybe they're just transferring us to another train?"

The uneasy crowd pours out of the train car down a board that's thrown from the car to the ground as a gangway. Zuleikha is last to go, grasping at her bundle of things with one hand and at her large belly, which faces sharply up, with the other. In the bustle of gathering their belongings, nobody notices that Izabella's emerald-colored hat remains lying under the bunks: it's fairly worn but still bright, its iridescent peacock feathers shining.

They are met by a lot of soldiers and every other one has a large dog that's quivering with tension and barking hoarsely. The barking is so loud it's impossible to talk.

Holding his ever-present "Case" folder under his arm, Ignatov observes from a distance as the exiles leave the train. The folder has faded during the long months of the trip, and its government-issued cover is now obscured by dark blue scars from stamps and seals, violet dates, signatures, penciled additions, and squiggles. A distinguished folder, decorated with honors. He will now hand it over – along with the deportees – to some local official. No doubt he'll still dream of the folder at night and it will throw its maw open, hurling its rudimentary insides in his face: a couple of thin, worn little sheets with dense columns of surnames, four hundred of which have been boldly crossed out with uneven pencil lines. That's fine; he'll dream of it for a couple of nights and then stop. Out of sight, out of mind.

How loudly they bark, those dogs …

"You're greeting them as if they're criminals being transferred," Ignatov says to the soldier who's come running over.

"We greet everybody that way," he responds with pride. "With music. Welcome to Siberia, as they say!"

He smiles cordially. And the teeth in his mouth are metal, each and every one of them.

THE BARGE

Zinovy Kuznets, senior employee for special assignments at the Krasnoyarsk office of the State Political Administration, outright refuses to accept Ignatov's charges.

"Here's a barge for you," he says. "And there's the Yenisei River. Take them."

"It's in my orders, in black and white – 'hand over to the authority of the local office of the State Political Administration.'" Ignatov is seething.

"Wake up! Read one line higher: 'deliver to point of destination.' First 'deliver' and then later 'hand over.' Well then, deliver, don't shirk. Take command of the barge and sail up to the Angara. We'll meet there in two days and I'll accept your sorry lot."

"So where is it, your point of destination? In the taiga? In some godforsaken place? I was only assigned to look after them on the railroad! I brought them halfway across the country. Six months squandered on the rails! And you don't want to accept them in your own city. That's not our way, not the Soviet way."

"Want to, don't want to ... The only thing I've wanted since winter is a good night's sleep!" Kuznets spits thickly and loudly by his feet, and looks off somewhere to the side, but his eyes truly are dazed and red. "You think because you're sensitive and pretty you're the only one in Siberia who should get a break? I receive a dozen barge loads every week, sometimes two. Where

196

should I find escorts for all of them? So look here, Ignatov, as your superior officer, I order you to go aboard and deliver the entrusted cargo in the quantity of – you yourself know how many heads – to the place where the future labor settlement will be founded."

"I'm not yet under your direction!"

"Well, consider yourself under it as of now. Or do you need a little piece of stamped paper? I'll obtain it quickly, don't think I won't. Just don't hold it against me later, my dear man …" Kuznets raises his reddish eyes, the black pupils like little needles, at Ignatov.

Ignatov slaps his hands on his knees: *I'm done for!* He takes off his peaked cap and wipes his sweat-soaked forehead. This might be Siberia but the heat is hellish.

They're standing on a steep, high riverbank and can see everything from here. The dark blue cupola of the sky is reflected in the river's broad mirror, which breathes with a slight ripple. The Yenisei's water is dark, heavy, and lazy. The green left bank rears up in the distance. Bony berths stick out of a lopsided pier like fingers. There's a stir by the pier as people swarm, dogs bark fervently, escort guards shout, and bayonets gleam in the sun. Exiles are being loaded onto a low, wide barge.

Kuznets takes an ivory cigarette case out of his jacket.

"Here, this one's better."

Ignatov initially refuses, then grudgingly accepts one. Kuznets's cigarettes are good, expensive.

"You lost a lot along the way – four hundred heads. Did you starve them or –"

"If they'd been fed better, I'd have brought more!"

It's too bad he's lit the cigarette. The aromatic smoke is stuck in his throat; it's not pleasing.

"And wasn't there an escape on your train?" Kuznets winks

unexpectedly, hiding a smirk in the flourishes of his rounded black mustache. "And he wants to teach me what's the Soviet way and what's not ..."

Ignatov flings his unfinished cigarette into the river.

"Well, now you understand," Kuznets concludes in a superior tone. "Fine, don't get steamed up. There're lots of kulaks here, no harm done. They'll dig the land there, plant wheat." He nods at a long chain of soldiers carrying armloads of shovels, saws, and axes wrapped in old rags, plus crates bristling with other tools. "There's a large, natural stock of them, you can see it yourself. You won't even be able to blink before they multiply."

Lots of tools are being loaded on the barge, and there's even a couple of sturdy utility carts with wooden wheels. (*In the taiga? Are they going to harness elk to it?* Ignatov wonders cheerlessly.) Equipment, sacks with provisions, bunches of kettles – everything's being piled on the flat roof, wrapped in tarpaulins, and tied with ropes. They're working in unison, the way they always do. The escort guards up on the roof hold their rifles horizontally. You can't miss from there if anything happens. One waves his arms, commanding. The others walk around, occasionally glancing down from on high at the deportees swarming beneath them. They're driving people somewhere below. They crawl along the gangway like ants and disappear, disappear into the bowels of the hold. The dogs' agitated barking carries after them from the shore. They're raging, the bastards. Are they fed human flesh or something?

"What, you can't wait to go back?" Kuznets notices Ignatov's gloomy gaze. "Yes, our life's harsh here. But don't you worry – you'll deliver your people and I'll let you go home to your wife's warm side."

"I'm not married," Ignatov tells him coldly.

*

During loading, it turns out that the exiles won't all fit on the barge. They've packed more than three hundred into the hold – so tightly they can scarcely breathe – and this violates all the guidance and regulations by greatly exceeding the allowable limit (the barge has settled low and heavy in the water), though several dozen are left outside even so.

Kuznets has suggested they transport the oldest and frailest on deck – the old ones, he says, won't jump overboard – but Ignatov won't budge on this, not for anything. One escape is enough for him. That Kuznets is a son of a bitch after all. Of course he knew one barge wouldn't be enough. Did he hope they'd all fit? Or that Ignatov, from inexperience or pity, would agree to take people in the open air?

A second barge has already arrived at the pier and attached its blunt snout of a bow to a berth; it will take the second batch. Criminals, explains Kuznets. Judging from all the dogs barking, the convicts are already close by – they've been somewhere on the high shore waiting for Ignatov's barge to cast off.

"You fall asleep or what!" the official on the pier rasps at Ignatov. "Go on, out! You've created a line here, you Trotskyite …"

"Up yours," Ignatov snarls at him. "And yours, too." (That's for Kuznets.) "Do what you want but I'm not taking people in the open air. I'm the one responsible for them after all."

"Screw it," says Kuznets, waving him away. "Give me the excess, for the launch. And take the barge away right now – get it out of my sight."

For the excess, they select the weakest, most tired, and unlikeliest to escape. Kuznets himself points a finger, taking many of the Leningrad remainders and several gray-haired peasants. They're rounded up into Kuznets's roomy launch, into a hold for storing fish. Kuznets is supposed to leave the next night, follow Ignatov's barge, and catch up to it somewhere around the mouth of the

Angara. In addition, he's demanding Ignatov assign someone very reliable to watch over the group and report any trouble. They have three days' journey ahead and who knows what might happen. Ignatov smirks and gives him Gorelov.

"I'll take people, yes, I will," Kuznets declares, "but I'm not shouldering your responsibility, Ignatov. You'll be accountable for them during the trip, remember that."

Coward.

Kuznets takes the "Case" folder anyway, just for now, "to have a read." Ignatov feels relieved when he passes it into Kuznets's sun-browned hands. It takes a load off his mind.

They finally head out. The motorized barge moves off along the channel like a large black cucumber, cutting the Yenisei in two. It creeps heavily and slowly under its excessive weight. The motor wheezes and sputters, belching thick smoke from its large-striped stack again and again. High waves extend in both directions like straight white mustaches.

The barge's name is *Clara.* The long, neat letters were painstakingly traced out on its rounded bow at one time, but the paint flaked off and was eaten away by rust long ago, so now it's barely visible on *Clara*'s dark brown side. More recently, someone decided to give her a surname and painted an unprepossessing, slightly leaning "Zetkin" below. But those letters have peeled off, too, almost erased by the waves.

First of all, Ignatov checks the doors of the huge hold in which his batch of people has been housed; the hold extends the entire length of the barge, and there are doors at the bow and stern. The doors in the bow are useless so were boarded up long ago, meaning that passengers – exiles and political prisoners shipped on the barge before 1917 and then exiles and criminals who are transported now – are loaded in and out only through the stern. Which is proper because fewer doors mean fewer anxieties. Ignatov feels the fat boards, digs his fingernail at the half-rusted clamps fastening them, and tugs at the metal girders that crisscross them. Sealed off well, solidly. You couldn't knock it out from inside, no matter how you tried. He puts a watchman there, just in case.

The sharp, strong smell of male urine assaults his nose when he comes to the doors at the stern. That smell hovers everywhere on the barge, surrounding it like a cloud, but is especially acrid and cutting here, by the doors: it comes from the hold. It blends many generations of political and criminal prisoners. It's a sort of final memory of them, a monument not made by human hands. Many of these people no longer exist: they've perished, but their smell remains.

There are two watchmen, not just one, by the doors at the stern. The opening of the square doorway is covered from the inside by a strong wrought-iron grate: the fat rods are sunk into the walls and hold the grate right up against them – it can't be loosened or knocked out. On the outside are metal doors closed with a wide bolt the thickness of a hand. Thought out practically. You could keep bears here, to say nothing of people weakened from long months of travel.

"And this, why isn't it locked?" Ignatov notices a half-open padlock in the bolt of one door.

"There was no order," a watchmen exhausted from the heat lazily answers. "They say it doesn't open well, needs to be repaired."

Utter sloppiness. Ignatov takes the lock in his hands. The key's sticking out of the keyhole and he turns it in one direction, then the other; the key clicks obediently when it turns. He hangs the lock on the door and closes it. Now everything's in good order and a mouse couldn't slip through. He pockets the key.

The people in the hold come to life and pound their fists when they hear voices.

"Chief!" carries, muffled, from behind the doors or maybe from under the boards of the deck. "Chief, we're roasting!"

"There's nothing to breathe!"

"If you opened the doors, we could at least take a little breath!"

"We're already baked!"

Ignatov pulls at the collar of his uniform tunic. It truly is hot; it makes you want to dive right into the Yenisei.

"Don't open the doors," he tells the watchmen. "But you can open the little windows."

A small row of low, tightly closed ventilation hatches stretches the length of the deck. The watchman kicks the little doors with the toe of his boot and they open, one after another. Sighs, sobs, and curses carry from the hatches.

"Were they given water?"

"There was no order," the watchman shrugs.

"Water every hour."

The last thing he needs is for someone to die of thirst on the final day.

Ignatov can now be more attentive as he gets his bearings. He continues his rounds. Towering over the deck are two squat wooden crew quarters held down by a flat roof. There are guards inside the quarters; provisions are kept there. On the roof is equipment, a couple of upside-down boats, and coils of rope. A few watchmen are wandering on the roof – their deep-blue shadows sway on the waves along the side of the barge and the merciless creak of boards is audible overhead. Everything creaks here: the deck (the boards gape with crevices that move underfoot as if they're alive), the walls of the crew quarters (which have been eaten away by beetles, to dust in some places, and blackened from rot in others), and dried-out gangways. A low hum comes from railings, red from thin, rusty scabs on paint that was once white. It's scary to lean against those. They leave a thick, dark red mark on your hand if you touch them.

"My grandfather sailed on this one," says a barefoot sailor as he runs ahead of Ignatov.

"Your *grandfather*, well, that makes sense," says Ignatov, shaking his head.

The closer to the engine room, the stronger the vibration under their feet. The engine room's crooked door is wide open and the machinery inside lets out a monotonous metallic clanging and a blaze of heat. Somewhere below, in darkness that breathes out jets of flame, two blackened stokers are singing, their white eyeballs and bared teeth flashing angrily. "*The sea stretches so wide ...*"

The motor is loud but it's also strained and uneven, as though short of breath.

"Do you have a mechanic here?" Ignatov calls to the barefoot sailor.

"No need." The sailor smiles. "My grandfather told me the *Clara* has a mind of her own. No mechanic can convince her if she stops."

Well, there you go. That's that, then. Quite the tub.

When Ignatov hears that the pregnant peasant woman in the hold has taken a turn for the worse, he allows her to be brought up on deck. He comes over and has a look as one of the guards leads Zuleikha, yellowish and pale, into fresh air and sits her down in the shadow of the crew quarters. Her face has narrowed over the months. It seems as if her eyebrows and lashes have thickened and darkened, and her eyes are rimmed with thick blue paint. These eyes are all that's left on her face.

But what do you know – she survived. The fat redheaded battleaxe from car number six with the big scarlet birthmark on her cheek died way back at Shchuchye Lake, unable to sustain life force even with her solid body. The mullah's stout wife, the cat lover, didn't withstand the journey, either, and departed near Vagai. But this one's alive. Not only that, she's carrying a child. What is her soul holding onto?

Why hadn't he left her with the investigator back in Pyshma?

Ignatov couldn't answer that question for himself. Most likely for the same reason he'd scuttled down the back stairs to avoid the unfamiliar official left in charge at Bakiev's office. His heart had faltered and raced ahead of his brain so he'd gone and done something stupid. If he'd cooled off and thought things through … well, it wouldn't have resulted in him running or removing that woman from the investigation. What did she have to do with him, anyway? That's right, nothing. Ignatov couldn't even recall her husband's face, no matter how he tried. He got angry at himself every time − why torment himself? Life isn't long enough to recall all the peasant men who've come at him with axes and pitchforks. An entire division of them have already taken up residence in his head as it is. The folder is called "Case K-2437" and it contains several hundred souls. Damn, he'd like to toss all those faces out of his memory but it doesn't happen. Fine, he'll take them to the Angara, hand them over to Kuznets, and *basta*, the end. They'll be forgotten; with time they'll definitely be forgotten.

"Stand watch over her, comrade Ignatov?" The guard nods at Zuleikha. Her belly's a mountain in front of her and she's holding it with both hands, arranging herself more comfortably, breathing heavily.

Ignatov waves a hand, letting the guard go. Where's someone like her going? He suddenly remembers carrying her in his arms, how light and slender she was, as if she weren't a woman but a girl. Nastasya's another matter, with a body that's fleshy, supple, and rolls around in your hands, undulating, so you want to squeeze, knead, and smooth it. Ilona's body is different, too; it's soft, languid, and pliant, but a woman's body all the same. This one's just air, though. And why, he might ask, was he so scared he sent for a doctor during the night? It's clear why: he was afraid she'd breathe her last, that's why. He felt sorry for her.

All the same, she'll die in the settlement. Taiga, midges, work … she won't make it, no. Her strength is waning, you can see it in her eyes. Ignatov has recently realized that he can tell from their eyes who still has strength and whose strength is running out. Sometimes he guesses when doing his rounds: this one will be a stiff soon, the eyes are completely cold and dead; this man will still live a while, this woman, too. He guesses right, by the way. Basically, he's turned into a fortune teller. An awful thought, ugh. That's what a long trip does to a person …

Zuleikha turns around and raises her exhausted eyes to Ignatov. It's as if she's looked into his soul. And those green eyes have already made their mark on his heart.

"Don't you dare give birth on my watch," he says sternly and walks toward the bow of the barge.

He'll hand her over to Kuznets; let her give birth then.

And so they leave Zuleikha on deck. She sits there all day, leaning her back against the wall of the crew quarters and gazing at ridges of green hills floating past in an uneven stubble of pines and spruces. The forests are dense here, dark. And they're not just any forests but the *urman*. The watchman brings Zuleikha's bundle of things up from the hold and she covers up for the night with her winter sheepskin coat. It's August but the nights are cool and nippy.

Carrying the baby is difficult. Zuleikha's belly has become large and cumbersome, and her legs are unwieldy, like iron. The baby is growing into someone restless, sometimes spinning like a spindle, sometimes kicking with all its might, sometimes leaning its little paws into her belly. The child apparently resembles its elder sister, Shamsia, who was also a naughty girl and a fidget. Or maybe the baby's just hungry. Zuleikha herself has lost a lot of weight over these past months, like during the time of the Great Famine in 1921. Even her fingers are thinner, weakened, and stretched with translucent skin. And so it follows that the baby can't be getting enough food, either.

She often looks at her belly with the fabric of her smock tightly stretched over it and imagines the tiny girl inside wrinkling a nose the size of the nail on a pinkie and opening her little mouth. Then her breasts fill with milk, growing heavy, like male flesh before a romantic meeting; two dark, round spots the size of a tenke coin show through on the fabric. The baby's only seven months old but the milk has already come in. This happened once before, when she was expecting Sabida.

Zuleikha attempts to forbid herself from thinking about her daughters but it doesn't work. *Shamsia-Firuza, Khalida-Sabida,* the water splashes against the side. *Shamsia!* – a gull in the sky screeches heartrendingly. *Firuza!* – a second one answers. *Khalida! Sabida!* – the others join in.

She's tired of fighting that. And tired of starving. And tired of always traveling somewhere. The imperious black-mustached Red Hordesman had kept Leibe, Izabella, Konstantin Arnoldovich, the hard-to-love yet familiar Ilya Petrovich Ikonnikov, and even the horrid Gorelov all back somewhere on the pier. It is doubtful Zuleikha will see them again. They have already been consigned to the past and turned into spectral recollections, like Murtaza or the Vampire Hag. She is so tired of losing people close to her. And living in fear of parting, in constant expectation of a quick death for the child, of her own death. She is tired of living in general.

Her only joy and comfort lies in her pocket. Zuleikha gratefully remembers the moment her death appeared to her in the railroad car, to the rhythmic clacking of wheels. It was lying on her palm, as a heavy lump of sugar with sharp edges, and it has been with her ever since, like a loyal friend or dedicated mother. In her roughest moments, Zuleikha would grope at the folds of her clothes for that cherished lump and feel relief. Apparently, this truly was her very own death, hers alone, sent from above through a supreme gesture. While all around her people were dying from illness or hunger, others losing their minds, their deaths didn't touch her: they felt distant, passing her by. Those who had died on other trains and couldn't be buried in time lay along the railroad and saw their fellow travelers off with frozen gazes. Others who'd heard about the daring escape carried out near Pyshma and wanted to repeat it had been caught and executed on the spot, by the train cars. But Zuleikha was still living. That meant this very death had been predestined for her; it's small, sweet, and smells – subtly and appealingly – of something bitter. Maybe it's too bad she didn't eat the sugar back on the train; she could have brought her suffering to an end long ago. *I'll eat it as soon as things become completely unbearable*, she'd decided. It would be better to do it, of course, before the child is born, so they can pass away together, never parting.

Zuleikha opens her eyes. All the objects around her seem to ripple and float in dawn's light-pink mist. A sturdy, white-breasted gull is sitting on a railing, the glistening amber buttons of its unblinking eyes watching. Behind the gull, vague outlines of distant shores show through the cottony morning fog that's formed. The motor is silent; the barge drifts noiselessly downstream with the current. Small waves splash tenderly against the side. And then there's a familiar voice at the bow: "Go ahead!"

The gull spreads its wings, rustling almost soundlessly, and dissolves into the fog. Zuleikha looks out from behind the wall of the crew quarters. She sees Ignatov at the bow, bare to the waist. A sailor is splashing river water on him from a bucket. Ignatov laughs and shakes his wet head so spray flies everywhere. His hands rub his ears, his sharp ribs, and shoulders bulging with muscles. He has a nice smile after all. It's white, like sugar. And there's a deep scar on his back, under one shoulder blade.

They toil their way down the Yenisei for a day and don't enter the Angara until the following morning. The day turns out hot and sweaty again as they chug upstream; they feel sleepy in the afternoon. Ignatov sits on a tightly coiled bundle of rope, leaning his back against the wooden covering of the crew quarters. Out from under the bill of the peaked cap that's pulled down over his eyebrows, he can see the spines of hills tinged bluish-green and the stony cheeks of precipices. Thin ripples of sunlight burn hot on the water, like fiery fish scales.

Now, at last, there can't be much longer. He's already counting the minutes until he sees the distant red dot of a flag on a boat; until he hands people over to Kuznets, counting heads so they don't torture themselves with lists (or have to look at their faces – why do that yet again?); until this is out of his hands so he can breathe freely and calmly for the first time in half a year. *That's it, Kuznets, you're in charge now. May those bearded faces haunt your nights now. I've had enough. I'd like work that's a little simpler and more understandable. If they're enemies, then cut them right down, mercilessly; but look after them if they're friends. For enemies to be looked after and fed and pitied and doctored ... well, spare me.* And then it will be home, home! Get enough sleep on the train and go straight to Bakiev from the train station to report, and then to Nastasya in the evening – to Nastasya, sweet, dear, and passionate. He wasn't overly concerned that she might have found someone else during this half-year. That one would disappear, just like he'd shown up. Anyway, he, Ignatov, would figure things out quickly. He'd have to find time for Ilona, too, to stop by, since things hadn't ended nicely.

The barefoot sailor is tinkering nearby, repairing a rotten gangway covered with black spots of mildew.

"You been on the Angara before?" he asks.

It's so hot Ignatov feels too lazy to answer. Dozing to the monotonous plopping of waterwheels is sweet and languorous. *You were right, Bakiev, my friend*, Ignatov admits to himself. *Oh, this business of nannying a train turned out to be far from simple ...*

"My grandfather told me there's nothing on earth prettier than the Angara," says the sailor, not giving up. "Or more treacherous, either."

Ignatov barely raises an eyebrow in response ... He'll admit to witnessing the search in Bakiev's office, too. He'll tell Bakiev he didn't doubt for a second that they'd release him soon, that's why he left then. They'll laugh about that together and slap each other on the shoulders.

Flattered by the merest attention given by a commander from another place, the sailor abandons what he's doing and turns to Ignatov, continuing to drive his point home: "The Angara, she's like ... a mother for some, a sister or stepmother. And for others, she's a downright grave."

Ignatov rests his chin on his chest. He'll need a gift for Nastasya, for the long wait. Some kind of headscarf, maybe – or what is it women like, anyway? His head falls to his shoulder; the light rocking lulls him, puts him to sleep.

"My grandfather, he drowned here himself," says the sailor, winding up his story. "Uh-huh. Didn't help that he could swim like a pike."

Lightning cuts the sky open lengthwise, along the whole horizon. Violet clouds rub up against one another, breathing blackness. There's a low, rumbling peal of thunder but no rain.

The storm seems to have sprung up spontaneously, in an instant. A gust of wind knocks the hat from Ignatov's head. He wakes, darts after it, and lo and behold – sweet mother! – it's already all around: the horizon's rocking, waves are hurling foam, gulls are darting in the air like arrows, and the sailors are rushing around like cats with their tails on fire. You can't hear the screams over the wind.

"Comrade commander!" A watchman has appeared next to him and is shouting into his ear. "Over there …"

He points a finger at the stern, the dolt, unsure what to say. Ignatov heads toward the stern. The metal door is shaking from being pounded.

"Open it!" they wail inside. "Open it!"

"A rebellion?" says Ignatov with a nervous start. "You want to organize a revolution for me, you bastards?"

He yanks his revolver from its holster. The watchmen are aiming their rifles at the doors.

"Sons of bitches!" carries from the hold. "We'll drown, open up! You drowning us on purpose? Sons of bitches! Sons of bitches! There's water in here! Water! Aaaah!"

"You're playing tricks," hisses Ignatov. "You won't fool me. Go on, back, you lowlifes! I'll shoot!"

The barge's horn is low and booming, and reverberates across the water. *What's going on? Why are you honking, you devils?* Ignatov races to the wheelhouse but it's hard to run because the deck is jumping under his feet, the boards are cracking, and there's spray in his face.

There's nobody in the wheelhouse. The ship's wheel is spinning like crazy.

"What is this?" Ignatov shouts in the face of a sailor running past him.

"We're going down!" the other yells back. "Can't you see?"

Going down? How can that be? So the ones in the hold weren't lying?

A crate of tools slides off the tilting roof with a loud crash – it cracks but doesn't spill. Whistling and spinning, it sweeps along the deck past Ignatov and disappears into the water. And then suddenly, falling like rain, like hail, are handles, crowbars, and shovels ... Axe blades gleam past (Ignatov just manages to press against the wall – they would have hacked him as they flew!), scythes screech, pitchforks scatter overboard with a thin groan, and nails jingle along the wood. Carts leap into the water, their wheels turning. An entire stockpile of goods is flying, flying, into the Angara, toward all the demons in hell.

The deck is keeling, keeling. The horizon suddenly tips, one end rearing into the sky. The barge's stern settles, its blunt snout raised into the air.

"Jump!" carries from the bow. "Go! You'll be dragged down!"

Over there, several sailors and stokers are springing into the Angara, as fast as frogs.

What's that about? Jump? What about the people in the hold? Ignatov gropes in his pocket for the key and takes it out. He races toward the stern. The watchmen are thudding unsteadily toward him.

"Halt!" shouts Ignatov.

A wall of wind silences him and his shout can't be heard.

The escort guards hurl their rifles in the water, jump after them, and disappear in the waves. They've abandoned their post, the dogs! The final watchman tears a red-and-white life ring from a nail, tosses it in the Angara, lets out a harrowing wail, crosses himself, and plops into the water below.

The deck jerks desperately and Ignatov falls and grabs at some kind of clamp. The key flies out of his hand, drumming along the boards. Ignatov throws his chest on it before it slides away. There it is, the dear thing! He puts it in his mouth: *Now I won't let it go.* He continues crawling toward the stern, hanging on with his hands.

Something above him sighs loudly, then slaps violently,

booming. Ignatov looks up and sees the tarpaulin is beating at the roof like a giant sail and the ropes are flung up toward the sky, like hands in prayer.

To the hold, to the hold, Ignatov! Let those kulaks out. Let everybody out, and the hell with it! What, did you bring them all this way for nothing?

Through the space between the crew quarters, he notices the pregnant woman on the other side of the deck. She's gripping a railing with her hands and gawking at Ignatov. She's too far away; he can't reach.

"Jump," he cries at her, pulling the key from his mouth and attempting to yell over the wind. "Jump into the water, you fool! You'll be dragged under!"

A large wave hangs over the side of the barge and crashes flat on the deck. After flowing back, there's neither woman, nor railing. Only broken, rusted stubs sticking out.

Crawl further, Ignatov, further! That was one woman. You need to let many go.

As he crawls up to the door of the hold, he notices water gushing into the open ventilation hatches. Someone's fingers are stretching into the gaps, attempting to catch hold but a wave washes them back inside.

The deck under Ignatov wails with hundreds of voices.

His chest shudders from blows to the boards – someone's attempting to knock them out.

Groans drift up from below.

Thunder claps. Rain falls in thick sheets and sloshes on the deck. Ignatov crawls toward the door but everything around him is suddenly becoming loose and slippery from the rain. *Now, now, you sons of bitches, I'll let you out, don't wail.*

The moment he seizes one of the door handles, something cracks loudly and ominously, and the barge begins submerging into the water.

Ignatov manages to keep his fingers clenched, holding onto the handle and not dropping the key. The only thing he can't manage is to take a deeper breath. Water is pouring into his ears, nose, and eyes. Ignatov is descending into the Angara – *Clara* is dragging him down with her.

Where are you, you damned keyhole? He pokes with the key, looking for the hole in the lock. *Chk-chk!* He found it, put the key in! But it won't turn. It's jammed. He's desperately turning the key in the lock but the *Clara* is revolving slowly, plunging deeper.

Come on, Ignatov, come on! Water makes his hair billow, stings his eyes, and gets in his mouth.

There! It turned! He pulls the door. It opens slowly, as if in a dream.

There's the grate behind it. Damn! Dozens of hands stretch through it, reaching toward Ignatov, seizing at the bars, and shaking them. Water is pouring into the hold through the grate, swiftly, relentlessly.

The door handle slips out of his fingers. Ignatov wants to catch it and reaches out, his muscles straining, but the force of the water hurls him aside. He sees wide-open eyes and wide-open mouths through a green layer of water behind the grate.

"A-a-a-a-a-h!" are their low, scared cries, and thousands of large bubbles surround Ignatov, sliding along his body, licking his chest, neck, and face.

In each bubble, an "A-a-a-a-a-h."

Dozens of hands reach, reach toward him through the grate, wiggling their fingers. They sway like a huge sheaf of grain. They're going deeper, deeper. Vanishing into the dark.

The water twists and tosses Ignatov in various directions, finally hurling him out, up to the surface.

"Aaaah!" he howls at the low sky, where shaggy clouds are billowing. "Aaaaaaah!"

Rain lashes at his open mouth.

"*Ee! Ee!*" answer the gulls.

Zuleikha is carried off somewhere below, through layers of water. Her eyes grow heavy as its thick greenness dissolves into them, darkening her view. A blizzard of bubbles spirals around her, beating at her face.

She's clenching her teeth: *Stay still, don't breathe.*

A faint light dances, flashing, sometimes below, sometimes to her side. It dwindles. Large, dark silhouettes are swimming in the distance – maybe they're above, maybe below. Wreckage? People? Fish?

She presses her arms to her chest and pulls up her legs. Her braids are knotted around her neck.

All-powerful Allah, all is at Your will.

She is spun, somersaulted, and hurled side-first into something hard.

Allah heard your prayers and decided to cut short your life's journey, so that you vanish without a trace in the waters of the Angara.

In the name of God, the Lord of mercy …

Water begins flooding her mouth. It's a little bitter and her teeth crunch on sand.

Thanks be to God, Lord of heaven and earth …

Maybe she swallowed that water or maybe she breathed it. Her body has begun twitching, dancing.

Amen … Amen …

Her body jerks once more and goes still. Her arms hang like whips and her legs slacken. Her braids stretch upward, swaying slowly, like water plants. Zuleikha is sinking, her face down, her braids up. Lower, even lower, to the very bottom. The soles of her feet drop into soft silt, raising a lazy, murky black cloud around her. Ankles. Knees. Belly.

The child wakes up sharply, abruptly. Beating with its little feet, a second time, a third. Squirming with its little hands, turning its head and fidgeting. Zuleikha's belly quivers from the small heels pounding inside.

Zuleikha's legs shudder in response. Again. And again. They push off from the bottom. Tighten and slacken. Her arms tighten and slacken, too.

She kicks toward the surface. From an agitated and swaying silty cloud toward a distant light ripple. Up, higher and higher, through the malachite layers.

She thrashes harder with her arms and legs, and rises faster. Some sort of cool, buoyant current catches and carries her up.

A blinding wall of white light hits her eyes. Zuleikha batters the water with her arms, shouts, and coughs. There's a sharp pain in her throat, from her nose to her very innards. Wind bites at her face and she hears gulls shrieking and waves pounding her ears. She catches sight of a shred of vivid blue sky. Could she really have swum up?

Water roils around her, buffeting, slipping through her fingers. There's nothing to grasp. Zuleikha doesn't know how to swim. Her feet are pulling her downward again. Is she really going back to the bottom? The horizon keels and ducks as her head goes under. *Allah* –

Hands pull her up by the braids.

"Lie on the water!" says a familiar voice next to her. "Belly on top!"

Ignatov!

Zuleikha attempts to wriggle free, to catch onto him with her hands, and at least grasp hold of something.

"You'll drown us both!" Ignatov pushes away but doesn't let go of her braids. "Lie back, you fool!"

She coughs and wails; she can barely hear. But she's trying and she turns over so her belly's on top and she's lying on the water.

Her belly rises above the surface like an island. Waves whip her face, as does rain falling from above.

"Legs and arms extended, make a star with them! A star! Do what I tell you!" Ignatov's face is right next to her but she can't figure out where. "There you go! Good job, you fool."

Zuleikha extends her arms and legs and rocks like a jellyfish. She has an unbearable urge to cough but holds back. She's breathing loudly, convulsively. If only she could get enough air to breathe, if only there were enough.

"I'm holding you," says the voice next to her. "I'm holding your braids."

The baby has calmed in her belly and isn't bothering her. The waves are subsiding little by little, too, diminishing. The lightning is creeping away beyond the horizon, and a small wedge of blue sky is widening and growing. The clouds are dispersing in various directions.

"Are you here?" Zuleikha is afraid to turn her head; she doesn't want to gulp down water.

"I'm here," says the voice next to her. "How could I get away from you now?"

At first Ignatov wants to swim to shore but Zuleikha can't. And so they toss around in the channel, drifting with the current. They're fished out a couple of hours later, chilled through, their lips inky-blue. Kuznets's nimble launch had come tearing along to meet the *Clara* but had found only her survivors. Other than Zuleikha and Ignatov, just a handful of sailors have been saved. Including the barefoot one – the one who kept talking about his grandfather. Apparently his time had not yet come.

When all of them – weakened and shaking from the cold – have been safely settled on the deck of the launch and ordered to remove and hand over their wet clothes for drying, Zuleikha shoves her hand in her pocket for the sugar. She pulls out only a handful of white sludge. She straightens her fingers and the goop immediately drains through them. She puts her hand over the side and the milky white drops flow off into the Angara.

The home brew glugs cheerfully as it's poured from a tall, round green bottle into a crooked tin mug. Ignatov's standing in the middle of the crew quarters, naked but for the burlap sacking he's holding to his chest with his hand; there are still bits of river plants in his wet hair. He's gazing evenly, unblinking, at that steady, cloudy stream. He grabs the mug without waiting for the last drops to fall from the bottle's mouth and tips it into his gullet. Alcohol burns his larynx, plops into his stomach, and spreads to his head in a slow, warm wave. Green sparks instantly explode before his eyes. Home-brewed liquor's strong, it's good. He exhales slowly and quietly, and looks up at Kuznets. Kuznets's eyes are mean, like a dog's, and his mouth is a straight line.

"She was rusty, like" – Ignatov squeezes the burlap in his fists, kneading at it – "like …"

Kuznets takes the mug from Ignatov's hands and refills it.

"I can't!"

"Drink!"

The tin rim clinks against Ignatov's strong teeth: he's grasping at the mug and drinking. The home brew pours in as easily and smoothly as if it were oil. The green sparks in front of his eyes fuse, flow, and beckon. So what now? Get soused, completely blotto? He's never once in his life been genuinely drunk, blacking out, falling down. Feeling regret, Ignatov takes the empty mug from his mouth and breathes out. His eyelids grow heavy, closing.

"Now, you listen." Kuznets's voice is stern and clipped. "I have no obligation to relieve you of your poor goners."

"Huh?" Ignatov has trouble lifting his eyelids. Kuznets flickers, warps, and doubles. There are already four, not just two, mean, unblinking eyes driving into Ignatov.

"I'll drop off everybody that's left at the location."

"Wh-where?"

"Somewhere! We'll find a suitable place."

"Erm …"

Ignatov's looking through dirty window glass. Out there, on a distant shore, the pointed tops of endless spruce trees extend beyond the horizon and rock in the wind.

"Hold on a minute …" Ignatov turns back to Kuznets. He can't manage to catch his gaze at all – he has too many eyes, the angry devil. "In the taiga? Without equip … equipment?"

"It's an order," Kuznets say flintily.

The burlap nearly slips from Ignatov's chest and he catches at it, wrapping himself up again.

"They'll croak," he says quietly.

Now they can hear the loud rattling of the boat's motor.

"You have to understand that we need that settlement!" Kuznets, who'd divided in two, finally merges into one.

"You want to put a dot on the map?" Ignatov takes the bottle by its narrow neck to splash something into the empty mug for himself. "Conquering the shores of the great Angara? And the people? The hell with them? New ones will be born?"

Kuznets grabs the bottle's thick middle but Ignatov won't give it back.

"Quiet!" Kuznets pulls it toward himself. "Who sank the barge?"

"It was a leaky barge! Leaky, as leaky as a rotten old stump!"

"Were your railroad cars leaky, too? Half the people scattered along the way, half escaped … Or maybe it's your hands that are leaky, Ignatov? Or your head?"

"But I brought them all the way across the country!" Ignatov groans and attempts to pull Kuznets's tenacious fingers from the slippery glass. "I dragged them along the rails for half a year to deliver them to you, you ass. And now you want to send them right off to the taiga? To feed the wolves?"

"No, my dear man, you're going to feed the wolves," Kuznets hisses right into his ear, his hot breath enveloping Ignatov. "Because you're staying with them. As the commandant."

The bottle slides away, remaining in Kuznets's big paws. Kuznets sputters, steadies his breathing, and wipes his drenched forehead.

"Temporarily, of course," he says, not looking at Ignatov as he pours home brew into the mug for him with evil generosity. "What, you want me to fuss around with your invalids? A couple dozen old people? Who shoved them in the hold? Me? Wasn't that you? If you'd brought them in the open, on the deck, you and I wouldn't be having this conversation right now. But you cooked up this mess so you're going to eat it. You'll sit with them a week and guard them until I bring a new batch and a permanent commandant."

After a loud thud, the bottle's standing back on the table.

"What're you doing, Kuznets?" Ignatov's voice is husky, as if he has a cold.

The burlap falls to the floor and Ignatov is left in his birthday suit. Kuznets casts him a stern gaze:

"That's an order, special assignments employee Ignatov."

He hurls the familiar gray "Case" folder on the table and leaves. Ignatov grabs the mug with both hands and pours home brew into himself. Its coolness streams down his chin, neck, and bare chest.

"Matches. Salt. Fishing tackle."

Kuznets crouches as he opens each of the sacks and parcels that lie on the rocks, poking a firm finger into them. Ignatov's standing alongside him, teetering slightly. He's wearing a uniform that's still half-damp and wrinkled (it's clear they've wrung it out hard and flapped it in the wind), and his holster is attached crookedly, but he doesn't notice. Kuznets's voice reaches him from a distance, as if from the other shore. Green sparks are still floating before his eyes, blocking out a distant horizon of boundless hills jagged with spruce trees, the dark gray Angara water, the launch rocking in it, and the wooden rowboat by the shore, where a couple of soldiers are waiting.

"Saws. Knives. Kettles." Kuznets looks at Ignatov's sleepy face with its drooping eyelids. "I'm telling you, you're going to boil up fish soup."

Some sort of recollection weakly stirs in his memory.

"And grouse!" Ignatov raises a shaking finger. "And grouse in champagne sauce, is that possible?"

"It's possible." Kuznets stands up and brushes off his knees. "Sorry, but I'm not leaving provisions. You'll somehow take care of that yourselves. There's ammunition" – he kicks a small, taut sack and something clinks heavily inside – "enough for all the wild beasts in the taiga. Well, and your wretched people, too, if they don't obey. And this" – he takes a heavy, nearly full bottle from one soldier's hands – "is for you. So you're not sad at night."

Ignatov recognizes it right away. He smiles, takes it, and embraces the cool glass; the liquid splashes promisingly inside: *Thank you, brother.* Kuznets slides the gray "Case" folder between Ignatov and the bottle.

"Well, commandant," he says, "stay strong. I'll send assistance soon."

Ignatov stoops and neatly, slowly, places the bottle on the rocks, so as not to spill the treasure. The folder falls next to it.

"W-wait …" His tongue is tied, as if it's not his own. "I wanted to ask you about, to ask …"

He straightens up and looks around, but Kuznets is gone. There are just two oars gleaming in the distance. The rowboat is headed toward the launch.

"Where are you going?" Ignatov whispers in surprise. "Kuznets, where are you going?"

They're already lifting the boat onto the launch. Ignatov takes an unsteady step and his foot clangs against something: long, thin one-handed saws lying on wet burlap. Are these really *saws*? They're going to saw lumber with these flimsy things?

"Where are you going, Kuznets?" Ignatov raises a hand, waves, and takes a couple of steps along the shore.

The launch lets out a high, sustained whistle in parting. The motor sneezes and barks, then chugs evenly, and the launch turns around.

"Where are you going?" Ignatov yells, continuing to run in pursuit. "Where? Wait!"

The launch leaves, shrinking.

"Wait!" Ignatov runs into the water. "Where?"

His fingers grope wildly for the holster and tear out the revolver. A cold wave splashes into his boots. Ignatov is trudging in water up to his knees, then to his waist.

"Where've you taken us, you son of a bitch? Where?"

"Air ... air ... air ..." responds the echo, flying along the Angara in pursuit of the dark blue dot of the launch. But it's already dissolving on the horizon.

"Where? WHERE? WHERE?"

Ignatov squeezes the trigger. The shot crashes, loud and booming.

Someone behind him is sobbing, frightened. The exiles are standing on the shore, huddled together and clutching lean bundles with their things, their faces gaunt, dark. Ignatov can feel their fearful eyes boring into him – the huge eyes of pregnant Zuleikha, the peasants' gloomy stare, the lost gaze of the Leningrad remainders, and Gorelov's crazed glare.

He helplessly slaps the water with his revolver and looks up at the sky. Something small and white is floating toward him from a black cloud. Snow.

Part Three

To Live

THIRTY

When viewed from the cliffs, the Angara is plainly visible. The splendid green left shore swells steeply, like risen dough in a vat, and its bright emerald reflection falls into the river's leaden mirror. The water twists around lazily like a wide piece of heavy fabric before departing for the blueness of the horizon, toward the Yenisei. To where Kuznets's launch recently departed from.

The right shore, where the exiles have settled, spreads low and obligingly at the water's edge then boils up into a sprawling knoll, where it grows into hulking hills, and bares its cliffs like fangs. Ignatov is standing on one of those cliffs now, gazing at the taiga below. The camp isn't visible from here; it's somewhere below, deep down in the folds of the hill.

Ignatov doesn't want to see anybody, though. Up until now, he's been oddly removed from himself, taking in the situation like an onlooker. Who is that standing, clothed, in water up to his waist, brushing away snowflakes stuck to his hair? Is that really him? Who's giving orders ("Light a fire. Break branches for a shelter. Not one step away from the camp, you bastards!") then going out into the taiga to hunt? Is that really him? Who's trudging along animal trails, snapping fallen brush, and creeping up to the cliff along rocks overgrown with moss and dry grass? Is that really him?

Now he sits down on a boulder heated by the sun and squints. He feels the stone's warmth through the chill of his still-damp clothing. The fragile stubble of lichen pricks his palm. A couple of mosquitoes hover by his ear but the wind blows them aside and their buzzing departs, dissolving far away. Freshness from the large body of water floats into his nostrils along with the tart smell of the taiga: spruces, pines, larches, and various fragrant grasses. And that's how it is. He, Ivan Ignatov, is here, in Siberia. He drowned more than three hundred enemy souls in the Angara. He's been left on a knoll as commandant of a handful of half-alive anti-Soviet elements. Without foodstuffs or personnel. With an order to survive and await the arrival of the next barge.

Let's say he didn't drown them but attempted to save them. "Attempted" is a word for weaklings, according to Bakiev. A communist doesn't attempt, he does. *But I couldn't save them, couldn't! I tried my best, there was nothing else I could do. I myself nearly drowned …*

But you didn't! And they all drowned, so now they're feeding the fish on the bottom …

Would it really have been better if I'd drowned along with them? And who were they anyway? Kulaks, exploiters, enemies, a burden for the Soviet authorities. They'll multiply again, like Kuznets says …

You want to assuage your guilt with someone else's words? And whose words? Kuznets's, that son of a bitch.

Negative thoughts drive into his brain like nails, splintering it. Ignatov takes off his peaked cap, gathers his hair in his hand and pulls, as if he wants to tear it from his skull. *As you were,* he orders himself. *Busy your hands with work and your feet with walking. Exhaust, expend, and enervate the body, so as not to think. Or at least think about something else.*

He looks at the blurry, blue-gray edge of the horizon. That's where the next barge will come from. When? Soon, Kuznets promised. It took them three days to get here. Kuznets had gotten here faster in his launch, in a day. Let's say he needs a day for the return trip, a day or two for bureaucratic delays at the office and loading a new barge, then three days to return to Ignatov. A week total.

He'll have to hold out for a week.

And what if Kuznets is late? That son of a bitch won't hurry. He might well not even come for a week and a half or two weeks. Toward the end of August, maybe. And snow already came down today. It's not like summer here at all, just a ripe, cold autumn.

How far had they come from Krasnoyarsk? They'd floated two days along the Yenisei – that's about three hundred kilometers, if not more – almost an entire day going upstream along the Angara – another hundred kilometers or so. So four hundred in all. Four hundred kilometers of water travel separate him from Kuznets. And a boundless sea of taiga. Every now and then, Ignatov spotted settlements sheltered along the Yenisei's shores – he kept wondering if they were active or abandoned – but not one on the Angara. There are no people here.

He flicks angrily at a beetle that has crawled out on the blue-gray stone; it flies off into the abyss. Ignatov stands and straightens his uniform tunic, which is still damp at the hem. *Why did you get in the water then, you fool? You drenched yourself for nothing.* He should have thought it through earlier, on the boat. Grabbed that rapscallion Kuznets by the scruff, by the neck, by the hair and not let him go, not let him go for anything. Let them tie him – Ignatov – up, put him under guard, bring him to Krasnoyarsk with escorts, then reprimand him for overreaching his authority. Somehow that would be better than what he has here now.

"A week," Ignatov says sternly to the abyss gaping under him, wagging his finger. "I'm waiting exactly a week, no more. So you'd better watch out!"

The abyss is silent.

The black grouse here are pudgy and stupid. Their big, round black eyes gawk at Ignatov under fat, red arched brows and they don't fly away. He approaches to a distance of several paces and shoots them point-blank. Their soft little bodies explode in fountains of black feathers, their wings shudder belatedly, and their tufted little heads fall into the grass. And their kin are already gaping with curiosity from neighboring trees. *What happened there, what? We want to see, too. And so do we.* He's nailed six of them, the number of shells in the cylinder. He binds their little throats together with a piece of string left in his pocket and it turns out to be two hefty bundles. He goes back to the shore.

He had painstakingly noted the route from the camp. *You won't get lost if you don't go too deeply into the* urman *– the Angara's right there, next to you, everywhere – but it's possible to stray.* He thus committed to memory all the markers, whispering to himself under his breath, as if he were unwinding string. Now he's winding it back into a tight ball as he returns: from the cliff, go down along the rocky path between the boulders – some are pinkish, some are whitish-green from the soft, curly moss – to the clearing that's bright, almost as if it's balding; further through sparse pines, walking along huge, flat rocks with smatterings of grass, to a gently sloping descent; through reddish candle-like pines and black brush-like spruces, down, a long way down, to a small, round clearing where a once-huge birch, now burned by lightning, stands, with its legs awkwardly sprawling; from the birch, walk along a cold and burbling brook, descend further toward the Angara; cross the brook at the large boulder that looks like a sleeping bear and go deeper into the forest. He should soon see an opening between the trees – that's the shore, where the handful of exiles has found shelter.

Ignatov makes his way through the taiga. He strides loudly, crunching. His feet are squelching in his boots because he couldn't hold on when he was jumping across the brook, on the rocks, and had taken a spill into the water. A heavy bundle of dead birds dangles from each hand. It will be an outstanding dinner. *Here you are, citizen enemies, chow down. You'll feed yourself on grouse all week with me and eat your fill after the hungry road.*

He doesn't even notice when evening falls. A thick brown dusk suddenly settles on the taiga. It has grown sharply colder. Carefree daytime birds have gone silent, and now there are sorrowful, distant night voices calling. All the sounds – the murmur of leaves, the whisper of evergreen needles, the hum of branches in the wind – seem closer and more resonant. Even the crunch of dead wood underfoot has turned to a loud crackling.

Something large, soft, and light-colored scuds past his head with a lively hoot, fanning his face with its wings. Ignatov's stomach shudders with an unpleasant chill and he holds his breath. An owl, he understands with belated relief; he quickens his pace. Some sort of chirring, high screeches, and urgent snuffling carry from a thicket. There's a low, velvety roar somewhere far away.

So, where's the site? It feels like it should appear any minute if he just peers between the trees. Spruce, spruce, spruce … And suddenly the crazy thought flashes that he'll come out on the familiar shore but nobody will be there. Not one person; they're dead, every one. What if all of them – green-eyed Zuleikha and the pathetic Leningraders and the bootlicking Gorelov – drowned there, in the middle of the Angara along with the barge? And only he, Ignatov, is left among the living? And only he was abandoned here on the deserted shore?

He breaks into a run. There's a deafening crack underfoot and then something gets into his eyes, hitting his cheeks. One foot lands in a hole, the other catches a dead branch. He nearly falls but stays on his feet. He runs faster. He thrusts his elbows forward to protect his face from branches. The grouse are suddenly getting heavy and large, as if they've been swelling along the way.

Finally there's an orange flame flickering between the tree trunks. Ignatov bounds forward a couple of times and runs out to the clearing by the river. He's panting and his heart is pounding, either from fear or from running so fast. And there they are, the people; they haven't gone anywhere. Some are finishing building a shelter under the branches of a huge, sprawling spruce and others are swarming around the fire. He slows his pace and calms his labored breathing. Without hurrying, he approaches the women crouched by the fire and casually flings the grouse, which are still warm, at their feet.

As the women busy themselves with supper, Ignatov decides to finish up an unpleasant but necessary task. It concerns the shabby gray "Case" folder mottled at the top with muddy-purplish rectangular stamps and seals, which contains within its gaunt depths all the bitter history of their long journey. He needs to cross out all the departed.

He takes the folder and sits by the fire. He imagines flinging it into the flames and it flaring up instantly, flapping its pages as if it were alive, writhing, blackening, and shrinking, dissolving in the hot yellow tongues and disappearing in the black sky as light smoke. Leaving no smell, no trace at all.

He can't. He's the commandant here, so he has to keep order. Which means having a precise list on hand with the names of all the camp's residents. Or is it more correct to call them prisoners? But what kind of prisoners are they if their only guard is a commandant in wet jodhpurs with a single revolver? He decides to stick with what he's accustomed to. The exiles.

He uses a stick to remove a couple of burning embers from the fire. He waits for them to cool. Then he grasps the end of the longer, sturdier piece — it feels greasy to the touch. He takes a breath and decisively opens the folder. In Ignatov's gray, tong-like fingers, covered with brownish spots and blotches, are four wrinkled sheets, yellowed by time. The paper is rough in places, where water and snow dropped on it, and the corners are tattered and torn. The fifth sheet, underneath, and in better condition, lists the Leningrad remainders. Some eight hundred names in total, scattered in slightly crooked columns that dance recklessly across the pages. Black pencil lines run just as cheerily, diagonally crossing out more than half the surnames. In the semidarkness by the fire, the sheets are reminiscent of a finely embroidered towel.

He begins with the easiest, the Leningraders. He crossed off a couple of the fifteen or so names long ago, while they were still on the road; the rest won't need to be because they're all here. Those "remainders" foisted on him at the beginning of the journey have turned out to be surprisingly hardy. You'd expect that with the social degenerates, Gorelov being the sort who can adapt anywhere, change his colors to any hue, switch sides to whomever he needs, latch on, gnaw through a couple of throats, and survive. But the intelligentsia! Polite to the point of leaving a bitter taste, sometimes cheeky when speaking, but also timid, listless, and submissive in their actions. Pathetic. And *alive* – unlike many peasants, who hadn't withstood illness and hunger. So there are your "remainders." Kuznets was taken in by their pale look, too, and selected them for his launch as the most emaciated, infirm, and incapable of escape. Basically, Leningrad was lucky.

Ignatov's gaze runs through the surnames, checking them with the faces around him.

Ikonnikov, Ilya Petrovich. There he is, dragging a gnarled, nearly bare spruce branch. (*Where're you carrying that, you blockhead? A branch like that isn't fit for a shelter. It won't protect from the rain.*) He's obviously clueless, unaccustomed and unsuited to labor, weak of body, and spineless. Someone like this won't go on the run or incite rebellion; he's not dangerous. Gorelov reported that Ikonnikov is a famous artist, drew Lenin for posters. That's something; he drew revolutionary posters but ended up here. There must be a reason why.

Sumlinsky, Konstantin Arnoldovich. A quiet little old man, good-natured. He's fussing by one of the shelters, waving his arms around. He's trying (*nice job, Gramps*) even though he's a scholar, either a geographer or an agronomist. Of course there won't be much use for him but his zeal pleases Ignatov for some reason; it warms his heart. This one's not dangerous, either.

Brzhostovskaya-Sumlinskaya, Izabella Leopoldovna (her papa bestowed quite the surname and patronymic here!) is his wife. She's sitting by the fire next to Ignatov, attempting to pluck a bird. Her slender fingers – dry, translucent skin stretched over bones – grasp helplessly at resilient grouse feathers that are apparently extremely stubborn. *You'll croak from hunger before you can deal with it, you old bag.* This haughty personage has pretension in every gesture and her tongue is intemperate. Gorelov complained that she berates the authorities, but he can't communicate the exact words because the criticism's in French. Sneaky, clever. But this decrepit cobra has nothing beyond cleverness and a sharp tongue. So she's not dangerous.

Gorelov, Vasily Kuzmich. He's found himself a long stick and is swinging it as if it were a baton, simultaneously taking command of the building sites for all three shelters. He's strolling from site to site, poking with his stick, shouting so loudly it makes the ears ring. The rascal appointed himself boss. Everything's obvious about this one. A most repugnant and loathsome character, the sort Ignatov would have gladly crushed in his normal life. Here, though, he needs to associate with him. On the road, Ignatov constantly summoned the minders from the railroad cars to see him, questioning them about the mood, and Gorelov was the fiercest, most obsequious speaker of all. Whoever's strongest is the master for this dog. He'll lick your hand and wag his tail as long as you're in power and have a revolver, but he'll bite or even tear out your throat if you ease up for a minute. This one's dangerous.

And so Ignatov gradually reaches the end of the Leningrad list. Several of them are either school teachers or university instructors, and there's a print shop worker, a bank employee, a couple of factory engineers or mechanics, a housewife, and a couple of people lacking specific occupations (social parasites, ulcers on the body of society), and goodness knows how a milliner wormed her way into this society. Basically, odds and ends, moth-eaten old folks who've been stored away, history's dust. Other than Gorelov, not one is dangerous.

Now comes the more complex task of sorting out the dekulakized. First find all those alive on the list and mark them, then cross out the rest.

The small Tatar woman, Zuleikha, is kneeling just a few steps from Ignatov, dressing the grouse he shot. He finds her name on the sheet and circles it with the charcoal. The line comes out bold and fat, densely black. Like her brows, he thinks. He scrutinized her face well then, in the water. No, he hadn't just scrutinized it, he'd memorized it, learned it by rote. He'd kept peering: *Is she alive? Breathing? Not too tired?* He couldn't allow her to die. Her life seemed to him to be the only forgiveness for the others, who were destroyed. When he saw her being lifted onto the launch and laid on the deck, he felt such sudden exhaustion he could have died, but only one thing was in his head: *I saved her, I saved her, pulled her out, led her, dragged her the whole way.* A mean thought flashes: *Do you think that will be taken into account? I let three hundred go to the bottom and pulled one out. I'm quite the savior, there's no denying it ...*

As you were, Ignatov commands himself, tiredly, already habit-ually. *As you were and back to work.*

And so. *Avdei Bogar*, one-armed. An invalid but works quickly, deftly laying branches on the shelter's roof, telling the others what to do as he points his finger. *Well, now there's one who's actually leading the construction!* They obey him, nod. Obviously a sensible guy. His eyes are keen and tenacious, and they're constantly lowered around Ignatov, as if he fears Ignatov will see something in them and figure him out. This one might be dangerous. The others will listen to someone like this even though he only has one arm.

Lukka Chindykov, a red-bearded Chuvash, is pottering around near Bogar. Chindykov is unprepossessing; it's as if all of him leans and lists to one side, plus he's desperately ugly. He lost his whole family along the way and is scared to death, haggard, and confused. Even now he's looking around wildly, as if he doesn't understand where he is. A broken person, not dangerous.

Musa-hadji Yunusov's white beard hovers close by. He is as thin and flat as a reed. At the beginning of the journey, there was a blindingly white turban glowing around his head, but then it disappeared somewhere, possibly used as rags. Ignatov smirks as he imagines Yunusov sawing spruce branches in his glowing turban. Yunusov's face is always bright and detached – he's thinking already about the eternal, not the earthly. That's exactly why he's a hadji. Also not dangerous.

Leila Gabriidze, a plump Georgian woman, short of breath …

As he peers into their faces, Ignatov recalls the names of everyone working in the camp. He finds them on the list, circles them with the charcoal, and counts again. There are twenty-nine people, including the Leningraders. Russians, Tatars, a couple of Chuvash, three Mordvins, a Mari woman, a Ukrainian man, a Georgian woman, and a German man whose mind is gone and has the fanciful and sonorous name *Volf Karlovich Leibe*. In short, an entire international organization. Ignatov crosses out the rest. As he draws the coal along shabby sheets that look greasy from wear, he tries not to look at the surnames. Toward the end, his fingers are black and almost velvety, leaving bold round marks on the paper.

As soon as the job's finished, Ignatov jumps up from the log with a start and swiftly walks to the riverside. He wants to wash it off his hands as quickly as possible. He wants to breathe in the cold river air. He wants very much to smoke.

Zuleikha has adjusted to plucking birds with a large sliver of spruce – of course a knife would be better but both knives are in use at the shelter construction site. The work can be done with a suitable piece of wood, though. Her mother was right when she said that head and hands are the most important tools for any work. Zuleikha holds the sliver firmly in her hand and quickly pulls the feathers from the bird's soft, pliant body, pinching them between the wood and her thumb. First come the long, firm ones, the contour feathers, then the smaller, softer ones. The carcasses haven't had a chance to cool yet and they pluck nicely, willingly.

Izabella is right beside Zuleikha. The two of them – the pregnant woman and the oldest woman – were assigned the role of fire tenders and cooks. The others are assembling shelters and arranging the camp.

"Zuleikha, my dear, I'm afraid I can't keep pace with you." Izabella is watching, bewildered, as the sliver of spruce flashes so quickly in the air it almost dissolves.

"Gather the feathers instead," says Zuleikha. "They'll come in handy."

She's pleased she can do this work better. It's good to be useful. Her conscience would bother her if she just sat by the fire and added wood while everyone else was working. But going back and forth between the camp and the spruce forest for branches would have been difficult for Zuleikha as her belly has grown heavier since swimming in the Angara; it's as if it had swelled with lead. The baby is constantly moving and fidgeting, her own legs are very weak, and her forehead sweats. A couple of times Zuleikha has felt something start to hurt down in her belly – a cramping, aching, and churning – and she's begun praying to herself, thinking she's going into labor. But they turned out to be false alarms.

Murtaza's gift of poisoned sugar flowed off into the Angara. This means she'll give birth no matter how much she fears the outcome. She will endure if Allah sends her the death of yet another child. The Almighty's will is sometimes capricious and incomprehensible to the earthly mind. Of all the traveling companions on the deadly barge, she was the only one Providence left among the living. More than that, it sent her husband's killer, the arrogant and dangerous Red Hordesman Ignatov, to save her. Perhaps Fate wants her to live?

Zuleikha felt a tremendous happiness, the likes of which she'd never experienced, when Ignatov's distorted face suddenly flashed beside her in a furious whirl of spray after she'd been tossed up from the water's depths to the surface. She was shuddering from wheezing and coughing, and almost choked. She'd never been that glad to see her husband, may the deceased Murtaza forgive her those thoughts. She's had time to think about how Ignatov might have swum past, not noticed her, or not wanted to save her; but there he was, already next to her, helping and calming. She wouldn't have been surprised if he had dragged her under by the braids and drowned her, but he held her, held her firmly, saying something, even joking. When it became obvious she couldn't swim to shore, he didn't start cursing and didn't abandon her. He saved her.

If a savior turns out to be a good person, one should probably kneel before him and shower his hand with kisses. If Murtaza were alive, he would have endowed that person with rich gifts. If the mullah were alive, Zuleikha would have requested that he say a prayer of thanks in her savior's honor. She has none of those "ifs." She has only herself and the harsh, unapproachable Ignatov. He's sitting next to the fire, scrawling something in his papers with charcoal, frowning, and clenching his jaw. Zuleikha simply wants to say thank you, but she doesn't dare interrupt his thoughts. Soon he exhales, abruptly and angrily, slams the folder shut, and goes off to the riverside.

Zuleikha threads the plucked carcasses on a long stick and they sear over the fire. It's already completely dark when she sets to cutting the meat into pieces and the exiles settle in around the fire, one by one, to wait for dinner after they've finished their work. Their nostrils hungrily inhale the sweetish smell of singed feathers.

They had enough time to build three shelters under a canopy of wide-boughed spruces. The large tree branches served as a beam on which to lay, crosswise, sizable shaggy boughs with slightly thinner branches over them; the same boughs were used for bedding. Someone proposed tossing birch branches and armfuls of grass on the tree needles inside the shelters for softness, but they didn't have either the energy or the time for that. They prepared firewood for the night, bringing over a mountain of brushwood and fallen dead wood. There was no axe and the large branches had to be sawed. The one-handed saws squealed, bent, jerked, and broke free from unaccustomed hands; it was awkward to work with them but the exiles somehow prevailed and cut up the wood. Before dark, they dragged logs from the thicket and arranged them around the fire. Now they're all squeezed together on the logs, propping each other up with chilly shoulders and warming themselves, their mouths releasing shaggy clouds of steam. It cools towards evening.

A large bucket on two flat rocks at the center of the fire is sending out steam and waiting for meat. Zuleikha tosses generous pieces of the birds into the bubbling water and the inviting smell of food floats over the fire and flies up into a black velvet sky with stars like large beads.

"Such illumination," Ikonnikov quietly says, extending work-worn hands with a couple of fresh cuts toward the orange fire. "It's pure Rembrandt."

"It's meat," Gorelov corrects him, surprisingly kindly, blinking oily eyes that are riveted on the bucket with the soup. "Meat."

The others are silent. Their sunken eyes gleam in the darkness and their pinched-looking faces, with sharp, angular features, flare in the light of the sparks.

Zuleikha sprinkles half a handful of salt in the bucket and stirs the concoction every now and then with a long stick. It will be a thick soup, hearty. Her stomach is shuddering from the anticipation of food. She hasn't had meat in half a year and she's ready to eat the raw meat right now, pulling it out of the boiling broth with her bare hands. It seems as if everyone sitting around the fire is experiencing the same thing. Saliva pours into the mouth, flooding the tongue. The stick knocks against the sides of the bucket. Branches crackle in the fire. A long howl sounds somewhere far away.

"Wolves?" asks one of the city dwellers.

"On the other shore," answers one of the village dwellers.

Footsteps sound and Ignatov emerges from the darkness. People move, freeing up a spot. They'd felt like they were sitting very close together, but after the commandant comes and takes a seat on the logs, there's so much space around him it seems like five people must have got up.

Ignatov takes something loose and jingling out of his pocket and tosses it on his palms: cartridges.

"This," he says, as if he's continuing a conversation begun long ago, "is for anyone who wants to escape." Two fingers pick up a round cartridge that's blazing like gold in the firelight.

He inserts it in the revolver's cylinder – the cartridge slips in softly, with a gentle sound, like a kiss.

"This" – he raises a second cartridge – "is for anyone who tries to start a counterrevolution."

The second cartridge enters the cylinder.

"And these" – Ignatov inserts four more – "are for anyone who disobeys my orders."

He spins the cylinder. The even metal clicking isn't loud but it can be heard distinctly above the crackling of the fire.

"Is that clear to everyone?"

The soup is gurgling desperately, bubbling over the brim. It needs to be stirred but Zuleikha is afraid to interrupt the commandant's speech.

"Count yourselves off, one at a time," commands Ignatov.

"One," answers Gorelov, as lively as if he's been waiting only for those words.

"Two," another chimes in.

"Three."

"Four."

Many peasants don't know how to count and the city dwellers help, counting for them; they lose track, start the count again, and somehow finally manage to do it.

"Citizen chief!" Gorelov leaps from his spot, sticks out his chest, and points his splayed hand at his shaggy head. "A detachment of migrants numbering twenty-nine persons –"

"As you were!" Ignatov makes a face and Gorelov plops back down on the log, offended. "So, a total of twenty-nine heads," he says, looking around at gaunt, creased faces with prominent cheekbones, hollowed cheeks.

"What do you mean?" says Izabella's soft voice. "Counting you, citizen chief, it's thirty."

Zuleikha looks down quickly, expecting a shout or at least a reprimand. Quiet again hangs over the fire, crackling and hotly snapping with sparks.

Ignatov is still looking at Izabella when Zuleikha dares glance up. *Glory be to Allah*. It seems to have passed. Zuleikha exhales noiselessly, raises herself up a little, and extends the stick to stir the soup in the bucket. The baby awakens in her belly at that moment and begins tearing her to pieces inside. She wants to shout but it's as if there's no air in her chest and her throat is constricted, making it hard to breathe. She sinks to her knees and falls backward. She's seeing stars.

"Looks like these people are already starting to … reproduce," says Gorelov, sounding bewildered and somehow very distant.

"Boil some water or something!" comes Ignatov's anxious voice.

"I think it's best for the men to leave us." This is Izabella.

"We'll freeze to death without the fire. What, you think we've never seen a woman give birth …"

And then there are other voices and shouts, but they gradually float away, float far away, merge, and disappear. Or maybe she's the one floating away, carried upon waves of overwhelming pain? The stars are growing; they come closer, and crackle loudly. Or is that the fire crackling? Yes, yes, it's the fire. It blazes up and sears the eyes, engulfs her; Zuleikha closes her eyelids tightly and escapes, tumbling into a deep and silent blackness.

CHILDBIRTH

Volf Karlovich Leibe has been living in an egg.

It developed around him on its own over many years, possibly even decades ago, though he'd never troubled himself with counting because time didn't pass inside the egg so had no meaning.

He remembers when its iridescent top first began shining – it was something like a halo or an umbrella – over his vulnerable bald spot. That happened a short while after the October Coup. Professor Leibe had just walked out onto Voskresenskaya Street, pushing very hard to open one side of a massive, shiny, varnished oak door at Kazan University; the uniformed doorman by the main entrance had already been gone for several weeks, for the first time since the day the educational institution opened in 1804. Through a forest of white columns, Volf Karlovich saw a crowd running. People were screaming and falling, and behind them galloping horsemen were shooting them, point-blank. He didn't manage to discern if these were newly minted insurgents with red armbands on their sleeves or simply the bandits who had multiplied in Kazan by that time. The people they were firing on were civilians, though: a peasant woman in a checked headscarf with a basket (the basket fell and eggs rolled along the road, breaking into star-shaped yellow blots); a woman in a frivolous lacy turban; a couple of ungainly grammar school students in green uniforms;

and some beggar with a dog on a raggedy rope leash (a shot pierced the dog and the beggar kept dragging its shaggy body behind him, not letting go) ...

The crowd was already tearing past, shouting incessantly, so Volf Karlovich didn't manage to duck back under the cover of the university walls. The woman in the turban suddenly cried out and raised her hands theatrically, embracing one of the columns, slowly sliding down it. She was so close that Leibe could have touched her with his hand. He sensed an astringent aroma of perfume blended with the light, slightly bitter smell of sweat. The crowd and the horsemen in pursuit hurtled on, toward the kremlin, but the woman kept sinking slowly downward, leaving a long, glistening red trail on a column that had once been snow-white but was now covered in a web of cracks and speckled with shots.

The professor rushed to her and turned her face upward. He recognized her as a patient he'd recently operated on, gallbladder removal. He hurried to take her pulse, though he knew from her glassy pupils that she was dead. Have mercy, how could she be dead? What about the complex five-hour operation? The sixth cholecystectomy in his life and so successful, no complications. This woman still wanted to have children, certainly boys. And her husband wanted that. After she'd been released from the university clinic, her husband sent a ridiculously large bouquet of lilies as thanks; Leibe had to put them out on the balcony so their scent wouldn't intoxicate the department. And now here she was herself: lying there, smelling like lilies. And dead.

Volf Karlovich pulled a handkerchief from his breast pocket and started rubbing the long red stain on the column. The stain didn't wipe off, it only spread under the rough motions of his strong surgeon's hands. People soon appeared, carried off bodies scattered on the road, and led the professor away. And he kept thinking that the woman had died, granted, and you couldn't return her to life, but couldn't this stain at least be wiped away?

As he approached the university the next morning, he wondered if they'd managed to wash it off. It turned out there had been other things to do. The stain gaped on the white column like an open, bleeding wound. The next day, too. And the day after.

He changed his route and started making a big detour so as to approach the university from the other side, by walking via Rybnoryadskaya Street. The stain taunted the professor, though. It was as if it crept around the column and leapt into his eyes, throwing its arms wide open for an embrace no matter how he approached the building. The stain smelled of blood and death, screaming, "I'm still here!"

Leibe attempted to convince the university steward to whitewash the column. The steward just smirked unkindly and shook his head because war isn't the best time for repairs. Leibe went to the rector and argued that blood on the snow-white face of a cathedral of knowledge profanes the lofty idea of education. Dormidontov half-listened, nodding absentmindedly. The next day, the university's main entrance was locked and a sign greeted professors and students: "The university is closed temporarily, until further notice." Volf Karlovich never saw the rector himself again. And the stain remained.

Unable to bear it, one night Leibe went to the closed building with a wet rag and bucket he'd stolen from Grunya and attempted to scrub the column with soap and water. But during the time that had passed, the blood had indelibly eaten into the whitewash. The stain had faded slightly but hadn't gone away. Utterly enraged, Volf Karlovich hurled the heavy bucket at the column in a fit of desperate powerlessness. The bucket's sharp rim struck the column's smooth shaft, knocking out a piece of plaster about the size of a hand and lining its white surface with a sharp-toothed lightning bolt of cracks.

It was at that moment that it appeared for the first time. It started shining gently and iridescently over the professor like a thin hemisphere the size of Grunya's little bowl for straining *tvorog*. Bright, lightweight, and exceptionally comfortable-looking, it was only asking to be tried on like a hat. Intrigued, Leibe was not against that. When he permitted himself to extend his neck ever so slightly, the egg sensed that, neared, and lowered itself on the top of his head. A soft warmth spilled from his crown down to his cheeks, chin, and the back of his head, then further, along his neck and over his chest and his legs. And then everything suddenly began to feel piercingly calm and bright for the professor, as if he'd returned to his mother's womb. As if there weren't a war, either next to him on the street, in his country, or anywhere else in the world. There was no fear. There wasn't even sorrow.

The egg was almost transparent, with a touch of light iridescence. Through its shining walls, which reached to chin level, Leibe saw the square in front of the university gleaming with cleanliness under golden sunbeams, leisurely students smiling deferentially at him, and absolutely smooth columns glimmering with unsullied whitewash. There was no bloodstain.

"*Mein Gott*," Volf Karlovich whispered from gratitude, and headed home, cautiously carrying the egg on his head.

The egg nearly blew away a couple of times but little by little the professor learned to control it. Each time a gust of wind swooped in, Leibe applied his will and the egg remained on the top of his head by reading his thoughts and obeying his wishes.

It turned out that the egg was extraordinarily intelligent. It let in sounds and images that were pleasant for the professor and tightly blocked everything that might cause him even the slightest anxiety. So life all of a sudden became good.

"You're in a cheery mood," panted Grunya as she polished the floors in the hallway with thick wax from her old prerevolutionary supplies.

"It's spring!" The professor smiled significantly and flirtatiously, holding back from swatting her haunch, which was hoisted up steeply. He had never permitted himself this sort of thing with the servants but now his blood was suddenly racing.

"They knifed another three, at the lake, you hear about that? Gracious Lord, all is at Your will," said Grunya, crossing herself without raising her flushed face, as she focused on floorboards that gleamed with a heavy, oily sheen.

"Yes, yes, a wonderful day," muttered Leibe, retiring to his office.

Neighbors who'd gone mad from fear, incessant rallies on the streets, endless detachments of servicemen in the city, gunfights, nighttime fires, more frequent murders at Black Lake, Red Guardsmen and Czechs in the White Army giving ground to one another multiple times in the city, riffraff and poverty spilling out of every crevice, and frenzied profiteers who'd occupied the Tatar capital – all this had ceased frightening or annoying Leibe. Because he didn't see them.

The professor wasn't perturbed in the slightest when, under a decree from the Council of People's Commissars that was approved in August 1918 "On the rights of acceptance to institutions of higher learning," it wasn't impertinent and haughty students in dandyish green uniform jackets who surged to the university (which was finally re-opened) but rather peasants and workers of both genders who were young and not very young. Most of them had no elementary or secondary education and were, simply put, illiterate. Leibe walked into a lecture hall stuffed full of newly minted students who were loudly blowing their noses and scratching themselves. He shoved his way to the front, stepping on people's boots, bast shoes, bare feet, baskets of food, bundles, and peaked caps. He stood at the blackboard, smiled meekly, and began speaking of the cyclical changes of the endometrium of the human uterus.

Leibe didn't raise an eyebrow when a new method of assessment was established in place of traditional individual exams (which the Red student body weren't unaccustomed to). He obligingly received the confused and blushing representative of a student group who held out a heap of examination papers and mumbled an unintelligible answer to each question, confusing "adenosis" and "atheism," sincerely attributing "hirsutism" to a little-known offshoot of Christianity, and, with spirited indignation, pushing "menarche" into the same family of words as "monarchy," something contrary to the representative's proletarian consciousness. Each time, the professor would nod approval and mark a grade of "satisfactory" in all the exam papers. This "rotational method" assumed one test taker and one collective grade for all.

His colleagues – who had formerly carried the titles of "meritorious," "ordinary," and "extraordinary" professors, but were intermingled by this time into one frightened human medley under the general and anonymous name "teaching staff," without any distinctions in titles or degrees – were astounded at the changes that had occurred in him. Rumors soon began spreading around the university ("Professor Leibe – how shall I put this kindly? – is not quite himself."). But Professor Leibe's mental state was the least of the worries for the rectors, who were replacing one another in those years at a truly revolutionary, cavalry speed.

The rectors didn't concern Professor Leibe, either. Thanks to the egg, he simply didn't notice them. He met only those he wanted to see at general gatherings that took place every now and then. In the university's large hall, which glimmered with thousands of candles and a mirror-like parquet floor, friendly rector Dormidontov smiled at him from the presidium's table as before, bearded philanthropists nodded importantly from their places in the auditorium, and the sovereign emperor squinted, fatherlike, from a claret-colored gilded armchair in the front row, spoiling this deserving educational institute with his fairly frequent visits. Professor Leibe was likely the only one who continued toiling at Imperial Kazan University. All his colleagues had long since moved on to serving at Kazan State University.

And that's how the egg was.

The professor ended up having to renounce his practice because of the egg. It turned out that the egg and practical medicine were absolutely incompatible. Delivering a lecture or discussing diagnoses was possible even with the shell on his head. But examining a patient certainly required its removal because the professor couldn't see disease through its thick, merciful walls, instead noting a patient who was extremely well fed and brimming with health.

Leibe initially attempted to engage in a balancing act by taking off the shell for a couple of minutes during an examination then hurriedly putting it back on again, then taking it off again during a follow-up examination. He conducted operations without the egg, but this became genuine torture for him because Volf Karlovich's psyche, which had become pampered, was wounded by seemingly innocuous remarks made by student observers or those assisting the doctor during the operations. It was in this extraordinary manner that a profession that had previously granted enjoyment and delight unexpectedly became the cause of pain and suffering.

Volf Karlovich quickly sensed that the egg didn't like this sort of juggling. The egg became lackluster and its shine grew sad and dimmed after yet more rounds at the clinic where it was repeatedly removed from the professor's head and then replaced. Leibe was even frightened one time after an operation when he noticed hairline fractures on the egg's smooth surface, but his alarm turned out to be unfounded. He had only to wear the egg without removing it for several days for the fractures to heal. The problem, however, was obvious: the egg was forcing him to make a choice.

The professor chose in favor of the egg. He renounced his practice at the clinic and stopped receiving patients at home. A short while later he left the university department, too, without the slightest regret, since teaching no longer brought as much joy as observing an ideal world through the merciful shell. The grateful egg helped Leibe expunge everything unpleasant from the present as well as the past. His memory was cleared of what was painful and foul, and what had passed became just as bright and cloudless as the present. His own notion was that he remained a respected professor and a practicing surgeon who was successful and in demand. He was of the constant, joyful conviction that he had conducted his latest operation yesterday and would deliver his next lecture tomorrow.

Leibe didn't notice the changes at his own apartment: loud residents who'd been assigned living quarters and were supplemented by numerous progeny, the disappearance of the greater part of the family silver and furniture, the absence of heating in winter and the switching off of the gas lamps. He lived without leaving his father's office and he directed the skimpy remnants of his emotional warmth toward his beloved and selfless friend, his one and only faithful companion, the precious egg.

Sometimes he would wake up at night in fear. Had the egg gone away? No, the egg had not gone away. To the contrary, it gradually grew and strengthened, fitting ever more closely on its host and becoming one with him. Walls had grown out of its fairly flat crest – first down to the chest, later to the waist – so now Leibe was more solidly and dependably shut off from the surrounding world. Apparently the egg would soon grow out along the entire length of his body and close up. The professor did not know what would happen after that. Absolute happiness would likely ensue.

From time to time, however, moments did arise that forced Leibe to, well, not to remove the egg, no, but to thrust the tip of his nose out from under the shell for a short while and glance at the true world. Some sort of restless little bell occasionally dinged, high-pitched and alarming, in a little corner of his consciousness. The professor would look around in surprise, thrusting his head out from under the large, dependable egg dome as if he were a turtle that had awakened. *What is this? What happened?* Most often, the stubborn little bell summoned him to patients. After peering out for an instant, Leibe would see the patient, grow frightened, and immediately pull his head back. But his tenacious brain had already managed to make an initial diagnosis or advance a couple of hypotheses, and then the flywheel of debate would begin to spin. "Stop!" the professor would command himself. And he would try to bury recollections of those moments somewhere in out-of-the-way parts of his memory as quickly as possible. He wished he could have ripped from his head that unbearable little bell that disturbed his peace but he didn't know where it was located. With time, however, the ringing sounded more rarely and he hoped it would soon abate forever.

The professor and the egg were happy together. Their joint life flowed along, evenly and unhurried, just as inexorably as a billiard ball directed by skilled hands rolls into a pocket. And then, suddenly – the cue's hard counterblow! – there was the indelicate visit of a young personage in a rapturous state who was, by all appearances, suffering from infertility. This event marked a change in direction for his joint existence with the egg, and Leibe's life unexpectedly became more varied and full, though no less pleasant. After tiring out a little in his seclusion, the professor enjoyed the changes, observing them through the egg's solid, transparent walls, which by this time already came to knee level.

The university sent a smart automobile with glistening black finish and chrome handles for him. The interior was stupendously soft and the ride was both smooth and swift.

During the time Leibe was absent from Imperial Kazan University, the building itself had undergone considerable renovations and was nearly unrecognizable. The professor's experienced eye divined in the harsh new lines of the architecture the remnants of details and contours that were of the past and very dear to his heart: the bend of a formal staircase, a half-removed bas-relief of a two-headed eagle on a wall, the festive patterned layout of a parquet floor, and a crystal chandelier that flashed inside a doorway.

The students who now accompanied him everywhere were unfailingly polite and spoke little. This modest reticence, which was moving to the point of tears, touched him more than anything, because these students were no match for their impertinent, talkative predecessors, who were ready to express their point of view on the tiniest question or enter an argument for the paltriest of reasons. Their businesslike concentration struck him, too. The students hurried along marble stairs and long corridors so energetically, even desperately, that it was as if they were ready to explode from the craving for knowledge that overflowed in them. It turned out that green student uniform jackets had been exchanged for gray jackets with horizontal patches on the chest and broad collar tabs where the students wore distinguishing badges, apparently in accordance with their course of study or achievements. Professors' uniforms were now gray, too. Nobody, however, reproached Volf Karlovich for his dark blue uniform of the old design, which made him very grateful to the new leadership.

Leibe met the rector that day. A certain Butylkin, whose appearance was rather simple and who was overly direct in conversation but charming, you couldn't take that away from him. Beyond that, he turned out to be quite a Germanophile, holding lengthy conversations with Leibe about German politics and economics. They became fairly close on that basis and Leibe was sincerely sorry to leave the hospitable walls of his alma mater when duty called him to head up a large military hospital.

They drove him along Voskresenskaya Street to a hospital situated right by the kremlin and the descent toward Black Lake, and the edge of his building flashed through the automobile window on the way. Leibe sighed yet again about his good fortune to have Grunya. She'd look after the apartment while he worked on matters of state importance.

During a lengthy excursion through endless hospital corridors, the quartermaster announced that the hospital entrusted to him had huge, even strategic, significance. "I ask that you not worry, gentleman officer," Leibe assured him. "I will do everything within my power." And he kept his promise, taking up residence right away in one of the hospital departments so as not to waste time on trips home, since he would disappear into the operating room for days at a time. He didn't ask himself who was now fighting whom; that was of little interest to him. His concern was to operate, to pull patients from the deadly abyss and not allow life to abandon weak bodies mangled by gunshots. Volf Karlovich fought on the side of life.

Not one to bear open admiration and flattery, the professor was forced to endure the ecstatic gazes of one of the medical nurses who often watched him with a long, wide-eyed stare – he could clearly see the black pupils dilate in the depths of her green eyes. It's possible she was in love with him. There would not have been anything unusual in that, since female assistants and nurses often fall in love with surgeons during operations. Lengthy stints alongside one another, practically forehead-to-forehead, and the maximal exertion of physical and mental energies all cause strong, uncontrollable flares of vivid emotions that a young, inexperienced heart can easily take for deep feelings among team members who operate together.

Shortly thereafter, the command decided to transport the hospital to the rear and appoint Leibe the director of the special train. Trembling with emotion and pride, he agreed. Fourteen railroad cars were entrusted to his care. Five of them held the seriously wounded, six had people with wounds of moderate and light severity, one contained an operation room and triage, and one was a pharmacy combined with a utility area. The train's staff and guards were located in a separate car. Leibe was rarely in his own compartment, sleeping there only in fits and starts, collapsing on a mattress and dropping into a deep slumber. His work required twenty-four hours a day. He was working like the devil. He lived for his work.

The special train hurtled through blazing forests and steppes burned to the ground, and over tempestuous rivers, crossing bridges that smoked and exploded behind it. His face black with soot and his hair disheveled, Leibe raced through the railroad cars like a winged demon, giving commands, scolding negligent male nurses, offering advice to the general practitioners, and cheering up patients. He would pop into the operation room like a whirlwind, like a flash of lightning, and then the doctors would sigh with relief, the orderlies would smile, the patients would stop yelling, and the green-eyed nurse's timid doe-like eyes would look up at him.

He'd noticed long ago that she was pregnant. The despicable little bell's offensive ring had called him to the real world one time and, based on the nurse's appearance, the professor's experienced eye had picked up special signs of future motherhood that were thus far elusive for the rest. Leibe even announced this to his negligent student, Chernov, who came to visit one time, catching up with the special train to retake a medical school examination. The conversation with Chernov brought Leibe no pleasure since the professor didn't like students whose eyes showed no readiness to give themselves over to medicine as passionately and selflessly as he himself.

One time, the special train was captured by the enemy army and the professor's fatherly, work-weary hand blessed several dozen passengers' escape from captivity to search for their people and deliver a message written in Leibe's hand requesting the train's liberation. The operation was successful and the train was soon taken back from the enemy. Leibe even spilled a solitary tear when the liberated train set off to run the rails again, headed toward danger and adventure.

This was when he noticed that during his glorious journey the egg had begun growing at a speed hitherto unprecedented. Its walls had thickened and strengthened so much that they could probably withstand a strong strike. Their transparency had taken on a much stronger iridescent tinge that slightly distorted his peripheral vision, though their luminescence had become bright and powerful. The egg already nearly touched the floor, fully covering Leibe to his toes, so it had become extremely challenging to peer out from underneath it when the little bell called. Each night before bed, the professor thought with a soulful tingle about the morning he would awaken to discover the egg's walls had joined underneath the soles of his feet.

Meanwhile, the war was picking up speed. At the front, the heroic professor was steeped in deserved glory and then sent on a new assignment, commanding a naval flotilla in the murky yellow waters of eastern seas.

"I am not an admiral, I am merely a professor of medicine," he said, listlessly resisting and chilled at the presentiment of grandiose assignments, which he simultaneously feared and desired. "I don't even know how to shoot."

"Nobody but you can handle it," the adjutant answered confidently, narrowing his gray eyes in respect and pointing a firm hand at the shining gangway.

A gangway gleaming with a thousand scrubbed cleats soared up to a huge snow-white liner bristling with the steel muzzles of weapons. At the swing of the adjutant's glove, a brass band of one hundred instruments festively struck up a tune on shore. A chorus of three hundred select dogs joined in with the melody, barking with such feeling and harmony that Leibe's soul trembled. He made his decision, stepped onto the gangway, and began walking up, to the deafening applause of the crowd remaining on dry land. After climbing up to the liner, he suddenly realized that they needed to shoot from onboard the ship at those very people, the ones making the rapturous ovation.

"Hold on," he muttered to the adjutant, who followed unceasingly at his heels, "this is happening very hastily, as if everything's on fire."

"Soon, professor, soon!" said the adjutant, revealing sugar-like teeth in his smile and ordering, "Fire!"

"Let me catch my breath," said Leibe, stalling for time and backing away.

"Fire!" insisted the adjutant.

"Your ship's bells are ringing over there," he said, attempting to distract the relentless adjutant.

"Fire!" the other shouted as loudly as a donkey at a Sunday bazaar. "Fire and your damned egg will finally close up! Isn't that what you wanted?"

The ship's bells truly were ringing, though.

But this isn't the ship's bells at all. This is the professor's little bell. For the first time, Leibe is glad about the ringing, which is usually unwelcome. He crouches. He lifts the egg's dome slightly and it's as heavy as a stone. He pokes his head out, leaving the liner, the bad-tempered adjutant, and the people (who continued applauding deafeningly) inside the shell.

He needs to catch his breath for a couple of seconds. His heart is pounding erratically. And it's cold outside. It's night and an orange fire is crackling. People are bustling around him.

"They've started ... reproducing," mutters one.

"Boil some water or something," shouts a second.

"I think it's best for the men to leave us," says a female voice.

"We'll freeze to death without the fire," says a bass voice. "What, you think we've never seen a woman give birth ..."

The maternity patient is lying with her face tilted up toward the sky, moaning quietly. Moaning in a bad way, Volf Karlovich understands. Weakened. She'll lose consciousness soon. When childbirth begins, a woman should shout in anger, from the depths of her soul. She could use some smelling salts under her nose right now.

The egg's heavy, warm dome presses at his spine. It quivers slightly, calling him back inside. *Right away*, thinks the professor, *right away. I'll just tell them to give her smelling salts and bring her to the clinic immediately.*

The maternity patient raises herself slightly on her elbows, turns her face toward the fire with her eyes wide open, as if she's searching for someone's gaze, and falls on her back again. Why, it's that very same nurse from the special train, the green-eyed one, the one in love! How did she end up here in the woods, surrounded by strange people? And Volf Karlovich himself, how did he land here? What nonsense. It's time, time to return home to the egg.

He's already begun lifting the bulky edge of the merciful dome to duck inside when he has a sudden thought that her eyes have been searching for him! Leibe freezes with indecision then casts one more glance at the woman after all. And he feels himself beginning to anger.

The maternity patient moans again, very quietly, wheezing slightly. Her feet are scraping along the ground as if they're looking for something to prop against, and her belly is shuddering sharply – it's large and overly broad at the bottom so the child is apparently lying sideways. She can't give birth to that baby on her own.

"What the devil!" Leibe cries out loudly and distinctly. "To a clinic, immediately! What, don't you realize the full seriousness of the situation?"

A dozen eyes are gawking at him with such surprise that it's as if he's speaking a foreign tongue or crowing like a rooster.

"There's nowhere to go," says a tall man in a military uniform, uttering each syllable individually, gingerly, and cautiously. He bears a resemblance to the professor's adjutant from inside the egg. "This is the clinic," he says.

This is the clinic? Well, this is just …

Leibe stands and looks around, dissatisfied. The forlorn egg remains hanging in the air behind him. In his fit of indignation, the professor doesn't notice.

And what if this really is the clinic? He's never once seen a clinic without walls or a ceiling. Where the medical staff are dressed in tatters and so muddle-headed they can't lay the maternity patient down properly. Where the operating room is lighted by a campfire instead of a bright gas light. He's spent so much time in the egg, though, that maybe customs have changed outside and people have become barbarous. It doesn't appear that the high military officer is either joking or misleading him – this is not the time for that. The devil take it – this apparently really is the clinic, no matter how improbable that seemed at first glance.

The egg floats up behind him and affectionately touches his back as if to say, "I'm here, I'm waiting." The maternity patient mumbles quietly and lets her head drop to one side; a strand of saliva falls from her mouth. That is not good at all. Leibe abruptly pushes away the egg: *A little later, I'm busy.*

"Why is it dark in the operating room?" he sternly asks the bearded old man in the torn shirt standing next to him.

The people around him are quiet and continue staring at him with astounded eyes. Quite the medical staff. Who the devil knows what they are …

"I asked for light in the operating room!" Volf Karlovich commands, a half a tone louder and harsher.

Some elderly nurse with a high hairstyle hastily flings an armload of spruce branches on the fire. A sheaf of sparks soars up, and it becomes lighter and hotter. At least there's one sensible worker to be found in this herd of blockheads. The professor hurriedly rolls up the sleeves of his uniform and addresses only the sensible nurse:

"Hands."

Blinking in astonishment, she presents him with a bucket of warm water from the fire. People help her, lifting the bucket higher and painstakingly pouring water on the hands the professor has placed under it. Leibe frenziedly rubs his hands together. There's neither soap nor lye; truly only the devil knows what this is.

"Disinfection."

A murky liquid smelling sharply of alcohol pours out of a large, rounded bottle onto his hands.

"Smelling salts." He's reciting things over his shoulder, carefully bathing his hands in the generous, strong-smelling stream. "Bandages, lots of bandages. Cotton wool. Warm and hot water. Scalpels and clamps, sterilized in flame. The maternity patient should be placed with her feet absolutely toward the light. Onlookers must leave the operating room."

What am I doing here? is the despairing thought rushing around somewhere at the edge of his consciousness. Operating room, maternity patient, bandages – what silliness. The egg is already tired of waiting over there; it's shining impatiently, even shaking. It's time, it's time to go there. But Volf Karlovich is too occupied to listen to all his thoughts. When he's standing by the operating table, he hears only the patient's body. And his own hands.

He's already kneeling by the woman, who's prostrate on the ground. His fingers are warming, filling with a taut, joyful keenness. His hands do everything on their own, even before he manages to mentally give them orders. They fall on the living, swaying mountain of her belly so that his right hand is on the hard bulge of the fetus's head, the left on its trembling little feet. Transverse presentation, the devil with it. He'll need to remove the fetus before the uterus tears. From somewhere the words surface, like a long-forgotten prayer: *Do I have the right? I do not have the right not to attempt.* Joy, some sort of youthful elation, suddenly grips him. Leibe pants a little and tears at his collar. And right then, like a bucketful of icy water: *But I haven't operated in a long time. How many years, five? Ten? So much time lost,* mein Gott ...

Left without any attention, the egg is rubbing more insistently against his back. The professor just jerks his shoulder as if to say: *Whoever's there, I beseech you, not now.* He casts back a heap of skirts and moves apart the maternity patient's paper-white legs, which resist weakly. *Just as I thought: the uterus is fully open.* It's ready to release the child and its large, dark hole is gaping like a wide-open mouth in the fire's bright light. The child is writhing inside, though, incapable of turning around and coming out of the maternal womb.

Leibe places his hand in the warm and slippery opening, first two fingers, then his entire hand. The woman moans. He's putting her on his hand as if she were a puppet. He extends his hand inside the uterus, groping at something delicate, taut, and filled: the amniotic sac. It's good luck that it's intact, because that means the fetus is still in the water and still moving around. *And now I need …*

He feels something poking, demanding and hard, at the base of his neck, between his shoulder blades, along his spine. He casts a sidelong glance over his shoulder: it's the egg, blast it. He abruptly pushes it away with his shoulder: *I told you, later! I need to lance the sac now.* He bends his index finger and scratches the surface with a piercing motion. Warm fluid immediately surrounds his hand. It's thick to the touch, the amniotic water. The sac has burst. Leibe's fingers touch something velvety, slippery, and moving. The child. It's time to take it out. *So, my dear, where's your little leg?*

Something envelops Volf Karlovich from behind, softly yet strongly. He turns around. The egg, which has lifted its dome over the ground and turned its base toward Leibe, has attached itself to his back like a huge pulsating sucker that wants to imbibe. His hands are occupied so he can't pick it off himself and toss it further away. He jerks his back and shoulders heavily, as if he's shaking off a predatory wild animal that's grasped the nape of his neck. A faint, low-pitched humming floats from the egg; something inside it is shouting, whistling, and whimpering. *I have time*, thinks Leibe. *I have time.*

So, where do we have that little foot? His fingers grope at a tiny paw with little splayed digits, four facing in one direction, the fifth facing in the other: it's a small hand. *Your foot, little one, give me your foot!*

Leibe feels the egg pulling him in, harder with every second. Its warm, slippery edges envelop his shoulders and neck, settling on the back of his head. All he has to do is manage to pull out the child. When the baby is fully liberated from the mother's womb, even the most muddle-headed nurses can finish the job by cutting the umbilical cord and seeing that the placenta has been expelled. He needs only to succeed in pulling the child out.

Another paw. All five little digits on this one are facing in the same direction. *Bravo, little one! Thank you. Now let's verify if this is the upper or lower leg. I certainly need the upper one, so you don't catch your chin on the pubic symphysis when I pull you outside.*

The edge of the egg is settling on Leibe's forehead, creeping toward his eyes, and reaching his brows. He squeezes his eyes shut and works by feel after sensing the egg's slippery mass engulf his eyes, forcing them shut. *You stupid egg, you think my eyes are smarter than my hands?*

Leibe's fingers creep up along the baby's tiny leg and reach a rounded little belly. Meaning this leg's the lower one after all. *Give me the other leg, little one.*

The egg has now fully possessed Leibe's head, after slipping itself on like a thick stocking. The professor feels warm slime in his mouth and a heavy, rotten smell in his nose; there's an even chomping sound in his ears coming from the egg's vibrating walls. He senses its edges creeping toward his neck. *It's decided to suffocate me*, he belatedly understands, *for betrayal.*

His hand has already found the second leg, though. *This is the one we need, the upper one. This is the one we'll pull.* Leibe places his thumb along the baby's thigh and his four fingers around it. *And now we'll pull and pull. Come on, little one, work, turn around so the back of your head faces up. Come out …*

The edges of the egg extend to the professor's Adam's apple and suddenly tense, filling with strength, and hardening as if they want to rip Leibe's head from his body. Just a few seconds more …

One baby leg is already outside, tightly clasped in Leibe's hand. The second is coming out on its own, right into the professor's other hand. A sharp turn and a downward motion, pulling the baby out to the corners of the shoulder blades. One arm, a second arm. And a small head.

His throat feels tight, his eyes go dark, and some kind of light bulbs flare and extinguish in his brain, one after another. *And that's that*, thinks Volf Karlovich, squeezing the baby's slippery little body in his hands. *I made it.*

The newborn opens its mouth and screams for the first time, at the very moment the edges of the egg begin quickly and implacably tightening. The baby screams so hard that even the professor can hear it in the egg's innards, though he's weakened and half-choked. The scream swells, resounding and filling with strength, and then the egg suddenly bursts on Leibe's head like an overfilled balloon. Shards of the shell, scraps of membrane, pieces of slime, and heavy spray fly everywhere. Volf Karlovich coughs and wheezes, inhaling air with a whistle. His lungs are breathing again, his eyes see, and his ears hear. After recovering his breath, he looks around, seeking out the remnants of the exploded egg, but there aren't any.

A bright-pink baby is bellowing in his arms.

Later, Leibe goes down to the Angara. The inky sky to the east is tinged a delicate blue and pale pink. Dawn is near. A black wave splashes as quietly as a whisper. It's delightfully empty and clear inside his head, and his body is light and young. His ears are like a wild animal's, discerning the slightest sounds: the murmur of stones under his feet, a fish tail hitting somewhere in the middle of the river, the noise of spruces in the forest, and the high squeak of a bat. And all kinds of smells – a large body of water, wet grass, earth – swarm in his nostrils.

Leibe sits down by the water and bathes his hands. Either his sharpened vision is noticing or he's imagining thick, dark blood washing from his fingers and going into the opaque water. He rubs his hands hard until they're icy-white, until the joints crack. There's a rustling close by, and it's the commandant, sitting on the rocks next to him.

"So what happened there?" he asks.

"It turned out to be a boy!" Leibe says emphatically, raising a sharp, long finger.

Ignatov exhales with a gasp and pulls his peaked cap over his face.

"Imagine," says Leibe, speaking cheerfully, quickly, and freely. "Baby Yuzuf! Just think about that, here, in this damned backwood – Zuleikha and Yuzuf. How about that, eh!"

He looks at the commandant's hat-covered face and grunts, flustered.

"Tell me," Ignatov says, taking off the hat and pointing his face into the faintest breath of a breeze. "Without you, would she have … ? I mean, she wouldn't …"

A wolverine yelps, muted, on the other shore.

"Do you often think about the 'what ifs'?" Leibe shakes off his hands and an unseen sprinkle flies from his fingers into water as black as tar.

"No."

"And that's the right thing." Leibe stands and looks at his own hands, so white in the darkness. "There's only what there is. Only what there is."

He walks back to the camp. He stops on the slope and turns to say, "We left you some soup. Eat."

Only the fire sentry is dozing when Ignatov climbs up to the knoll. Everyone else has dispersed to the shelters to sleep. He takes the gray folder from a pile of things and opens it, not even noticing the smell of meat coming from the pot, which is still warm. On an empty corner he writes with the charcoal in large, crooked, slanting letters: "Yuzuf."

THE FIRST WINTER

Ignatov wakes up an hour later with the thought that they should dig an underground house. Everyone's still asleep and sounds of snoring and someone's groans carry from the shelters. Impatient birds expecting daybreak occasionally call out in the thicket and a wave splashes lazily at the shore. Realizing that sleep has left him for good, Ignatov decides to go down to the river to wash.

They'll get by for a week in the shelters. They won't just melt away, he convinces himself, sitting on stones at the riverside and furiously wiping his face with icy Angara water. *And then when Kuznets comes, they can even put up two-story wooden mansions if they want. Without me!*

And if they have to get by for two weeks? Or longer? After all, nature here knows no calendar and winter could even descend in September.

He looks at the Angara's flawlessly smooth, mirror-like surface breathing with an almost invisible morning fog. A transparent blue sky gleams to the east, waiting for the sun. It will be a hot day, sultry. There's such quiet that the sound of drops falling from Ignatov's face are audible. He looks down. A gloomy, unshaven face with black circles under the eyes gazes out of the water. His beard will soon grow out, as the exiles' have, and they'll become indistinguishable. Ignatov slaps his palm at his reflection, which shatters into small pieces and disperses in circles.

Ignatov takes his peaked hat, which he'd set aside on the rocks, and puts it on. They'll start digging an underground house today. They can't sit around the whole week with nothing to do.

His exacting gaze examines their site as if he's looking for the first time. The Angara takes a smooth bend at the place where they landed and the shore seems to jut out, forming a broad, gently sloping promontory. The earth by the water is dense and clayey, with lots of large and small rocks mixed in. It spreads low, then flares up into the spacious knoll where they've now made their camp. A good place, the proper one. Not right next to the water (where the river's coolness would chill their shelters) but still close enough to the Angara that it's not far to run for water. It's inconvenient, though, since the descent from the knoll is steep and crumbly. Ignatov decides they'll need to make steps out of rocks.

The knoll itself is so wide that an entire village could fit on it. It faces the river and a dense line of spruce trees borders its back. Jagged spruce tops rise upward, forming a wall; the forest is clambering up the high hill. The cliff from which Ignatov observed his surroundings yesterday protrudes somewhere there, too, up high, but it's not visible from the shore. Several lanky, broad-boughed spruces are scattered along the knoll, which is covered with bushes and waist-high grass. It's as if the trees ran out of the forest toward the river but just froze there. The tattered shelters stand like large, green nestled haystacks under three of them. Two shelters are already tipping to one side, their shaggy roofs a little disheveled; but one still stands evenly and tidily. Ignatov notices it's the shelter that one-armed Avdei built.

The tools and other items Kuznets left are lying in a messy heap by the fire. Kuznets had apparently scraped together everything that was on the boat, either the remains of his own supplies or surplus from someone else's stockpile of goods. There's a sizable but depleted box of matches (they need to be used sparingly; being left without fire would be trouble); a sack and a half of salt (they could salt all the animals in the taiga and then all the fish in the Angara on top of that); a scruffy clump of nets all tangled up with hooks, ropes, floats, and wires whose intended uses Ignatov doesn't understand; a generous armful of thin, flimsy one-handed saws (Kuznets should be forced to saw firewood with those himself!); a couple of sturdy fisherman's knives and kettles blackened with soot; several buckets and ropes rolled into coils; the half-empty bottle of home brew; and a bulky sack with revolver cartridges. That's all. Well then, thank you for that. Ignatov pulls his cap a little lower, right down to his eyebrows.

They need a large, spacious underground house that holds everybody. It will be crowded, but it will be warm. And for him to have everyone in sight will make things easier. He'll appoint Avdei head of building and Gorelov to keep order. The majority of them will be busy with construction and the rest will be sent into the forest once a day to prepare firewood. They'll always have one person in charge of the fire, not allowing it to go out under any circumstances. Everyone is to work, men and women, with no exceptions for age. Rest strictly during breaks. Unauthorized absences in the forest forbidden. Criticism, complaints, and other troublemaking conversations to be cut short immediately. All violations of procedures will be punished with loss of food privileges. Ignatov himself will go hunting again and bag as many black grouse as he can. He'll examine the taiga more carefully as he does. He'll take the sack of cartridges with him – he's decided to hide it in the forest so none of the exiles get any nasty ideas into their heads.

He pulls his revolver from the holster and pounds the handle on a bucket standing by the fire: *Time to get up, you sons of bitches! Get to work!* The loud tinny sound of the alarm carries over the sleepy clearing. Birds go silent in the forest. The shelters shudder and shake as frantically as anthills when the frightened exiles crawl out, pushing each other and looking around wildly.

There you go. He's not going to spoil anybody by letting them break the rules.

Avdei turns out to be a surprisingly sensible and skilled guy. He builds the underground house as if he's been doing this his whole life. He sends all the men into the forest to get logs for the framework. He keeps the women with him for digging – without any negotiations, they've appointed Zuleikha as ongoing cook and keeper of the fire, until the baby gets stronger. Avdei finds a suitable place and drives in four tall pegs to form the corners of a long rectangle, carefully measuring the distance with string. He uses a stick to draw in the outline. That's the base.

They neatly cut out the sod and set it aside; it will come in handy. They begin digging, poking around with sticks, rocks, and hands, whatever works for them. Seeing that the job isn't going well, Avdei proposes they pull blades from a few saws and use them to scrape at the ground. The work starts moving faster as some scrape and poke, while others use kettles to remove the softened earth and throw it away outside. They finish in two days, digging out a pit so deep that the whole of stocky Avdei, including his head, can get fully inside when he goes down there. Not even his shiny bald pate sticks out of the ground. Wielding a homemade plumb line made from stone attached to a string, Avdei painstakingly evens the walls, smoothing in some spots with his hand. *Lick it with your tongue, too*, Ignatov thinks angrily. He's been urging, hurrying, and swearing at them, wary of rain that could halt work and flood the pit. The days have been dry and warm thus far, though, so the weather isn't impeding them.

Cursing the one-handed saws, the men somehow prepare and haul logs to the camp. The stronger ones saw the wood, the weaker ones strip off branches and bark. A couple of days later, everybody's hands are calloused and covered in red spots from splinters and squiggly scratches, and their backs and shoulders ache unbearably.

They lower logs into the pit and begin lining the walls. They drive in fat logs, horizontally along the perimeter, laying long beams behind them, all the way up to the very ceiling, as a retaining wall. They stuff the wall's crevices with pieces of spruce so earth won't sprinkle in.

"Braces, girders, supports, purlins, rafters, joists ..." Ikonnikov mutters under his breath, vigorously knocking on the top of a log with a heavy stone to force it into the ground. "But oh, has my vocabulary been enriched."

"The main thing is the experience," puffs Konstantin Arnoldovich alongside him, placing spiky spruce branches in the gap between the retaining wall and the earthen wall. "How your practical experience has been enriched, colleague! It's one thing to paint clouds and fields of wheat on the walls at some cultural center and something else entirely to build a real house. Don't you find that?"

"A house?" Ikonnikov is looking at half a fat pink worm sticking out of the ground. "Well, I suppose!"

"You are intending to live here," says Konstantin Arnoldovich, gasping slightly for breath. He wipes his sweaty forehead with his hand and looks up questioningly. Green spruce needles gleam playfully in his narrow beard, which has grown out in a half-year. "Or aren't you?"

Sinking support poles for the roof's ridge beam turns out to be a difficult and unexpectedly lengthy task because the soil becomes dense and rocky, and the holes for the posts just don't want to reach the proper depth. Wary of clouds swooping in from the north, Ignatov demands they continue working and embed the posts in the resulting shallow holes, but Avdei displays an unexpected rigidity.

"I was hired to dig an underground house, not a grave," he says, tugging his sparse blue-gray beard with his only hand and looking out from under his brow at the commandant. "If you've decided to bury us, commissar, then there's the pit, it's ready. No need for us to wear ourselves out more here."

Ignatov backs off. They just manage to dig down to the required depth for the holes, embed the supports, strengthen them with stakes, and reinforce them with stones.

Overhead they lay a long log as a purlin and secure it with rope. On that they place poles as rafters, smoothing them at the joints with stones for stability. For the roof covering they decide to take spruce branches from the shelters, which have already collapsed by this point. They place boughs across the rafters, constantly strewing earth and cementing them with clay that Avdei spent half the day searching for before finally finding what he needs – the clay is thick, black, and dense to the touch.

The arrival of the clay brings out an unusual liveliness among some of the builders. The previously apathetic Ikonnikov suddenly becomes cheerful and excited, and his eyes start glistening. He keeps tilting his head toward Konstantin Arnoldovich, who's flushed with pleasure, and Ikonnikov shows him something in his hands, then they explode in fits of loud, irrepressible laughter. No matter how he tries, Gorelov can't determine the reason for their jollity. Each time he sidles up to them, he sees only small clumps of clay in Ikonnikov's hands.

They place two layers of sod on top of the triangular roof so the first layer has its roots up and the second has its roots down. From front and back, the underground house now resembles a small hill rising out of the ground.

That's the first night they spend in the half-finished underground house. They sleep poorly, freezing terribly, either from the dampness of the deep-set earthen floor that's still completely uncovered, or because autumn is approaching so relentlessly with every passing day. In the morning, many are coughing and the Georgian woman with the aristocratic name Leila has come down with a fever. They decide to assemble a stove before finishing construction, and the women are sent down to the riverside to find large stones suitable for the purpose. Leibe asks Ignatov's permission to go into the forest to collect medicinal herbs and Ignatov squints at the pale professor in his absurd dress uniform, which is torn to shreds in places, and agrees.

A very basic stone stove, with a chimney, rises up in the middle of the underground house. It's like a magical vessel, an Aladdin's lamp that fulfills only one wish, albeit the most important, giving warmth. While they're at it, they fortify the path down to the river with large flat rocks, making it more convenient to go for water. Gorelov now hums a song about stone stairways each time he goes down to the Angara. He always puts his hands in his pockets as he goes, holding his chin high, slightly tilted.

It requires a few more days to lay the floor, construct the bunks, and complete the exposed sides of the house at each end of the roof: one has an entrance burrowing down to the doorway and a vestibule below. They've just finished digging small drainage channels along the sloping roof when a persistent rain begins to fall.

In the evening the exiles sit, huddled together in the dark and still rather damp underground house. "In a couple of days it'll be baking inside and dry out," Avdei promises. They aren't warm but it's not very cold, either. They haven't managed to eat even once today but a bucket of black grouse meat is already bubbling on the stove. Their faces have darkened in the sun, become weather-beaten, and been covered with blistering mosquito bites. Some have no strength left and are already asleep, their heads laid on a neighbor's shoulder, while others watch the bucket of soup with a fixed stare. The stove drones and there's a strong smell of smoke, half-raw meat, and the herbs the professor gathered. All their simple belongings – tools, buckets, tackle, and bundles of clothing – are piled up in the corner. The loud beat of heavy rain carries through thin little windows formed by gaps between the house's roof and side walls.

"What good fortune that we're under a roof," Izabella loudly says. "And have matches and salt and everything else … Thank you, Avdei. You simply saved us."

Ignatov is lying on his bunk, which was built at some distance from the others, and he's gloomily thinking about how they haven't been able to prepare enough firewood. What they have will only last through the night. If the bad weather continues until morning, they'll be forced to go into the forest in the rain.

The seventh day of their stay on the riverbank is ending.

A son.

She's given birth to a son for the first time in her life and he's tiny, completely red, and by all appearances premature. When the professor held out the newborn to her – still wet, slippery, and covered in her own blood – she placed him to herself, under her smock, clasped him to her breast, and pressed her face to the top of a head as soft as bread, and felt the rapid beating of his heart on her lips. The soft spot on the crown of infants' heads isn't usually large, only the size of a coin, but it was huge, hot, and greedily pulsating on this child.

She instantly sensed that he was very beautiful, even before she could make out the child's face in the night darkness. Eyelashes stuck together in clumps of dried mucus, half-blind cloudy little eyes, neat nose holes peering up, the small pleat of a mouth always open partway, wrinkled, flat little clumps of ears, and thread-like fingers without nails stuck together – all that was beautiful, bringing tingling and butterflies to her stomach.

She looked him over more closely at dawn. A large head the size of a man's fist. Small legs gnarled like a frog's and slightly fatter than her fingers. A rounded belly like an egg. Thin little bones showing through so much in places that it seemed an incautious touch could break them. His skin was creased, bright-purple with marbled light- and dark-blue blotches of veins, as soft to the touch as a flower petal, and covered in places by wispy dark hairs. He was the most beautiful of all the children she had given birth to. And he was still living.

Zuleikha decided to simply carry him on her chest, on her bare body under her smock. She didn't sleep the first night. She kept clasping him to herself with all her might and then relaxing her arms, fearing she'd squeeze too hard. She kept opening the edge of her smock a little to let her son breathe fresh air, then closing it when the air seemed much too cold. In the morning she felt as fresh and strong as if there'd been neither childbirth nor sleepless pre-dawn hours. She could have sat like that for another year, warming the tiny little body with her own heat and listening to his weak, barely discernible breathing. In the morning she adjusted herself to carry him by arranging her newborn's head between breasts swelled with milk, spreading his little body over her belly, and then binding him to herself with a rag. Then she could move around and even do her work while her son was always with her. She kept bending her face to the unfastened buttons on her chest, peering into her slightly opened smock collar and listening. The child was breathing.

She feeds him often, a lot each time. Glory be to Allah that the milk stands so high and taut in her breasts; just watch it doesn't spurt. Sometimes her breasts fill so much that they harden, pulling at her shoulders. She doesn't wait then; she hurriedly thrusts a swollen nipple oozing white drops into his mouth, not waiting for the child to wake up; but the baby smacks his lips without opening his sleepy eyes and latches on. When he takes a liking to feeding, he sucks greedily and quickly, moaning, and her breast empties and shrinks, feeling more comfortable for a while.

Zuleikha is glad when the child urinates and she feels something hot and wet on her belly because this person is living, his little body is working. She is even ready to kiss the spot on her dress and the pink squiggle of male flesh between her son's tiny little legs.

As before, she constantly wants to eat. The forest unexpectedly bestows a lot of fatty meat upon them. When she catches sight of Ignatov's tall figure at the forest's edge with a colorful bunch of killed birds in his hand, she restrains herself from shouting, running out to greet him, and kissing his hand. *Food has come! Food!* She plucks the birds fiercely, in a frenzy; guts them, fighting the saliva gushing in her mouth; flings them in boiling water, then salts, stirs, and casts a spell over the fire to burn hotter, stronger, faster.

Gorelov had wanted to take the food allocation into his own hands here, too, but Ignatov sullenly looked at him and nodded at Zuleikha, saying to let her serve. She pours the prepared soup from the large bucket into kettles that are slightly smaller, and the exiles sit in several circles, grasping scorching hot pieces of poultry in their hands, and tearing it with their teeth, dirtying their smiling faces with fat and soot. After dispensing with the meat, they gulp down broth from the kettles using spoons made from shells attached to sticks. They leave a double portion for Zuleikha and she isn't embarrassed. She eats it up quickly and gratefully, sensing that the meat now in her gut is already filling her blood with strength and her breasts with milk. She doesn't like soft bird rumps or thick grouse skin covered on the inside with layers of fat, but she eats them so her milk will be fatty and hearty.

She stops thinking about everything unrelated to her son: about Murtaza, who remains somewhere far behind in her past life (she has forgotten that the newborn is the fruit of his seed); about the Vampire Hag with her scary prophecies; and about her daughters' graves. She doesn't think about where Fate has cast her and what will happen tomorrow. Only the present day is important, only this moment, with quiet snuffling on her breast and the heaviness and warmth of her son's little body on her belly. She has even stopped fearing that one morning she won't hear weak breathing inside the opening of her smock. She knows that if her son's life is interrupted, then her heart will instantly stop, too. This knowledge sustains her, filling her with strength and some sort of unfamiliar courage.

She has started praying faster and more infrequently, as if in passing. It is frightening to admit, but a thought that is essentially sinful and horrifying has settled in her head: what if the Almighty has suddenly become so busy with other matters that He's forgotten about these thirty hungry, raggedy people in the wilderness of Siberia's *urman*? What if He turned his stern gaze away from the exiles for a little while and then lost them on the boundless expanses of the taiga? Or (this is possible, too) that they have floated off to such a distant place at the edge of the earth that the All-Powerful's gaze doesn't reach because there is no need. This offers Zuleikha the strange and wild hope that perhaps Allah – who has taken four children away from her and is apparently intending to take away the fifth – won't notice them, that He will overlook them and forget the disappearance of a pitiful handful of creatures worn out from suffering. She can't forgo praying completely (that would be scary!) but she tries to utter her prayers quietly, whispering, or even only muttering them to herself so as not to attract attention from on high.

Surprisingly, she is content during these days, with some sort of incomprehensible, fragile, and fleeting happiness. Her body freezes at night, suffers from heat and mosquito bites during the day, and her stomach demands food, but her soul sings and her heart beats with one name. *Yuzuf.*

Kuznets hasn't come, not one week after the exiles came ashore, not two.

Ignatov goes to the cliff each morning, cursing himself for doing it, but unable to keep away. His hands cling to the rough ledges of boulders edged in coarse, blue-gray lichen as he clambers to the top, rapidly on clear, dry days and cautiously on rainy, cloudy days, constantly slipping on the wet rocks. He'll stand for a long time, resting his gaze on the edge of the firmament where the river and sky come together and flow into one another. He'll wait. Then he'll abruptly turn and go hunting.

There's no explanation for what's happening. Maybe there's been trouble with the launch and it's vanished in the Angara's waters, following the *Clara*? Maybe Kuznets has come down with typhus and is lying delirious on an infirmary bed, pouring out hot sweat. Maybe (and Ignatov likes this version most of all) Kuznets has turned out to be an enemy of Soviet power and has been taken into custody and sentenced. Maybe he's even been shot?

Sometimes when Ignatov is on that peak, he'll think he can discern the dot of the launch in the blue distance. Some evenings, when he's already lying on his separate bunk in the underground house, he'll suddenly leap up and run to the shore because he's distinctly heard the sound of a rattling motor and anxious voices. At those moments, he's prepared to forgive Kuznets for the endless days of waiting and the hunger and cold of the weeks that have passed, to embrace Kuznets and slap him on the shoulders, saying, "We'd grown tired of waiting for you, brother." But that exciting instant would pass when the dot on the horizon dispersed, dissolving into the blue of an expanse of sky or water, when the roar of the motor turned into a drake quacking, and the voices became splashing water.

The exiles see his concern and probably guess at the reasons but they don't ask anything. Only Gorelov, the scoundrel, once asked, conspiratorially narrowing his Kalmyk eyes at Ignatov, "Comrade boss, what do you think, will the launch bring reinforcements of gals? We only have old women in the camp, after all – there's nobody to have a little stroll to the forest with." Ignatov didn't reply and just looked coldly at Gorelov. *You*, he corrected him mentally, *you have only old women.* The swine had gobbled down lots of meat and now he wanted broads. As if he had everything else and it pleased or suited him. One time Ignatov heard someone in the forest saying, "It's time, let's go home." That was jarring. Did anyone really, truly consider this crowded, stuffy underground house with its lopsided little stove that looked like a fat-bellied toad to be a home? They'd quickly grown accustomed to it, resigned themselves. Ignatov can't, though, and he hates Kuznets all the more with each day of waiting. The malice – muffled and confused – would rise in him, and he'd brandish his revolver as he shot at defenseless grouse. *There you go! Die, you bastards!*

The taiga birds quickly recognized the predator in Ignatov and a close death in the thundering shots. They have become more careful. They flap their soft black wings in fear and take flight as soon as they hear his footsteps. It has become more difficult to bring back food. The time of easy procurement has ended and the time for genuine hunting has come.

Ignatov has never hunted in his life. *I hunted for Denikin's men*, he gloomily jokes to himself as he makes his way through thickets in search of any kind of animal suitable for food. *And the Czechs who fought for the White Army, and the Basmachi. But not wild game – there was no need.* Now he wanders the forest for entire days, his hand holding a loaded revolver in front of himself, his eyes scanning for edible targets. Chipmunks' striped little backs blaze between bushes, squirrels streak in tree branches like reddish flashes, mice of various colors dart underfoot, and unfamiliar gray-and-yellow birds with fancy ornate tufts scamper up and down tree trunks. It's a shame to waste cartridges on such small prey. He needs something larger, heftier, like a deer or five grouse. But his stride is too heavy and loud, so neither Siberian deer nor roe deer nor any other large wild animals cross his path. It chills Ignatov's heart a little to think he could encounter prey more powerful than himself – a bear or a boar – and he doesn't know if his small revolver's bullet could pierce a thick hide. Toward evening, when his eyes are already flickering from constant strain and his feet throb and ache, he usually somehow manages (after missing a few times and wasting about five cartridges) to shoot down a couple of squirrels or some grouse that lost its vigilance. Sometimes he's lucky. Once he came out by a forest lake hiding among pleat-like hills and shot an entire family of beavers, whose meat turned out to be surprisingly tender and juicy, and another time he shot down a pair of ducks flying over the taiga. But their rations are becoming more meager with each day.

In the evening of the final day of summer, 1930 (Konstantin Arnoldovich is keeping a calendar on the wall of the underground house, sawing out a tiny notch in a log each day, a short one on a weekday, a slightly longer one on weekends, and the longest at the end of the month, so the exiles can keep track) they are in the house discussing the question of foodstuffs after a thin supper of an old, lame, and extraordinarily tough badger.

Ignatov is lying on his bunk with his eyes wearily half-closed. He sees fiery squirrel pelts, finely quivering pine needles, and zigzagging spruce branches among splashes of sunspots that are all breaking and falling away as if they were in a kaleidoscope. He listens in on the exiles' quiet conversation through his drowsiness.

There are no hunters to be found among them (and even if there had been, Ignatov smirks to himself, they wouldn't have received firearms) but one fisherman has turned up, the red-bearded Lukka, who's as puny as an adolescent, all rumpled, worn down like a sliver of soap, and toothless. They ask Lukka if he could catch fish tomorrow and they lay out for him the tackle that Kuznets left behind. Lukka speaks Russian poorly but immediately understands what's required of him. Without looking at the tangle of tackle and hooks on the floor, he answers in a small voice that crackles like a fire, "I need to look at the river, to listen and speak with it. Then to wait. If it gives, there will be fish. If not, there will be no fish."

They send the diplomatic Konstantin Arnoldovich to Ignatov's bunk to negotiate with the commandant and request permission to excuse Lukka from his labor obligations for a couple of days so he could fish. At Ignatov's instruction, all the exiles have been preparing firewood from morning until night and have had no right whatsoever to be absent.

"Let him," says Ignatov, not opening his eyes or waiting for Konstantin Arnoldovich to choose his words and state the overall request. "Let him go. I'll give him two days for those conversations. If he doesn't bring fish, then he'll work it all off by sawing wood for me at night."

The next day, Lukka catches horseflies and assembles fishing rods. He walks along the shore a while and has a talk with the Angara. In the evening he brings to camp a bucket with hefty silver fish bodies that quiver between velvety green burdock leaves. This is very welcome because it's the first day Ignatov returns from hunting empty-handed.

September greets them with sun, breathing yellow and red on the hills. The sky turns entirely blue, making the earth's colors look even warmer and cheerier. The days are dry, clear, and crisp, but the nights are already cold and winterishly long.

Gnats come.

There's no escaping them. The mosquitoes and deerflies that the exiles had previously thought were the taiga's harsh punishment for invading its territory have disappeared, yielding their place to their smaller brothers. The gnats swoop in like a cloud, like fog, filling the taiga, clearing, shore, and the underground house. They cram in under clothing, into folds of skin, the nose, mouth, ears, hair, and eyes. People eat them up with their food (they turn out to taste sweet, like berries) and inhale them with air. They are the air itself.

A person can run from deerflies and swat mosquitoes. But tiny gnats the size of a grain of sand? People swell from the bites (the gnats leave large, bleeding lesions) and lose their minds from the incessant itching on their bodies. Those with the strength swing their arms and legs or run along the riverbank like madmen – the running blows the midges off their skin – and some bathe arms and legs they've scratched raw in the icy Angara water. Yet others smoke themselves in the pungent smoke of a fire, which causes violent coughing and reddens eyes but rescues them a bit from the insects. Work is at a standstill because nobody can even contemplate going for firewood or game in the depths of the forest, where the cloud of midges has come from.

They'll eat us alive, Ignatov thinks absent-mindedly as he plunges puffy hands covered with bold red dots into transparent and impossibly cold water. His hands go numb, either from the cold or from the bites. He senses someone standing behind him and turns to see Leibe. His lips are swollen and protrude like a camel's, and his eyes are tiny because of his puffy pink eyelids.

"Pitch," he says, "we need birch pitch. It's a well-known insecticide. It's just that I don't know the method for preparing this pitch. It's usually sold in pharmacies, in glass vials, thirty-two kopeks each."

The peasant men know a method for preparing it. They immediately equip themselves to go for birch bark and strip all the birches near the clearing from top to bottom. They heap the bark in a kettle, cover it with a bucket, and surround it with firewood. They smoke the bark for a long time, right until sunset. The resulting liquid, which is as thick as honey and absolutely black, gets mixed with water and smeared over them from head to toe. They look dark-skinned, with only their eyes and their teeth gleaming white. The venerable Musa-hadji looks most hilarious of all since he had no desire to smear his beard with pitch like the other men, so it glows like a white flag on his glossy face, which resembles a generously polished boot.

The gnats retreat and the exiles are able to get some sleep that night.

For Yuzuf's tender skin, Leibe suggests that Zuleikha mix the pitch with breast milk. From that day on, the title of "doctor" fastens itself to Leibe in her mind.

After mid-September has passed, Ignatov begins thinking about whether to prepare an expedition to Krasnoyarsk.

The exiles have settled in and made themselves at home during the past month. The underground house – where the stove burns hot and never goes out – has dried from within and thoroughly baked. Following Avdei's advice, they've constructed wood piles in stacks on tall stones around the house: the firewood lies in circles, one circle on top of another, forming high towers. Someone proposed covering their tops with spruce boughs but Avdei forbade it because the firewood would rot.

Each morning, even before sunrise, Ignatov knocks his revolver on the bottom of an empty bucket to raise the camp for work. Grumbling and coughing, the sleepy inmates head out for firewood under Gorelov's supervision. Ignatov sets a daily quota for wood processing and nobody dares return to camp until it's fulfilled. One time they tried, complaining of cold, rainy weather. Without saying a word, Ignatov grabbed the bucket with the supper Zuleikha had prepared and flung the contents in the Angara. The quota has been rigorously fulfilled since then, and people crawl into camp worn out, barely alive, and sometimes not until night, but they bring the required quantity of sawed logs and ready kindling. The stacks of firewood are growing like mushrooms around the underground house, but Ignatov thinks there's never enough, and that they absolutely need more.

"We're preparing firewood as diligently as if we're planning to feed ourselves with it all winter," he heard Izabella say one time. The old witch was hinting that they had no edible supplies whatsoever. And where would those supplies come from if thirty mouths ate up absolutely everything he managed to shoot and Lukka could catch? Ignatov thought a bit and from that day on ordered that Lukka divide the catch in two, half for fish soup, the other half to be dried for future use. People tried to protest against reducing the fish ration – "We're already living half-starved!" – but no one could really argue with the commandant.

The women have asked several times for permission to be excused to pick berries because when working on firewood, they often encounter bilberry and lingonberry patches in the forest and come upon rowan trees strewn with orange bunches. Konstantin Arnoldovich maintains that cranberries could certainly be found here. Ignatov is adamant that there's not much satiety to be had from those berries and the working day would be lost. So much firewood could be prepared in that time!

Only Lukka the fisherman and Zuleikha, too, don't go to prepare wood. Sometimes Leibe asks to be excused to gather herbs and Ignatov lets him go; he's warmed slightly toward Leibe because of the gnat incident. The others work every day. One time, Ikonnikov started a conversation about how factory workers in backward tsarist Russia were provided with days off even under moribund capitalism but Ignatov quickly cut off that showboating: "You can talk about imperialism with a blizzard this winter."

Firewood, firewood … The humble sight of scruffy woodpiles gladdens Ignatov immensely. The bundles of dried fish, which are growing little by little, do, too. Zuleikha hangs them outside on sunny days and brings them inside the underground house on rainy days. But clothing is worrisome.

Many of the dekulakized had managed during their travel to keep warm things they'd taken from home and Ignatov has noticed that some even have a pair of felt boots and a reddish shaggy fur hat. But the Leningraders have no winter clothing and their bundles contain mostly useless junk, like thin between-season coats with gleaming round buttons, wrinkled brimmed hats with bright-hued silk linings, iridescent-colored mufflers that are slippery to the touch and have long delicate fringes, and suede and light cotton gloves.

Ignatov, too, has only the clothes he's wearing: his summer officer's State Political Administration uniform with a tunic for a shirt, light jodhpurs, and boots. And a peaked cap, of course. And so his alarm grows as he tracks long, inky clouds moving along the horizon. They promise rain and snow. These clouds have appeared recently, floating in from the north and circling the firmament for several days; they're now covering and obscuring it from all sides, breathing cold air. When the last piece of clear sky dissolves between the shaggy sides of low-hanging clouds, Ignatov realizes Kuznets isn't coming.

His insides seem to crackle with hoarfrost from that thought, and his head throbs and heats up, filling with rage. *Away with the suffering,* he orders himself. *Away with it. Just think about what can be done.*

Should he send out scouts? They really can't overwinter here. He could send a couple of the most sensible men to Krasnoyarsk (maybe Gorelov and Lukka). Slap together a boat for them and away they go along the motherly Angara and then the fatherly Yenisei, too. But three-quarters of the journey's four hundred kilometers is upstream, in the cold and rain, and without food supplies. So they wouldn't make it.

And what if they did make it? What would they report upon arrival? *We were dekulakized,* they'd say, *and exiled to the Angara by Soviet power, but out of the kindness of his heart, our temporary settlement commandant let us come to Krasnoyarsk in a boat for an outing – he's impatient, don't you see. He's waiting for his replacement so he can head home ...*

His scouts wouldn't reach Krasnoyarsk. It was as plain as day that they'd run away. Even if Ignatov were to appoint Gorelov as their minder. In fact Gorelov would be the first to propose it. It's around Ignatov, who has the revolver, that he's so obedient and zealous. And if something were to go wrong, he'd go into hiding without blinking an eye. He's a hardened criminal.

Or should Ignatov go on the scouting trip himself, leaving the exiles here? Even worse. He and Kuznets would return to an empty camp: the peasants would all run away and the Leningraders would all die the hell off during that time.

One way is bad, the other's worse. No matter what happens, he – Ignatov, the commandant – would be to blame. And he's already gotten into so much trouble, more than enough for three. He'll have to answer to the fullest extent before the Party and his comrades, for the attrition on the special train and for the escape and for the sunken *Clara.* No matter how he looks at it, he has to sit here and wait, whether for Kuznets or for the damned devil himself so Ignatov can account for himself with deeds rather than words.

Another thought tosses and turns in the depths of his consciousness and for some reason it makes him uncomfortable: he *must* save them. He's often dreamt that he's drowning in the Angara again, and as he's being submerged into its cloudy cold waters, there are hundreds of hands stretching toward him from the black depths, with their long white fingers billowing like seaweed, saying, "Save us, save us …" He always wakes up abruptly, sits up on his bunk, and wipes off his damp neck. That same "Save us" then rustles and rolls around in his head all day. And though he is afraid to admit it, it makes him realize that what he wants, desperately wants, is to save these enemies so they will actually live to see a new barge and survive, every last one of them. And he wants that not for them, nor for Kuznets, nor the impending tribunal for the mistakes he made. He wants it for himself. And that's why he's uncomfortable.

Ignatov picks up a hefty stick and knocks it on the scaly, reddish pine trunks as he strides back to camp. Then he swings his arm and tosses it into a thicket. He imagines it falling on Kuznets's head – smack dab on the top – and his soul begins feeling brighter.

The first snow falls that evening and these aren't the light grains that sprinkled down on them from the sky on the first day of their life on the riverbank, but the real thing – large, shaggy snowflakes. Frost hits during the night, ice glistens like fragile glass at the bottom of a bucket inadvertently left outside, and a thin hoarfrost nips at brush-like spruce boughs.

It's impossible to observe the exiles leaving in the morning for work without laughing – they put on all the clothes they possess. The peasants wrap themselves in head scarves, pull on fur coats and sheepskin jerkins, and the city people wear once-dandified plaid coats, gloves and mufflers of delicate hues, extremely wrinkled kepis, and hats with broken brims. The heavyset Leila wears a pot-shaped hat embroidered with colored glass beads and burrows her nose in a matted boa that looks as if it's been plucked. Konstantin Arnoldovich models a pie-shaped hat that's slightly deformed from having been transported so long and is made of very smooth, extraordinarily fine fur the color of strong coffee with cream. Izabella discovers she's lost her emerald-colored hat with the feather and this vexes her thoroughly because she has to cover her head using a shawl that already has holes worn in it in several places. They all carry identical one-handed saws in their hands.

One of the peasants has given Ignatov an old leather jacket that's cracked at the elbows – it was left behind by his son, who escaped from the ill-fated eighth train car. The jacket's a little narrow in the shoulders and Ignatov's arms stick out of the sleeves quite a bit, but it warms him. Ignatov – who's been openly freezing in recent days and had begun placing dried grass and leaves under his shirt in secret – did not refuse the gift.

That same day, while walking as usual through the taiga in search of prey, he has the idea of killing a bear. They could salt the meat and use the hide for clothing. The peasants have promised to handle it by fleshing, pickling, and tanning the hide nicely. An extra fur coat wouldn't hurt in the winter. And if he comes across a large bear, they can even cut a couple of hats from the hide.

He has to act quickly because the animals could settle in for hibernation. For three days, Ignatov digs a pit in the taiga, until his palms are worn to bloody blisters. The peasant men offer help that he refuses ("Firewood, the firewood, who's going to saw it?"). He covers the steep walls with smooth poles and pounds a sharpened stake into the middle. He places brushwood and boughs on top, and blankets it with grass. He begins waiting. No bear comes.

Ignatov tosses in bait a couple of times, either a squirrel he's shot or half a grouse. There's no bait to be found in the pit in the morning because lynxes or martens have dragged it off, scattering the brushwood Ignatov had placed so carefully. No bear ever visits. Ignatov stops by the pit to check from time to time but then he abandons it. He's not sorry about his work, though he's very sorry about the three days spent in vain.

At the end of October, snow falls in the taiga and stays for good. Winter has set in.

It's decided to work in two shifts. One group leaves in the thick, dark blueness of early morning to saw wood, pulling on all the warm clothes they have in the underground house. They return a half-day later, hastily dry their wet, sweaty clothes, and give them to the second shift. They work until late, until the stars come out.

Ignatov orders those who sit at camp to weave baskets. The evening shift has things easier because people wake up to Ignatov's never-changing alarm – his revolver on the bucket – and sit down to weave without leaving their bunks. The morning shift, though, works off five hours in the fresh air, comes back, collapses on the bunks from exhaustion, and falls asleep. Ignatov is usually foraging in the taiga during that time. He orders Gorelov to wake up the lie-abeds and deny supper to those who disobey. Supper is the only feeding in the camp, so large, medium, and small baskets soon fill the already crowded underground house. One day, when the exiles cautiously inquire of Ignatov if they might have enough baskets, he replies that they do, then instructs them to weave snowshoes and sleds for wood instead. In answer to their eloquent silence, he shouts, "Winter's around the corner – how are you planning to go for firewood, you bastards?"

He's ill-tempered, people whisper. They've resigned themselves to it.

Some get sick and burn with fever for a long time, coughing incessantly during the nights, keeping the others awake. Leibe gives them curative drinks with repulsively reeking herbs. Ignatov chases them back out to work, though, as soon as the patients' eyes begin twinkling from feeling better, their foreheads are no longer covered in perspiration, and they can plod independently to the latrine installed in the underground house's "entrance hall."

"It's ungodly," Izabella says one morning after Ignatov has demanded Konstantin Arnoldovich, who's still bluish-white from the fever he's recently endured, go with everyone else to cut wood in a forest seized by ringing hoarfrost. "You'll kill us."

"Fewer mouths to feed will make it easier for the rest," says Ignatov, baring his teeth.

At times Ignatov reads something resembling meek hatred in the eyes of these elderly people exhausted and emaciated by hunger and suffering. If he hadn't had a revolver, it's possible they might have even attempted to kill him.

At the beginning of winter, Ignatov's life grows complicated in a way he didn't anticipate at all. He doesn't go very far from camp that day. He inspects work in the clearing, where the exiles are laboring away felling trees and preparing logs that they drag to the camp on a sled, piling big branches into bundles, small kindling into large baskets, and birch bark, pine bark, pine cones, and pine needles into their own baskets – and then he heads off to his own work: hunting. The lumbermen's voices, the screech of the one-handed saws, and the crack of felling timber are still audible and very close by, but then he hears a sudden rustling and quivering of branches in the juniper bushes. It sounds like a large animal.

Ignatov freezes and slowly, very slowly, reaches for his revolver. His fingers creep along the holster as noiselessly as shadows. The cold weight of the weapon is in Ignatov's hand.

The bush is still quivering steadily, as if someone's plucking at it from the other side. A branch crunches under a heavy paw. A bear? That means it's come to visit. He prepared a pit and bait but it came on its own, uninvited, to feast on little juniper cones.

Shoot now, blindly? He might wound but not kill. The beast could either turn nasty and tear him the hell up, or get frightened and run away so Ignatov can't catch up. He'll have to wait until the animal shows its snout. Then he can shoot at a weak spot – its open jaws or an eye – to be absolutely sure.

The quivering in the bush moves closer. The bow-legged animal is walking right into his arms! Ignatov raises his revolver, places his second hand on top and prepares to cock it. He can't now, though, because the bear would hear. As soon as the bear sticks its nose out, Ignatov will pull the trigger and fire into its snout, the snout!

His throat is dry and he struggles to swallow. When he does, the sound seems deafening. The bush shudders abruptly again and out walks Zuleikha. Ignatov mumbles angrily, then quickly lowers the revolver. For an instant, it's as if he can't get enough air.

"And what if I'd shot you down!"

A couple of frightened crows fly from a branch and dart behind the tops of spruce trees. Zuleikha is backing away, her hands covering her dress where it protrudes on her belly, and staring, frightened.

"And so out of consideration for you, we kept you in the kitchen to tend the fire. But here you are, strolling in the woods?"

"I wanted to gather some nuts or berries," she whispers. "I want so badly to eat."

"Everybody wants to!" shouts Ignatov. They can probably hear him at the lumbering site.

"It's not for me." She continues backing away until she runs into an old birch bursting with torn black spots. "It's for him."

She looks down at the dark top of a head that's peeping out from her chest. Ignatov strides right up to Zuleikha and hovers over her. His breathing is still heavy and loud.

"Obey me," he says, "without exception. If you're ordered to stay in the camp, then sit there. If I order you to go for berries, you'll go. Clear?"

The baby on Zuleikha's chest suddenly yelps restlessly, stirring and grumbling. A tiny, wrinkled little hand with hook-like fingers appears in the opening of her dress for a moment and then disappears.

"See? It's 'Give me milk' again." Zuleikha unfastens the buttons on her chest. "Go on, then, go. I need to feed him."

Ignatov stands, angry and unmoving. The baby is crying, snuffling his little nose and rooting around with his open mouth.

"I said go! It's a sin to watch."

Ignatov doesn't budge; he's looking straight at her. The baby is bawling, sobbing, as if from bitterness and offense, wrinkling his old man's face. Zuleikha takes a heavy breast out of the opening of her dress and places a swollen nipple with trembling drops of milk on the end into his wide-open mouth. The crying ceases immediately and the child feeds hungrily, moaning as he quickly stretches and squeezes his taut, bright-pink little cheeks. White milk flows along them, mixing with tears that haven't yet dried.

Her breast is small, round, and full. Like an apple. Ignatov is watching that breast and he can't tear himself away. Something hot, large, and slow stirs in his belly. They say a woman's milk is sweet to the taste. He takes a step back. Sticks his revolver in the holster and fastens it. He walks off into the forest and turns after a couple of steps:

"Go to camp when you finish feeding. Bears want to eat, too."

He strides away along a path that's already been trodden between the spruces. He sees before him a small hand diving into the opening of the dress, clasping and reaching a taut, round, milky-white sphere of a breast with light-blue lines of veins and a large, shining, dark pink berry of a nipple that's burning, quivering with rich milk.

Some joke, half a year without a woman.

And so Ignatov tries not to look at Zuleikha after that. It's not easy in the crowded underground house. When their eyes happen to meet, he feels that same hot stirring in his belly again and turns away immediately.

Ignatov has selected the best snowshoes for himself. The exiles wove several dozen pairs but these, produced by the gnarled fingers of Granny Yanipa, a taciturn Mari woman with a brown face and small eyes lost amid shaggy eyebrows and deep wrinkles, are the best for walking because they sit nicely on the foot, don't fall through a thin crust on top of the snow, and don't let snow through. He's already been wearing them for three months. The birch cane has worn on the curves and is in shreds. Ignatov wants to order a second pair from her but she's been sick and hasn't gotten out of bed for several weeks.

The snowshoes the other peasants make are heavy and clumsy so they're suitable for short trips to fetch firewood but not for long, fast-moving hunting outings. The Leningraders' handiwork is so unsightly that it's difficult to recognize them as snowshoes; they're reminiscent of either an intricately shaped twig broom or an unsuccessful basket. "It's an example of Suprematism," Ikonnikov once said incomprehensibly, scrutinizing the shaggy woven something his hands had just created. The zealous Gorelov had wanted to throw Suprematism out of the house but Ignatov wouldn't allow it, ordering that it be hung under the ceiling because there was no longer any space on the floor.

Ignatov is stepping, placing his snowshoes on a dense, hard crust of ice. He's listening to the sound of his feet. The January sky is gray and cold. Dark clouds hang motionless, their inner white linings showing and a pre-dusk sun shining golden through them. It's time to go back.

He's returning empty-handed today.

Ignatov has not embraced hunting during his months in the taiga. He can tread quietly, hear keenly, and shoot accurately. He can already distinguish tracks in the snow as if he's reading dispatches left by the animals. Long and sparse are hares', larger and heavier are badgers', and light and sweeping are squirrels'. Sometimes he even senses the animals and he thrusts out his hand holding the revolver, squeezing the trigger before his head manages to grasp that it, his prey, is flashing between the bushes. But he hasn't been able to genuinely come to love hunting. He likes chasing and shooting but in a different way, where there's an open and comprehensible target. As in a battle, when you see an adversary and fire at him or chase him and hack him with a saber. Everything's clear and simple. But hunting is complex. Sometimes he imagines forest animals crawling out of their burrows and dens, and skipping along a huge field in even rows without hiding, meandering, or covering their tracks. He's behind them on a horse. He aims his revolver, shooting one after the other, one after the other. Now that would genuinely be hunting. But this?

Hunting fortune has been harsh for Ignatov, rarely gladdening him with success. Of course the largest prey was the elk. That happened in December, just before the new year. By chance, Ignatov had wandered to the bear pit he'd dug and forgotten about in the autumn and seen that something had landed inside. Dumbfounded by the premonition of sizable prey, he peered in at something large and dark gray that was lying there, tired. Its shaggy long legs with hooves as long as fingers were shaking slightly. Brownish-crimson guts, still lightly steaming, were entwined on the sharpened stake that stuck out over the elk. Ignatov dashed right off for camp. He ran in, panting and wild-eyed, scaring everybody. They gathered the men, grabbed sleds and homemade torches, and quickly went back into the woods. Ignatov was afraid the smell of meat would attract wolves but they encountered only a lynx in the pit. It had already torn at the carcass pretty well and it bared its crooked fangs wickedly, bubbling elk blood at them. Ignatov killed the lynx, too, and they dragged the animals to the underground house and ate for nearly a week. That was how they celebrated New Year's.

Nothing else has landed in the pit. There has been only small, insubstantial prey since that elk, which seems to have expended Ignatov's entire allotted share of hunting successes all in one go. There is help, thanks to Lukka. The Angara was already covered with ice in November but the men sawed about a dozen large holes under Lukka's supervision, so Lukka has been spending days at a time on the ice ever since. He brings back bream that are as broad and flat as dishes and shimmer like copper, spotted green pikes with spiteful bared teeth, and fishes unknown to Ignatov that gleam with pearlescence and have large, rhomboidal fins on their fatty backs.

Lukka has recently fallen ill, though. Many have taken to their beds since New Year and only Ignatov is hanging on. He's been forced to abandon sending two shifts into the forest for firewood so now only one shift works, only the healthy people, which really means those who are least ill. With misgivings, Ignatov excuses Professor Leibe from his labor duties because someone has to look after the sick. Because of Lukka's illness, they've been forced to feed themselves with stored fish. The dried fish doesn't last long; they've eaten everything they prepared in autumn within a couple of days. Ignatov is now their only hope.

He is striding through the taiga. Spruces float past him, their broad boughs pillowed in snow and bent toward the ground, resting against snowdrifts. Bushes swell like steep white boulders, and golden trunks of pine trees flash with a coating of thick hoarfrost. He goes down to the familiar clearing, where the giant skeleton of a lightning-charred birch tree stands in the corner, and he crosses a frozen stream where mounds of rocks are frosted with drifted snow. The camp is already close and the faint, bittersweet smell of smoke touches his nostrils.

In sunset's meager light, Ignatov sees tall poles on which two gray skulls bare their teeth between the trees. One skull is large and long, with a bent nose, large, flat chewing teeth, and the sturdy roots of horns growing right out of small, oval eye sockets – the elk. The second skull is small and round like a potato, with a hideous hole of a nose and fanged jaws that are thrust forward and tenaciously lying on top of one another – the lynx. Lukka hung up the skulls to scare off forest spirits. Ignatov had wanted to remove this appalling counterrevolution but gave up and left it after noticing the peasants' imploring looks. He thought it would be better if the skulls scared off illness. But there they hang, seeing Ignatov off for hunting in the morning, their black eyeholes gawking after him. They greet him in the evening, peering indifferently into his hands. What are you bringing back? Is there something to feed the people? Or has the time come to die?

Ignatov turns away from the skulls' unblinking gaze, gloomily hurrying past them to the underground house. As he walks, he again counts, out of habit, the tall round drifts – the woodpiles – that cover the clearing like mushrooms. There are fewer of them now than a month ago because the exiles have begun using up the firewood supply. Blizzards sometimes cover the taiga, howling over the house for several days, singing and shrieking in the stovepipe, and sending snow flying over the earth in a dense burst, carpeting the sun overhead. You'd perish in foul weather like that, so there's no going into the forest. They even go out to the woodpiles on a tether: they grope with their hands in search of the wood, trudge through waist-deep snow, and return to the underground house, pulling a rope with one end tied around their middle and the other to the entrance. Their supplies began melting away faster when illnesses arrived, and even when the weather was good, the exiles couldn't prepare as much firewood as before.

Ignatov sticks his snowshoes in a drift by the entrance, kneels, and crawls into the house. The outside door, woven from birch switches and reinforced with a mixture of turf and clay, is lying on the ground; it needs to be lifted and squeezed into a slot. Now Ignatov is in the cold "entrance hall." He goes down the earthen steps, throws back curtains made of bast fiber and elk hide and ducks into the underground house's crowded space, which is filled with heavy, warm air, the smell of herbs, fish, tree bark, spruce needles, smoke, scorching hot stones, and the sounds of coughing and quiet conversations.

He's come home.

Somewhere in the depths of the house, listless voices go quiet right away. The uneven light of a splinter lamp burning brightly over a kettle of water illuminates somber faces with distinctly drawn angular cheekbones and wrinkly folds. A dozen eyes stare at Ignatov and his empty hands.

He makes his way to his bunk without looking in their direction. From underneath his homemade pillow of boughs he removes the sack of cartridges, which has been shrinking tremendously over the winter. With the onset of winter, he stopped hiding it in the forest and began keeping it with himself, at the head of his bed. He loads his revolver. Without kicking off boots wound with scraps of lynx hide, he lies down, placing the hand with the revolver under his head. He closes his eyes, continuing to sense the gazes directed at him.

In moments like these he usually feels rising tides of fury and wants to start waving his weapon and shout, "What are you staring at, you bastards?" But today he doesn't have the strength. An unhurried, somber sort of tiredness has overcome him. He needs to dry out his boots and clothes, and at least drink some hot water to fill the sucking emptiness in his stomach. *Right now*, thinks Ignatov. *Right now, right now.*

"Very well, we'll have some *soup du jour*, then," says Izabella. She scoops a spoonful of salt out of a fat sack and drops it in a kettle that's been bubbling away on the fire. The clear water clouds and turns white as if someone had mixed in milk, then it sputters and clears again a moment later. The salty soup is ready.

Not many people like it. The majority turn toward the wall and don't even get out of their bunks. Only Konstantin Arnoldovich and Ikonnikov take seats by the pot.

For a long time, Konstantin Arnoldovich scrutinizes the bowl of his spoon, made from a pearlescent shell, then suddenly smiles:

"I feel like I'm on Avenue Foch. Saturday evening, oysters on ice, a glass of Montrachet ..."

"The best oysters, though," chimes in Ikonnikov, sipping his salty soup with gusto, "were to be found on Rue de Vaugirard. You won't argue with that, will you?"

"My dear Ilya Petrovich! How would you know? You were just a youth then and saw nothing but your études. It's surprising you even left your Montmartre!"

"*Messieurs, ne vous disputez pas!*" Izabella laughs as she knocks her spoon on the edge of the pot, as if she's flicking off fatty pieces of meat, translucent lemon slices, and small olive rounds that have stuck to it.

Gorelov plops down alongside them, takes a spoon out of his shirt, licks it, and looks ravenously at his companions. The conversation dies down.

Zuleikha buries her face in Yuzuf's hair. Ignatov came back from hunting empty-handed again. There's nothing for supper tonight, meaning her milk won't come in. Lately her milk supply has even been sparse after food.

It began running low in mid-winter. At first she thought it was from the meager food but she understood her milk was ending when they ate their fill of fatty, fragrant elk meat for a whole week in January and her breasts remained as weak and soft as before. She started giving her son meat and fish as a supplement. Potato or bread would have been better, of course, but where could she get that? She'd place a small piece of something in a rag and slip it into a space in his tiny toothless gums. Yuzuf spat it out at first but then he recognized the taste and sucked at it. He didn't like salty things – he cried – so Zuleikha didn't give him dried fish. When several completely hungry days came, she tried stewing some aromatic yellow cones that were left on the branches of a bough but that plant food gave her son sticky lumps of emerald green diarrhea and Doctor Leibe scolded her like nothing on earth. She hadn't even known he could shout so loudly and threateningly.

Since all the illness, when Ignatov abolished the severe twice-daily outings into the forest, many of the exiles now stay in the house during the day – and so Izabella often relieves Zuleikha at the stove. Zuleikha can lie for a while without moving after she's lowered her tired gaze to her sleeping son; she listens to his quiet, measured breathing. Yuzuf's sleeping minutes have become a delight for her but they make the minutes when he wakes up and cries all the harsher and bitterer. Her little boy wants to eat all the time.

She can't wait for him to start walking. She shuts her eyes and imagines Yuzuf when he's grown a little: after being bow-legged and skinny, his legs have become sturdy and are padded in resilient baby fat, round pink fingernails have grown out on his small fingers, his head is covered in dense, dark hair, and he stamps through the underground house to greet her. He picks up one little foot after the other and waddles like a duck – he's walking. Will she live to see that? Will he?

Zuleikha thinks so much about her son that she often forgets about her own groaning stomach and the weakness that sometimes overcomes her. She's very afraid of getting sick. Who would look after Yuzuf then? Her past life – Yulbash's open spaces, the threatening Murtaza, the nasty Vampire Hag, the long trip in the railroad car with the smells of hundreds of people – has slipped so far away, remaining behind such sharp turns, that it seems like a half-forgotten dream, a vague recollection. Did all that really happen to her? Her life now is catching the doctor's calm gaze ("Everything's fine with Yuzuf, don't worry, Zuleikha …"), waiting for Ignatov to return from hunting and Lukka from fishing ("Meat! We're going to eat meat today!"), and curling up on the bunk like a ring around her sleeping son and inhaling, inhaling his delicate smell.

It's quiet in the underground house. The exiles are already pressed up against one another, sleeping. After eating their fill of salty soup and embracing one another, Konstantin Arnoldovich and Izabella are wheezing a little, Ikonnikov is gently snoring, Gorelov is lost in a heavy, tense slumber, and Ignatov is lying on his separate bunk like a dead man, not moving.

Yuzuf shudders and his little nose moves sleepily – he's looking for Zuleikha. She's recently stopped carrying him around and he's been getting used to living on his own, without maternal warmth and scent surrounding him from all sides. As soon as she ends up alongside him, though, he seeks to press into her like before, worm his way in, and stick all his skin against her. As he does now. After his face has found his mother, he burrows himself in her chest, flattening his nose. He lies calmly for a minute or two then starts fidgeting away and his lips begin smacking. He's sensed the smell of milk. He'll wake up now.

And he does. He grunts and moans a little, sobs a couple of times and bursts out in hungry, demanding wailing. Zuleikha shushes her son affectionately and takes him in her arms. Her fingers get tangled in the frayed fasteners on her smock as she hurriedly opens the collar. She takes out a soft, flimsy breast and places it in the baby's hungry, wide-open mouth. Yuzuf hastily chews the limp nipple and spits – there's no milk. He cries louder. One person coughs hoarsely in the depths of the bunks and another turns over with a groan, mumbling unintelligibly.

Zuleikha shifts Yuzuf to her other arm and gives him her second breast. He goes silent for a moment, his toothless gums frantically yanking at the second nipple. *It hurts so much*, she notices with joyful amazement. *Could it really be his first tooth?* She doesn't have time to think that through, though, because Yuzuf spits out her breast, which has deceived him with its familiar smell. Now he's crying loudly, sobbing. His little face instantly floods with blood and his fists twist in the air.

She leaps up and rocks Yuzuf, bending so she doesn't hit her head on baskets, bunches of feathers, rolls of birch bark, bundles of pine cones, and other junk hanging from the ceiling.

Sometimes he can be successfully rocked, settled down, convinced, and whispered to so he'll fall asleep without even eating, giving Zuleikha the gift of a few more hours of precious silence. One time, she tried rocking Yuzuf in a cradle, a large basket hanging from the ceiling, but he completely refused to fall asleep by himself. He always wants to be in his mother's arms.

She presses her lips to his small head, which is very warm and damp from sweat. She mumbles half-forgotten lullabies in his tender little ear and whispers, casting a spell. She rocks him, first gently and evenly, then harder, more abruptly, and swinging more. She puts a homemade fabric pacifier in his tiny mouth but he spits it out and continues screaming. Between lips that are wide open and already covered with a slight nervous blueness she can see his tiny dark pink gums, glistening with spittle and completely smooth: there's no first tooth on them. Yuzuf is already almost six months old but his teeth haven't grown in.

Zuleikha jiggles his tense, arched little body. His crying is so shrill and loud that it hurts the ears. People roll over on their bunks, sighing, but continuing to sleep. They're used to this.

She takes someone's spoon left from supper and scrapes the bottom of the pot for a couple of drops of salty soup and places that in Yuzuf's mouth. He makes an offended face, spits, and chokes from crying so hard. His voice is already tired and a little hoarse, and the soft spot on his head pulses frequently and heavily, as if it wants to explode.

Zuleikha's back aches and she places Yuzuf's bellowing little body on the bunk and sits beside him. She lowers her head to her knees and plugs her ears, but it's no quieter because it's as if her son's crying has settled in her head. In moments like these, Zuleikha sometimes thinks it would have been easier for Yuzuf if he had departed during childbirth.

Out of the corner of her eye, she notices a slight motion in the middle of the underground house. It's as if a breeze has wafted, making the long shadows that extend from the stove door give a start, sway, and begin fidgeting. Zuleikha raises her head. The Vampire Hag is sitting right by the stove, on a gnarled wooden block made from a piece of an old pine stump, her elbows leaning into sharp knees set far apart.

Yellow specks of light from the fire tremble on her parchment-like forehead, streaming over hilly cheeks and flowing away into the hollows of her mouth and eye sockets. Her braids hang down toward the earthen floor like gaunt, shaggy ropes. Crescent-shaped earrings of dulled gold swing ever so slightly in her droopy, wrinkled earlobes, splashing light on the dark walls, the bunks, and human bodies sleepily tossing and turning.

The Vampire Hag stirs the remainder of the salty soup for a long time, then taps the spoon thoroughly and places it on the edge of the pot.

"My son never cried that hard," she calmly says. "Never cried that hard."

White drops of salty soup flow from the shell spoon and fall back in the pot, plinking. Surprised, Zuleikha wonders how she can hear it through the crying.

Yuzuf is still bellowing and wheezing beside her. A fine spasm runs through his twisted little body and his lips are rapidly turning a rich blue.

Large, hefty drops continue falling from the spoon into the pot. Each is like a hammer striking. They're no longer plinking but thundering. So loudly they muffle her son's voice.

Zuleikha walks over to the kettle and takes the spoon. She grasps the handle in her fist and hits the sharp side of the pearlescent shell exactly at the center of the middle finger on her other hand. The small but deep semicircular gash is like a crescent and it spurts out something thick, dark, and ruby red. She returns to the bunk and places her finger in her son's mouth. She feels his hot gums squeeze right away, biting and seizing at her fingernail. Yuzuf sucks greedily, groaning and gradually calming. His breathing is still rapid and his little hands still shudder from time to time. But now he's not crying: he's busily feeding and he grunts every now and then, as he used to when he drank milk. Zuleikha watches the blueness leave his tiny lips, his cheeks grow pink, and his eyes eventually close from exhaustion and satisfaction. Taut red bubbles swell in the corners of his tiny mouth from time to time, bursting and running to his chin in little winding streams.

It's not painful at all.

She looks up but now there's nobody at the stove.

Spring arrives suddenly, unexpectedly – it's loud, booming, and strong-smelling. All morning, rambunctious bird chirps have been bursting through the pieces of rags that stop up the house's little windows. The chirping is a teasing invitation that finally turns into the heavy, distinct thought that Ignatov has to go hunting.

His eyelids open. His body has lightened of late; it's as if it lacks bones, though for some reason it's difficult to carry. It's even become hard to think. His head is empty, as if it's flat and made of paper. His thoughts are somehow weightless and fleeting, too, like shadows or smells, so if you don't seize them, you won't fully think them through. That's why this morning's thoughts are unwieldy, stirring in his skull like a lazy fish, and seeming so important and necessary. He has to get up and go hunting.

He didn't go anywhere yesterday; he lay on his bunk the whole day, resting. Now the persistent chirruping has woken him, stirred him up, and forced him to hope again. What if he manages to kill one of those birds? He has to get up now and go hunting.

Ignatov throws his feet off the bunk and an icy crust crunches on the floor; the water's been running for a long time, ever since the snow started melting a little. He finds his revolver at the head of the bed and rummages around in the sack for a long time, groping for a cartridge. It's the last one. What did Kuznets say when he was leaving? Enough for all the wild beasts in the taiga? It's ended up not being enough. But that's funny, so he should laugh, laugh to his heart's content at what turned out to be Kuznets's hilarious practical joke, though he somehow lacks the strength. He'll have a laugh later, when he gets back from hunting. He just can't let himself forget it, that joke. Ignatov flings the empty sack away, has trouble opening the drum, and inserts the cartridge. Coping with the revolver has also become difficult of late; it's too heavy. Just like the obsessive thought in his head that he absolutely has to go hunting and bring something back.

He leans his hands against the edge of the bunk and comes to his feet. His head spins and the air disappears from his lungs. Ignatov is standing with his hands propped against a vertical support log and he's waiting for the walls to stop rocking. He adjusts his vision and breathing, then walks toward the door.

The exiles are lying on the bunks in tight bunches, embracing. They're not moving. Maybe they're sleeping. He ordered those on watch to check people in the mornings. If there's a corpse, bring it outside immediately. They should probably make the checks more frequently, twice a day.

A small mound of tatters stirs weakly by the stove: it's Gorelov. He spits, occasionally tossing firewood into the stove. He's on watch today. There's not much firewood, only enough for a half-day, and that's all that remains of the magnificent woodpile stacks that were once so tall. They've been heating frugally lately, a little at a time, and supplementing the firewood with woven baskets and snowshoes. They've burned everything they wove in the autumn, even Ikonnikov's Suprematism, after cleaning off the soft birch bark, which they pounded, boiled, and drank beforehand. The firewood went quickly even so; it practically melted away. The indifferent thought that flashes is: *We'll freeze to death at night.*

Konstantin Arnoldovich's invention, the sawed calendar, is on the log by the door. Half of August, September, October, November, December, January, and even February were applied by a firm, stubborn hand. In March, the marks became irregular, uneven, and not very noticeable, and by April they completely went missing. It doesn't matter now since April is probably over.

Ignatov makes his way under the elk hide, which is as rigid as tree bark and has been mercilessly slashed by a knife. They cut leather off many places and boiled it for a long time but couldn't eat it anyway because it was too tough. They ate both bast curtains, though, and needles from the boughs they'd used to cover their bunks for softness. As well as the medicinal herbs Leibe had prepared.

Ignatov rests the top of his head against the outside door, pushes, and crawls outside: fresh air and the pattering thaw splash through the gap that's opened up. The clearing is in front of him. It's spacious and bundled in snow in some spots but already breathing reddish brown earth in others, and there are black circles made of river rocks, the remnants of the foundations for the woodpiles. The forest is quiet and transparent in the distance, with delicately gray trunks of spruces that have frayed over the winter, occasional black-and-white birch trees with branches like thin hair, and the brittle, reddish lace of juniper bushes.

The earth's thick, fusty fragrance makes his head spin again. Still crouching by the entrance to the house, Ignatov rests and scrutinizes the darkening Angara below through his half-closed eyes. The river frightened them all winter, making its way toward the knoll with its ice standing on end. Then it began glimmering in places, large gray spots appeared, and the river started sparkling in the sun. A few days ago it suddenly thundered, breaking into angular pieces of blindingly white ice that floated away. *You tried, but you could not defeat me,* Ignatov thought then, observing the rapid, menacing flow of ice chunks along the swelled river. Now it has already calmed, darkened, and eaten up all the ice. It's as blue and shining as last summer.

Ignatov strides into the taiga to hunt, shuffling his feet in boots that have fallen apart and lost all form, and holding his revolver in his outstretched hand. From their stakes, the skulls bare their teeth behind him – there are his old comrades the elk and the lynx, a couple of toothy wolverines, and a badger with a flat forehead.

And there's the chirping, up above. Something's ringing, singing, and murmuring where thin branches swollen with buds and shabby spruce boughs cross. Ignatov looks up as spots of light blue, reddish-brown, and shades of yellow swing, hop, and fly. The birds are so high he can't discern or reach them. He'll need to tear off the buds on his way back, though, for supper.

Ignatov slowly pushes forward, into the depths of the forest, holding onto tree trunks and branches as he walks around puddles with motionless black water and snowdrifts that have melted a little on the sides. His feet are leading him somewhere on their own, and he's submitting to them, walking. He makes his way across a brook that recently thawed and now jangles deafeningly on the rocks. He walks up along gray land with lumps from last year's pine cones and between pine trunks that burn with reddish fire. The taiga beckons. Soon, soon there will be prey.

He leans his back against a tall old larch, breathing loudly. His chest is heaving and his legs are buckling, folding in half because he's unaccustomed to walking so much now. And he's gone a long way. Will he make it back? Ignatov closes his eyes partway and there's an unbearable ringing in his ears from the babbling birds. Apparently the taiga is deceiving and enticing him, not allowing him to go back.

There's a sudden rustling beside him. A squirrel is on a branch right next to Ignatov's face: it's thin, dirty gray, with scanty white fluff, yellow cheeks, and long scampish tassels for ears. Meat! A shining brown eye darts and – zoom! – it's up the tree trunk. Ignatov's shaking hand reaches upward with the revolver but it's instantly way too heavy to hold. A shabby tail like a miniature broom flashes mockingly up above, teasing as it blends in with brush-like branches, layers of bark, and needly sunbeams, before disappearing. The sky suddenly starts spinning faster and faster, and then everything's spinning, the treetops, the clouds …

Ignatov shuts his eyes tightly and his head droops. Turn back? The birds call up ahead, chirping and promising. Ignatov walks forward, half-squinting, lowering his gaze, and not looking at the sky gone mad. He stumbles on a pine root and falls. Why hadn't he figured out before that crawling is easier? He moves ahead on all fours, looking only at the ground.

A delicate little pink back flashes and a pair of curious eyes sparkle very close, between knotty pine roots: a large jay is busily hopping somewhere. So that's who's been singing the whole time! That's who lured him here! Ignatov aims an uncertain hand at the jay. Whoosh! It's flown away. Ignatov's gaze follows but quickly looks down after seeing the spinning firmament again.

He suddenly understands he's been making his way up the cliff this whole time. He hasn't been here in a long while, since autumn. And there's only a little further to the top. If only the damned sky would stop spinning for just a second. Ignatov gathers his strength and crawls up.

Even from a distance, he notices there are blindingly green shoots of fresh grass with bright yellow, star-shaped flowers at the very top, on a shred of earth that's warmed by the sun between some rocks. He contracts his muscles, darts forward like a snake, falls face-first on the grass, tears it with his teeth, and chews. He mumbles from enjoyment as a wonderful fresh taste fills his mouth, spreads through his veins, and rushes to his head like young wine. Happiness! His stomach shudders hard and relentlessly. Poorly chewed emerald greens with little yellow flowers sprinkled in, mixed with mucus and gastric juices, spill out on the grass. Ignatov howls and coughs convulsively, pounding his revolver on the ground. He's puked it all up, to the last blade of grass. His breathing is labored and his face drops in the grime, into the grass his innards rejected, and he understands. This is the end, he won't make it home, he has no strength.

He didn't keep the exiles alive. Didn't save them.

Exerting himself, he brings the revolver's cold, heavy body to his face and sticks the long barrel in his mouth: his teeth chatter against the metal and the sharp front sight scratches the roof of his mouth. *Bastards*, is the last thought that flashes through his mind.

He suddenly feels like the sky has stopped rotating above him. He looks up. In the distance, dark against the bright blue Angara water, is the long brown spot of a barge and a bold black dot alongside it. It's the launch.

THE SETTLEMENT

Kuznets springs out of the boat. Big, cold splashes of water fall on sturdy boots carefully polished with wax, then skitter away and roll back into the Angara. He walks along the riverbank, unhurried, as his imperious gaze takes in the rocky beach and the knoll hanging over it. Other boats sputter behind him as their bows land against the shore. Oars knock, chains clank, and escort guards' shouts carry, blending with their charges' meek voices.

"What the ... ? Where the hell're you taking all that? Toss it over by the water, let them sort it out themselves!"

"Stand still, you dogs! Closer together! Straighter!"

"Don't you cry, Dima, we're here now, see ..."

"Comrade Kuznets! Should we put them in formation or let them stand like this, like rabble?"

"I thought we were going to a real settlement, where there are people, but there's ..."

"The lists, where're the lists?"

"Count those heads again, Artyukhin! Some mathematician you are ..."

The voices abruptly drop off. Kuznets turns his proud profile to the tense quiet that has set in behind his back.

A strange, dark figure is walking down from the knoll, reeling and bobbing oddly, as if it's dancing on legs that won't bend well. A person. The person's wearing dirty, worn-out, and colorless rags, and something's wound around his formless boots. There's a threadbare woman's shawl criss-crossed over his chest, his hair is like a mane, and his beard is scraggly. He's walking slowly; it requires exertion. Soon they can see his mud-smeared face, along with his bugged, completely wild eyes, and the revolver in his tensely extended hand.

Kuznets narrows a brown eye. Is he imagining, or is it really … ?

"Ignatov, it's you! Holy Mother, he's alive! I didn't even think …"

Ignatov trudges along, seeing just one target in front of him: Kuznets's radiant, round, ugly mug, which looks like it was outlined by a compass, with its dumbfoundedly wide-open slots of well-fed, kindly eyes. The despicable sky is spinning again, pulling Ignatov into its frenzied whirl but he stubbornly plods along, not giving in. The ugly round mug approaches for a long time, a very long time, hurriedly muttering something. Kuznets's voice is carrying from far away, maybe from the forest, maybe from underwater.

"How're you doing here, my friend? Where are your feeble buddies? They survive? Well, well, look at you, you devil, huh? Oh, you won't believe how crazy things got after we left you! They've been dumping the kulaks on us by the trainload. There was no time for you, forgive me."

The ugly mug is finally right alongside him. Ignatov wants to say some final words but they've all left his memory. He mumbles and places the shaking revolver to Kuznets's broad chest. The trigger is heavy and tight, as if it's taken root. He clenches his teeth and directs all his will, the remainder of his energy, into his index finger. He squeezes the trigger and the revolver dryly clicks.

Kuznets's mug laughs, its eyes nearly shutting:

"Let bygones be bygones, as they say …"

Ignatov's dry throat swallows and he squeezes the trigger again. Yet another click.

"Stop being offended, Ignatov," says Kuznets. He's laughing hard. "That's it, your new life is starting. Look at these charges I brought you: you can plow away at the land with them."

Someone's hands carefully take the revolver from Ignatov's bent fingers. Kuznets's smile blurs and dissolves in the unbearably bright sunlight. The sky takes one final spin and covers Ignatov like a bedspread.

Kuznets's round, satisfied face is the first thing he sees when he comes to. Ignatov starts moaning, as if from pain and Kuznets slaps him on the arm. "It's fine, brother," he's saying, "you'll be back to your old self soon. You slept through," he adds, "two days. You woke up yesterday for a little while, chowed all my officer's chocolate, then went back to sleep. You really don't remember anything?" Ignatov shakes his head and raises himself a little on his elbows. He's lying by a large spruce on some sort of sacks under a tarpaulin. Covered by a sheepskin coat. He's surrounded by screeching saws, thudding axes, tapping hammers, and salty language.

"Where am I?" he says.

"Same old place," laughs Kuznets. (*Enough laughing, you mustached ass!*) He's sitting on a slab of wood next to Ignatov, scribbling in his map case.

"Where are my people?"

"Your deceased are alive, have no fear. Every last one of them. Hardy, the devils! I've never seen such gaunt people. We left them in the underground house for the time being so the wind doesn't blow them away."

Ignatov settles on his back again. He could lie like this forever, looking at the evergreen needles lazily stirring above his head, sensing the smell of spruce pitch, and hearing people's businesslike voices. His hand gropes at the taut sides of the sacks under him.

"What's this?"

"New provisions." Kuznets pronounces this as simply as if he were speaking about water or air.

Ignatov turns on his side with a quick motion, ending up on the ground. His weak hands fumble with the ties, pull, and tear toward him, opening one of the bags. There's fine loose grain inside; it's sharp and dirty gray, in scrappy silvery husks. He plunges a hand into the sack's cool depths and takes out a whole handful so a bitter, mealy, and slightly dusty smell touches his nostrils. Oats.

Kuznets is looking at Ignatov in a fatherly way, as if Ignatov were a small son delighted by a new toy. "Even better, take a look around – take a look."

Ignatov overcomes his weakness, sits next to the sacks – he can't lie on the grain – and leans his back against a spruce trunk sticky with pitch so he can look around. The camp has been transformed during the days that have passed. The underground house is still in place, with a thin creased ribbon of smoke spiraling out. ("They heated the stove up," he sighs with relief. "Something to be thankful for.") And life is simmering away around him. Unfamiliar people – a hundred? more? – are scurrying around, dragging logs that display even, shiny, creamy-yellow saw cuts, waving axes, and pounding hammers. The ground is generously sprinkled with sawdust and woodchips, pieces of bark, and scraps of wood, and the air is so thick with the fragrance of pitch that you could eat it with a spoon. A dozen rank-and-file soldiers, wearing gray and carrying weapons, are right there to oversee, urge on, and shout from time to time. Foundations for three long, broad structures – future barracks – are growing in the middle of the knoll.

A couple of women are stoking a fire and a hearty smell is rising over two buckets boiling on the flame.

Under the spruce where Ignatov and Kuznets are sitting there's a heap of crates, boxes, sacks, bundles of shovels and pitchforks covered in burlap, large baskets, buckets, and kettles. Yes, it's a genuine stockpile.

"Outstanding," is all Ignatov can say. "You've really taken charge here …"

"You bet I have!" Kuznets motions significantly with his powerful Roman chin, cleft by a lengthwise dimple. "After all, what was I before? A guarding function. And you? An accompanying function! And now you and I are unquestionably in charge. All this kulakdom is now ours, my friend."

This is how Ignatov learns that, in 1931, all labor settlements established for habitation and labor-based re-education of the dekulakized were handed over to the Joint State Political Administration and entered into the Gulag system, which had been officially created only a half-year before but was already demonstrating its efficacy. Responsibility for oversight, organization, and the management, regulation, and use of the exiles' labor had been placed upon this young and successful administration.

"You and I, Ignatov, won't fall flat on our faces. We'll go all out. We'll teach the exploiters about proletariat labor and show them what genuine Soviet life is. We'll build an infirmary out of logs over there, by the forest. And a dining hall by the barracks, to the side. And the commandant's headquarters on the hill." Kuznets looks long and hard at Ignatov.

"When do I go home?" Ignatov is scanning the river and finds only Kuznets's launch, bobbing at anchor not far from shore; the barge apparently left straight after unloading the people.

"I'm leaving this evening." Kuznets places his pencil in the hard leather map case, firmly fastening the strap. "I've already been sitting too long here with you."

Ignatov feels his jaws tighten until they slowly and painfully crunch; there's even an ache in his temples.

"We," he says a minute later through his teeth. "*We're* leaving in the evening."

"You planning to go far?" Kuznets is calm and peaceable, as if he were discussing whether the two of them should go berry picking.

"Home," hisses Ignatov. "I'm planning to go home, you grinning bastard."

"Uh-huh, go on then. This happens to be a very heated time back in your Kazan. Another day, another underground cell uncovered. It's either 'wreckers' or Mensheviks or German spies or English ones, the devil alone knows who they are. Things got rolling as soon as the mayhem started last spring. There are thirty from the Tatar Central Executive Committee already in jail, the crooked bastards. And the Administration's not without its Judases. They've arrested everybody at your State Political Administration, Ignatov. It's unclear who's left at work. There was even an article in *Pravda* called 'The Tatar Hydra.'"

"You're lying, you son of a bitch!"

"Then I'll bring it for you, that newspaper." Kuznets is imperturbable, even affectionate. "I'll sit at the library all night if I have to, I don't mind spending the time. I'll find it – you can read it yourself."

You're lying, Ignatov says over and over to himself, *lying, lying.* But he already sees Bakiev's office before his eyes, turned upside down, two soldiers with tense gazes by the door, and a gray silhouette sorting stacks of papers on the desk. Could it really be they hadn't let Bakiev go back then? Is he the *hydra?* Stupidity. Nonsense. Gibberish.

"But you wouldn't make it there anyway," says Kuznets. "I've seen your file. It's just like a bedtime story – *A Thousand and One*

Nights, it's called. There's the overwhelming attrition on the train and an organized escape to the count of around four dozen souls and harboring an important witness from an investigation (and not simply a witness, a kulaker woman, mind you!) and – just think, Ignatov! – giving bribes to a public servant, a train station director. You really outdid yourself. Nobody else could keep pace."

Ignatov's hitting the ground with his fist; his eyes are closed. Kuznets is right. Right on all counts.

"So you stay put, my friend. We'll register you here officially, add you to the rolls. You'll stay for now and pray behind my broad back, atoning for your sins. In a couple years, when they notice you're missing, well, there you'll be – a respected commandant, a big shot fulfilling a plan they could only dream of. The toiler of Siberia! Who'd touch you then?" Kuznets stands, adjusting his belt and the map case on his hip. "Let's go. I'll turn the documents over to you, introduce you to people. Give yourself a wash first, though, and change into clean clothes or you'll frighten the personnel. They'll take you for a hobgoblin."

"Why do you need me?" Ignatov asks this wearily, looking up at Kuznets's powerful frame.

"There aren't enough people. There'll be about a hundred settlements around the taiga soon. Who can you leave them with? Who do you trust? And it's on me if anybody asks. It's obvious looking at you, Ignatov, that you're committed right down to the fingernails. That's why I can calmly turn two hundred souls over to you. You kept your no-hopers alive during the winter – you'll keep these alive, too."

"How do you know?" says Ignatov. He slowly rises, leaning his hand into white streaks of sticky pitch on the spruce trunk. "Maybe I'm a hydra?"

His legs are still weak and they shake, but they're already holding him. He can walk.

"You're a dense one, Ignatov. A hydra's got a lot of heads, more than you can count. You could be one baby snake on the hydra's head but you can't be the whole hydra, oh no. You should know things like that."

Kuznets does bring the newspaper. He shows up a month later, in early summer. Ignatov's window has a good view of Kuznets's long, black launch with antennas like a rapacious mustache and lamps like bugged eyes when it suddenly takes shape on the dark blue mirror of the water. The commandant's headquarters are on the knoll's very highest point so the settlement, the broad ribbon of the shore, and the Angara itself can be surveyed equally well from here.

I won't go and greet him, thinks Ignatov. He quickly tosses some rusks, sun-dried fish, and a kettle with yesterday's leftover porridge stuck to the sides on the overturned crate he uses as a table so it'll look like he's been eating lunch. Hiding behind the window opening – the frame and glass haven't been installed yet, but they've promised to bring them by mid-summer – he observes as the craft quickly, proprietarily, casts anchor by the shore and spits a small wooden boat into the water.

On shore, a figure runs hastily and intently toward the boat. Pebbles are even flying out from under his feet. Gorelov. In his hurry to show his face to the chief, he's left the area entrusted to him – construction's finishing up on the infirmary. He should be slapped with a couple days in an isolation cell for that, the bootlicker. But there's no lockup in the settlement.

Gorelov darts into the water without taking off his shoes. He catches the boat's pointy bow and pulls it to shore. He hurriedly says something, his shaggy, dog-like head nodding slightly and his spine bending to one side, then the other. He's trying to win favor. The chief's not listening. He jumps ashore, tosses the line to Gorelov, and strides off to the commandant's headquarters.

Ignatov sits at the table and places a tough little fish with white streaks of salt on a half-crisped, crumbling rusk. He doesn't have a chance to take a bite before Kuznets abruptly flings the door wide open without knocking. He enters quickly, as if he's at home. He looks at Ignatov, frozen with the rusk in his hand, and plunks a newspaper folded into quarters on the table in front of him. "Read," he says, "and I'll take a look around here on my own – don't worry about me." And out he goes.

The newspaper is worn along the edges, badly yellowed, and coming apart at the folds. Ignatov takes it as carefully as if it were a snake and unfolds it. There's a violet stamp of the Krasnoyarsk Municipal Library in the upper right-hand corner and two ragged holes in the side, as if the newspaper had been torn out of a binder. Ignatov's heart thumps low and cold in his chest. No, Kuznets hadn't bluffed about the library.

The front-page feature tells of a speech by Kalinin about heroes of industrialization. Further on, there's a group letter from female weavers in Paris that calls on female workers in the Soviet Union to envelop the Red Army's fighters with special love and care, as well as a plea from unemployed people in Germany for the 'wreckers' who sabotaged socialist construction in Soviet Siberia to face the firing squad. Ignatov pages through rough, brittle paper that smells of sweetish dust. "Achieve the Five-Year Plan in Four Years!" "Let's Produce More Steel!" "Exemplary Tending of Sugar Beets!" In the feuilletons are pieces from worker correspondents and worker-peasant correspondents, a poem about a tram …

And then suddenly, huge letters hurry, slanting, across the center spread: "They Sheltered the Hydra." Unknown and vaguely familiar faces flash from an array of photographs. (*Maybe we met in the hallways?*) And there's Bakiev, his face stern and solemn. He's taken off his glasses so his gaze is a little childlike and dreamy; the Order of the Red Banner is silvery on his chest. This photograph of Bakiev was taken for his Party membership card. The article is long and detailed, with the small type spilling over the double spread. There's a drawing in the corner of someone's powerful hand squeezing the neck of an old woman whose insane eyes are bugging out and who has a good dozen snakes instead of hair. Her neck is skinny and flabby, like it'll snap any minute now, and the snakes are as mean as demons, baring their fangs and attempting to bite the hand that's caught them.

Ignatov rubs his throat, which is suddenly ticklish and starting to itch.

And so Bakiev sent him on this trip specially. Yes, that's obvious now. What did he say back then? "It's for you, you damned fool ..." something like that? He wanted to save him, that was it, pull him out of danger, send him far, far away. And Bakiev had been acting strangely around then, downcast, because he knew. He knew but hadn't fled, sitting in his office, sorting papers, and waiting.

Ignatov takes his head in his hands. *Mishka, Mishka ... Where are you now?*

The half-strangled hydra gawks from the table.

The freshly planed door swings open and Kuznets's broad smile is in the opening.

"Well, how about that, comrade commandant," he says. "Nice work! Your dining hall's a palace. The infirmary, too – you could put everyone in there at once. You're straightening out these exploiters' lives. It's about time to talk about regular workdays now. They'll need to labor doubly hard to earn a dining hall like that."

Ignatov smoothes the newspaper with his hand and throws a couple of fish on it.

"Sit down, chief."

"I thought you'd never offer," smirks Kuznets. He sits, plunges his hand into the voluminous map case on his hip, and pulls out a long, narrow, transparent bottle.

"They still haven't brought glasses," says Ignatov, trying to cut the little fish bodies. They're as tough as wood on the newspaper. "We'll have to swig from the bottle."

Kuznets waves a hand – *well, of course!* – and uncorks the bottle, inhaling the smell from its thin neck with delight. Ignatov saws at the dense fish fibers and bones using a crooked knife made from a former one-handed saw. It's right on the scared hydra's face and the blade keeps clunking at the newspaper, cutting the hydra, slashing and hacking it to shreds.

In June of 1931, the population of the still-unnamed settlement totals one hundred and fifty-six inmates, including the old-timers who survived the first winter. Plus ten guards and the commandant.

They live in three barracks that seem unbelievably spacious and bright after the close quarters in the underground house. Walls of long, even logs have been planed and the doors are hanging on hinges. There's a promise of iron stoves from the city. Each person has their own – very own! – bunk, though people still line them with boughs and cover themselves with clothing. Women and children have been settled in one building; men are in the other two. The guards share a small log house that's been added on, kitty-corner, to one of the barracks. The commandant, as chiefs should, lives separately, in the commandant's headquarters.

They eat in the dining hall (or "the restaurant," as Konstantin Arnoldovich likes to call it). Food is still cooked over a fire but they're already savoring taking meals in a civilized manner, sitting under a roof in even rows at festive yellow tables smelling of pine pitch. They eat fish soup (they've established a three-person fishing artel, working under Lukka) and game less frequently (Ignatov sometimes allows the guards into the taiga to stretch their legs), and even more rarely they get porridge, rusks, and macaroni brought from the city. The standard serving is small, as if it were a child's portion, but they have food! Sometimes they come into some sugar and once there were even splendid, nearly rock-hard, plain crackers. They are fed twice a day. Lunch is brought in buckets to the work site in the forest, and they eat supper in the dining hall. They still eat with spoons made from shells. They have dishes and mugs now, but the spoons were forgotten in an oversight. Happiness isn't about spoons, though!

They've built a large, ten-bed infirmary from logs. In the front there's a waiting area and bunks for the patients (one-tier, at Leibe's insistence), and in the back there's a cubbyhole for staff. This is where Leibe has taken up residence. He gave Kuznets a list of two hundred items – medications and instruments – for purchase. Kuznets smirked and on his next visit he brought a dilapidated, flat traveling bag with the red cross half worn off and something clanking and rolling around at the bottom. Maybe not two hundred items but even so.

Under an agreement concluded between the Joint State Political Administration and the government agency overseeing the timber industry, the settlement has been handed over to the agency for timber work. Each morning, to the guards' brisk shouts, the inmates crawl out for the morning roll call then go into the taiga.

The detested one-handed saws have been relegated to the past and they now work using two-handed saws and axes in teams of three. Two fell the tree and the third lops off the small branches and collects them in bundles; they saw the trunk into lengths (six meters or two meters long, for different construction purposes), and drag them to a sled, to which three workers are harnessed.

They bring the sled to the timber landing on the shore, not far from the settlement, where the wood is stacked and tied together.

They return in the evening. Hardly anyone achieves the set daily target for processing logs – and women basically never do, so their rations are often cut. New people complain and the old-timers mostly keep quiet, like Ikonnikov, or joke it off, like Konstantin Arnoldovich. They want relentlessly to eat, and many hurry back into the taiga after supper for nuts, berries (cloud-berries and bilberries in summer, lingonberries and cranberries in autumn) and mushrooms (there are abundant ceps and bent milk-stools near the settlement, sometimes saffron milk caps, too, among the other types of milk cap). They have no aversion to cattails (they boil young shoots, which have a flavor somewhat reminiscent of potato, and dissolve its strong-smelling brownish-yellow pollen in water to drink); and they dig up meaty lily bulbs.

The administration doesn't object. The guards are cheerful and spirited. They might shoot jays for supper so the soup will be richer or catch one of the settlement women in the bushes for a romp. They are down-to-earth, simple fellows. They'll beat people for disobedience, and once they shot someone, maybe for planning an escape, maybe for something else. They're afraid of the commandant (he's horribly strict), but the forest offers a sense of freedom where they can relax.

They've installed an agitational propaganda stand at the center of the settlement and the bright-colored posters, which smell sharply of paint, keep changing. The agitation's directed at accel-erating the process of re-educating the exploiting class.

In short, life is taking shape.

The women ceded a lower bunk to Zuleikha and Yuzuf, one further from the entrance and away from the draft of the constantly opening door. Izabella's bunk is nearby and Granny Yanipa's, and several other Leningraders, too: the old-timers have tried to stick together whenever possible. Leila, the Georgian woman, settled on a top bunk, despite her solid age and weight. They had to nail a couple of strong beams on the frame so she can climb up to the second tier, as if on a ladder.

The efficient Zuleikha has been kept in the kitchen. As her supervisor, they've appointed Achkenazi, who isn't yet old, though he's already as withered as tree bark and stooped enough to be hunched. He's one of the new people, with a skull that appears very fragile – it was shaved to bareness at one point and is now overgrown with sparse black shoots. He's taciturn; his eyes are listless, scared, and half-closed; and his chin is lowered, as if he's exposing the shaved back of his head to anyone who might want to take him by the scruff. Achkenazi was an excellent cook at one time (or so people say). He never cut but "julienned," didn't shuck but "peeled," didn't fry but "sautéed," didn't parboil but "blanched," and didn't stew but "simmered." He calls soup broth "bouillon," rusks "croutons," and strips of fish are even "goujons." He doesn't converse with Zuleikha other than to exchange brief remarks. He most often uses gestures. She's slightly afraid of Achkenazi since he's one of several who've landed in the settlement under a commutation of sentences, meaning he should have been sitting in prison or a camp now, along with genuine thieves and murderers. Zuleikha doesn't know his crime but she tries to fulfill his requests quickly and diligently, without annoying him, just in case. It's nice to work with him, though, because he knows his craft and treats Zuleikha fairly, not quibbling over anything.

At first he had looked critically at his new assistant's left hand, wondering if her injuries would impede her work. The ends of all five fingers are slightly mutilated and covered in strange short and crooked scars that look like commas. "It went into the thresher," she explained to her new supervisor without waiting for his question. He stopped worrying about that after seeing how deftly she handled the game and fish.

The two of them are responsible for all the cooking, with Achkenazi as the "*maître*," as Konstantin Arnoldovich puts it, and Zuleikha working alongside him, at his beck and call, washing, peeling, plucking, gutting, dressing, cutting, grating, scraping, and washing again. She carries lunch into the forest, too. A bucket with soup in one hand, a bucket with drinking water in the other and it's onward, to the first work station then back, to the second station then back, to the third … By the time she's run to everybody and fed them, it's time to start supper. She only just makes it to her bunk in the evening, to collapse. And she thinks it's good fortune that she's in the kitchen.

Yuzuf grew slowly, if at all, during the winter's starvation, which Zuleikha doesn't like to recall. Her son's hair was then weak and sparse, his skin pale blue, his nails as transparent and brittle as a bee's wing, and he didn't have a single tooth. He moved little and then only reluctantly, as if he were conserving his energy; he always observed things sleepily and moodily; and he never learned to sit up. She was grateful he stayed alive. In the summer, though, as soon as the sun showed itself and food appeared, he suddenly started making up for lost time and quickly began growing. Now he eats a lot, almost as much as an adult, and Achkenazi notices Zuleikha giving him extra food, but turns away without saying anything. Yuzuf has started smiling – showing wide, strong, blade-like teeth that have cut through – and babbling. He has learned to sit up and crawl quickly, like a cockroach. The hair on top of his head has darkened and became curly, and his arms and legs have grown out, even taking on a little baby fat. He doesn't want to stand and walk at all, though. He will soon turn one.

He's painfully and utterly attached to Zuleikha. She always

feels his lively, clinging little hands at her hem when she's working in the kitchen. He will crawl out from under the table, touch his mother, and crawl back. She knows he'll look for her while she's running her errands to the back yard or to the river for water. She hurries back, panting and sweaty from running, and he'll already be sitting on the threshold and howling, his grubby little fists smearing plentiful tears on his face.

At first, she took him with her when she brought lunch into the taiga. It exhausted her because hauling two full pails and a hefty year-old baby turned out not to be an easy task. Nearly impossible. Not only that, but mosquitoes mercilessly devoured Yuzuf in the thicket and then he wouldn't fall asleep for a long time, tormented by the bites covering his tender skin.

Only grudgingly did she first leave him in the kitchen for a long stretch. After feeding lunch to everyone from the settlement, she ran back to the kitchen several hours later and flung the door open, her heart pounding. Silence. She dashed in to find her son, and there he was, sleeping under the table, his face puffy, striped white from tears, and burrowed in the rag she usually used to wipe the counter. After that, she started leaving him her headscarf – it was better for him to burrow into that. She has to go around with her head uncovered.

Zuleikha has been doing many things of late that would have seemed shameful and impossible before.

She prays rarely and in haste. She became convinced during the recent starvation that Allah neither saw nor heard them, because if the Almighty had heard even one of the thousand tearful prayers that Zuleikha had dispatched to Him during that harsh winter, he would not have left her and Yuzuf bereft of His kindly care. Which means the supreme gaze doesn't reach this out-of-the-way place. Living without the constant attention and stern supervision of an all-seeing eye was initially terrifying, as if she'd been orphaned. Then she got used to it and resigned herself. By habit, she sometimes sends hurried little prayers to heavenly heights; it's like sending postcards from distant, savage places without any real hope they'll reach the addressee.

She goes into the *urman* alone and for long periods. That this truly is *urman* – gloomy and dense, with trees felled by wind – is something she understood on the very first day serving the lumber teams, her belly chilled from fear when she set off running to the felling area along a barely defined trail. She knows that prayers in the *urman* have no effect so she wastes no time on them, flying between trees like a shadow, not noticing the branches lashing at her face, her jaw clenching and eyes bulging from horror, and thinking all the while of her son waiting for her in the settlement, which means she must return. She remains alive; the *urman* doesn't touch her. Soon she grows bolder and begins walking instead of running. She'll notice a marten that flashes like black lightning in reddish-brown needles or a nimble yellow crossbill hurrying somewhere along a spruce branch or the giant hulk of an elk crowned by a branching bush of horns and solemnly floating between red pine trunks, and she grasped then that the *urman* is gracious to her, not angry about the intrusion. When she finds several bilberries by an old stump overgrown with shaggy moss, she picks them with gratitude, puts them away in the pocket of her smock for Yuzuf, and calms because the *urman* has accepted her.

She doesn't know the local spirits so doesn't know how to honor them; she just greets them silently when she enters the woods or goes down to the river. That's all. It's possible all sorts of forest and river imps can be found here, too, like long-fingered *shurale* rascals, darting around the forest's thickets in search of travelers who've lost their way, or loathsome *alabasty*, who crawl out from under the earth at the smell of human flesh, and *su-anasy*, those shaggy water-dwellers known to grab people and drag them down to the riverbed. Zuleikha encounters none of them in the *urman*, so either spirits don't live in these remote parts of the universe or they're quieter and more submissive than their kin in Yulbash's forests. One could try to feed them so they'll let themselves be known, make an appearance, and then take you under their protection. But Zuleikha can't even contemplate giving a piece of food – be it leftover porridge, boiled fish skin, or soft grouse gristle – to some imp instead of her son.

She's stopped her daily commemorations of her husband, mother-in-law, and daughters. She doesn't have the strength because she gives whatever's left to Yuzuf and it seems silly and unwise to spend valuable minutes of her life remembering the dead. It's better to give her time to the small living being who waits greedily all day for his mother's affection or smile.

She works side by side for days at a time with a man who isn't her kin. Her shoulders often bump into Achkenazi and their hands even touch – their working space in the dining hall is cramped.

Everything her mother once taught her – what was considered correct and necessary in her half-forgotten life in her husband's house, and what seemed to constitute Zuleikha's essence, foundation, and substance – is being taken apart and destroyed. Rules are being broken, laws are turning into their own opposites. New rules are arising and new laws are being revealed in exchange.

No abyss is opening up beneath her feet, avenging lightning isn't flying from the heavens, and wild beasts from the *urman* aren't capturing her in their sticky webs. People don't notice those transgressions, either. They don't see them because they have other concerns.

Zuleikha also brings dinner to the commandant's headquarters every evening.

Inmates and guards eat supper together in the dining hall, workers at their tables, guards at their own separate table. Ignatov always eats alone in his own quarters. He rarely eats lunch, which is a meager snack of a couple of rusks or a piece of bread, but he asks that a hearty hot supper be brought to him.

After reheating leftovers of the lunch soup in a small kettle and tossing the fattiest, largest pieces of fish or the thickest porridge, from the bottom of the pot, into a large bowl, Zuleikha places all that on a wide board and carries it up the knoll from the dining hall, to a neat little house, the only one in the settlement with glass windows. The path upward is long and takes time, and Zuleikha walks along it slowly, carefully placing her feet and gathering her courage. She doesn't know what's happening. No, she knows. She knows what's happening. There's no point in hiding it from herself.

At first it seemed Ignatov didn't notice her at all. She would enter after timidly knocking and hurriedly place the food on the table without hearing a word in response and she felt how stuffy and dense the air was there, as if it were water instead of air. After she'd ducked back out the door, she'd fly down the path, relieved and breathing deeply, understanding she'd been holding her breath in the commandant's headquarters for some reason, as if she truly had been underwater. The commandant would stand by the window that whole time, facing outside, or lie on his bed with his eyes covered. Not only did he never look, he never once raised an eyebrow.

One time, though, he suddenly stared at her. She felt that gaze without looking up. "Is everything all right?" she asked. "Is the food salted enough?" Ignatov didn't answer, he just looked. She slipped out and took a breath. As she walked down the path, she sensed that gaze on her neck, in the place where the hair starts to grow. She's started wearing a headscarf to go to Ignatov's. And he's started looking at her. Now the air isn't even water, it's becoming honey. Zuleikha is in that honey, gliding, tensing all her muscles and stretching her sinews, but everything's moving slowly, like in a dream. Try as she might, she cannot possibly move any faster; she wouldn't be able to even if there was a fire. She walks out the door, tired, as if she's been chopping firewood, and she needs something to drink.

She knows what's happening because Murtaza had looked at her that way many years ago, when the youthful Zuleikha had just come into his house as his wife. Her husband's killer is looking at her with her husband's gaze.

If only she didn't have to go to Ignatov's, then she could stay out of his sight. But how could she get out of it? She couldn't send Achkenazi to him with plates. And so she goes, slowly climbing up the path, opening the heavy door, inhaling deeply, and then ducking into the thick, viscous honey. She senses herself, all of her, gradually turning to honey. Her hands, which place the pot on the table and seem to flow along it, her feet, which stride along the floor and seem to stick to it, and her head, which wants to drive her right out of this place but softens, fusing and melting under her very, very tightly tied headscarf.

Her husband's killer is looking at her with her husband's gaze and she's turning to honey. This is agonizing, unbearable, and horrendously shameful. It's as if all her past and present shame has merged, absorbing everything she hasn't felt shameful enough about during this mad year: the many nights spent side by side with unknown people, unknown men, in the darkness of dungeons and the crowdedness of the railroad car; her pregnancy, borne in front of others from the first months until the end; and giving birth around people. In order to somehow escape that shame and overcome the improper thoughts, Zuleikha often imagines a large black tent made of thick, crudely dressed sheepskins and resembling Bashkir yurts. The tent covers Ignatov and the commandant's headquarters like a solid lid, and when the door curtain is drawn at the entrance, everything carnal, shameful, and ugly remains there, inside. Zuleikha leaps on a large Argamak horse, digs him sharply with her bare heels, and speeds away without looking back.

It's already dark when Konstantin Arnoldovich comes to the commandant's headquarters; the hushed settlement is sleeping after supper. He scratches meekly at the door for a long time and then, after not receiving an answer, he takes small, shuffling steps around the building, and finally peers in a window. There he encounters the commandant's stern face, with the bold reddish spark of a hand-rolled cigarette in his teeth. Ignatov's sitting on the windowsill, smoking.

"Well, Sumlinsky?"

"Comrade commandant," says Konstantin Arnoldovich, pronouncing the vowels with special care, letting them fully develop in his mouth, so they come out long and smooth. "Comrade commandant, we have a matter to take up with you."

"Well?"

Konstantin Arnoldovich steals closer and wraps his soiled, completely buttonless little jacket around his chest.

"Our settlement doesn't have a name."

"Doesn't have a what?" Ignatov doesn't immediately understand.

"A name. A title, if you like. There's a settlement but there's no title. We've living in a populated spot that's unnamed and unplotted on the map. Maybe it'll cease to exist tomorrow but today – today! – it exists. And we exist in it, too. And we want our home to have a name."

"And you don't want plumbing and hot water?"

"No, we don't want plumbing." Konstantin Arnoldovich sighs, serious. "A name requires no material expenditures. The settlement will be given a name sooner or later. And so we ... hmm ... as its very first residents, would like to exercise the right to name it."

Ignatov inhales. The orange cuff on the tip of his hand-rolled cigarette flares and Sumlinsky's sharp cheekbones catch fire for a second and then dissolve back into the darkness so only his eyes glisten. He lost his pince-nez in the forest back in the autumn and has had to get by without; his eyes have seemed overly piercing, even impertinent, since they've been deprived of their customary gold frame.

"So what do you want to call ... all of this?"

Konstantin Arnoldovich grins, flustered, and nods his head for some reason.

He finally utters it, solemnly: "Vila."

"What?"

"It's an acronym," says Sumlinsky, whose speech suddenly becomes hurried. "You see, it's an abbreviation formed by joining initial letters. We took four names: Volf, Ivan, Lukka, and Avdei. It works out V, I, L, A, Vila. It's all very simple!"

Ignatov knows three of them but Ivan? There's no Ivan at all among the old-timers, Ignatov remembers that for sure. He releases smoke into the darkness, where Konstantin Arnoldovich's anxious breathing is audible.

"The four people who saved our lives that winter – it's worth naming the settlement after them, don't you think?"

A hefty fish splashes loudly somewhere on the Angara.

"There's one other thing ..." Konstantin Arnoldovich takes a step toward the window, pressing his intertwined hands to his chest. "They don't know we want to, hmm, immortalize them. Neither Volf Karlovich nor Avdei and Lukka. But now you know."

How did the exiles find out his name is Ivan? Nobody calls

him anything but "comrade commandant," only the overstepping Gorelov sometimes says "comrade Ignatov." And what is this? A labor settlement carrying his name? Damn it all to hell ... Ignatov crushes the cigarette butt against a flat stone on the windowsill and flings it into the darkness.

"No," he says.

"We're proposing a completely different official explanation!" Konstantin Arnoldovich bobs up toward the window and his wizened little paws catch at the frame. "We understand. Don't think we don't. We'll state that we're naming the settlement in honor of Vladimir Ilyich Lenin: Vi-la!"

He giggles, satisfied, rubbing his hands together.

"No," repeats Ignatov. "No villas and mansions here."

"Excellent!" For some reason, Sumlinsky, the "remainder," is as cheerful as if he's received approval. "We thought as much, that you wouldn't agree! So we prepared a reserve option – hmm, something more clandestine."

"Go get some sleep, Sumlinsky," says Ignatov, taking hold of the open window.

"Sem' Ruk, named after your seven hands!" Konstantin Arnoldovich blurts into the closing window. "Because there are seven hands among the four of you. Let's name the settlement that way – nobody will ever guess it, you hear me? And the name resonates. It's possibly even unique."

The window slams with a crash. Through a layer of glass, a skinny figure with drooping shoulders takes small steps down the path to the settlement.

It was as if Sumlinsky had known something in advance. A couple of weeks later, during another round of visits to his holdings, Kuznets says to Ignatov in passing:

"We want to give your settlement a name, commandant. You'll now be Angara Twelve. That's what we'll put on the map."

"It already has a name," objects Ignatov, surprising even himself. "There wasn't anything to do in the underground house during the winter and people thought it up."

"Well? Why'd you keep quiet?"

"Who was I to tell? And you didn't ask."

"So how are you now to be named and extolled?" Kuznets's gaze is attentive and persistent.

"Sem' Ruk," is Ignatov's delayed response.

"Tricky. Did a priest fit you out with that name by any chance?"

"What?"

"You're a nut! That name reeks of religious prejudice, that's what. Of six-winged seraphs and the like."

"You're a fool, Kuznets, even if you're my chief." They'd recently switched to using first names, but when they argued they lashed each other with surnames, as before. "My contingent is entirely Tatars and Mordvins and Chuvash who've likely gone their whole lives without ever seeing a priest, not to mention a seraph."

"To hell with you." Kuznets waves his arm. "Sem' Ruk it is!"

And so the name Konstantin Arnoldovich thought up survives, and zips through all the paperwork and the chain of command. Among the complete and extremely long list of newly formed populated spots – by that time there are already a good hundred in the Eastern Siberian territory – their name falls to the chairman of the Irkutsk Oblast Committee of the Party for approval. An empty-headed woman in the typing pool who's hugely upset that she hadn't been able to buy more longed-for lisle stockings at three rubles a pair from a greedy profiteer the day before, makes a mistake in the name, writing it all as one word and making it look like yet another bureaucratic neologism. The lists are approved. The typesetter at the printing house doesn't see the mistake and so a no less sonorous, albeit slightly altered name for the settlement – Semruk, for "Sevenhands" – is entered into all the directories and maps.

It happens the first time in late June. Zuleikha doesn't realize anything at the time. She's just carried two buckets full of water into the kitchen and is dragging them to the worktable where Achkenazi is bent over like a fishhook and already practicing his magic on pearlescent fish fanned out on the table.

Yuzuf, who's been crouching by the door waiting for his mother, darts toward her like a wild animal, but then suddenly collapses on the floor and lies motionless, as if he's been shot. Zuleikha rushes over, grabs him, and shakes him. His face is white, his lips are gray-blue with an inky tinge, and he's not breathing. "To the infirmary, fast!" says Achkenazi. Zuleikha picks up his motionless little body, which has cooled in an instant, and flies off.

Leibe has been examining some old man whose skin has begun peeling off in layers, like pine bark, from exhaustion. Zuleikha places her son on the table right between the old man and the doctor, catches hold of Leibe and howls, unable to explain anything. He examines the little boy, listens, frowns, and gives him a shot of some sort of sharp-smelling medicine from a glass syringe as long and thin as a finger.

"It's just as well that they brought all this last month," he says, "both the medicines and the syringes."

Yuzuf comes to a minute later, sleepy, and his little eyes blink. Zuleikha's still howling; she can't calm down at all.

"All right, that's enough, now …" Leibe catches his breath, unbuttons his collar, and drinks half a mug of water. "And if anything happens again, come straight to me."

Zuleikha carries Yuzuf back to the kitchen. As she walks through the settlement, everything rocks around her, and she's clutching her son to herself; she just can't hug him enough. She starts cleaning fish and her eyes are constantly drawn under the table, where sleepy Yuzuf has crawled. She crouches down every minute to check that everything's all right, that he hasn't fallen again. He's curled into a ball and gone to sleep. Zuleikha leans over him and listens. Is he breathing? "I'd let you go home today, Zuleikha, but the administration might not like that," Achkenazi tells her, as if apologizing. That's the longest sentence he's ever said to her.

The problem repeats several weeks later, this time in the evening, as Zuleikha is putting Yuzuf to bed. She again brings him to the doctor, who gives another injection.

She stops sleeping at night. How can you fall asleep if that can happen at night, too? She lies alongside her son, listening to his breathing, guarding him. Her periods away from Yuzuf, when she takes lunch to the workers at the logging sites, have become torture. Zuleikha runs along the path with full buckets, worrying, wondering if it's happening again. Or will in a minute? Or two? Achkenazi doesn't look up from the cutting board so he wouldn't notice. And Yuzuf's constantly resting under the table. She comes back in a lather every time, her heart exploding from the running, and then she throws herself under the table. Is he alive? She's begun handling her kitchen tasks poorly. She's afraid Achkenazi will complain and they'll banish her from the kitchen, for general assignment work. But Achkenazi turns out to be a person with heart and puts up with it.

It happens again one night in August. Zuleikha's open eyes are gazing into the darkness, and she's listening to Yuzuf's breathing. It's as if she's rocking on waves: *inhale-exhale, inhale-exhale, up-down, up-down*. The exhaustion of the past weeks is dragging her by the feet, down into a heavy, heavy sleep. It feels sweet and cozy to close her eyes for a moment and give up resistance. The water's rocking and persuading her and then Ignatov's face is suddenly alongside her, calm and affectionate. *Give me your hand*, he says. *Come on, you'll drown in the honey.* Lo and behold, everything around her is yellow, as if it's made of gold. She sticks out the tip of her tongue and it truly is honey. It wakes her up. Her mouth is thick with saliva and she can taste sweetness. The sounds – her neighbors' breathing and snoring and nocturnal stirrings – are all far away, not with her. It's quiet and serene next to her.

Yuzuf isn't breathing.

She shakes him. No, he's not breathing. Barefoot, with her braids undone, she rushes him to the infirmary. The moon in the sky is as round as a coin, the wind is whipping off the Angara, and there are pine cones, sticks, rocks, and soil underfoot, but she doesn't notice anything. She pounds on the front window first, almost knocking out the newly installed glass, but there's nobody there. After coming to her senses, she runs around to the back of the building, to the living quarters.

Disheveled from sleep, Leibe runs to her in just his drawers, which are threadbare and almost transparent. He lights the kerosene lamp and puts the boy on his own bed. Yuzuf's hands, forehead, and the tip of his nose are already ice cold. After the injection, he begins breathing, groaning, and crying. He calms in his mother's arms then falls back to sleep. And Zuleikha's own arms are shuddering hard, not in a good way; she nearly drops the child.

"Lay your son here," Leibe whispers to her. "And calm down."

She places Yuzuf on the doctor's pillow, a shaggy fur hat turned inside out. Her legs buckle, not supporting her. She positions herself so her knees are on the freshly planed floorboards, her torso's on the bed, and her face is by her son's warmed-up little fingers.

"It worked out fine this time, too," says Leibe, extending a mug of water to her. "It's good you noticed. If it had been another few minutes ..."

Zuleikha grabs the doctor's wrinkled hand, sprinkled with brown spots, and stretches to reach it with her lips. Water splashes from the mug to the floor.

"Stop that immediately!" He angrily tears his hand away. "You should take a drink!"

She takes the mug. Her teeth chatter loudly against the tin; she doesn't want to wake Yuzuf so she sets the water aside to drink more later.

"Doctor," whispers Zuleikha, without rising from her knees (she surprises herself: are these her lips speaking?), "let us live in the infirmary for a while, me and Yuzuf. I couldn't bear it if anything happened to him. Don't send us away, let us stay. Save him. And I'll do everything for you. I'll launder, tidy up, and pick berries. And I can help with patients if you need. Just so Yuzuf will be here at night, closer to you."

"Live here as long as you want," shrugs the doctor. "If the commandant's not against it."

A half-hour later, Zuleikha has dragged her simple belongings to the infirmary and Yuzuf hasn't even had a chance to wake up – he's slept calmly through the whole night, all the way until morning, on the doctor's furry pillow.

Leibe goes to the commandant himself rather than waiting for questions. "Here's how it is," he reports. "The patient requires care in the infirmary. This situation will not affect Zuleikha Valieva's capacity for labor in any way." Ignatov looks at him sullenly and unkindly, but doesn't object.

Zuleikha and Yuzuf are allotted a bunk walled off by a curtain. After the stuffiness of the communal barracks, the strong-smelling air at the infirmary – with carbolic acid, alcohol, juniper, lingonberry leaves, St. John's wort, and Labrador tea – seems clean and fresh. In the mornings, Zuleikha runs off to the dining hall with Yuzuf under her arm. In the evenings, she hurries back and cleans the infirmary rather than taking her usual outings into the forest for bent milk-stool mushrooms or cattails. She washes the floors, walls, tables, benches, windows, and bunks (even those that are empty), battling unsanitary conditions. Then she makes her way into the residential half, where she scrubs the floorboards and the large stove made of stones, and scours the front steps. She washes all the doctor's clothes in the Angara. She learns to boil bandages and basic medical instruments in a kettle.

"Don't strain yourself, I beg of you!" Leibe tells her, raising his long withered hands toward the low ceiling. "You should get some sleep!"

They take turns watching over Yuzuf's bedside, half the night each. Leibe maintains that he's already sleeping an elderly person's short hours, making nightwatch duty easy for him. If he had been anyone else, Zuleikha would not have been able to go to sleep, but she trusts the doctor. She goes to bed and drops into the blackness of sleep, without thoughts and without dreams.

The doctor himself suggests she bring Yuzuf back to the infirmary from the dining hall during her afternoon absences at the logging sites, and Zuleikha gratefully agrees.

When a lemon-yellow man with a constant violent cough and black circles under his eyes is admitted to the infirmary, Leibe orders that they move into the residential quarters, with him. Zuleikha hesitates at first – what will people say? – but when she meets the doctor's stern gaze, she hurriedly brings her son into the back of the infirmary, behind a solid door.

That happens in late summer. The second year of the exiles' stay in the settlement is beginning.

Zuleikha places a kettle with bandages inside the hot stove. She always launders and rinses the bandages in the running water of the Angara; her hands feel wooden after that, aching, making it all the more pleasant to hold them against the hot side of the stove, sensing the flow of blood into her hands and feeling the skin on her fingertips again. The fire crackles under the base of the blackened kettle, greedily eating the rest of a log that's been tossed in. Zuleikha will have time to run out to the yard for firewood while the water comes to a boil – the bandages aren't supposed to boil for long but she likes to keep them in until they're white.

Yuzuf is frolicking on the floor, crawling and playing with clay toys that Ikonnikov sculpted. First he'd made a round-bellied baby doll resembling a fat spindle with plump lips that look like they've been turned inside out; then came a pompous tufted bird with shaggy legs and funny wings not designed for flight; and finally there came a sturdy, hefty fish with insolently bugged eyes and a stubborn lower jaw. The toys are good since they're neither too large nor overly small, each fitting comfortably into a child's small hand, nor heavy, and – most important – each one has a living gaze. In addition, they have the extraordinarily convenient benefit in that the legs, wings, and fins that Yuzuf breaks off have a habit of growing back after Ikonnikov drops in at the infirmary while going about his errands.

While Yuzuf's enjoying knocking together the fragile clay foreheads of eternal rivals – the bird and the fish – Zuleikha rushes to go out to the yard so her son won't notice she's gone. The door opens on its own a moment before Zuleikha has a chance to touch it. A tall, dark silhouette stands in the opening, coming through rays of sun that beat at Zuleikha's face. A wide, floor-length dress flaps in the wind and a crooked staff sternly bangs at the threshold.

The Vampire Hag.

She strides into the house. Her nose leads her, its broad nostrils twitching, inhaling air.

"It smells of something," she says.

Zuleikha jumps away, her back screening Yuzuf, who's playing on the floor. He's crawling, babbling something under his breath, ramming the little hand that's tightly squeezing the fish at the bird, who's rapidly retreating under the enemy onslaught. He doesn't notice a thing. Zuleikha's mother-in-law walks about, sniffing loudly and using her stick to toss things that fall in her path. It's as if she clearly sees them. An overturned chair crashes, an empty bucket rolls and clanks, and empty little clay dishes fly from the table to the floor.

"It smells!" she repeats, loudly and insistently.

There are strong smells of scorching-hot stove stones and boiling bandages in the house, and weaker smells of smoke, seasoned firewood, and fresh wood. The faintest smells of carbolic acid and alcohol hover, and a spicy, flowery aroma comes from fat bunches of herbs hanging under the ceiling.

The old woman is coming toward her. Zuleikha sees her flat, white eye sockets, coated with a bluish film like the skin of a freshly cleaned fish and covered with a thick network of knotty red blood vessels. Her soft and very sparse hair the color of dust is parted at the exact middle of her forehead in a neat path, and wound into long, thin braids.

The Vampire Hag breathes hard and her nostrils make a snuffling sound. The tip of her stick reaches for the hem of Zuleikha's dress and lifts it, baring pale, naked legs that seem to gleam in the duskiness of the house. Zuleikha made her baggy pants into diapers long ago, back last autumn. The old woman smirks so the corner of her mouth creeps upward and sinks into the large folds of her wrinkles.

"I found what smells," she says. "It's *fekhishe*, the smell of whore."

Nobody had ever called Zuleikha that. A horrid, suffocating heat rises from her chest, over her neck, cheeks, and forehead, to the very top of her head.

"Yes," the Vampire Hag repeats louder. "The smell of a whore who thinks at night about the Russian man Ivan, murderer of my Murtaza ..."

Zuleikha shakes her head, squeezing her eyes shut. There was no denying it.

"... and is living with a German man, the infidel Volf!"

"I need to raise my son," Zuleikha whispers through her dried throat, "to put him on his feet. He's already over a year old but doesn't walk. He can't even stand. And that's your grandson."

She steps to the side, revealing her son sitting on the floor for the Vampire Hag, as if she truly could see him. Yuzuf keeps playing – the fish and the bird are united in his persistent little hands and jointly attacking the poor doll, who already lacks an arm.

The Vampire Hag squeamishly pulls her walking stick away from Zuleikha, as if she's been dirtied by muck.

"You forgot about sharia law and human law. I used to tell Murtaza, 'That woman's unfit, unclean in both body and thought –'"

"Murtaza died. I have the right to marry a second time!"

"And before the eyes of all the people, she's spending the night under the same roof as a man who's not her husband! Who is she after that? A whore is who!" The old woman loudly and juicily spits under her feet.

"I'll become the doctor's lawful wife!"

"*Fekhishe!* Whore! Whore!" The Vampire Hag shakes her head slightly and the bulky flourishes of her earrings jingle softly in her fleshy earlobes.

"I swear!" Zuleikha's head sinks into her shoulders and she quickly lifts a hand, defending herself.

When she lowers her hand, there's no longer anyone beside her. Yuzuf is peacefully frolicking, enjoying knocking his clay toys together. The wood in the stove crackles as it burns; water is burbling loudly, spilling out of the kettle, and hissing on scorching-hot coals. Zuleikha sits down on the floor alongside her son, buries her face in her hands, and whimpers quietly, like a puppy.

On the last day of summer, white clouds are floating like apple blossoms, and the Angara is dark, a deep blue verging on black that rises from its depths on particularly warm and sunny days. There's a light, dry autumn warmth.

Zuleikha is striding along a forest path. Yuzuf is on her back, wrapped in a shawl, and she has a basket in one hand and a staff in the other. Reddish tree needles and the first fallen leaves, fragile and already tinged with a sickly yellowness, crunch underfoot. She is grateful to Achkenazi for letting her go into the taiga today to pick berries for compote. It's already darkening early in the evenings, so she can't go after dinner. This is an excuse devised by the *maître*, since they could have gotten by without compote today – it's not a holiday and the chief isn't expected to arrive. But Achkenazi felt sorry for her so decided to give her a day off. He sees she's not herself lately, isn't sleeping much, and works enough for three.

Zuleikha is afraid to go too far away from the settlement – just in case something happens with Yuzuf – so she walks to a familiar stand of bilberry plants in the pine forest. She steps on large, flat rocks to cross a brook that roars resoundingly (she thinks of it as the Chishme), then strides further along it, to the base of the large cliff where there sprawls a broad, light clearing, which she's privately named "Round Clearing." There's a patch of plentiful berries hidden here, guarded by a huge old birch scorched by lightning and a detachment of red-trunked pines. Large, beady bilberries grow so plentifully, like stars in the sky on a clear night, that you can just sit and gather them. The berries are heavy and purple and they look like they're covered with light-blue velvet; touch one and a dark trace remains on its round side. They're juicy, sweet, and honeyed, too. Zuleikha has plenty to eat herself and feeds Yuzuf. He's smiling and his teeth shine with the berries' ink. This is delicious, and joyful, too, because he has his mother's attention for so long without her leaving.

"That's all, *ulym*," says Zuleikha, wiping smudges of sticky red juice from his chin. "We've played enough. I need to get to work."

She spreads the shawl in the shade of the pines and sits Yuzuf on it. She tosses a scarf on her hair so her head doesn't get too hot. Then she starts crawling around like a snail, picking berries. The basket is large and deep, and she can fill it if she puts in the effort.

Yuzuf is babbling something, telling stories to the flowers. Although he hasn't yet learned to talk, not a single word, he goos and gahs away at the flowers in his own language, while examining them. This scared Zuleikha at first because she wondered if he'd grow up to be an imbecile. Her son's eyes are smart and thoughtful, though, so she's decided that maybe a time will come when he begins speaking. If he remains mute, fine, she'll love him that way, too. She'll feed and raise him. Just so long as he stands and starts walking.

She reaches for heavy berries languishing in the sun, her fingers moving apart thin, wiry bilberry shoots among round, green petal-like leaves. Suddenly there are boots in the bright, shiny greenery. They're black, new, and have been rubbed to a thick, mirror-like shine with wax polish; they're right next to her so she could just reach her hand out and touch them. Zuleikha slowly looks up and sees broad gray breeches growing out of tall narrow boot tops, the hem of a brown shirt, a reddish belt tautly tightened at the waist. And two hands, one holding a long hunting rifle with a burnished barrel. Higher are two chest pockets with flaps, and sitting between them at a slant is a thin strap for a holster. Even higher, buttons that shine in the sun prop up a high, tightly fastened collar. Raspberry-red collar tabs, broadly sweeping shoulders. And somewhere in the distant heights, under the dome of the sky, is a face framed by the halo of a peaked cap, with a fiery-red cap band and dark blue crown.

Ignatov's looking at her.

Pine needles softly stir overhead, moaning a little in the light breeze. The chirr of grasshoppers is loud, heavy, and deafening in the grass. Honeybees are buzzing in the clearing and hefty bumblebees rumble around, flying from flower to flower.

Ignatov leans his rifle against a bright-red tree trunk that looks filled with sunlight, takes off his peaked cap, and drops it in the grass. He unfastens the top button of his shirt, then the second and third. He removes his belt, the buckle on his chest, and the buckle at his waist. Rips his shirt off over his head.

Zuleikha crawls backward a little, still on her hands and knees. Dry autumn grasses sway around her; the ripe seeds inside them turn them into rattles.

He takes a step toward her and crouches down, his face rapidly descending from the sky until it stops very, very close to hers. He extends a hand and his large, long palm completes its seemingly endless journey by touching her chin. When his fingers pull the knot of her headscarf, the tightly tied fabric easily gives way, separating, flowing along her cheeks, and baring her head. Ignatov takes the ends of her braids in both hands and pulls. Zuleikha's hands catch at the braids and she pulls them to herself, not giving them up. He slowly runs his fingers through her hair and the braids slacken, unplaiting.

"I wait for you, every night," he says.

He has a dry smell, of warmth and tobacco.

"Well, don't."

If only she could take his fingers from her hair, but there's no way; they're persistent. And hot, like they were around her fist clenching the loose grains back in the forest in Yulbash.

"But you're a woman. You need a man."

His face is smooth; the wrinkles are as thin as hairs. There's a faint red mark on his forehead, from his peaked cap.

"I have a man. I found one."

His eyes are bright gray with green in their depths and the pupils are broad and black.

"Who?"

His breath is pure, like a child's.

"A lawful husband. I married yesterday, the doctor."

"You're lying."

His face is on hers. Zuleikha squeezes her eyes shut, presses her feet into something, pushes away, and rolls along the ground. She leaps up, grabs the rifle leaning against the tree, and points it at Ignatov.

"He's my husband, before people and heaven," she says and motions with the rifle barrel to go away. "And I'm his wife."

"Lower it, you fool," he answers from the grass. "It'll fire."

"A faithful wife!"

"Lower the barrel, I'm telling you."

"And don't you follow me into the *urman* again!"

Zuleikha squints and clumsily takes aim at Ignatov. The thin black end of the barrel trembles, wandering from side to side. Ignatov groans as he lowers his back into the tall grass.

"You're a fool, what a fool …"

She finally manages to catch the disobediently quivering tip of the front sight in the notch of the back sight. She guides the barrel slowly, looking through the back sight, and the world seems different and more distinct, vivid, and bulging. The grass is lusher and greener over the spot where Ignatov is lying on his back. The butterflies circling the clearing and the dragonflies sitting on spikes of grass are larger and prettier, and Zuleikha even discerns web-like lines on their transparent wings and iridescent spheres in their tiny bulging eyes. The back of Yuzuf's head is further away. Blood vessels form a marble-like pattern on the petals of his little pink ears and a heavy drop of sweat slowly rolls out from under his dark, curly hair to his white neck. Even further is a shaggy brown triangle. A bear's snout.

A huge, glossy bear is standing at the edge of the clearing, gazing lazily, sideways, at Yuzuf. Its damp round nose shakes every now and then and its two lower fangs shine in its half-open jaw like splayed fingers.

"Ivan, how do I shoot?"

It's as if her throat has filled with sand.

"Decided to exterminate me?" Ignatov's angry face rises from the grass. He turns and sees the bear.

"Raise the hammer first," he whispers.

Her wet fingers slide along the cold, sticky metal. Where is it, that hammer? The bear growls, not loudly, first examining the baby sitting in front of it, then Zuleikha and Ignatov, who are frozen at a distance. Yuzuf is watching the animal, rapt.

Zuleikha pulls the hammer toward herself and there's a loud click. The bear growls louder and stands on its hind legs, growing into a powerful, shaggy hulk. They can now see a sunken and light-colored belly with uneven gray dappling, a barrel-like chest that juts forward, and the crooked sickles of claws on long front paws that nearly reach the ground. The beast bares its teeth and a shiny black and pink tongue flashes between yellowed fangs. Yuzuf screeches with joy and stands, too.

Zuleikha squeezes the trigger and a shot bangs. The butt of the rifle strikes her hard and painfully in the shoulder, throwing her backward. Gunpowder sharply hits her nose. Her son's short, frightened shriek is like a bird call.

The bear takes a step toward Yuzuf. A second. A third. Then it collapses to the ground, parting the grass on both sides in broad, green waves. The shaggy carcass continues shuddering for a time, like a huge piece of brown aspic, before going still. Yuzuf turns his puzzled face toward his mother then back toward the beast.

"There, there." Ignatov places his hands on her fingers, which have turned to stone on the rifle butt, and unhooks them one by one. "Now that was good ... good ..."

He finally releases the rifle and sets it aside. Zuleikha doesn't notice because she's watching as Yuzuf toddles over to the dead bear, wobbling a little on his slightly crooked little legs. His first step, second, third ...

A shining bear eye clouds over with a murky film and a thick gray foam flows out from behind yellowed fangs. Yuzuf walks over, loudly slaps his little hand on the bear's bumpy forehead, grabs at its hairy ears and pulls, then turns toward his mother and jubilantly laughs, firmly standing on both feet.

A Good Man

"Leave." Ignatov slows his rapid breathing and rolls on his back; there's a tired emptiness in his body.

"Something happen, Vanya?" Aglaya adjusts her rumpled dress and sits on the bed.

"Leave."

She looks at him a little longer as her slender fingers run through the fasteners on her stockings (the creamy skin of a magnificent thigh flashes among dark woolen folds). Did they come undone? No, there wasn't time. She stands. The soft soles of her feet noiselessly tread over to a tin washbasin, where a crooked sliver of mirror has taken refuge between the logs.

"You're going crazy, Vanya," she says, primping short red ringlets that barely cover her ears. "More and more every day."

Without getting out of bed, Ignatov gropes on the floor for her heavy shoe, a man's shoe with a thick sole and squared toe. He hurls it, hitting her in the back, right, as it happens, on the spot where the dark little delicacy of a beauty mark sits on a round shoulder blade that looks like marble under threadbare cotton. Aglaya cries out and steps backward.

"I told you to leave!" He hurls the other shoe.

"You really are a madman!" Aglaya hastily gathers up her shoes and scampers out the door.

Ignatov stretches an arm under the bed and pulls out a

long, narrow-necked bottle. There's still something cloudy and yellowish splashing like oil at the bottom – not much, though, no more than a finger or two.

"Where … ?" he tiredly asks the ceiling, as if he's repeating it for the tenth time. "Gorelov, you dog … where are you?"

Tangled in a balled-up blanket, rumpled pillows, and his own feet, he falls out of bed. He has trouble rising and holds the walls as he trudges to the door, which he opens wide. A mean, cold wind hits him in the face; the summer of 1938 happens to be cool. Semruk is sprawled below. In the middle are three broad, long barracks that take up almost all the settlement's area, and a couple of dozen outbuildings that cluster around them, forming the semblance of a crooked little street. A small cook in a white apron hits a gong with a ladle, and the harsh, quavering sounds fly along the knoll, rolling further, beyond the Angara and into the taiga. Small figures hurry from every corner of Semruk to the dining hall for supper.

Standing on the front steps in just his underclothes and shaking the empty bottle, Ignatov screams into the evening settlement from the heights of the commandant's headquarters:

"Where are you? I'll kill you, Gorelov! Where are you?"

Gorelov is already running out from behind a corner. He's out of breath and lugging a second bottle, pressed carefully against his chest, where something viscous and gray with an orange tinge gurgles heavily inside, bubbling from being shaken.

"There!" he says, panting with his mouth open, like a dog. He places his burden on the front steps. "It's made from cloudberries, nice and fresh."

Reeling, Ignatov bends, drops the empty bottle, lifts the full one, and goes inside, miraculously not stumbling on the threshold.

*

"My master's dissertation, back in Munich in 1906, was devoted to ideas about the nourishment and cultivation of cereal crops. I saw my work as mostly theoretical, having strategic rather than concrete practical importance. I never imagined for a moment that I would one day cultivate that same wheat myself!" Konstantin Arnoldovich Sumlinsky shakes the brownish flatbread he's clutching in a withered hand with broken fingernails. "Moreover, to eat bread prepared from it!"

There's a quick, even clatter of metal spoons all around them. The exiles are eating supper, sitting at long wooden tables that their elbows and hands have buffed to a pleasant, almost homey smoothness over the years. Two hundred mouths hurriedly chew, wasting no time on unnecessary words. They'd expanded the dining hall several years ago, adding on a second log building that's longer and broader than the first, but four hundred people still won't fit, so Semruk's residents now eat in two shifts, taking turns.

The guards' table, which is spacious and spread with a clean checked tablecloth once a week, remains in its previous spot, not far from the serving area. They eat there watchfully, without hurrying, enjoying the simple but thoroughly decent flavor of the food that's served. It's here – at one end, not taking much space, and prepared to leap right up when summoned – that Gorelov gulps down his thin soup. None of the guards remember when and under whose permission he'd started eating with them, but they tolerate him and don't send him away. He's sitting there so there must be a reason.

"And you consider all this," says Ikonnikov, waving around a worn metal spoon whose handle is a spiral twist and whose sides look like they've been bitten, "reasonable payment for the opportunity to, as you stated it, cultivate wheat?"

Ikonnikov gulps angrily from his bowl. He chews and removes a thin, crooked fish bone from his mouth using fingers stained with ultramarine and cobalt.

"No, not at all, nothing of the kind!" Konstantin Arnoldovich fidgets on the bench, squashing the bread in his small hand. "Now you, Ilya Petrovich, what truly important thing did you create when you were at liberty? Twenty-three busts with mustaches?"

"Twenty-four," Izabella corrects him, neatly tilting her bowl away from herself and spooning out the last remaining brownish leaves in cloudy gray broth.

"And you would have sculpted that many more!" Konstantin Arnoldovich's hand hammers threateningly at the table.

Gorelov rises at the guards' table and surveys the dining hall, looking concerned about the noise.

Izabella slaps her husband's hand affectionately.

"And here" – Sumlinsky can't calm down so he's speaking quickly and loudly – "you're Raphael! Michelangelo! You're not painting a clubhouse, it's the Sistine Chapel. Do you yourself realize that?"

"By the way, Ilya Petrovich, my dear fellow!" Izabella is firmly and significantly squeezing her husband's hand. "You promised to show us –"

The gong – made from a large tin plate that hangs by the dining-hall entrance – suddenly groans, swings, and quivers from a strong strike. A revolver is vigorously pounding it. People exchange glances, set their spoons aside, rise from the tables with their heads down, as usual; some pull the caps off the tops of their heads. The commandant bursts in, wearing wrinkled, mud-spotted breeches he's somehow pulled over his drawers, and a dirty undershirt tautly caught up in uneven suspenders. A lock of brown hair, slightly touched with white, hangs over his eyebrows and his sharp cheekbones wear a brush of uneven stubble.

"Get up!" the commandant booms. He seems to reel slightly from his own shout. "To work! You think I'm going to spoil you?"

Gorelov hastily wipes off his hands on his brown minder's uniform jacket, gets up from the table, and hurries to Ignatov.

"They've already finished their work, comrade commandant!" Gorelov's standing at attention, with his chest bulging and his short-fingered hands stretched at his sides.

Ignatov casts a muddled glance at two hundred bent heads and two hundred dishes of unfinished thin soup on the tables.

"You're gobbling it down, you sons of bitches," he bitterly concludes.

"Yes, sir, comrade commandant!" Gorelov answers, with such resonance and passion it makes the ears ring.

"Insatiable vermin." Ignatov's voice is quiet and tired. "You feed and feed them … When will you ever get enough …"

"They worked up an appetite, comrade commandant! Striving to meet their daily quotas. Fulfilling the plan!"

"Ah, the plan …" Ignatov's brows gently rise along his wrinkled forehead. "And so?"

"They exceeded their quotas, comrade commandant! By an entire ten cubic meters!"

"Good." Ignatov is walking through the rows, peering into sullen faces with lips pressed together, eyes lowered, and cheekbones tense. "Very good."

His unsteady hand slaps the sunken scoliotic chest of a skinny, stooped man with a closely shaven head and large ears that stick out like a child's. Ignatov takes a bowl from the table – clumps of something grayish-green splash around in it – and puts it on the man's head, like a hat.

"We must abide by the plan!" From his warrior-like height, Ignatov bends toward the skinny man, looks confidingly into eyes narrowed from fear, and whispers into ears with thin soup trickling into them. "We won't get anywhere without the plan!" He shakes his head with grief and knocks the bowl with his revolver. The sound is muted and dulled, unlike the gong.

Greens mixed with fish heads are sliding down the skinny man's face. Ignatov nods with satisfaction and threatens everyone else with the barrel of his gun, as if it were an index finger telling them to watch out. He turns and slowly goes to the exit. Finally, he swipes his revolver at the gong. Now that sounds better!

After Ignatov's footsteps have faded, the exiles sit down one at a time, silently take their spoons, and continue eating. Vibrations from the gong hang in the air, creeping into their ears. Still standing, the skinny man pulls the dish from his head, breathing shallowly and wiping his dirty face with his sleeve; someone warily touches him on the shoulder.

"Here," says Achkenazi, sullen as usual. He holds out another dish, filled to the brim with soup that's thick, obviously from the very bottom of the kettle. "Take it, Zaseka. I'm giving you seconds."

"Our commandant's essentially a decent person," says Konstantin Arnoldovich, leaning across the table toward Ikonnikov. "He's moral in his own way. He has his own principles – even if he's not fully aware of them – as well as an undeniable inclination for justice –"

"A good man," Izabella cuts him off. "It's just he's very troubled."

The faces started appearing to him in 1932. For some reason it was before falling asleep that he remembered the first time he'd seen Zuleikha, sitting like a sack on the large sledge, wrapped in a thick headscarf and an oversized sheepskin coat. Then her husband's face suddenly flashed, with bushy brows gathered in a lump on his forehead, a nose with wide and fat nostrils, and a chin like a split hoof. Ignatov saw him as clearly as a photograph. He placed no significance on it and fell asleep, but then Murtaza up and appeared in Ignatov's dream, looking at him silently. Ignatov woke up from that gaze and rolled on his other side, irritated, and then he dreamt of the husband again. He wouldn't leave.

It had gone on from there. The dead began coming at night and watching him. Each time he looked at yet another guest, Ignatov excruciatingly recollected the where, the when, and the how. He would wake up from the pressure of each memory, which would remain fresh, even after turning the pillow over for the tenth time so the cold side was on his cheek. That one was near Shemordan, winter of 1930; that one was in Varzob Gorge, near Dushanbe, in 1922; that one was on the Sviyaga River, in 1920.

He'd killed many in gunfights and battles without seeing their faces, but they came and watched him, too. He recognized them in some strange way that's only possible in dreams, by the turn of a neck, the shape of the back of a head, slouched shoulders, or a saber's stroke. He recalled them all, from the very first, in 1918. They were toughened, dangerous, out-and-out enemies to a man: Denikinites, Czechs in the White Army, Basmachi, and kulaks. He reassured himself that not one was to be pitied. If he were to meet them, he would kill them again without hesitation. He reassured himself but he's almost stopped sleeping.

Those strange, silent dreams – where faces long-forgotten and completely unfamiliar look at him wordlessly and impassively, not asking for anything and not wishing to tell him anything – are more agonizing than the nightmare about the sinking *Clara*, a dream that Ignatov has stopped having in recent years for some reason. His long-term, insomniac tiredness doesn't help, nor does the warmth of a female body beside him. Sometimes home brew helps.

And so Ignatov is glad of Kuznets's unexpected arrival. It's much more pleasant to drink with him than alone or with Gorelov, who's growing more insolent – and more brazenly so – with every passing year.

Ignatov's standing on the front steps of the commandant's headquarters when he throws his arms wide open and shouts,

"He's here!" after seeing the chief's long black launch beyond a hill.

"Huh, so you were expecting me, my good man," Kuznets smirks as he jumps ashore, accurately assessing the strength of the stale alcohol on Ignatov's breath and the circles under eyes as black as coal.

Kuznets shows up for regular inspections every month or two, and after the formality of taking a walk around Semruk and the logging sites, they head to the commandant's headquarters to sit for a while. They sit thoroughly, sometimes for two or three days. Gorelov doesn't participate, though he does provide ample assistance. He himself will bring food from the dining hall. Under Gorelov's personal supervision, Achkenazi takes from his pantries sun-dried bream and preserved lingonberries stored away for the occasion, and braises herbs and game procured in the forest in short order; fruit puddings and drinks are also served "for a sweet and pleasant start to the day." In addition, Gorelov will command bathhouse preparations, ensuring the fire is stoked and bundles of leaves readied (the bathhouse was built the previous year beyond a river bend some distance from the settlement and they take turns bathing: men one Sunday, women the next); and he will make the women scour Kuznets's launch, moored at the tiny wooden berth, until it sparkles.

By all appearances, their get-together can be expected to be genial this time. Gorelov sweats profusely as he drags Kuznets's case up from the shore and it's as heavy as if it were stone, with something clinking and gurgling inside, sounding muffled and expensive. Kuznets is wary of the local home brew so usually brings his own drink with him, something he has purchased.

They take a walk along the shore and inspect the timber landing by the river, which is swarming with people and filled with high piles of logs as tall as a person. They go inside the freshly constructed log building that will be a school; classes are set to begin in September. They admire the uprooting of stumps on new land for crops. Their experiments with cultivating grains have been successful and it's been decided to use another piece of the taiga as a field. They look at each other with relief: *Well, so, is it time to sit for a while?* And they go.

Their conversations at the table turn out to be warm, even heartfelt. Ignatov knows Kuznets is taking detailed mental notes of everything he says, whether sober, tipsy, or passing out from drunken intoxication, but Ignatov isn't afraid of that because he has nothing to hide. All his sins are as prominently on display as Kuznets's mustache. There's even something attractive about that, some special joy that smacks of vengeance – drinking with a person from whom you have no secrets and can no longer keep secrets, but who might himself have secrets. So let Kuznets tense up, keep himself in check, and hold his tongue, afraid of letting something slip. He, Ignatov, sits down at the table with ease and joy, as if he's offering up his own bared soul for show.

"Where's this from?" Kuznets takes a small yellow turnip the size of a child's fist, with a long and fluffy green tail like a comet, from a table set with dishes, bowls, cups, and kettles of various sizes.

"Well, I have this … agronomist here," says Ignatov, gulping impatiently as he pours crisp-sounding Moscow vodka into glasses with sharp, gleaming facets.

They usually drink from mugs but Kuznets brought glasses with him this time; he apparently wants to sit for a while in good taste, the urban way. A lush green label the color of young conifer needles on the bottle's round side promises pure fifty-percent enjoyment, guaranteed by the USSR's Glavspirtprom trademark. They finally clink glasses. The turnip is sharp and juicy, with a hint of gentle bitterness, so it turns out to be just the thing with the vodka.

"Let's consider our meeting open," says Kuznets. He eats his turnip whole, leaves and all, and waves his fat fingers over the glasses, gesturing as if to say: *Come on, hurry up with the second now.* "Here you go, Vanya, first item: kulak growth, damn it to hell."

Kulak growth is what the authorities have begun calling the rapid accumulation of wealth among exiled peasants. After being sent thousands of kilometers from their native homes, they're the ones who've recovered six or eight years after the blow, adapting somewhat in alien places and contriving, even there, to earn an extra kopek, set it aside, and use it later to buy up personal inventory and even cattle. In brief, the peasantry that lost absolutely everything is kulakizing all over again, and of course that's completely intolerable. And thus a wise decision was made at the highest levels of government to stop the growth immediately, punish those guilty, and organize the kulaks (who practiced their ineradicable individualism so craftily even in exile) into collective farms. A wave of punitive actions for permitting so much rekulakization had already swept through the ranks of the People's Commissariat for Internal Affairs, adding to the relentless flow of repressions during 1937 and 1938.

They tackle the first question on the agenda quickly. The bottle doesn't even have a chance to empty, for what is there to yammer about anyway when everything's clear? Forbid private construction (in Semruk, a few especially nimble people have already finished building themselves small, solid houses, moved out of the barracks, and started families) and hold a general meeting with an explanatory discussion, cautioning against kulakization.

"Oh, yes, we will hold one," Ignatov promises the green label, picking at its fancy edge with his fingernail. "Oh, will we caution ..."

Their session's second item for discussion flows organically from the first: organizing a local collective enterprise.

Back in January of 1932, the USSR's Council of Labor and Defense issued a resolution "On seeds for special migrants," under which labor settlements were to be regularly supplied with grain seeds so they could independently produce their own bread and cereals. Seeds have been provided to Semruk, too. There's oats, barley, wheat, and, for some reason, even warmth-loving hemp, which doesn't have enough time to mature in the meager Siberian sun. Sumlinsky has taken on agronomist responsibilities and has been handling the job fairly well. Ever since receiving Ignatov's cautious permission, he has had the audacity to order additional seed resources from the central office over the last two years (the insolent man even indicated specific sorts!), and thus turnip made its appearance at the settlement, along with carrots, bulb onions, and radishes. Sumlinsky has been obsessed for two years with the idea of growing melons but Ignatov, fearing ridicule, has forbidden him from including melon seeds in the order. Their harvests cannot be considered abundant, though they should be worth the working hours invested. They eat their own bread at the settlement and occasionally vegetables, too. It's true the grain they prepare doesn't last the winter, but they're now readying another field where Sumlinsky intends to grow autumn-seeded crops.

The second bottle has emptied; ten of Kuznets's expensive cigarettes have been smoked; all the turnips and radishes, which were as small as peas and awfully sour to the taste, as well as the supper that Gorelov brought (flaky fried fish in breadcrumbs, still sizzling with smoked pork fat) have been eaten; and the kerosene lamp is already burning lemon-yellow through the thick blue-gray smoke: but the question still isn't closed. Kuznets wants the Semruk collective farm to supply products not only to the settlement but also to the "mainland."

"What am I going to supply you with?" Ignatov shakes a pale green scallion with feathery, white-tinged leaves in front of

Kuznets's raspberry-colored face. "These vegetables are only enough for one meal for the settlement. The wheat barely matures! We work for a year and eat for a month! Four hundred mouths!"

"Then try harder!" Kuznets tears the onion from Ignatov's fingers, stuffs it in his broad maw, and grinds it with his teeth. "What do you think, my dear man? That we're establishing a collective farm so it's just your own kisser chowing on turnip? You've got four hundred pairs of hands! Be ever so kind! Labor along and share with the state!"

They send for Sumlinsky. He runs up, disheveled from sleep and wearing a jacket he's tossed on to cover his underclothes. They splash something into a mug for him but Konstantin Arnoldovich refuses to drink and just stands by the table, frightened, with his cheeks wrinkled and his hair sticking up. After grasping the essence of the question, he grows pensive, furrows his brow, and smoothes his long, sparse beard, which has taken on an utterly goat-like look over the years.

"Why not supply?" he says. "We can supply, too."

Ignatov slams his hands on the table out of annoyance. *Here I am protecting these fools and then they go sticking their necks in the noose on their own.* After the hand gesture, he lowers his head to the table, too; all the talking has worn him out. Kuznets is roaring with laughter: *Nice job, old man. I love people like you!*

"But," adds Sumlinsky, "there's a series of necessary conditions."

And so he counts on his pointy fingers. "No fewer than fifteen people as workers in the collective farm, the sturdiest and handiest men, and they have to be on a permanent basis, not like now, as volunteers and with other assignments on their days off: that's first. The seed stock has to be in strict accordance with the preliminary order I personally compiled. And I need the right to refuse rotten or spoiled grain if that's what's supplied under the guise of seed stock, like in 1934. That's the second thing. Bring new metal tools for uprooting trees because the wooden ones are torture. Sometimes we work with rocks, like primitive people, but we need pickaxes, crowbars, spades, hoes, and pitchforks of all sizes. I'll compile a list. That's third. Agricultural tools are another matter. A lot of these are needed, too. I'll specify those in a list in a separate section so nobody's confused: that's fourth. Definitely beasts of burden, five or more oxen – we can't plow without them; they could come toward next spring, toward the beginning of sowing: that's fifth. Now fertilizers ..."

As Kuznets listens, his neck, which is already crimson, is gradually turning purple, too. Kuznets can't contain himself by the time all the fingers on one of Sumlinsky's hands have been used and he's moving on to the next.

"Who are you anyway," he hisses, "you bastard, setting conditions for me, Zinovy Kuznets?"

Konstantin Arnoldovich lowers his hands and wilts.

"Probably nobody," he says. "But at one time I was head of the applied botany department at the Institute of Experimental Agronomy – there is such a place in Leningrad. And a very long time ago – one might say in a previous life – I was a member of the scientific committee at the Ministry of Arable Farming and State Property. That was back in Petersburg."

"I'll set the conditions for you; you won't do it for me, you minister of arable farming. When I give the order, you'll improve the collective farm on your own, without the sturdiest and handiest men and without oxen, too. You'll plow the land with your own rod, not some tools."

"You can give an order to me," Sumlinsky says to the floor, "but you can hardly give an order to the grain."

Ignatov tears his heavy, unwieldy head off the table.

"Let's have a drink, Zin. And that one" – Ignatov's dulled gaze has trouble fumbling around for Konstantin Arnoldovich's frail figure, which seems to be soaring over the floor in the dense cigarette smoke – "toss him out of here. Let him put it all in writing."

Kuznets is breathing loudly; he throws a parsley leaf in his mouth and rolls it along his teeth.

"Let's drink," says Ignatov, pounding his hand on the table and not calming down. "Drink! Drink!"

"Let's," Kuznets finally agrees, raising his glass and staring straight at the pale Sumlinsky. "To the future collective farm. To it blossoming like a magnificent socialist flower and as soon as possible. Fine, minister, I accept your conditions. But if you let me down …"

They clink glasses. As they're drinking, Sumlinsky vanishes outside without a sound. And that's how the seeds of the Semruk collective farm were sown and the second agenda item for the day was closed; midnight has already rolled past by this time.

The third item is so serious they head off to the bathhouse for discussions. They bring the vodka with them and chill it in a bucket of icy-cold Angara water. This point is called "informant and agent work," which Ignatov has set up outrageously badly. The situation must be rectified. Moreover, immediately.

"Who am I supposed to recruit as agents, anyway – the bears?" Ignatov listlessly resists as Kuznets whacks his back with a splendid bundle of birch leaves that's been conscientiously soaked three times in boiling water.

"It can even be elks and wolverines," grunts Kuznets, the thick pearlescent air wavering around his powerful torso like a live cloud. "Just be ready to hand over five informants, that's what I need."

When Ignatov was in charge of the special train, he regularly called in the minders from each car for a conversation. But it was one thing to talk and listen, and another thing entirely to note down observations and send them to central office, understanding that when your paper was placed in the person's individual file it would remain there for a long time, likely forever, outliving both the person himself and his observer.

They lash themselves to the bone and run down to the Angara – naked, they don't get dressed – to take a dip. They shout in the icy water, scaring away all the nocturnal fish in the vicinity, splash around, and scurry back to the bathhouse to warm up.

"Understand, Zin, brother," says Ignatov, trying pitifully to pour vodka into small wooden dippers (they forgot to bring the glasses from the commandant's headquarters and are too lazy to run back for them), "this agent … agent business … makes me sick …"

Kuznets gulps from the dipper, chasing the drink with a dark brown birch leaf that's stuck to Ignatov's forehead, then spits out the leaf stem.

"Look, Vanya, here's what you have to do."

He kicks the door and night coolness blows in from outside; a creamy-yellow half-moon is dangling in the dark blue sky. Kuznets whistles briefly, like a master calling a pet dog. Gorelov's concerned face appears in the doorway a minute later.

"The women," he reports, "are already sitting at the commandant's headquarters, waiting on the front steps. One's dark-complexioned, the other's light, like last time. If they need to be brought over here for you, just say …"

Kuznets's finger beckons to Gorelov, who cautiously makes his way into the crowded little bathhouse, which is filled with the smells of smoke, white-hot stones, birch leaves, vodka, and sturdy male bodies. He averts his eyes from the delicate parts of the naked chiefs' bodies, looking only at bright-red faces covered with glistening sweat.

"What's your … ?" Kuznets is snapping his fingers in the air.

"Gorelov!"

"Gorelov, why're you cooling your heels here in the settlement instead of working off your term in a camp? The camp's crying out for you, pouring bitter tears."

"I'm not a felon." Gorelov's bristling like a wild animal, backing away toward the door. "I'm just not part of a social class …"

"You're lucky, you dog." Kuznets smiles. He splashes some vodka in a dipper and extends it to Gorelov, who nods with cautious thanks and drinks, his sharp Adam's apple measuring the swallows like a piston. "I'd have put you in as a felon. Anyway, fine, don't be a scaredy-cat. You're better off telling me who's breeding anti-Soviet ideas here in Semruk."

Gorelov sneers and squints out from behind the ladle with distrust, wondering if he's being tested.

"There's a lot."

"Ah!" Kuznets meaningfully lifts a tensed finger. "And can you write them all down?"

"I've learned to read and write."

"And might there be people who could help you, fill you in on details – the who, what, and where? The things you yourself might not have seen?"

"I'll find them, you can be sure I will." Half of Gorelov's mouth grins as if he still can't believe the leaders are appealing to him with such an important request.

"Good!" Kuznets waves his hand like a king. "Go, you're dismissed for now."

And he looks victoriously at Ignatov, who's collapsed by the wall: *So what do you think of that? A lightning-fast recruitment in two steps, even just one and a half.*

"I can do it right now! Right now!" Gorelov's bursting with concealed knowledge that he absolutely wants to report, in its entirety, to chiefs who look on him favorably at this anxious moment. "I can show you the main one! He's not sleeping yet – he's painting up his anti-Soviet stuff, that turncoat. I know it!"

"Who?" Ignatov's heavy gaze comes out from under his puffy eyelids and bores into Gorelov.

"Ikonnikov! They say he has done 'quite something' at the clubhouse!"

"Well, if it's quite something, then go on, show us." Kuznets stands. Reeling a bit, he ties a white sheet around his muscular purple torso. He takes on an immediate resemblance to an ancient Roman patrician in the hot springs at Caracalla.

They built the clubhouse five years ago when there was an order from on high requiring labor settlements to establish domestic as well as agitational and cultural elements of life for the re-educated peasantry. Ignatov would have been more eager to put his workforce into expanding the infirmary or storage space, but an order is an order so they built it.

In all honesty, the building came out botched. The tall, rectangular log frame building could hold two hundred people at most, and only standing. They initially held general gatherings there, but with Semruk's rapid population growth, the gatherings were moved outside to the square, by the agitational board, meaning the clubhouse was empty most of the time. Ignatov proposed using the building as a school instead, or at least a storehouse, but Kuznets was adamant that the clubhouse exist in the settlement as its own entity. In other labor settlements, interest groups met in clubhouses: the Union of the Militant Godless, the Down with Illiteracy Society, and even Automobile Roads, a group focused on the development of automobilism and road improvements. It wouldn't hurt to bring clubs of this sort to Semruk. *No way in holy hell*, thought Ignatov, picturing red-bearded Lukka diligently listening to a paper about a month-long campaign to fight roadlessness in Turkestan or Granny Yanipa in the ranks of the godless demonstrators. *It's better if they're felling trees.*

They'd recently decided to decorate the clubhouse with agitational art. More importance has been placed on agitational work of late, though until now it's been limited to just supplying bright posters wound in tight rolls. Watching the settlement's residents from the posters are curly-haired collective-farm women driving steel tractors with one hand while insistently and meaningfully pointing somewhere with the other (Konstantin Arnoldovich just sighed dreamily, running a finger along the carefully traced side of a jagged tractor wheel and explaining its mechanics in simple terms to peasants who'd never seen an iron horse). Others show well-fed male and female figures directing their inspired profiles toward an infant with splotchy red cheeks and chubby little hands waving in support of its own "joyful and happy childhood" (1938 was significant for Semruk in terms of demography because the birth rate exceeded the death rate that year for the first time since the settlement's founding, apparently thanks in part to the powerful agitational influence of the poster). There are also red-hot Komsomol members striding along giant long-fingered hands that have been raised toward them in hope (under a special Gulag circular from 1932, it was forbidden to organize Young Pioneer squads from children of special migrants, but a reversal of policy in 1936 allowed this, and even declared it highly desirable, with the recommendation that future members of the Komsomol organization be diligently cultivated from those newly converted Young Pioneers). For some reason, a packet of posters from the Moscow Zoological Garden ("Entry fee only twenty kopeks!") was sent from the central office along with three posters advertising squirrel coats from Soyuzmekhtorg for the ladies, although nobody considered hanging those on the board.

Then came a sudden order to use agitational art – the lusher and heartier the better – to beautify places for leisure activity. The clubhouse was the only such place in Semruk. And so a decision was made to decorate it. Ignatov wanted to limit decorations to standard posters and a couple of street banners with full-throated inscriptions, but then Kuznets remembered something. Isn't there an artist here, one of the "remainders," somebody well known? Let him sweat a little and portray something a bit more original. Kuznets knew that inspectors from Moscow, who were sure to descend upon them one day, would duly appreciate the fact that places for public cultural uses existed in this out-of-the-way Siberian settlement, and not only that but that a creative approach had been taken to the complex matter of agitational art.

Kuznets himself brought canvases, paints, and a small canister of turpentine from Krasnoyarsk. As Ikonnikov ran fingers coarsened by tree felling and shaking with excitement over the treasures that had fallen to him – Neapolitan yellow, cadmium, and Indian paints; ochres light and dark; mars, sienna, and umber; cinnabar, chrome, and Veronese green – he had a fit of creative inspiration and unexpectedly proposed that they start a mural for the ceiling.

Kuznets narrowed his eyes balefully. "Like in a church?"

"No, like in a subway station!" said Ikonnikov.

So a mural it was. They brought plywood and covered the ceiling. *More medicine or fishing gear would have been better than this indulgence,* brooded Ignatov, observing the pensive Ikonnikov as he wandered among scaffolding standing in rows in the clubhouse's empty space and incessantly grumbled to helpers who were nailing thin sheets of plywood to the log ceiling "too roughly." They didn't understand how you could hit "more softly" and "more gently" with a hammer, and they cast suspicious sideways glances at the eccentric artist and exchanged significant looks among themselves.

Ikonnikov was anguishing. He was weary from a surge of emotions that blended inspiration, pining, long-forgotten youthful elation, despair, and some sort of aching tenderness for a mural that had not yet been created nor even fully visualized. Only a week before, when he was finishing sawing the eleventh pine trunk for the day or harnessing himself into rope to drag logs to the timber landing, he couldn't have possibly imagined he'd be standing like this with his face raised toward the ceiling, toward a boundless space on which faces and cities and countries and times and all human life, from its very origin to spectral future horizons, were already glimmering for him and beginning to show themselves on the yellow plywood.

"Agitational art should be simple and understandable," Ignatov declared. "And without any of your tricks, so watch out."

During a week of creative torment, Ikonnikov's face thinned and his pendulous nose sharpened, lending their master a resemblance to a large and sullen bird; his eyes flared with a rather wild fire. He primed the plywood day and night, lying under the ceiling on wooden scaffolding and only occasionally taking breaks to sleep and eat. With the commandant's permission, he slept at the clubhouse, too. He completely stopped drinking the home brew that some of the exiles had learned to make from berries; Ikonnikov was known to imbibe. He used up his monthly supply of candles in five days; working at night was somehow jollier and more wicked. Finally, he began on the mural.

Ignatov, who'd initially made daily stops at the clubhouse to inspect the creative process, was surprised to realize that agitational art was no quick matter. A month after work began, the ceiling had only been ruled into some kind of little squares, streaked with incomprehensible lines, and partially covered with colored dots whose intended use was unclear.

"Will it be ready soon?" Ignatov asked Ikonnikov, with a sense of doom.

"I'll try to have it done by the November holidays," Ikonnikov promised.

It was the height of spring. Out of annoyance, Ignatov gave up and stopped going to check. He'd heard that Ikonnikov was using his free time away from agitational art to indulge himself by painting his own pictures on canvases that had ended up at his disposal. Ignatov hadn't placed any particular meaning on that, but it turned out he should have.

They pound on the door so hard that the scaffolding shakes and shudders under Ikonnikov.

"Coming!" He speeds down the rungs in a hurry, his feet missing slats from nervousness.

He forgets his candle above, so now it's burning right under the ceiling, illuminating someone's large, half-drawn hand with long Raphaelesque fingers and casting angular black shadows in all directions as its light catches scaffolding that towers high and threateningly, a homemade easel Ikonnikov had crafted from beams, and Ilya Petrovich himself, who's scrambling to the door. He finally gropes at the bolt and unlocks it, just as the door swings open from a powerful blow, nearly flying off its hinges.

"Greet your visitors, it's a search!" booms out of the dark blue night.

Gorelov rolls into the clubhouse holding a kerosene lamp in his extended hand and obligingly giving light for someone behind him. Two others enter, dressed so strangely and with such crimson faces that Ikonnikov doesn't recognize them at first. Commandant Ignatov is wearing underclothes he's pulled on haphazardly and he's barefoot, with wet, tousled hair and a couple of birch leaves stuck to his forehead. Alongside him is Kuznets, the chief from the central office, but the only ordinary clothing he's wearing is boots pulled onto bare legs covered with woolly black hair; his body is wound in a damp white sheet, over which he's donned a reddish officer's holster for some reason. Both men are carrying large wooden dippers that they click together zealously from time to time. They're drunk, Ikonnikov understands, thoroughly smashed.

"Well?" Kuznets inquires with a threatening playfulness, lightly scratching at dark, tightly curled thickets of hair on a chest as broad as a sail. "What do you have here? Show me!"

Gorelov darts among the scaffolding like a mouse, making shadows from the lamp rush along the walls like a jumbled round dance.

"I can smell it," he mutters. "I smell it, it has to be here." Then there's a sudden, triumphant, "Found it!"

Ignatov and Kuznets force their way toward his voice, entangling themselves in intersecting planks and knocking down some boards and tools.

In a yellow patch of kerosene light, several canvases stand haphazardly by the wall and on the windowsill. There are narrow, cobbled little streets with large, yellow crystal-like streetlights and café tables huddled together on crowded sidewalks; three-story buildings of bakeries and greengroceries wound in ivy and flowers, their first stories dressed up in awnings as if they were purple skirts; festive palaces with roofs covered in a noble emerald patina; and a river shackled to sand-gray embankments and steel bridges.

As Gorelov draws the lamp right up to one of the pictures, he sniffs at hardened, thick, glistening daubs of paint and digs at them with a fingernail.

"There it is," he whispers, "absolutely pure, out-and-out anti-Soviet activity! Realest you'll ever see!"

On the canvas is a long, narrow triangle, a tower of lacy metal set against a backdrop of malachite-green hills flowing toward the horizon.

"Hmm?" Kuznets's face nears the tower and his overbearing gaze runs from the top of the tower's head to its short-legged base, then back. One must admit that the look of this structure really is completely bourgeois.

"You're dead meat!" Gorelov explodes, grabbing Ikonnikov by the jacket. "We excused him from work and didn't spare the paints. There's a whole container just of turpentine! And he's doing this? Off to the logging site tomorrow! You'll give me fifty percent over the quota, you louse!"

"As you were!" Ignatov swings broadly and whacks Gorelov in the chest with a dipper, as if asking him to hold it. Straining, he focuses his gaze on the canvas then shifts it to Ikonnikov, who's skulking in the shadows. "What is it?" He asks this sternly, poking a calloused finger at the picture.

Ikonnikov looks at Ignatov's hard fingernail that's pinning the top of the Eiffel Tower to a transparent, dark blue Paris sky.

"That …" He feels his legs weaken, go numb, and scatter like sand as his insides sink down somewhere close to the ground. "That's Moscow."

Three pairs of eyes addled by alcohol fix their gaze on him.

"Moscow," he repeats, throat dry. "The building of the People's Commissariat of Heavy Industry."

Eyes skip back to the canvas, attempting to discern some sort of inscription or placard on the tower's wrought-iron veins.

"And here, at the bottom, see this? That's administrative offices and there's the Yauza River. Behind it is Sokolniki and the hills further away, that's Elk Island."

Ignatov exhales loudly, with a whistle, and shifts his gaze to Gorelov, whose legs are bent at the knees from bewilderment. He's crouched and his mouth is agape.

Kuznets takes the lamp from Gorelov and illuminates another picture, where there's a lively, festively lit street and a large windmill with bright, ruby-red sails.

"And this," he asks, "is it Moscow?"

"Yes, yes, of course. I draw from memory. I'm a professional, my memory is almost photographic." Ikonnikov's feet are gradually starting to sense the floor and his insides are returning to their proper places. He turns the painting slightly and the Moulin Rouge flashes in all its red hues, from fiery red to purple. "That's Sretenka Street, not far from the Kremlin. The red windmill is a symbol of the victory of the revolution – it was built back in 1927 for the tenth anniversary. And that …" He pulls another canvas into the circle of light to show an intersection of the green and gray rays of boulevards and residential blocks, where the Arc de Triomphe towers over the city like an imposing Greek letter pi. "These are the Nikitsky Gates. Right behind Tverskoi Boulevard, off to the left. Lenin spoke there in 1917, remember? Do you happen to have been to Moscow?"

"We're Leningraders," Gorelov says quietly and irately, through clenched teeth.

"Leningraders!" Ignatov grabs him by the scruff of his neck but can't stay on his feet and drops to the floor, carrying Gorelov with him. Part of the scaffolding creaks, sways, and falls, scattering large pieces of debris on them both. Ikonnikov backs away, frightened, looking at the two muttering bodies bumbling around on the floor. Kuznets is laughing so hard he's pressing his hands against his knees so he won't fall, shaking his black head, and snorting from deep inside his gut.

Ignatov doesn't have the strength to stand and he's the first to crawl out, creeping on his belly.

"Let's get out of here, Zin," he mutters. "Gorelov, you fool, all we did was waste our time." His gaze settles on an empty bathhouse dipper lying on the floor and he examines it in aston-ishment. "What, there's nothing to drink?"

The guilty party writhes behind him, and the debris crunches.

"What do you mean, nothing?" Gorelov shouts eagerly. "Just ask Ikonnikov – he must have a supply!"

A supply really does turn up at the clubhouse and it's not small. They drink right away, using the dippers. Kuznets forgets his squeamishness about local alcohol products and Ignatov's mouth joyfully senses the sharp berry flavor he's grown accustomed to. They're sitting on the floor, scrutinizing spots on the future mural that's flashing dimly on the ceiling; the spots sway and dance some sort of subtle, intricate tango or foxtrot.

"You'll make me such agitational art," Kuznets says, breathing the hot smells of vodka, fried fish, and home brew into Ikonnikov's ear. "Such art that it makes people shiver! Their spines will tingle! To the very heels of their feet! You got that?"

Ikonnikov nods submissively. How could he not get it?

The tiredness that had been descending upon Ignatov suddenly eases after the home brew. He feels a wave of strong, furious joy rising from somewhere deep inside. He feels like laughing and now everything is funny: the scaffolding spinning in the nearly dark clubhouse, and Ikonnikov's frightened, sober little face and his pendulous nose, and the hole Gorelov tore in his uniform jacket when he tumbled to the floor, and the sheet around Kuznets's torso that keeps trying to slide off and bare the chief's imposing loins. Ignatov jumps to his feet and sways but remains standing. He spreads his arms wide – "I feel so good, Zin!"

Kuznets is already rising, too. He's regally tucking in the end of his sheet that had come loose so it's under his holster, and he stomps to the exit, knocking over something heavy (maybe it's crates, maybe it's buckets) and booming along the way.

"Forrrrrward!" he shouts. "Hurrah, comrades!"

Revolver taken from holster, door kicked with boot, and out. Ignatov and Gorelov follow.

The sky is already a smoky, pre-dawn blue. The stars are dimming quickly, one after another. Ignatov runs forward, behind his commander's white back, and feels joy expanding and growing in his body. The ground springs underneath his feet, tossing him up so he flies forward, lightly and swiftly. This always happens during an offensive. Who's hiding up ahead, waiting in ambush like a coward? White Army? Narrow-eyed Basmachi? For some reason there's neither a revolver nor a saber in his hand. He picks up a blade that someone has dropped on the ground and waves it. The saber cuts the air with a whistle.

"For the revolution!" he shouts at the top of his lungs. "For the Red Arrrrm—"

Kuznets shoots. The echo slams along the river like thunder, rolling.

In the buildings ahead, faces distorted by fear are peering out of windows. *Uh-huh, they're scared, the sons of bitches!*

"The enemy," screams Kuznets. "I'll slaughter them all!"

"I'll slice them up!" Ignatov chimes in and starts hacking everything around.

They burst in, but where? Voices squeal loudly and shrilly, people scatter in all directions. Ignatov slices at something white and soft (the air fills with down, grassy debris, and dust) and at something hard and wooden (the saber in his hand breaks off for some reason but he finds a new one) and at something human and soft (someone screams, swears, howls).

They abruptly end up outside again and there they are up ahead, the enemy, hopping in all directions, escaping as they wail, and running fast – *those sons of bitches!* – so they can't catch up. Kuznets shoots after them again, then again and again, and the shouts become more desperate, changing to a screech. Kuznets suddenly falls, either overwhelmed by a treacherous bullet coming from the other side or from simply stumbling.

Ignatov, who's been running behind Kuznets, trips on his large body, and drops to the ground alongside him, where his face gets stuck in something slimy and viscous (mud?) and his skull cracks, exploding with pain. The joy disappears immediately, evaporating as if it had never been there, and a familiar, loathsome, and gnawing anguish is again sloshing in his chest. He looks at the saber in his hand. It's not a saber, it's a stick that he tosses it away. Ignatov wipes his face with his palm and finds sludgy clay. He crawls toward Kuznets's body, stretched out near him. It's hard to move because it feels like his body has been replaced with gluey aspic.

"Zin," whispers Ignatov, the mud crunching distinctly on his teeth, "let me out of here. I can't stay here any longer, you hear? I can't."

Kuznets is snoring, his shaggy chest swelling toward the heavens.

THE SHAH BIRD

Zuleikha opens her eyes. A ray of sun is pushing through shabby cotton curtains, creeping along a reddish curve on a log wall, over a flowered, coarse cotton pillow with the black tips of grouse feathers poking through, and further, toward Yuzuf's delicate ear, rosy in the shaft of light. She extends her hand and noiselessly pulls at the curtain – her boy still has a long time to sleep. But it's daybreak, time for her to get up.

She carefully frees her arm out from under his head, lowers her bare feet to a floor that's cooled during the night, and places a scarf on her pillow so when her son decides to wake up, he'll stretch, nestle his face into her scent, and sleep a little longer. Without looking, she takes her jacket, bag, and rifle from their nail. She pushes the door – the babbling of birds and the racket of the wind burst in – and noiselessly slips out. In the hallway, she puts on simple leather shoes that Granny Yanipa crafted from elk skin, quickly braids her hair, and then it's onward, into the *urman*.

Zuleikha has always been the very first among the camp's hunting artel – a work group of five – to go out into the taiga. "Your animal is still sleeping, dreaming, but you're already set for work," grumbles the red-bearded Lukka. Sometimes they meet when he's coming to the settlement after night fishing and she's leaving to hunt. She doesn't deny it, she just silently smiles back; she knows her quarry will never escape from her.

She has fond memories of her first bear, the one she killed in 1931 at Round Clearing: if it hadn't been for that bear, she would never have discovered how accurate an eye and steady a hand she has. All that remains of the bear is a yellowish-gray skull on a pole. She visits it occasionally and strokes it, in thanks.

The settlement's hunting artel was founded back then, seven years ago. Achkenazi had tried to change Zuleikha's mind when she decided to leave her job in the kitchen. He had even scolded her: "How will you feed your son?" That evening, she brought him a brace of wood grouse for the evening soup. He accepted the meat and stopped trying to change her mind. They found him another kitchen helper.

In the spring and summer, she comes back from the taiga carrying fat grouse and heavy geese with thick, tough necks. A couple of times she's been fortunate to take down a roe deer and, once, even a quivering, frightened musk deer. She sets snares to catch hares, and for foxes she sets traps sent by the central office, at the artel's request. In winter she hunts animals whose thick, glossy fur has already grown in – squirrels, Siberian weasels, and occasionally sables.

In summer, the hunting artel's capacity goes primarily toward the settlement's needs: they eat and preserve fowl, baking the feathers and down in the sun for use in pillows and quilts. The only thing they send to the central office are beaver pelts, but those don't turn up often. The areas around Semruk aren't for beavers.

Winter is another matter, the most hectic time. Headquarters takes all the fur animals, whether they're ordinary squirrels and martens or rare sables that sometimes need to be tracked for two or three days. The settlement is paid for the pelts, most often in money transfers, only rarely in hard cash. The majority of the money goes toward the settlement's budget, with some offset by taxes and other deductions (as well as state taxes, there are settlement fees of five percent added on, plus payments on the settlement's credits), and the remainder is given to the hunters themselves. Zuleikha has already been earning money this way for seven years.

People say it's best to hunt with dogs but the settlers aren't allowed to have them, "as a precaution." Even rifles are permitted only reluctantly, probably because hunting wouldn't work out very well at all with just snares and bear spears, but no firearms. All five of Semruk's guns are registered with the commandant's office. Strictly speaking, they're supposed to be given out in late autumn, only for hunting season, and then returned to the commandant in early spring, but Ignatov doesn't follow the rules as tightly as he should. The hunters supply the settlement with meat in the summer and everyone eats well during those three warm months, making up for the long, hungry winter, which takes away a good quarter (if not an entire third) of Semruk's population each year, as if winter is licking them away with its tongue. Those who perish are generally newcomers, the ones who arrive toward the beginning of cold weather and don't have time to adjust to the harsh local climate.

At first they processed the pelts themselves, each on their own, but then they banded together, putting everything in Granny Yanipa's hands. By that time, there was little use at the logging site for an old woman who was half-blind, but she didn't need to see to remove membranes and boil the pelts, afterward drying and combing them. And so they count the working group as five and a half people, meaning five hunters plus one half, Yanipa.

Zuleikha is a full-fledged unit of labor for the artel, but another half of her is registered as an aide in the infirmary, so there's not just one of her but an entire one and a half. Leibe has explained that she needs an official occupation, on paper, for the summer season. The bureaucratic mathematics don't trouble her; if that's the way things have to be, fine.

It's more complicated for other members of the artel: there aren't many "vacancies" for a hunter who disappears in the taiga for days at a time. Formally registering them for lumbering jobs would mean having to automatically increase a work quota that already takes tremendous effort to fulfill and sometimes isn't fulfilled anyway. They get around the system however they can: one person might be made a file clerk, another an assistant to the settlement's bookkeeper. They're forbidden from joining the staff in the kitchen, lest the team there get too large. The hunters try to work off their half-time jobs at least partially, however and whenever they can, so that the summer assignments aren't pure deception; this additional burden on them is considered worth it, though, for the opportunity to remain an artel member without restrictions. Back at the central office, Kuznets graciously closes his eyes to these hidden violations (the problem with the hunters is resolved the same way in all the other labor settlements), though he doesn't miss chances to remind Ignatov that, "Yes, my dear man, I know everything about you and I see through you, as if you were a glass of you know what."

Zuleikha works off her half honestly. She returns from the taiga before supper, when it's still light, and goes to the infirmary to scrub, scour, clean, wipe, and boil. She's also learned to apply dressings, treat wounds, and even poke a long, sharp syringe into skinny male buttocks covered in hair. At first Leibe waved her aside and sent her to bed ("You're on your last legs, Zuleikha!") but then he stopped. The infirmary has grown and he can no longer get by without her help. Zuleikha truly is on her last legs but that's only later, at night, when the floors are clean, the instruments sterilized, the linens boiled, and the patients rebandaged and fed.

As before, Zuleikha and her son are living in the infirmary, with

Leibe. Yuzuf's seizures are gone, and they'd gradually stopped sitting watch at his bedside during the night. Leibe hadn't turned them out, though. More than anything, he seems glad for their presence in the housing provided by his job. Leibe spends little time in his living quarters, only sleeping there at night.

Living in a small, comfortable room with its own stove is their salvation. Adults as well as children get sick in the freezing common barracks, with the wind blowing through. And so Zuleikha gratefully accepts this gift and works for her happiness every day until she's exhausted, with a rag and bucket in her hands.

In the beginning, she thought that because she was living under one roof with a man unrelated to her, that meant she was his wife before heaven and people. And was thus obligated to pay back a wifely debt. How could it be otherwise? Every evening after lulling her son to sleep, slipping out of his bed unnoticed, and thoroughly washing, she would sit on the stove bench, her belly chilled until it ached, to wait for the doctor. He would appear after midnight, barely alive from fatigue, hurriedly swallow, without chewing, the food she'd left for him, and collapse in his own bed. "Don't wait up for me every night, Zuleikha," he'd scold her, his words slurred from fatigue. "I'm still in a condition to cope with my own meal." And he'd quickly fall asleep. Zuleikha would sigh with relief and duck behind the curtain, to her son. Then she would sit on the stove bench the next evening, to wait again.

One time, after falling face down on his sleeping bench, as usual, without even taking off his shoes, Leibe suddenly grasped the reason for her night vigils. He abruptly sat up in bed and looked at Zuleikha, who was sitting by the stove, her hair in neat braids and her eyes cast downward.

"Come over here, Zuleikha."

She walked over to him, her face white, mouth a straight line, and eyes darting along the floor.

"Sit right here with me …"

She sat down on the edge of the bench, not breathing.

"And look at me."

She slowly looked up at him, as if her eyes were heavy.

"You don't owe me anything."

She looked at him, frightened, not understanding.

"Absolutely nothing at all. Hear me?"

She pressed her braids to her lips, not knowing what to do with her eyes.

"I order you to put out the light immediately and sleep. And don't wait up for me again. Ever! Is that clear?"

She nodded slightly and suddenly began breathing loudly and wearily.

"If I see you do this again, I'll send you to the barrack. I'll keep Yuzuf here but I'll send you the hell out!"

He didn't have a chance to finish because Zuleikha had already darted to the kerosene cooker, blown on the flame, and vanished into the darkness. That's how the question of their relations was conclusively and irreversibly resolved.

Lying in the dark with her eyes wide open and her loudly pounding heart covered with a pelt blanket, Zuleikha agonized and couldn't go to sleep for a long time. Would she fall into sin by continuing to live under the same roof with the doctor, not as a husband but as a man unrelated to her? What would people say? Would heaven punish her? Heaven kept silent, likely agreeing to the situation. People simply accepted how things were – the aide lived at the infirmary, what of it? She'd arranged things well for herself, been lucky. When Zuleikha couldn't hold back and shared her doubts with Izabella, Izabella just laughed in response: "What are you talking about, child! Sins are completely different for us here."

*

Zuleikha is making her way through the forest. The trees ring out in birdsong and the awakening sun beats through spruce branches, their needles blazing with gold. Zuleikha's leather shoes bound easily along the rocks to cross the river she calls the Chishme and run along a narrow path next to reddish pines, through Round Clearing, past the burned birch, and further, into the thick wilderness of the taiga's *urman*, where the animals are the most fattened and delicious.

Surrounded here by blue-green spruces, she must slip noise-lessly, barely touch the earth – not trample the grass, not break a branch, not knock down a pine cone – while leaving neither a trace nor a scent. She must dissolve into the cool air, the buzz of mosquitoes, and a ray of sun. Zuleikha knows how because her body is light and obedient, her motions quick and precise; she herself is like a wild animal, like a bird, like the wind as it sweeps between spruce boughs and weaves through juniper bushes and fallen trees.

She's wearing a gray double-breasted jacket with large, light gray checks and broad shoulders; it was left behind by one of the brand-new residents who'd passed into another world, and it warms her on cold days and protects her from the sun in the heat. Small, unintelligible letters – "Lucien Lelong, Paris" – dance in a circle on the shiny, deep-blue buttons the previous owner had sewn on very tightly with coarse thread. There is a faded lily on a lining that was once turquoise. It's a good jacket and reminds Zuleikha of the kaftans her father's guests from faraway Kazan wore when they came to visit.

A rifle, heavy and cold, nestles into her back; it will spring into her hands on its own if necessary, stretch toward the target, and never miss. "You cast a spell on it or something?" the others in the artel ask, half-joking, half-envious. Zuleikha keeps quiet. How can you explain that it's not a rifle at all but practically a part of her, like her arm or eye? When she rasies the long, straight barrel, resting the butt on her shoulder, squinting at the sight's opening, she's merged, fused with the rifle. She feels it tense as it anticipates the shot. She senses the bulky bullets waiting, still, preparing to fly out of the barrel, each one a small, leaden death. She squeezes the trigger lovingly and smoothly, without hurrying.

She'd grasped long ago that if her rifle doesn't shoot that squirrel or wood grouse, there will be another predator – be it a marten or a fox – that will tear it to pieces the next day. And in another month or year, the predator itself will die from illness or old age, feed the worms, dissolve into the earth, nourish trees with its juices, sprout up on them as fresh needles and baby cones, and then become food for the children of the killed squirrel or the wood grouse that was torn to pieces. Zuleikha hadn't grasped that on her own. The *urman* taught her.

Death is everywhere here but death is simple, understandable, and wise, even just in its own way. Leaves and needles fall from the trees and rot in the earth, bushes break under a heavy bear paw and dry out, grass becomes quarry for a deer, just as a deer is quarry for a pack of wolves. Death is tightly, seamlessly interwoven with life, so it's not scary. Beyond that, life always triumphs in the *urman*. No matter how terrible the peat fires rage in autumn, no matter how cold and harsh the winter is, no matter how rife the starving predators, Zuleikha knows that spring will come, the trees will burst with young greenery, silken grass will flood land that has been burned to black at one time, and cheery, abundant young will be born to the animals. Because of that, she doesn't feel cruel when she's killing. To the contrary: she feels herself part of a big and strong world, like a drop in an evergreen sea.

Not long ago she suddenly recalled the grain buried in the Yulbash cemetery, between her daughters' graves. And she got to thinking that it hadn't all been wasted. Some of the grains, if only a few, would have grown shoots through the cracks in the wooden coffin when spring came, and though the rest might have rotted, they'd have become food for the young sprouts. She imagined the tender shoots of the wheat spikes fighting their way between the uneven gravestones, overgrowing, hiding, and swaddling them. That warmed her soul, put her more at ease. Who can say if the spirit of the cemetery is still caring for her daughters?

She still hasn't figured out if there are spirits in the *urman*. She has never run into one during her seven years of making the rounds of so many hills, walking through so many ravines, and crossing so many streams. Sometimes it seems, for an instant, that she herself is a spirit …

Zuleikha first checks the snares and traps along paths she'd identified as favored animal routes to her Chishme River: one by a large, half-rotten spruce where, on close inspection, the grass is trampled a little (small animals apparently couldn't jump over the trunk, so they ran around it), and another near a deep, icy-cold pool as narrow as a crack and concealed in a spruce thicket. She makes the rounds to the snares twice a day, morning and evening, so a captured hare won't fall into a predator's clutches. Then she goes upstream, along the Chishme, toward the swampy ravines, to see the ducks' favorite spots. The trip isn't brief and she treks on until noon. She walks, perpetually on the lookout (any animal she runs into on the path, in the bushes, or on the spruce branches, could prove to be quarry), and thinks. Zuleikha didn't think as much during her entire previous life in Yulbash as she does now during one day of hunting. During her years as an unrestricted hunter, she has recalled her entire life and taken it apart, piece by tiny piece. She recently and suddenly grasped that it's good that fate has cast her here. She's taking shelter in a cubbyhole in a state-owned infirmary, living among people who aren't blood relations, speaking a language not native to her, hunting like a man, working enough for three, and she's doing fine. Not that she's happy, no. But she's fine.

Toward midday, when there's only a half-hour's walk left to the duck creeks, her thoughts habitually turn to a dangerous topic. She's tired of forbidding herself to think about it. But if she doesn't forbid herself, she could hit upon something too scary to imagine. Zuleikha throws her rifle over her other shoulder. Thoughts aren't a stream and you can't block them with a dam, so let them flow. She often recalls that day at Round Clearing, seven years ago. How black boots, part of a uniform, sprang from grass strewn with bilberries, how Ignatov sat down in front of her on the ground and stretched a hand toward her headscarf. And she wasn't afraid of him then but of herself, of how all of her, every bit, had turned to honey instantly just from his gaze, how she'd flowed toward him, blinded, deafened, having forgotten everything, even her son playing nearby. And she'd aimed the rifle not at him but at her fear, at her fear of committing sin with her husband's murderer. But she didn't commit sin – the bear had helped.

She left her kitchen job soon after, and Achkenazi's new helper started taking lunches to the commandant's office. Ignatov hasn't sought her out since, and whatever went on between them receded, remaining in the past, as if it never happened. Sometimes she thinks maybe it didn't. Maybe it just seemed to happen. But then she'll see in Ignatov's lowered eyes that it did. She knows by the way something inside her melts and thaws when she looks up at the commandant's headquarters that it happened. She knows because she thinks about this every day; it happened.

He began drinking soon after, and hard. Zuleikha can't stand drunks. There it was, she'd thought, her medicine. Seeing the commandant drunk, stupid, and berserk should have immediately snatched away all her unworthy thoughts. It didn't work. The sight of Ignatov's red eyes and his face, puffy from alcohol, made her feel pained instead of disgusted.

When yet another batch of new arrivals came, he picked out a slut with short red hair, sharp little breasts, and a firm rear end squeezed into the stretched fabric of a dress that was too tight. And when that same Aglaya began stopping by the commandant's headquarters at the sight of Ignatov's lighted cigarette at night, Zuleikha decided that was it: it was finally over. But was it really?

She shoulders her rifle and fires into a gap between shaggy spruce branches. A hazel grouse quivers its wings too late and its colorful body tumbles to the ground.

The day has flown by and has produced some success: a hazel grouse and a brace of ducks are bouncing on Zuleikha's belt (the hidden spot for ducks didn't let her down, giving her an emerald-headed drake with dressy white cheeks and a hefty black female), and a hare that got caught in the snare is in the bag on her back. She boldly strides home through the taiga, cracking branches and not hiding, since she's done hunting. As she crosses the Chishme along the rocks, the bushes explode at the water's edge and something small and nimble flies out, headlong. A small animal? No, it's Yuzuf!

Zuleikha flings her arms wide open. Yuzuf's long, long legs gleam out from under his short, patched pants as he flies toward her and embraces her, pressing his head into her. She lowers her face to the top of her son's head and inhales his beloved, warm scent.

"I forbade you to wait for me here, *ulym*. It's dangerous in the taiga."

He just pushes harder into her chest, the nape of his neck dangling like a floppy ear. She could have scolded him more strictly for defying her rule again, but of course she can't because she herself is glad he's come so they can have this brief time to walk along the path together, calmly and unhurried, as if there's an eternity ahead for the two of them, to gently jostle each other, listen to birds, talk, or keep silent. There won't be more of these solitary moments today. As soon as Zuleikha gets back, she'll clean the infirmary and Yuzuf will help her by lugging water from the Angara, burning garbage in the yard …

"You're not hungry?"

"The doctor fed me."

Yuzuf calls Leibe "the doctor," as does Zuleikha.

He unclasps his arms, releasing his mother. He'll be eight soon, and he's very tall, already taller than her shoulder, so if he keeps growing this fast, she'll have to lengthen his jacket sleeves again, take apart his pants, and let down the hem. His hair is shaggy – Zuleikha doesn't shave him bald, as people did in Yulbash, because his hair will keep him warm in winter, like a second hat – his nose is sharp, and his round eyes large. He's taken after his father in height and build, but it's immediately obvious his face is hers.

Yuzuf grandly takes her bag, grasping it with his hands, slinging it over his shoulder, and lugging it (he would have gladly carried his mother's rifle, too, but Zuleikha doesn't allow that); his fingers, the nails chewed off, are spotted with yellow and blue.

"Playing around in the paints again?"

He's recently taken to visiting Ikonnikov at the settlement's clubhouse, to draw. Remnants of plywood scribbled with charcoal and pieces of paper covered with fat pencil lines have started turning up at home. Yuzuf's clothes are gradually becoming covered with smears and spatters of bright colors. The paints Ikonnikov uses to make his agitational art are durable and don't yield to the Angara's cold water, remaining instead to forever brighten Yuzuf's pants and shirt, sewn from someone's old dresses, and on the large men's shoes inherited from some settlement resident or other. Zuleikha doesn't approve of her son's pursuits but doesn't forbid them either, since it's better that he dirty himself with paints than knock around the taiga alone. Yuzuf senses his mother's stance and doesn't talk much about the clubhouse.

"Tell me about Semrug, Mama."

"I've told you a thousand times."

"Then tell me a thousand and one."

Zuleikha has shared with her son all the folk tales and legends she heard from her parents when she was a child: about shaggy, long-toed *shurales*, who tickle tardy forest wayfarers to death; about a certain unkempt water spirit called Su-anasy, who can't untangle her mane of hair with a golden comb for a good hundred years; about the serpent Yuma, who turns into a beautiful girl by day to tempt young men and drinks their lifeblood at night; about fire-breathing *azhdakha* dragons that hide in the bottom of wells and devour women who come for water; about silly and greedy giant *devs*, who steal brides; about the powerful, narrowed-eyed Genghis Khan, who conquered half the world, casting the other half into fear and trepidation; and about his admirer and follower Timur the Lame, who completely destroyed a good hundred cities and built only one in return – the splendid Samarkand – over which huge golden stars shine from a sky eternally blue in any weather ... The story of the magical bird Semrug is Yuzuf's favorite.

"All right, listen," Zuleikha agrees. "Once upon a time there lived in the world a bird. Not just any bird but a magical bird. Persians and Uzbeks called the bird Simurg, Kazakhs said Samuryk, and Tatars say Semrug."

"The bird is named the same as our settlement?"

Yuzuf invariably asks that question and Zuleikha invariably answers, "No, *ulym*. The names are just similar. And this bird lived on top of the highest mountain."

"Higher than our cliff?"

"A lot higher, Yuzuf. So much higher that wayfarers, whether on foot or on horseback, couldn't reach its top, no matter how much they climbed. Nobody could see Semrug – not wild animals, nor birds, nor humans. They knew only that his plumage was more beautiful than all the worldly sunrises and sunsets combined. At one time, while flying over the faraway country of China, Semrug dropped one feather, clothing all of China in radiance, so the Chinese themselves turned into skillful picture painters. Semrug was not only splendidly beautiful but his wisdom was as boundless as the ocean."

"Is the ocean wider than the Angara?"

"Wider, *ulym* ... One time, all the birds on earth flew to a big celebration to revel together and rejoice at life. The festivities were spoiled, though, because the parrots started arguing with the magpies, the peacocks quarreled with the crows, the nightingales with the eagles ..."

"What about the hazel grouse?" Yuzuf touches the round little bird head that's dangling on his mother's belt and looks like a colorful egg.

"With the ducks," says Zuleikha, turning the dead drake's green-tinted black head toward the hazel grouse: the birds' motionless bills bump, as if they're pecking each other.

Yuzuf's laugh rings out melodiously.

"And from that great quarrel there arose in the world such a hullabaloo that all the leaves began falling off the trees and all the animals grew frightened and hid in their burrows. A wise hoopoe flapped his wings for three days, calming all the enraged birds. Finally, they settled down and let him speak.

"'What is the use in spending our time and energy on factions and feuding,' he told them. 'We need to elect a shah bird among us to lead us and bring quarrels to an end with his authority.' The birds agreed. But here was the question: who should be elected as their head? They began squabbling again and a scuffle nearly broke out, but the wise hoopoe already had a suggestion. 'Let us fly to Semrug,' he proposed, 'and ask him to become our shah. Who, if not he, the most wonderful and most wise on earth, should be our sovereign?' This speech went down so well that a large brigade of eager birds prepared right then and there to make the trip. The flock soared into the sky and set off for the highest mountain in the world, in search of his illustrious highness, Semrug."

"A flock as vast and black as a cloud," Yuzuf adds.

Yuzuf follows along attentively, not allowing even one detail to slip from his favorite story, and Zuleikha must retell it as she learned it from her father, word for word.

"Yes, that's right," she corrects herself. "A flock as vast and black as a cloud soared into the sky and set off for the highest mountain in the world, in search of his illustrious highness, Semrug. The birds flew day and night, not pausing to sleep or eat, until the last of their strength was all but gone, and finally they reached the foot of the mountain they had been seeking. There they had to abandon flight, as the path ahead could only be trodden on foot. For it was only through suffering that they could ascend to the top.

"The mountain trail led them first to the Valley of Quests, where birds who were not striving hard enough to reach the goal died. Then they crossed the Valley of Love, where those suffering from unrequited love remained and dropped down, lifeless. In the Valley of Insight, they lost those whose minds were not inquisitive and whose hearts were not open to new things."

Yuzuf strides alongside Zuleikha, silent and puffing from exertion (the hare in the bag is heavy after feeding well during the summer). "How can the heart open itself to knowledge?" Zuleikha wonders aloud. "The heart is the house of feelings, not of reason." She trails off for a moment, straightening the birds on her belt, and Yuzuf impatiently urges her on.

"In the treacherous Valley of Indifference … Come on, Mama!"

"In the treacherous Valley of Indifference," Zuleikha continues, "there fell the most birds of all – those who could not make equal in their hearts grief and gladness, love and hatred, enemies and friends, living and dead."

This part of the legend is the most incomprehensible to Zuleikha herself. How could anyone treat good and bad equally? And consider that correct and necessary, too? Yuzuf nods his head almost imperceptibly in time with his strides, as if he understands everything and agrees.

"The rest ended up in the Valley of Unity, where each felt himself to be all, and all felt themselves to be each. The tired birds rejoiced, tasting the sweetness of unity. But it was too soon!"

"It was too soon!" Yuzuf whispers, confirming it.

"In the Valley of Confusion – which was shaken by thunderstorms – night and day, and truth and untruth were muddled. Everything the birds had come to know through such hardship during their long journey was swept away by a hurricane, and emptiness and hopelessness reigned in their souls. The progress they had made seemed useless to them, the life they had already lived, worthless. Many of them fell here, defeated by despair. The thirty most steadfast remained alive. Bleeding, mortally tired, their feathers singed, they crawled to the final vale. And there, in the Valley of Renunciation, all that awaited them was a smooth, unending watery surface, with eternal stillness over it. Beyond, there began the Land of Eternity, to which there was no entry for the living."

Yuzuf and Zuleikha are striding along a path strewn with crunching evergreen needles and cones. There's already a blue gap ahead between the trees – it's the settlement. The closer they are to home, the slower Yuzuf walks; he wants his mother to be able to finish the story. When he sees the walls of the clubhouse, he stops so he can hear the end of the story in silence.

"The birds realized they had reached Semrug's dwelling place and they felt his approach through the growing gladness in their hearts. Their eyes squinted from the bright light that filled the world and when they opened them, they saw only one other. In that instant, they grasped the essence – that they were all Semrug. Each individually and all of them together."

"Each individually and all of them together," Yuzuf repeats. He sniffles and strides into the settlement.

After his mother goes to the infirmary to scrub the floors, Yuzuf makes his way to the kitchen to give today's birds to Achkenazi. The dead hazel grouse and the drake and the hen duck have come a long way in his hands without even knowing it: not just through a small taiga settlement – from a rickety log-house infirmary to a little kitchen smelling of fish guts and millet porridge. No. They've flown over red deserts and blue oceans, over black forests and fields spiked with wheaten gold, to the foot of a mountain chain at the edge of the world, then further, on foot this time, without using their wings (the hazel grouse quickly picking up its short, shaggy little legs, and the drake and hen duck, somehow or other, quacking any which way and waddling heavily on their broad, webbed feet), through seven wide and treacherous valleys, to the abode of the storybook shah bird. They don't have time to learn the essence of the matter and behold in one another the illustrious image of Semrug, though, because when Achkenazi sees out the window that the little boy is playing with the birds, he takes them away and gives Yuzuf a light, friendly cuff. The door to the kitchen slams shut with a bang and a huge feather tinged with emerald remains in the air, to soar.

THE FOUR ANGELS

The world is enormous and vivid. It begins at a pearl-gray, wooden threshold – ornately eaten away by a beetle – in the house that Yuzuf and his mother share with the doctor. It extends through a broad yard flooded with waves of lush grass: where cracked wood blocks rise like islands with axes and knives crookedly sticking out of them, a woodpile climbs like a steep cliff, a crooked fence stretches like a broad mountain ridge, and laundry drying in the wind flutters like multicolored sails. It flows around the house, and toward the squeaky infirmary door, behind which there's a kingdom of hidden floors his mother scrubs until they're yellow, cool white sheets, intricate instruments gleaming with an unbelievable shine, and bitter medicinal aromas.

From the infirmary, the world spreads further along a well-trodden path to the rest of the settlement: three very long log-built black barracks dominate; the agitational stand stretches broad wings where resounding slogans blaze on glossy posters; in the mysterious building with the kitchen something is constantly rustling and sizzling, shrouded in the smells of food; the gloomy commandant's headquarters gazes from the top of the hill like an unassailable bastion; and shining bright in the distance between blue spruces there stands the clubhouse, where Ilya Ikonnikov makes magic day and night with strong-smelling paints.

Yuzuf's world ends here because his mother has forbidden him to go further, into the taiga. He tries not to upset her so obeys. Some evenings, though, the wait for her to return from hunting becomes unbearable, so he hurries off, his eyes squinting from fear, past the clubhouse, past the crooked poles with cracked skulls (elks, deer, boars, lynxes, badgers, and even one bear), some baring long fangs, onward, following a barely noticeable little path toward the ringing Chishme, so he can hide under a trembling rowan bush and look out for his mother's slight figure flashing among reddish pine trunks.

The Angara is another border of this world. Yuzuf loves sitting on the shore and peering into its ever-changing depths. The heavy, cold water hides within itself every shade of dark blue and gray, just as the *urman* hides every shade of green and the fire in the stove holds red and yellow.

The world is so large you could pant after running from one border to another, and it's so vivid that Yuzuf sometimes can't get enough air. It makes him squint, too, as if the light were blinding him.

Somewhere far away, beyond the mighty backs of the hills, there's another world where his mother and the other settlement dwellers lived before coming to Semruk. In Yulbash, his mother told him, there were as many as a hundred houses – not ten and not twenty – and each was the size of the infirmary. It's hard to imagine such a giant settlement. It's probably even harder to live there because if you went out for a walk, later you'd be in the middle of a hundred houses, so how could you find your own? Strange, scary creatures that Yuzuf knows only through his mother's stories wandered the streets of Yulbash: *cows* trudged sedately accompanied by the rumble and boom of little tin bells tied to their necks (these beasts vaguely resembled elks but had fat, bent horns and long tails like whips); nasty, loud-voiced *goats* darted around (about the size of a musk deer but shaggy, their horns curving to their backs and their beards sweeping the ground); and mean-tempered *dogs* bared their teeth from under fences (these were tame wolves who would lick their master's hands and rip at a stranger's throat). Each time Yuzuf hears his mother's stories about her native land, he feels a chill in his belly and senses tremendous relief inside that she'd known to move from Yulbash to peaceable, cozy Semruk before it was too late!

From what he can gather, mysterious Leningrad, which Izabella keeps calling Petersburg and Ilya Petrovich calls Petrograd, is smaller than Yulbash – nobody ever marveled about the number of houses there. On the other hand, the buildings are all made of stone. And not just the buildings, either, but the streets, embankments, and bridges – everything, in fact, is made of granite and marble. Yuzuf pities the poor Leningraders who are forced to take shelter in cold, damp stone dwellings. He imagines Izabella and Konstantin Arnoldovich shuddering, their teeth chattering, as they crawl down from stone bunks on foggy Leningrad mornings, huddling together and going outside the stone barrack to the stone-covered shore of the narrow little Neva River, which is smaller than the Angara but larger than the Chishme. Attempting to warm up, they wander along the shore among crowded bunches of marble *lions* (large, shaggy lynxes with magnificent manes), granite *sphinxes* (lions with human heads), and bronze *statues* (huge dolls as tall as a person, similar to those Ilya Petrovich sometimes molds out of clay), past the barrack called the *Hermitage*, as green as grass and tall as a powerful spruce, past the yellow barrack called the *Admiralty*, whose roof is decorated with a long and even needle (like a young pine tree) with a sailing ship at its point, past the gray barrack called the *Stock Exchange*, and past the fat, red, log-like *Rostral Columns* on whose tops there burns a pale fire that gives no warmth. A dim sun peeks through clouds that keep sprinkling a fine, slanting rain.

It's good fortune that these cold and terrifying worlds of Yulbash and Leningrad are far from Yuzuf. They lie in roughly the same parts of the world as the shah bird Semrug, crafty and beautiful women called *peri*, fire-breathing *azhdakha* dragons, and the gluttonous giantess, Zhalmavyz.

Not long ago, Yuzuf saw a miracle. It happened one evening in early summer, just before supper, when Achkenazi asked him to take a dish of oatmeal stew to Ikonnikov. Since starting work on his agitational art, Ikonnikov often preferred to eat in his workplace, not taking a break from production. Yuzuf was rather afraid of the sullen artist, but he obediently took the dish from the cook and trudged off with it to the clubhouse. Diligently carrying the steaming bowl in both hands, Yuzuf pushed the door with his back, squeezed through the gap, shifted from one foot to the other in the darkness of the entrance, and finally ended up inside the clubhouse, which the light of the sunset was brightly illuminating.

The hot dish burned Yuzuf's fingers and the very delicious smell of oats boiled soft was in his nose; the oatmeal even seemed to be made with meat broth and have some fat. He needed to complete his assignment quickly and go back to the kitchen for his own portion.

The artist's stooped back was right by the window. Yuzuf was sniffling but Ikonnikov didn't hear; he was standing somehow crookedly, as if he were leaning forward. Yuzuf approached closer and peered over his shoulder. In front of Ikonnikov, on a lopsided triangular little house that was somehow slapped together from beams (an *easel*, Ilya Petrovich would explain later) was a small square of canvas that was a hand and a half wide and just as tall. On the canvas was Leningrad, where a street as wide as the Angara flowed along an austere stone expanse between metal fences and houses that were silvery in the dawn haze, and then flew over the Neva as a lace-like green bridge and disappeared on the other shore; church cupolas were concealed in greenery like flower buds and occasional people hurrying somewhere. A wave was hitting against the embankment's gray granite, and long-winged birds hovered over the river. There was a smell of fresh foliage, wet stones, and a large body of water. A shrieking "*Ee! Ee!*" was distinctly audible but Yuzuf didn't understand if that was an Angara seagull shrieking outside the window or a Leningrad seagull on the canvas. This wasn't a painting; it was a window into Leningrad. A miracle.

His fingers were suddenly burning unbearably. The dish banged onto the floor, the spoon bounced away and rolled, clinking, and the oats spattered everywhere. Yuzuf stood, his hands extended, fingertips scalded, his mouth wide open from fear, and his chilled heart beating in his belly. Rivulets of oat stew streamed along his bare knees and large shoes, tied with string at his ankles, then flowed through the floorboards to the ground beneath.

"Huh?" Ikonnikov took his brush from the canvas and turned around. His eyes were stern, his brows shaggy, and his pendulous profile menacing.

Yuzuf's heart – completely panic-stricken from horror – jumped into his throat. He scampered away and clattered through the door.

At the dining hall, Achkenazi later ladled out a full adult portion for Yuzuf ("Eat, helper!"), but the stew wouldn't go down his throat. Yuzuf attempted to sneak the dish outside and take it to the clubhouse, but the ubiquitous and grumpy Gorelov blocked his path and pulled painfully at his ear. "Where're you headed, you louse? That's not allowed!" He had to eat the whole thing, choking down the small, carefully boiled oats and not sensing the taste. If they'd served bread, Yuzuf would have been able to hide it behind his shirt and take it out, but there wasn't any bread that day.

A couple of hours later – after biting his fingernails and lashing a switch at all the nettles behind the infirmary – Yuzuf went to the clubhouse to face up to what he'd done. He was ready, so let the mean artist scold or punish him.

It was already darkening. The door squeaked louder and the shadows on the clubhouse's log walls were longer and more intricate. A yellow kerosene lamp burned in the window and the finished painting was drying on the easel. Ikonnikov himself wasn't there.

Yuzuf took the lamp and walked right up to the canvas. Warm light streamed along the bold, gooey brushstrokes and delicate strands of various colors blended and swirled in each, none repeating – everything breathed and flowed in iridescent hues. Yuzuf gently touched the Neva with the tip of a burned finger. A small, round indentation remained on the river and a cool, dark blue spot on his finger.

"And so what do you see?" Ikonnikov had entered unnoticed and was standing in the doorway, observing.

Yuzuf shuddered and hurriedly placed the kerosene lamp in its place. Nabbed! And he couldn't escape: Ikonnikov was right by the door and would catch him.

"I'm asking you: what do you see in the painting?"

"A river," Yuzuf forced out, then corrected himself right away. "The Neva."

"Well? What else?"

"Stone houses."

"And?"

"An embankment. People. Trees. Seagulls. The dawn."

"And?"

And? Yuzuf looked despondently at the canvas. There was nothing else there.

"Fine then, go," said Ikonnikov. "I took the dishes to the kitchen myself."

"My supper, I wanted to give it to you … Gorelov didn't let me …"

"Go on, now."

Ikonnikov took a brush and neatly smoothed the mark Yuzuf's finger had left on the waves. His eyes were warming, as if they'd been heated by the sun rising over the Neva.

"I also see it's not cold in Leningrad," Yuzuf said from the door. Ikonnikov didn't turn.

It became a habit after that: first Yuzuf brought Ilya Petrovich's lunches and suppers, then he began stopping in for no reason, to hang around the clubhouse for days at a time. He washed out brushes, scraped palettes, and even just sat, observing Ikonnikov at work.

Ikonnikov spent a large portion of his time high up, under the ceiling. Lying on the scaffolding, he would often stab the point of a homemade brush at the plywood, mumbling something under his breath. Sometimes he came down the steps, craned his neck, and ran around in circles to inspect his labors from the entrance, from the window, and from the center of the room. An excruciated expression would appear on his face, and his large, bony hands would scratch each other incessantly. After those inspections, Ilya Petrovich either grabbed a painting knife and frantically scraped off a piece of the mural (in moments like those, Yuzuf would sit quietly, taking refuge in the corner behind the easel) or purred with satisfaction and continued painting. Yuzuf didn't have to hide then and could climb up the scaffolding to examine the painting more closely and even ask a question or two.

Ikonnikov came down in the evenings. Stretched his numbed arms and legs, packed his wooden pipe with strong-smelling grassy dust, and smoked. Placed a clean canvas or piece of plywood on the easel. Yuzuf would hold his breath. There it was, it was starting.

Ilya Petrovich's fat brush first made several long, sweeping strokes, cutting the future painting's expanse into sections, then thickly covered the resulting pieces in various colors. The canvas now resembled an incomprehensible and untidy kaleidoscope, a rubbish heap. With careful touches of a thin brush, that disorderly accumulation of shapes suddenly acquired proportion and meaning so that vivid, distinct images that had initially hardly shown through now revealed themselves. This was "the window" swinging open.

Little boys in large black caps and torn trousers fished on the embankment of the River Seine, which was unknown to Yuzuf; half-naked female swimmers basked in the sun on the pearly stones of the Côte d'Azur; a sailboat sped along the big Neva, straight for the Vasilevsky Island spit; and bronze Graces spun in a round dance along the tree-lined paths at the deserted Oranienbaum. The places where those windows swung open dazzled Yuzuf. He would sit for hours, mesmerized, peering at the intertwined brush strokes, attentively listening to them, and sniffing. The distant world lying beyond the hills of the taiga was not so cold and forlorn after all. It smelled sharply of oil paint, but through that strong scent one could clearly sense the aroma of spring grass and warm stones and the wind and rotting leaves and freshly caught fish.

One time when Ilya Petrovich asked him what he would like to see in the next painting, Yuzuf responded without pondering. A cow. Ikonnikov coughed, tugged a bit at his long nose, and slapped his brush at the plywood a couple of times. A fat and affectionate creature with large eyes gazed at Yuzuf. It was soft to the touch and had horns like yellow commas over the top of its curly head. It was not scary.

Then Yuzuf requested a goat. Slap, slap! Alongside the cow there appeared a goat's sharp snout with a funny little beard and white stubs of horns sticking out.

"A dog," Yuzuf ordered. A dog appeared, panting after running, its pink tongue cheerily hanging out.

Yuzuf went silent. He had nothing else to wish for.

From that day on, Ilya Petrovich painted for Yuzuf. Churches and embankments, bridges and palaces were set aside. The time had come for toys, fruits and vegetables, clothing and shoes, household objects, and zoo animals.

Apple, lemon, watermelon, melon, and guavasteen. Potato, black radish, corn, eggplant, and tomato. There were various hats: this one's called a top hat; that one's a sombrero; and here's a collapsible hat. There were gloves: men wear leather ones and only in autumn but women wear them year-round, lacy white ones to the theater and for visiting, mittens without fingers in cool weather, and fur ones in winter.

The world surged so much and so rapidly from worn canvases and fragments of plywood that it threatened to deluge Yuzuf. At night he dreamt of cats in splendid tutus and giraffes carrying tattered primers in yellow leather satchels; seals greedily munched at ice creams in strange cones; and striped tigers smashed at a large leather ball with their blunt muzzles. They were all woven from light, raised strokes and were thus a bit rough and angular, reflecting hundreds of delicious, strong-smelling specks of light when they were moved. Yuzuf would wake up excited, his head heavy, his ears burning, and the end of his nose cold, feeling as if the colors and images he had absorbed were overflowing his skull and bursting from inside. They needed to be released back out.

Later, he couldn't remember exactly what he had drawn first. It somehow happened on its own when he began scratching scribbles on the floor with a pencil stub that was lying around. This brought him relief – his head cooled and felt lighter. The scribbles gradually crept toward the window, taking over the windowsill and part of a wall. One morning, he discovered a clean piece of plywood and a brush on the easel, as if they'd been prepared by someone and forgotten. He looked up and saw Ikonnikov lying under the ceiling, as usual, his nose in his agitational art, paying no attention to Yuzuf. He cautiously took the brush, poked at the palette, and drew it along the plywood, leaving a thick orange comet. And then another one. And another. That was the day he began painting with oils.

"*Quelle date sommes-nous aujourd'hui?*"

"*Le premier juillet mille neuf cent trente-huit, madame.*"

"*Qu'est-ce que tu faisais aujourd'hui?*"

"*Je dessinais, madame.*"

"*Et encore?*"

"*Je dessinais seulement, madame.*"

Yuzuf and Izabella are walking along the shore. He's kicking pebbles with the toe of his shoe and they're landing in the Angara with a plop; as always during lessons, Izabella is pacing sedately alongside him and one of the hands behind her back is holding a long birch switch.

"*Tu dessinais quoi, Yuzuf?*"

"A station and trains, lots of trains." They haven't gone over these words yet, so he answers in Russian. "First Ilya Petrovich drew them himself, then I did, after him."

She stops, looks intently at him, and sketches on the ground with the switch: "*Gare.*"

"*Gare* means station," she says.

Izabella always pronounces new words so calmly and distinctly that they etch themselves in Yuzuf's memory. The slightly crooked letters traced on the damp earth stay right in front of him, even after the waves wash them away. *Gare* is train station. *Billet* is ticket. *Quai* is platform. *Chemin* is road. *La destination* is where you're going. *Voyageur* is traveler. *Partir* is to leave. *Revenir* is to return. There are lots of new words today and he'll need to memorize them before the next lesson.

"Here's a saying for you about this topic," says Izabella. "*Partir, c'est mourir un peu.* 'To leave is to die a little.'"

Yuzuf already knows a lot of French sayings that are spirited and apt, about love and war, kings and sailors, sheep and fried eggs. But this one seems sad, as if it's not French at all.

"Isn't there a happier one?"

"Sorry, yes – I meant to give you a different one. How about this: *Pour atteindre son but il ne faut qu'aller.* 'To get to one's goal, one must get going.'"

Beautiful words. Yuzuf crouches and draws a finger along letters that are already half-dissolved in the waves that have lapped at the shore: "*partir,*" "*revenir.*" He wants to draw a tired person who's wandering stubbornly, who's been gnawing at his own lip, and is firmly squeezing a staff in his hand. He's going somewhere far away, maybe to his destination or maybe back home. Izabella ruffles the front of Yuzuf's hair and walks away from the shore, unexpectedly finishing the lesson earlier than usual.

Shortly thereafter, Volf Karlovich suspects that an interest in medicine has awakened in Yuzuf. He'd previously been indifferent to what was happening in the infirmary during the day and only ran there in the evenings because he needed to help his mother clean, but Yuzuf has suddenly begun frequenting the examination room, stealing in quietly behind Leibe, perching himself in the corner, sniffling and staring with huge eyes like his mother's.

By this time, the infirmary has already expanded to two buildings stuffed with bunks, and Leibe has finally divided the space into male and female sections, separating out a tiny isolation ward for patients with infectious diseases, too. The examination room is located in its old spot by the window not far from the entrance and partitioned from the main room, initially by a curtain made of bast matting, now by a durable wooden screen. There's a chair, a pine trestle bed for examining patients, and homemade shelves with instruments all laid out in a strict order. A table was added not long ago, too, and it immediately became Leibe's favorite place. Now he sits at it when he's maintaining his patient registry log; he had previously needed to settle himself sideways on the windowsill.

The huge gray ledger's appearance alone instills patients' deep respect. Their respect turns to awe when Volf Karlovich leafs through the thick, stiff, brownish pages, written all over in his tiny floating hand. Semruk's peasants deferentially call him "our doc."

Leibe always receives patients. There are no infirmary office hours, weekends, or holidays. If something happens during the night, people knock on the window and the sleepy Leibe hurries to the examining room, pulling on the white lab coat that has recently appeared for him; Kuznets brought it in gratitude for strictly confidential treatment of a disease in his male parts. Volf Karlovich treats everything: typhus, dysentery, scurvy, venereal diseases, and horrible pellagra, which strips skin from patients' bodies while they're alive. He pulls teeth, cuts off feet and hands maimed at the logging site, repairs hernias, delivers babies, and performs abortions (not in secret at first, but more covertly after the resolution of 1936). There's only one diagnosis he can't deal with, the one most commonly encountered: severe malnutrition. It's a diagnosis he's forbidden to make, which he thus notes in the ledger with a vague "cardiovascular inefficiency."

And here's the seven-year-old Yuzuf, who's tall but also as skinny as a pole, big-boned, and as long-legged as a compass, too. Volf Karlovich tries to feed him extra: grateful patients bring the doc a sack of berries or a handful of nuts or some fresh nettles for soup or dandelion root (which Leibe has long grown accustomed to brewing instead of coffee). But what's the use? Yuzuf's young body is growing and his arms and legs have remained as scrawny as before, like sticks.

One particular day, the boy is sitting quietly by the wooden screen, not stirring, as usual. He's looking, unblinking, at the patient, a stooped old man with wrinkled, large-pored skin like dried orange peel. The man has disrobed to his underpants, displaying for Leibe knobbly joints like large lumps and fingers deformed by arthritis that look as if they've been broken. Leibe prescribes bilberries, stone bramble, and rowan berries to the old man, in any form and at maximum quantities, plus a glass of home brew for serious pain. What other options were there? Home brew, a time-tested painkiller, has to be used in many cases.

Then Leibe turns to Yuzuf:

"So, are you interested? This is arthritis, a disease of the bones and joints. Did you know, young man, that there are more than two hundred bones in the human body and each of them can become inflamed, change its contour or size, get infected ..."

Yuzuf begins touching his own knees, ankles, and ribs; his entranced gaze doesn't budge from the doctor.

"Right here," says the doctor, taking Yuzuf by a skinny wrist, "is the ulna, which goes up to the elbow. And the one above, the humerus, going up to the shoulder. Then there's the clavicula, costae ..."

A sudden warmth rises to Leibe's cheeks: for a moment he felt he was back at the university rostrum, in the crosshairs of hundreds of young, attentive eyes. Recovering from his self-consciousness, he continues his story. That evening he hurries off to the commandant to ask for several agitational posters "for the ideological decoration of places offering medical service to the population." He returns to the infirmary after his request has been fulfilled and nervously spreads out on the table pictures of hale and hearty muscular athletes of both genders who proudly carry scarlet banners greeting the country's leadership. Volf Karlovich toils over them all night, muttering in both Latin and German, and tracing his pencil along well-fed, tanned bodies unthreatened by either malnutrition or pellagra. The anatomical diagrams are ready in the morning. The athletes are still parading with flags but they're also displaying for the world exactly four hundred and six bones – long, short, flat, and irregular – two hundred and three each.

Yuzuf appreciates the doctor's work. His lips move diligently as he memorizes the tricky names in a week, searching on his own body along the way, which seems destined for this type of study, since he can touch many of the bones through his skin – from the sharp little os nasale to the barely perceptible os coccygis.

Volf Karlovich prepares a second set of educational materials in which the athletes' trained bodies obediently demonstrate the musculoskeletal system: the sculpted vastus lateralis and gastrocnemius, the threateningly bulging pectoralis major. And Yuzuf memorizes all those quickly, too.

Inspired by his pedagogical success, Leibe proposes moving on to the structure of the internal organs, but Yuzuf unexpectedly refuses and asks permission to put the leftover posters to use as drawing paper. The disheartened Leibe agrees and Yuzuf relocates from the examination room to the wards to draw patients lying on bunks. To Volf Karlovich's bitter disappointment, Yuzuf's sudden fervent interest in medicine has ebbed and soon he's disappearing again for days at a time at the clubhouse with Ikonnikov. The athletes, finely chopped into muscles and bones, and written on with Latin terms, remain hanging up in the infirmary, immeasurably strengthening the Semruk doc's status, which is already colossal.

*

Ikonnikov has been painting his agitational art for exactly half a year. He has invited both Sumlinskys to the clubhouse for a "private view" before turning it over to the chiefs, who are out of patience. "Finally!" rejoices Izabella. "I haven't been out in society for ages."

The private view is imminent: tonight, under cover of darkness. Ikonnikov, who has become extremely emaciated of late and whose bloodshot eyes are surrounded by dark circles, has spent all day taking apart the scaffolding himself, leaving only one ladder by the wall. He locks the door, lies on his back on the floor, and begins waiting for his guests.

He lies and looks at the mural in dusky half-darkness. An orange square of light from the window creeps first along the floor, then along the wall, and later disappears entirely. Darkness comes. The lines on the ceiling disperse and dissolve in the dense night air but Ikonnikov sees them just as distinctly as during the afternoon, so he doesn't light the lamp.

He'll present the agitational art tomorrow. Kuznets will come, grope it with his predatory little eyes, estimate if there's enough of an ideological message – meaning he'll consider whether to leave it at the club or tear it the hell off to be burned and send the artist out of peaceable Semruk life, to the camps, or far beyond. Gorelov will tag along. He'll sniff around hungrily, looking for anything he might find fault in, and he'll surely find something. They'll part tomorrow. He'll leave behind this mural, a couple dozen city scenes (he's grown bolder, hanging them on the club's walls after the memorable night visit from the chiefs), a heap of leftover plywood scraps with pictures for Yuzuf, homemade brushes, palettes, painting knives made from the blades of one-handed saws, half-empty tubes of paints, and rags. He'll leave behind nocturnal vigils, the smell of linseed oil and turpentine, conversations with little Yuzuf, spots of paint on his fingers, all his thoughts, and his very own self. And welcome back to the logging site: *We'd grown tired waiting for you, citizen Ikonnikov.*

There's a heavy bottle hidden beyond a pile of junk in the corner. Open it? No, not now. It would be too bad to miss this moment.

Someone cautiously scratches at the door; it's the Sumlinskys. Ikonnikov lights the kerosene lamp and goes to greet his guests. Konstantin Arnoldovich is wearing a new jacket (the clothing problem in Semruk has been resolved in a simple way because the dying leave their wardrobes to the living as an inheritance) and Izabella, whose hair is carefully styled, is leaning on her husband's arm.

"*Bonsoir,*" she says sedately.

Then she cries out because Gare Saint-Lazare is looking at her from a rough, poorly planed pine wall. Next to it is Sacré-Cœur. The Tuileries. La Conciergerie. Izabella walks slowly along the wall, her long shadow floating beside her.

"Bella." Konstantin Arnoldovich is standing by the opposite wall, arms down at his sides, and not moving. "Look, it's Vasilevsky Island, the Sixth Line."

Izabella slowly turns her face and walks right up to the small, rectangular canvas.

"That's the Eighth Line," Ikonnikov says, bringing the lamp closer.

"The Sixth, Ilya Petrovich, my dear fellow, the Sixth." Izabella stretches her hand toward yellow and gray buildings with intricate little balconies, but she's not touching them, she's stroking the air. "We lived here, a little further, right in this building." Her finger goes outside the border of the canvas, creeps along the log and pokes at the wiry oakum.

Leningrad takes up two walls of the clubhouse; Paris, Provence, and seascapes have two others; and the rest of the world takes shelter in the corners, meagerly represented by a couple of small panoramas and everyday sketches. The Sumlinskys move from Vasilevsky Island to Île de la Cité, from Quai Branly to Petersburg's English Embankment, from Alexander the Third Bridge to Troitsky Bridge, from Bank Bridge to Pont au Change, along Canal Saint-Martin to the Lebyazhy Canal and then, further, past the Mikhailovsky Theater to the Neva …

"I'm never leaving here," Izabella finally says. "Ilya Petrovich, I'll live here as an apprentice, I'll mix paints for you or wash the floors."

"We haven't been mixing paints for a long time. They're sold prepared, in tubes. And this is my last day here. I'll turn in the agitational art tomorrow and it will be *finita la commedia*."

The Sumlinskys suddenly remember the mural – they still haven't taken a look at it! "Where is it, maestro? Show us."

Ikonnikov turns the wick in the kerosene lamp as far as possible – the flame flies up under the glass bell in a long, bright strip, flooding the space with yellow light – and he lifts it toward the ceiling.

There's a firmament of transparent dark blue where clouds float as lightly as feathers. Four people are growing out of the ceiling's four corners, stretching their arms upward, as if they're trying to reach something in the center. Under their feet, somewhere far below, there are fields undulating with dark golden rye and strewn with tractors like little black boxes, forests that look like grass and have kernel-like dirigibles soaring over them, cities bristling with factory smokestacks like matchsticks, and crowded demonstrations with banners like little red snakes. That entire tempestuous and densely populated world spreads in a narrow ribbon around the edges of the ceiling, like an intricate, florid frame inside which the four main characters soar after having pushed themselves away.

A golden-haired doctor in a starched white lab coat, an athletic warrior with a rifle on his back, an agronomist with a bundle of wheat and a surveying instrument on his shoulder, and a mother with a baby in her arms – they're young and strong, and their faces are open, brave, and extraordinarily tense, showing one single aspiration: to reach a goal. But what goal? The center of the ceiling is empty.

"They're reaching for what doesn't exist, right?"

"No, Bella." Konstantin Arnoldovich places a thin hand at his lower lip and tugs at his sparse little beard. "They're reaching for one another."

"But, Ilya Petrovich," Izabella suddenly remembers, "where's the actual agitational part?"

"It will come," he grins. "I still have one detail left to paint. As it happens, I'll have time to do that during the night."

After the Sumlinskys leave, he pulls the scaffolding ladder out to the center of the room, sits on the lower step, and squeezes a thick squiggle of blood-red cadmium on the palette with a pensive smile.

Creeaaak! The door swings wide open, letting Gorelov's stocky figure over the threshold. He was spying, the dog.

"Breaking rules, are we?" he hisses. "Leading a nocturnal life? Hosting guests?"

He's in no rush as he swaggers into the clubhouse. Sniffling loudly, his eyes roam the ceiling, the ladder, and Ikonnikov's motionless figure sitting on it. Gorelov stops in front of him, pressing his hands to his hips and pensively moving his heavy lower jaw.

"Come on, report to the minder, son-of-a-bitch citizen Ikonnikov. Tell me what you and the Sumlinskys were whispering about."

"We were discussing the agitational art," says Ikonnikov, raising his eyes to the ceiling. "The sum total of ideas placed in it, its sufficiency for concrete agitational and educational goals, and the potential subjective particularities of how certain individuals at our inhabited locality will perceive it."

"You're lying ..." Gorelov brings his face closer; his eyes are like wide-open slots. "Fine, you puffed-up dauber, just wait till you end up at the logging site with me, then we'll have a chat. Or are you thinking you might talk your way into staying here? Go on paintering away instead of doing honest labor?"

By all indications, Gorelov has somehow found out that Ikonnikov recently wrote a petition to the commandant, proposing to organize an artel of art producers in Semruk. That dispatch contained a detailed description of the type of production this artel could create ("high quality oil paintings with patriotic and agitational content, all possible topics, including historical"), who could be the consumers of their production ("cultural and community centers, village reading rooms, libraries, cinemas, and other places for the cultural entertainment and enlightenment of the working masses"), as well as an approximate calculation of income from the activity. The sum turned out to be impressive. Ignatov has chosen to resolve the matter after receipt of the agitational art at the clubhouse.

Ikonnikov keeps silent, rustling at his palette. Gorelov abruptly grabs the brush from him and pokes it under his ribs with a stealthy motion, as if it were a knife. For a moment it seems as if the sharp handle has speared his skin. Ikonnikov rasps hoarsely, seizes the brush, and attempts to deflect it from himself, but Gorelov has a firm grasp, as if he's caught the edge of a rib with a steel hook.

"Well, you might get to loaf around in an artel for a while." Gorelov's hot, sour breath is in Ikonnikov's ear. "But it's proven artists, not rebels like you, who paint pictures for the Soviet people in this country."

"Stalin … Twenty-four busts …" Ikonnikov is wriggling on the ladder like a pinned moth.

"You want to be an artist, then you need to prove you're worthy! Choose, you bastard. You're either with us or you're at the logging site tomorrow."

"What … do you want?" The brush has been driven into either his lung or his diaphragm and is ready to pierce; it's impossible to breathe.

"I repeat: what were you whispering about with the Sumlinskys?"

"About Leningrad!"

Gorelov takes a step back. Ikonnikov collapses to the floor, wheezing as he draws in air, and coughing incessantly.

"There you go!" Gorelov looks at the brush in his hands with disgust, breaks it on his knee, and tosses it into the darkness; the pieces bounce along the floorboards, rolling into various corners. "You'll write down everything, who said what, what you were all laughing about, any bad-mouthing …" He straightens his belt, which has slipped to the side, and pulls down his uniform jacket. "And you'll bring it to me tomorrow. If you do it before the chiefs come to inspect your agitational art, you'll have your artel. If you don't, then sharpen your saw. I'll see to it you're assigned to my shift. That's all, you son of a bitch, dismissed."

Gorelov's boots thud toward the exit and he disappears out the door. Ikonnikov crawls to the corner, still on his knees. He tosses around empty crates, scraps of plywood, and rags, and finds the hidden bottle. He tears the stopper out with his teeth and takes a couple of long, gurgling swallows. Shuffling uncertainly in the darkness, he returns to the ladder. He takes the kerosene lamp and palette, and crawls up under the ceiling. He sits on the upper step for a couple of minutes, observing the boundless dark blue expanse with transparent, fluffy clouds stretching across it. He scoops a generous amount of cadmium from the palette and smears it on the ceiling – an enormous, thick crimson blotch explodes on the firmament.

As soon as Kuznets arrives, he goes straight to the clubhouse to look at the agitational art. After stepping into the middle of the room and drilling his eyes into the ceiling, he stands, eyebrows moving and getting a feel for things. Ignatov is next to him. Gorelov trails along with them, too, and he's milling around by the door, casting shifty glances at the chief. Ikonnikov himself is on hand, holding up the wall. He's listless and downcast; he never did go to sleep last night, and his hand keeps grasping at his side, under the ribs, as if his stomach is seizing up. When the silence drags on, he decides to defuse the situation a little.

"Allow me," he says. "As the artist, I'd like to say a few words about the concept ... I mean about the main idea."

The chiefs are silent, breathing loudly.

"This agitational art represents an allegory, a cumulative image of Soviet society." Ikonnikov raises his hand, in turn, to each of the figures soaring in the sky. "The protector of our fatherland stands for our valorous armed forces. The mother with the baby is for all Soviet women. The red agronomist – a peasant engaged in farming – embodies working the land and the prosperity of our country that flows from it, and the doctor represents protecting the population from illnesses, along with all Soviet scientific thought."

Kuznets is rocking from heel to toe and back again, and his boots squeak from the strain.

"The army and the civilian population, science and agriculture are directed, in a unified impetus, toward the red banner, a symbol of revolution."

In the center of the ceiling, where yesterday the tall sky had been shining dark blue, there hovers a giant crimson streamer resembling a magic carpet. It's so large that it seems it will fall any minute, covering all the little people standing under it with their heads craned upward. The weighty inscription, "Proletarians of all countries, unite!" is emblazoned in thick gold and flows along its folds. It's as if the four figures in the mural's corners have immediately shrunk in size; they're now devoutly extending their arms in a set direction, toward the banner.

It came out beautifully, Ignatov thinks with surprise as he scrutinizes the inspired faces of the people soaring above them. *It's truthful, in a genuine way. Nice work, artist. You didn't betray us.*

He takes half a year daubing out those small people then does the flag in one night, Gorelov laments to himself. *He was loafing, the snake.*

"Well," Kuznets finally utters. "It makes a striking impression. I commend you. An artel can be entrusted to a master like this."

And he whacks Ikonnikov's slumped shoulder so Ikonnikov barely stays on his feet.

The chiefs leave but Ilya Petrovich stays in the club. He sits down on the ladder, lowers his head into hands smudged with paint, and sits that way for a long time. When he finally lifts his face, there's an unfamiliar breath of redness and heat from the ceiling – it's the banner.

Of course those are angels. Yuzuf's mother has told him about them – about *fereshte*: they soar high up in the sky, feed on sunlight, and sometimes stand behind people's shoulders, unseen, and defend them when they're in trouble, though they rarely show themselves, only to announce something very important.

Yuzuf has even asked Ilya Petrovich if he's drawn angels on the ceiling. Ilya Petrovich started smiling. "I might just have done that," he said.

One time, shortly before the mural was finished and when

Ikonnikov wasn't at the clubhouse, Yuzuf had climbed the scaffolding and carefully studied the mural up close. At first he lay there a long time, looking at the golden-haired doctor, who was looking at Yuzuf. The doctor's eyes were bright, a sharp dark blue, and his hair as luxurious as a sheep's. *He looks like our doctor*, Yuzuf decided, *only he's young and doesn't have a bald spot.*

Then he looked at the agronomist. This one was even younger, just a youth, and he was dreamy and tender, with velvety cheeks and a rapturous gaze. He didn't resemble anyone; there were no faces that joyful in Semruk.

The warrior was another matter: his eyes were stern and stubborn, and his mouth was a straight line so he looked exactly like the commandant. It was surprising how people and angels could look alike.

The woman with the child was green-eyed, with dark braids twisted on the back of her head, and the child in her arms was tiny and half-blind. Yuzuf didn't know children were that small when they were born. He wondered if an angel's child would be an angel, too, when it grew up. He didn't have time to think that through because Ikonnikov had come in.

"So," Ikonnikov asked, "did you examine it? And who are they, do you think?"

Yuzuf came down from the scaffolding and dusted himself off very seriously.

"Of course, they're angels," he said, "the most ordinary ones. Anybody can see that. What, you think I'm a little boy or something and don't understand things like that?"

THE BLACK TENT

A huge log, about one and a half cubic meters, crashes from the riverside timber landing into the water, its cut yellow end spinning. People are already running over to it, pressing their hands into it and pushing it away from shore. They lead it deeper, until the water's up to their necks, and release it where the Angara itself will catch the log and carry it off. Log drivers standing in boats and holding long pike poles will straighten the logs' course, gathering them closer together, toward the center. Metal hooks at the ends of their pikes catch logs that stray from the flock, returning them to the channel. The long caravan of floating timber will stretch down toward the mouth of the Angara, toward the anchorage point, with the log drivers following. Barges are already there by a log boom, and people are waiting to fish out the logs, transfer them across the Yenisei, and pull them toward Maklakovo, to the lumber mill.

Workers from Semruk float the loose timber when the Angara is at its lowest levels and has calmed – it's dangerous in high water and the timber would be damaged. Some roll the logs into the water, where another group rounds them up for the log drivers – the most reliable and tested – to take to Maklakovo.

They'd begun work today even before daybreak and the Angara is already teeming with the dark spines of logs; it's as if there's a school of giant fish jostling in the river. When the sun reaches its zenith, the log rollers are almost as wet (from sweat) as the rear crew, who wade around in the water pushing the logs; the first group of log drivers has already disappeared behind a bend in the river, heading toward the Yenisei.

"Lunch break!"

People sink to the ground. Some look at the remaining piles, others watch the spines of logs rattling along the river in the distance, or gaze at the clear July sky. Spoons clink and the reeking smell of homemade tobacco wafts around. From this part of the riverbank, there's a good view of the Semruk pier in the distance, where Kuznets is boarding his gleaming brown launch, barely staying on his feet thanks to a bad hangover. A half-dressed Ignatov clings to him, reeling, shouting, and waving his arms as if he's making a demand or wants to ask for something, but Gorelov holds the commandant, allowing Kuznets to break loose and jump on the launch. "I can't … ! Let me go! … I can't be here any longer!" carries Ignatov's desperate wail.

"Sons of bitches," one of the log rollers quietly says, with hatred.

The uproar they created back on that autumn night in Semruk – firing on live people – has been nicknamed Walpurgis Night. Fortunately, there were only injuries and nobody was killed.

The launch finally breaks away from the dock, coughs, picks up steam, and heads toward the bend in the river, carefully skirting the accumulated logs. Gorelov releases the commandant, then throws his hands in the air as if in apology and presses them to his chest. Ignatov isn't listening. He jumps into a small boat that's bobbing at a berth and rows after Kuznets's launch. The boat is just a small rowboat, so it flies quickly along the waves and the current carries it into the channel, pulling it into the tail end of a heavy flotilla of logs.

"He'll get caught the hell up," say dispassionate voices in the crowd. "Be crushed to pieces."

People look up from their dishes. Some peer and half-stand to have a better look while others continue gulping indifferently. The loud, terrifying cracking of logs can be heard at a distance.

Ignatov notices the danger too late. He's pulling the oars with all his might but can no longer row away and the boat smashes into a shiny jumble of moving logs in the middle of the river. He tries to push off one of them with an oar but the oar immediately snaps. A couple of seconds later, Ignatov appears to be crouching and shrinking in height, and then neither he nor the boat is visible. His brown hair flashes just once more among the frothy logs, and that's all.

"Die, you bastard," utters Zaseka, a frail little man wearing ragged overalls.

Someone suddenly darts away from the onlookers and rushes headlong toward the river, pushing a boat prepared for the log drivers into the water and jumping in. He goes after the caravan, desperately working a pole to drive the boat toward the churning porridge of logs and froth. It's Lukka. People watch from the knoll as he's flung from side to side, kneeling on half-bent legs, mashing at the Angara with the pole. He's rapidly carried downstream but manages to steer the boat a bit to the side, edging and pushing his way stubbornly between the logs to where Ignatov's wet head last flashed. He suddenly tosses the pole into the boat and bends toward the water.

"Has he found him?"

And now everyone has dropped their dishes, spoons, and unfinished hand-rolled cigarettes, and is dashing toward the river, crowding, making a racket, and running into the water. Several boats spring out into the Angara, tearing along the shore, downstream with the current, preparing to meet them, and help them out of the wooden jumble. People fling ropes, extend their pikes, yell …

"Come on, come on!" Gorelov shouts as hard as he can, his boots sloshing in water up to his ankles, and desperately waving at the tiny red-haired figure in the middle of the Angara.

Lukka catches his pike pole on one of the lines that's been tossed and then they somehow haul Ignatov's boat to shore and raise it to the Semruk pier. It's crushed like a little paper boat and already half-filled with water that's a rich red – Ignatov's lying on the bottom, wheezing large, bloody bubbles and his legs are as awkwardly twisted as a puppet's.

He comes to during the night, as if he's been struck. He sits up in bed. *Where am I?*

A taut gauze cap is stretched over his forehead, his right arm is immobilized against his shoulder, and his left leg feels like a dead weight. The pillows around him are dim white in the dull moonlight; people are breathing loudly. Ah, yes, the infirmary. It seems like he's already been here a long time, several days, maybe even weeks. He wakes up each night, regains consciousness – this is agonizing and takes a long time – and remembers; then he limply leans back and falls asleep again. Faces flash: Leibe, Gorelov, and other patients. Sometimes a spoon materializes in his mouth and he obediently swallows either cool water or a warm and liquidy stew that flows slowly down his throat. The same kind of thoughts – liquidy and viscous – splash listlessly in his head, too.

But everything's different today because his head is clear; everything inside it is in good order, quick, and precise, and his body is unexpectedly strong. Ignatov's healthy hand grasps at the strings digging into his chin and he pulls to unknot them, tearing the gauze over his head and throwing off the little cap. He peels off a couple of wads of cotton stuck to the top of his head and a light breeze from the vent window gently flutters at his shaved skull, caressing his skin. He's free!

He leans into the edge of the bed, wanting to lower his feet to the floor. His right foot somehow obeys him and creeps out from under the blanket but the second has become unliftable and shoots with sharp pain. He throws off the blanket and sees his leg is tightly wound in gauze, like a swaddled infant, and half his foot is gone.

He breathes deeply and rapidly, gazing at his bandaged foot, then turns away. He notices a freshly planed crutch leaning against the bed. There weren't crutches in Semruk until now. Meaning they'd crafted it themselves. For him? He grabs it and launches it into the darkness with all his might. There's a crash and the clang of some vials; one of the patients raises himself up, grumbles, and drops his head to the pillow again. Quiet returns.

Ignatov sits and listens to his own breathing. Then he stands up with a start (his ribs burn his torso) and hops on one foot to where the crutch flew – there it is, lying by the wall. He bends and picks it up. The crutch smells strongly of pine pitch and it's sturdy so it didn't break into smithereens. The hand grips are wound with rags for softness, and there's a heel from someone's boot nailed to the bottom so it won't thud too much. It was made sensibly, to last. (*Thank you for that, at least.*) Ignatov inserts the crutch under his arm and hobbles toward the door. There's a sound of shuffling feet behind him. The sleepy doctor, rubbing his eyes, has come out of the living quarters because of the noise.

"Where are you going?" he clucks behind Ignatov. "You have a traumatic brain injury! And what about the stitches? The broken bones? Your foot!"

Ignatov thumps the crutch at the infirmary door, which swings open with a crash, and walks out into the night.

The commandant lives in his own home from that day on. Leibe comes up once a day to examine him and Zuleikha changes his bandages in the evenings.

She arrives and, gazing at the floor, goes to place the basin of hot water on the table, setting it alongside rolls of bandages she laundered and thoroughly boiled the day before. Ignatov is already sitting up in bed, watching. Has he been waiting?

She begins with his head. The doctor has strictly forbidden the commandant to remove the dressing from his head and Ignatov submitted after making a bit of noise; they are no longer winding a little cap on him but making a simple circular dressing instead. Zuleikha places her palms on the warm back of his head, which is overgrown in thick brown stubble with sparks of gray, then unwinds a long bandage, runs a hot damp rag along his pale skin and around fresh, zigzagging burgundy-colored stitches, and wipes it dry. She swabs the stitches with home brew that smells very bitter, then winds a clean bandage over them.

Now it's time for the arm. Groaning from the effort, she somehow removes an uncooperative shirt from Ignatov's large, warm body; he doesn't help, not even with his healthy arm. She sees that his huge bruises are gradually changing color, lightening, and fading. Pale, flawless skin has appeared under them. She remembers Murtaza's curly-haired belly and hairy shoulders, and his powerful trunk, like a tree's, unembraceably broad in the shoulders and just as bulky at the waist. Everything is different for Ignatov, who has sharp shoulders pointing in opposite directions and a long torso that's narrow at the waist. She removes the bandage, bathes the heavy, supple arm, which is stitched substantially in two places (he winces from pain, tolerating it), and all the bruises and abrasions on his chest, ribs, and back. There's a conspicuous deep old scar under his shoulder blade and she averts her eyes at the sight of it, as if she's peeked at a secret not intended for her. Dry rag. Home brew. New dressing. Put the shirt back on.

She treats his foot last. She places the basin on the floor by the bed and kneels. She separates the stump from the gauze and bathes it, feeling Ignatov's heavy gaze on the top of her head. He holds his breath and groans, probably agonizing from fury rather than pain. She remembers washing Murtaza's feet, if you could call them that: they were fat, broad hooves with the toes splayed in various directions. The black soles of his feet, coarsened from walking on soil, flaked and shed skin in her hands, like tree bark. Ignatov's feet are long and slender with soles that are dry, smooth, and hard. His toes are probably handsome, too. Zuleikha doesn't know this; she hasn't seen his healthy foot.

She knows the rest of his body; she's memorized it.

Wash thoroughly, wipe, swab, bandage.

Ignatov sits silently the whole time, his face turned to her. It's as if he's tracing her scent. She also thinks there's an unbearable smell of honey. The hot water, the bandages, and even the home brew smell of honey. So does Ignatov's body. And hair.

She tells herself not to raise her eyes from the floor. Not to touch more than necessary. Not to turn her head. To ball up the soiled gauze, wipe up the floor after herself, and get out, get out of there, launder the dressing rags in the icy Angara water, cool the hands, cheeks, and forehead; clench the jaw, squeeze the eyes shut, summon up in the mind's eye a black tent that covers the commandant's headquarters like a densely woven rug, and gallop away at breakneck speed, escape from him on a fast Argamak; heat water again tomorrow and go back up the path, to where Ignatov is already waiting for her, sitting on his tidied bed.

*

417

And that's how they live for the whole remainder of the summer, until autumn.

In September, the doctor allows the dressings to be removed. By then, the sutures have already healed up and lightened. Today she'll go to the commandant's for the last time, to remove the bandages from his arm and head. They'll still leave the dressing on the stump but Ignatov can change it himself now that he has two healthy arms.

She arrives at sunset, as usual. Pressing the heavy, hot basin to her belly, she knocks her foot lightly at the door, which gives way and opens. Zuleikha enters and unburdens herself of the steaming basin, setting it on the table. Ignatov isn't in bed, though; he's standing by the windowsill, with his back leaning against the window, and he's looking right at her from the altitude of his warrior-like height.

"I came to take off your dressings," Zuleikha says to the basin on the table.

"Then take them off."

Zuleikha approaches Ignatov. He's very tall, probably taller than Murtaza. His head, wrapped in a white bandage like a turban, is just under the ceiling.

"I can't reach."

"You'll reach."

She stands on tiptoe and stretches upward, tipping her head back to see. Her fingers grope for the familiar bristly back of his head and unwind the dressing. It's hot in the commandant's headquarters, as if it's being heated.

"Your fingers are ice cold," says Ignatov.

His face is very close. She silently unwinds the bandage. After she's finally managed that, she lets her arms down, walks off to the table, and exhales. She submerges a hand with a piece of clean gauze into scalding water in the basin and walks over to Ignatov again, carrying the scrap of fabric, which is dripping hot water and steaming white.

"But I can't see anything."

"Then work by feel."

She raises the fabric, applies it to the stubbly top of his head, and leads it down the steep back. Hot drops of water flow down her arm, wetting her smock sleeves. Her hands truly are cold, though, despite the hot water.

Ignatov is wearing a shirt over his bandaged arm but has only slipped his healthy arm into a sleeve. He usually removes his belt before Zuleikha's arrival but today he hasn't. She fumbles for a long time, agonizing, as she handles the tight brass fastener, and the belt finally clangs, muffled, on the floor. She's angry and doesn't pick it up; then she abruptly pulls up the thin fabric of his shirt, stripping it from his large, motionless body.

"You'll break the other arm," Ignatov says without smiling. "Stay this time," he adds without a pause.

As Zuleikha furiously and quickly unwinds the endless long bandages, she feels her hands quickly warm from fury, heating and melting as a heavy, honeyed smell cloaks her, flooding her. Ignatov's arm is already free of bandages. He cautiously moves his fingers. He lifts a hand and places it on her neck.

"Stay," he repeats.

She breaks away, picks all the rags off the floor, and grabs the basin. She runs to the door, stumbling and spattering water.

"What about washing the sutures?" he shouts after her.

Zuleikha turns toward him and splashes hot water from the basin at his hairless white chest.

Zuleikha can't fall asleep that night. She lies, listening to the darkness with her son's even breathing at her shoulder, the doctor's light snoring in the corner, and the rumble of the wind in the stove. It's hot and stuffy.

She stands, greedily swallowing water from a dipper, then tosses a jacket on her shoulders and slips out of the house. It's a clear night, the stars are out, and the moon is like a lantern. A milky-white steam floats from her mouth.

She goes down to the Angara and looks at the moon's oily-yellow path, which is dabbled across the waves; she listens to froth murmuring by the shore and a distant yelping across the river. She braids her hair tighter, throws it on her back, and splashes her face with cold water. It's time to go home.

Along the way she notices a bright red dot on the hill by the commandant's headquarters. It's Ignatov smoking. The dot gets bigger, swells with light, and then diminishes, paling. It blinks like a lighthouse. And Zuleikha answers its call.

Ignatov notices her from far away. He stops smoking and the red dot between his fingers goes out for an interminably long time. She stops at the front steps, looks at Ignatov sitting on the stairs, and takes her braids in her hands to unplait one, then the other. His hand suddenly jerks because the cigarette has burned down and scorched his fingers. He stands and goes up into the house, leaning on the crutch.

The open door squeaks as it swings on its hinges. Zuleikha climbs the stairs. She stands. Then she extends a hand, draws aside a heavy curtain that's soft to the touch and smells sharply of sheep hides, and steps inside the black tent.

Time turns inside out within the black tent. It doesn't flow straight but sideways, slanting. Zuleikha swims in it like a fish, like a wave, either dissolving fully or appearing again within the boundaries of her own body. Sometimes after closing the squeaking door of the commandant's headquarters behind her, she'll discover a few moments later that morning has come. Other times, after placing her hand on Ignatov's broad back and pressing her face to the base of his neck, she senses an infinitely long flow of minutes measured by occasional ringing drops that fall into a bucket from the tip of a spout on the tin washstand. There's an eternity between the first drop and the second.

There's no place for recollections and fears in the black tent – its bulky animal hides reliably protect Zuleikha from the past and future. There is only today, only now. That "now" is so teeming and palpable that Zuleikha's eyes mist over.

"Say something, don't be silent," Ignatov has asked her, his face nearing hers.

She looks into his clear gray eyes and draws a finger along his even forehead striped with fine wrinkles, along his steep and smooth cheekbone, along his cheek and chin.

"So beautiful," she murmurs.

"Is that really the sort of thing you should say to a man … ?"

She seems not to have slept that autumn. She puts her son to bed, kisses the warm top of his head, and then quickly leaves the infirmary and climbs the path where the little red flame persistently summons her each night. They don't close their eyes; there are never enough hours in those nights. In the morning she comes to see her sleeping son, then she goes hunting, and in the evening there's the infirmary to clean. Zuleikha has no time to sleep. And she doesn't want to anyway. Her strength hasn't diminished, it's increased and overflowed. She doesn't walk, she flies; she doesn't hunt, she simply takes her dues from the taiga; and for entire days she awaits the nights.

She's not ashamed. Everything she was taught and learned by rote as a child has left her, gone away. What's new and has come in exchange has washed away the fears, just as a flood from melting snow washes away last year's twigs and decayed leaves.

"A wife is the tilled soil where her husband sows the seeds of his descendants," is what her mother taught her before sending her off to Murtaza's home. "The plowman comes to till when he desires and tills while he has the strength. It does not befit the land to defy its tiller." And she did not defy – she gritted her teeth, held her breath, and tolerated it, living that way for so many years, not knowing it could be otherwise. Now she knows.

Her son senses something and has become pensive and reserved when he peers into her eyes. He takes a long time to go to sleep, tossing and turning, constantly waking up, and not letting his mother go. He's also maturing rapidly and growing more serious.

Yuzuf started school that autumn. There are eighteen children in Semruk and all are gathered into one classroom and seated in two rows: older and younger. They study together. There are only five textbooks (all about arithmetic) for the entire school, but what books they are! They're hot off the presses, still crackling at the bindings and smelling deliciously of printer's ink. A certain Kislitsyn handles the teaching duties. He's from the latest batch of newcomers, maybe an academician, maybe some former official from the People's Commissariat of Education. Izabella had already taught Yuzuf to read so when he saw the author's surname on a textbook cover – which says "Y.Z. Kislitsyn" – he walked up to Yakov Zavyalovich, bewildered, and asked, "Do you have the same surname?" "Yes," the teacher cheerlessly smirked, "one might say I have the exact same name." Zuleikha is glad her son is busy at school during the day, since he's fed and cared for. When he helps her with cleaning in the evenings, she asks if he likes school. "Yes," he answers, "a lot." "Well, good, it's important to learn to count and write."

It tortures her that she no longer gives all her warmth to her Yuzuf, that her nighttime kisses are more ardent and plentiful than the evening ones for her son, that he could wake up at night in bed alone and be afraid, and that she now has a secret from him.

So she hugs Yuzuf harder and longer, smothers him with kisses, and showers him with caresses. Sometimes he breaks loose from his mother's arms when they grip him too tightly and looks out at her guiltily from under his brow. Is she offended? His mother just responds with a broad, happy smile.

People in the settlement evidently suspect something. Zuleikha hasn't given any thought to what they would say as she doesn't interact much with people, and then only with the old-timers, and she disappears into the forest for days at a time anyway. If not for Gorelov, she wouldn't have found out that people had noticed her relationship with Ignatov.

One morning, he catches Zuleikha on her way to the taiga. By this time, he has been living in his own small, squat log cabin for a couple of years (Gorelov was the first to put up a privately owned house, and settled in well, fencing it in and putting glass in the windows), and he's made an earthen bench at the front of the house, where he loves to relax, watching the settlement's residents pass by.

Zuleikha is walking through still-sleepy Semruk on a dark-gray autumn morning and Gorelov is already sitting by his little house, smoking every now and then. He has obviously risen this early on her account and has been sitting waiting for her.

"Well, hello there, hunting artel! Going to the taiga to hunt down your daily quota?"

"That's right."

"Here, have a seat, let's have a chat. There's something we need to talk about."

"I don't have time to hang around, my prey's waiting. So go on, just say it."

Gorelov rises from the bench – under the uniform jacket draped over his shoulders is a dirty, striped sailor jersey and legs like crooked matches dressed in close-fitting drawers and boots.

He slowly walks around Zuleikha with his loose gait, examining her as if he's seeing her for the first time.

"Not so bad," he says quietly, as if to himself. "Ignatov chose a woman for himself, a fine one. Nice job. I hadn't spotted that right away."

"You need something?" Zuleikha feels blood pounding in her face.

"Nothing from you, sugar. You just keep having your love affairs. Just come and see me every now and then, won't you, to have a chat about the commandant. Our man's a hothead. The chief instructed me to look after him. And you, hunting artel, you should take care not to have a falling out with the chief if you want to keep doing your artel thing instead of rotting at the logging site."

Gorelov's drilling his narrow, slightly flattened eyes into her and she sees their color distinctly for the first time. They're impenetrably black.

Aglaya runs out of the house wearing an old sheepskin coat over a beige lace slip and shoes on bare feet, and her red curls are corkscrewed in all directions. She's bringing Gorelov a quilted jacket. She tosses it on his shoulders and wraps it proprietarily over his chest: *See that you don't freeze!* She looks jealously at both of them and runs off, back into the house. Aglaya has been living with Gorelov for a year now, not hiding it, instead proudly showing off their relationship to the settlement at every convenient occasion.

Zuleikha adjusts the rifle on her shoulder and walks away.

"So can I expect you to stop by then?" Gorelov yells after her.

"No!" She's striding quickly, almost running.

"Watch out you don't regret it! You have a son! Remember him?"

She spins around and gives Gorelov a long, close look. Then

turns abruptly and her narrow back soon dissolves between the trees.

A couple of days later, Gorelov is walking through the woods. He loves taking walks during the workday. Instructions have been handed out, the shift is sweating away at their labor, and cubic meter after cubic meter of pitch-scented lumber is toppling to the ground with a crash and being placed in stacks, so now he can step away and breathe more freely, especially since his head's already ringing from the screeching saws.

He walks slowly through the autumn taiga, slashing with a small switch and knocking down ruby-red rosehips. It really was the right thing to appoint him for agent work. Kuznets has a good head on his shoulders and discerned Gorelov's wasted talent immediately. Within a month of their memorable discussion in the bathhouse, Gorelov had not only got that smug dauber Ikonnikov scribbling short notes composed in fancy language, but the accountant from the office began scratching away at detailed essays for him in his neat schoolchild's hand. There was also the little assistant cook at the dining hall, sweating from tension, who passed on brief phrases that Achkenazi said to him during lunch preparation; and various other people who hadn't been taught reading and writing were dropping by Gorelov's house in the evenings to whisper a little and talk about life. Everybody's covered: loggers, office clerks, and even the dining hall and the clubhouse. The only failure is with the commandant.

Gorelov hacks the switch as hard as he can at the sharp top of an anthill. It roils with agitated ants. Of course nobody's ordered him to look after Ignatov; that's simply become an interest for him. Would it work out, though? Something has gnawed long and pleasantly in his belly at the thought that the woman who'd been lying under the commandant about an hour before, still warm with his heat and still smelling of his scent, would tell him – the mangy, hardened criminal Gorelov – what the commandant had been saying. This is why it's all the sweeter to sleep with Aglaya. It makes Gorelov glow inside, nice and hot, to imagine Ignatov stroking her heavy curls shot with reddish gold, running a hand along her rounded back with the dark beauty mark on a shoulder blade, and burying his face in her soft white neck. All that is now his, Gorelov's.

If Zuleikha tells the commandant about their recent conversation, Gorelov will see to it she pays. But he's certain she'll keep quiet out of fear for her son.

He flings the switch and sits under a gnarled pine tree. A slight breeze is barely breathing on his face. Saws squeak and workers' shouts ring out somewhere in the distance. That's good.

There's a slight rustling close by. It's a dark squirrel already dressed in fluffy gray for winter and it's scratching along the ground, pricking up its sharp little ears. Gorelov slowly reaches into his jacket pocket, pulls out a cigarette butt he stashed away in the morning, presses it in his fingertips, and clicks his tongue: *Here, have some.* The animal approaches, extending its slim snout forward and twitching its shiny little nose. Carefully, so as not to frighten it, Gorelov hides his other hand behind his back and gropes among the pine roots for a hefty rock, grasping it comfortably in his fist.

The squirrel is already beside him, its hazel eyes glistening and its wrinkled little black fingers stretching toward the palm of Gorelov's toughened hand. He presses the rock harder behind his back and holds his breath. *Closer, sweetie, come on.*

Then a shot booms and the squirrel is suddenly lying motionless on variegated brown tree needles with a dark red spot instead of an eye socket. For an instant, Gorelov thinks the shot grazed him. There's nothing to breathe. He's frantically inhaling, having difficulty swallowing, and his throat feels twisted, as if a vise were pressing it. As before, he senses the crumbly softness of the cigarette butt in one hand and the cold hardness of the stone in the other. Is he in one piece?

There's a sound of lightly snapping branches at the edge of the clearing, then a small, thin figure slips out from behind rowan bushes that have already shed half their leaves, and comes closer. Gorelov feels a large, cold drop roll along the back of his head, down his neck, behind his shirt collar, and along his spine.

Zuleikha slings her rifle on her back as she comes right up to Gorelov. She crouches, with her knees spread apart like a man, picks up the lifeless lump, puts its little head in a loop of rope, and hangs it on her belt. She looks straight down on Gorelov from above, then turns around and goes into the forest.

After the light, nearly silent crunch of her footsteps has quieted in the thicket, Gorelov sticks the cigarette butt pressed between his fingertips into his mouth, fumbles in his pockets with a shaking hand, finds a match, and frantically strikes it on the sole of his boot. The match breaks, he flings it away, and spits out the cigarette butt.

She's a viper. Who would have thought? She looks so quiet. He leans his back against a rough pine trunk, exhales deeply, and closes his eyes. Well, screw it. Forget the commandant. Who cares?

Snow comes late, toward the end of October, and changes autumn to winter in a day. The animals already have their winter coats and are dressed in splendid fur. The season has begun but for the first time Zuleikha isn't glad of it. She doesn't have the strength to tear herself away from Ignatov's warm chest, slip out from under his heavy arm, and run off into the cold, dark blue morning. Leaving the commandant's headquarters is like cutting ties that bind. Before, there had been some joy in her skis gliding rapidly over the snow, in the frosty wind hitting her face, and in fluffy pelts flashing in the crown of a pine tree. But now the short winter days drag on like years. She waits them out, overcoming them like an illness. She hurries back when the sun reddens slightly as if it's sunset, the air thickens, and the shadows fill with violet. She goes to the infirmary but her eyes are already hurrying toward the hill, toward the high front steps where a small, hot flame flares, filled with impatience.

That night Ignatov says:

"Come live with me."

She lifts her face from his body and finds his eyes in the darkness.

"Bring the little boy and come."

She lays her head back without saying anything.

Snow is piling up early the next morning. The storm is blowing so hard and thick that it beats at the door, the windows are plastered in white, and the chimney howls like a pack of wolves. The lumbermen never go out into the taiga in blizzards like this; the hunters don't go out, either.

Zuleikha touches Ignatov's temple with a finger:

"At least, just this once, I can stay and look at you for longer."

If she could, she would happily look at him all day.

"What's to look at?" he says, covering her face with his own. "I'm afraid you'll have to keep looking some other time ..."

When she finally tears her head from the pillow, having fallen back into a deep slumber, the storm has died down and everything is absolutely still outside – no human voices, no knocking of axes, no dining-hall gong – as if the place were a ghost town. A dull yellow light's trickling through the half-covered windows. Ignatov is still asleep, settled on his back. She straightens a blanket that has slid off him.

There's a cautious crunch of footsteps around the house – someone's walking in the snow along the walls. Is that dog

Gorelov sniffing around again? A dark silhouette flashes in the little window. Zuleikha drops noiselessly from the bed, tosses a sheepskin coat over her bare shoulders, and slips outside. There they are, tracks – dark blue and deep, as if they've been scooped out with a ladle – running around the commandant's headquarters.

"The dirty dog," Zuleikha utters loudly and walks around the corner.

A large figure wearing long clothing is standing by the back window, leaning forward, and pressing their nose to the snow-powdered glass. The collar of a long-haired dog fur coat is raised, and a pointy-tipped fur cap towers over their head like the top of a minaret.

The Vampire Hag.

"You old crone." Zuleikha walks right up to her mother-in-law; she could reach out and touch her with her hand. "You've come to drink my blood again?"

The Vampire Hag pulls her pale face back from the glass as if she's heard and turns toward Zuleikha. Her forehead, eye sockets, and cheeks are all plastered in white snow, as if it were chalk, and that snow isn't melting. Only the nostrils on the white mask move – black holes taking in air – and her purple lips quiver, too.

"Go," Zuleikha says angrily and clearly. "Get away!"

The mask opens the hollow of its mouth, breathes out thick, raggedy steam, and hisses, barely audibly.

"He will punish ..." she says and a gnarled finger with a long, bent nail rises toward the sky. "He will punish you for everything ..."

"Get out of here!" Zuleikha is shouting; her body is consumed by the full force of her anger. The roots of her hair are heating up and her heart is beating so it pushes at her ribs. "Don't you dare come to me again! This is my life and you can't order me around anymore! Out! Out!"

429

Her mother-in-law turns her back and hurriedly hobbles toward the forest, leaning on her tall, gnarled walking stick. Her huge, heavy felt boots squeak deafeningly on the snow and the long, thin strands of her white braids swing behind her back, in time with her steps.

"Witch!" Zuleikha hurls snow after her. "You died long ago! And your son, too!"

The Vampire Hag lifts a bony finger again as she walks, shaking it threateningly and pointing upward without turning around. Her figure diminishes and the squeaking of her steps fades behind brownish, brush-like spruces. Zuleikha looks up at the copper moon burning solemnly on the stern dark blue-and-black horizon. The moon is completely round, like a freshly minted coin. Night? Already? So that's why it's so quiet around her ...

Yuzuf! Has he gone to bed? Did he fall asleep alone? She dashes to the infirmary, stumbling as she runs, her felt boots scooping up snow. Yuzuf isn't in bed, and his boots, sheepskin coat, and skis aren't there, either. Her son must have broken the rule again, today of all days – he probably thought she went hunting like always and went to meet her, and hasn't returned.

Zuleikha grabs her skis. She returns to the commandant's headquarters and makes her way inside, trying not to creak the door. She removes Ignatov's heavy rifle from its nail, takes a hefty cartridge clip out of the nightstand, and shoves it in her pocket, then thinks and takes another. She casts a glance at the peacefully sleeping Ignatov and slips out.

Two thin streaks from Yuzuf's skis wind along the rich blue snow. She races after him, recognizing his route. From the clubhouse at the edge of the settlement, Yuzuf went up toward the frozen Chishme, then skirted along the shore to the crossing at Bear Rock, where he usually lies in wait for her under the rowan bush. He marked time there for a while because there are lots of overlapping tracks in every direction. Her little boy froze by the forest brook, waiting for his mother as she was giving herself to her lover in a rumpled bed soaked in hot sweat.

The tracks lead further, into the *urman*. Yuzuf obviously went to find her when she hadn't turned up. Zuleikha dashes after him. Trees decorated in white tower around her, interfering; black shadows and yellowish-blue stripes of snow painted with moonlight flash in her eyes. Further, further. Deeper into the *urman*, deeper.

"Yuzuf!" she shouts into a thicket. A large shelf of snow falls from a high branch, crashing to the ground. "*Ulym!* My son!"

Yuzuf's ski tracks are growing fainter under drifts of snow. They appear again for a while then disappear, and soon they're gone completely. Where to now?

"Yuzuf!"

Zuleikha races ahead and little clouds of snow puff up from under her skis.

"Yuzuf!"

The inky-black tops of spruce trees are dancing on the dark blue firmament and bold sparkling stars glisten between them.

"Yuzuf!"

The *urman* is silent.

There it is, retribution for an impious life outside marriage with an infidel, with her husband's killer. For preferring him to her own faith, her own husband, and her own son. The Vampire Hag was right. Heaven has punished Zuleikha.

Sinking into the snowdrifts, she forces her way through crackling, thorny juniper bushes. She creeps over fallen birch trunks covered in slippery rime and struggles to make out the path through a spiky spruce thicket. Her ski suddenly catches a branch and Zuleikha flies forward, tumbling down some sort of steep hillock, churning up snow, and snapping her skis. The hard, prickly coldness pounds at her face, getting into her eyes, ears, and mouth. Her hands flail at the snow as she somehow makes her way out of the drift. She sees a piece of a broken ski in front of her. Not her ski but her son's.

"Yuzuuuuf!"

She's no longer shouting, she's howling. And someone in front of her is howling in response. Up to her waist in snow, with the splintered remnants of her skis tangled in low bushes, she makes her way to a small clearing that's tightly bordered on all sides by trees.

There, in a crowded, uneven ring clustered around a tall, old spruce with a tilting top, sits a sharp-nosed gray pack, looking intently upward. It's winter and the wolves are lean; their skin stretches over their ribs and their spines look bristly. They notice Zuleikha, turn their snouts for a moment, and growl but don't leave their spot. One suddenly leaps high, as if he's been tossed, and snaps his teeth at the sharp top of the spruce where there's a small, dark, motionless spot.

Zuleikha walks straight at the wolves, striding almost mechanically and loading the rifle along the way. Several animals stand and slowly scatter to greet her. They surround her, quivering their lips, showing their fangs, and jerking their tails. One of them, with transparent yellow eyes and a torn ear, breaks away and is the first to jump.

She shoots. Then again and again. She loads as quickly as she breathes, then again and again. She inserts the second clip, then again and again.

Yelping, harrowing squeals, whimpers, and wheezes. One of the wolves attempts to run away and hide in the woods but she doesn't allow it. One lies with a broken spine, jerking its paws, and she fires point-blank, finishing it off. She's shot all the cartridges, every last one. A half-dozen wolf carcasses lie around the spruce, on snow that glistens black with blood; there's a smell of gunpowder, burned flesh, and singed fur; gashed intestines steam. It's quiet. Zuleikha walks over the bodies, toward the crooked spruce.

"Yuzuf! *Ulym!*" she rasps.

From the treetop, a small body with the inanimate face of a doll, frosty brows and lashes, and eyes squeezed tightly shut falls straight into her outstretched arms.

Yuzuf lies delirious for four days. Zuleikha kneels beside his bed the whole time, holding his burning hand. She sleeps right there, her head resting against his shoulder.

Leibe attempts to move her to the next bed but she won't allow it. He gives up and just draws a curtain dividing Yuzuf's spot from the rest of the ward. Leibe has decided to put them here in the infirmary rather than at home, so he can always keep an eye on them.

Achkenazi himself brings food. He watches Zuleikha kneeling motionless by her son's bed, carefully places a dish on the windowsill, and removes the previous one, the food untouched.

Izabella stops by and firmly strokes Zuleikha's back for a long time but Zuleikha doesn't notice. Konstantin Arnoldovich comes a couple of times and attempts to draw Zuleikha into conversation. He tells her something about melon seeds they've sent him from the mainland after all, about agricultural helpers who will arrive any day, about the oxen and cows promised for the spring, for plowing ("I'll learn how to plow – just imagine me behind a plow, Zuleikha!") but no conversations come about.

Ikonnikov comes only once. He finds a place to kneel next to her and extends a shaking hand smudged with paints toward Yuzuf's shoulder. Zuleikha pushes his hand away and throws herself on her son, covering him with her body. "I won't give him up!" she snarls. "I won't give him up to anyone!" Leibe leads Ikonnikov away and doesn't allow him back in the infirmary.

Ignatov comes every day. Zuleikha doesn't notice him. It's as if she doesn't see him, and when he begins speaking with her, it's as if she doesn't hear. He stands behind her for a long time then leaves. On the fourth day, Ignatov is there when Yuzuf's little body begins cooling, releasing a generous, sticky sweat, and losing its crimson tinge. Ignatov sits down on the next bed, places his crutch beside him, lowers his face in his hands, and freezes, maybe dozing, maybe thinking. He sits for a long time.

"Leave, Ivan," Zuleikha says, suddenly calm and not turning away from her son's bed. "I'm not coming to see you anymore."

"Then I'll come here," he says, lifting his head.

"I've been punished. Don't you see?" She strokes Yuzuf along his nearly closed eyelids and along cheekbones that have grown prominent.

"By whom?"

She walks up to Ignatov, shoves the crutch in his hands and pulls him up, raising him from the bed. He yields and stands. Zuleikha was small before, not reaching his shoulder, but now she's absolutely tiny, as if she's shrunk.

"Whoever it is, I've been punished." Her weak arms push him toward the door. "And that's all there is to it. That's all."

Ignatov bends, grips her shoulders, and shakes her, searching for her gaze. He finally finds it but Zuleikha's eyes are frozen, as if they're dead. He carefully releases her, takes his crutch, and slowly thuds toward the door.

She turns to her son after the thudding has faded outside. Yuzuf is sitting in bed. He's pale, the skin is tight on his face, and his eyes are huge, set in purple circles.

"Mama," he says in an even, quiet voice. "I had dreams, lots of dreams. Everything that Ilya Petrovich painted – Leningrad and Paris. What do you think, can I go there someday?"

Zuleikha leans her back against the wall and looks at her son without tearing her gaze away. He's looking out the window, where large flakes of heavy snow are falling hard, without stopping.

Part Four

Return

THE WAR

The war comes to Semruk like a reverberation of a distant echo. It doesn't seem to exist, though people say it does. They unexpectedly begin to receive a regular newspaper delivery – once a month, in one big, thick packet – bursting with headlines: "We'll Close Ranks ..." "We'll Rout ..." "We'll Defeat ..." The newspapers themselves gradually get thinner, but the war makes them grow meaner, fiercer, and more reckless. They're now hung on the agitational board, where Semruk residents often stand in the evenings, reading with their heads together. Then they turn toward the Angara, watch seagulls circling in the clear sky, and quietly exchange remarks. It's strange to think that somewhere far away there are enemy planes cutting through the firmament instead of birds.

Kuznets, who was recently promoted to the position of lieutenant of state security, organizes rallies during his rare visits. He tells of fronts where the Red Army battles valorously and of the successes it has achieved; people listen, keeping quiet. It's hard to believe what he says, though it's also impossible not to believe it.

Not one person left Semruk during the first months of the war. In the labor settlements, the commandants' headquarters maintain registries of reserve corps for the rear guard who've reached draft age, but the lists have no practical use. Inmates aren't allowed near weapons, which means they're not allowed near army service, either, where the danger of their unifying in organized groups grows exponentially. The question of drafting them isn't even posed in 1941 since it's obvious that after reaching the front, enemies of the people would immediately desert to the fascists' side and begin fighting against their motherland.

And so the war goes on, but it goes on far away, passing them by.

Then the war unexpectedly does what the government has so feared and hasn't wanted: it opens, slightly, the heavy curtain separating Semruk from the world. During long years of fighting for survival on a tiny island-like patch in the depths of the taiga, deprived of ties to the "mainland," and devoting their lives exclusively to fulfilling an economic plan, the exiles suddenly see themselves as part of a giant, heavily populated country. The names of distant cities – Minsk, Brest, Vilnius, Riga, Kiev, Vinnitsa, Lvov, Vitebsk, Kishinev, and Novgorod – sound from the low stage of the Semruk clubhouse, like a song floating from the pages of a geography textbook or a fairytale heard in distant childhood. It's frightening because the enemy has captured all those cities. And there's simultaneously a sweet ache from the thought that these cities exist at all. The very fact of those names being uttered by Kuznets's broad, fleshy lips confirms that those cities have been there, growing, developing, planting greenery, modernizing, and living all this time. Kuznets's lips used to just repeat, over and over, information about the plan, the five-year plan, indicators, quotas, the labor front ... But now there's Kerch, Alupka, Dzhankoi, Bakhchisarai, Yevpatoria, Odessa, Simferopol, Yalta ...

"I'd almost forgotten there's a place somewhere on earth called Bakhchisarai," Konstantin Arnoldovich whispers, leaning toward Ikonnikov's ear.

"I lived there two months and could sketch you the Fountain of Tears from memory. I was trying back then to capture the streamage of water along the marble," says Ikonnikov.

"*Streamage* is an incorrect word, Ilya Petrovich. It doesn't exist."

"How can it not exist if I captured it?"

They learn about the blockade of Leningrad from Kuznets in October, after a month-long delay. They don't even begin to discuss it with one another because there's nothing to say.

In the spring of 1942, Kuznets makes a sudden appearance out of nowhere, as always. He's brought with him a barge packed with emaciated people who have dark-olive skin and distinct profiles: Crimean Greeks and Tatars. "Ivan Sergeevich," he says, "these outsiders are to be taken into your charge. And provide security measures. After all, they're a socially dangerous element in large numbers and of excellent high quality." He laughs.

Non-natives were being deported from southern territories in case the region should be overrun with occupiers and minority nations, giving such people the opportunity to desert to the enemy. This measure was, as they said, a precaution.

Well, Greeks are Greeks. Even if they're Eskimos with papooses, they're no strangers to Ignatov. Out of curiosity, he once counted up all the nationalities residing in Semruk and came to nineteen. This means there are two more now. They send these dark-skinned people to empty barracks to throw down their things. And then to the taiga. There's still half a workday ahead, socially dangerous citizens. Ignatov entrusts the outsiders to Gorelov, who's good at knocking sense into novices.

Kuznets and Ignatov retire to the commandant's headquarters, as is their established habit. Ignatov isn't drinking much of late but he's with Kuznets, so how could he not sit a while and indulge the chief?

"You and I need to talk, Vanya," says Kuznets, pouring strong-smelling alcohol into cloudy faceted glasses.

Ignatov wipes crumbs from the table with his palm, takes out what's left of last night's dinner – cucumbers, carrot, onion, all sorts of greens, and bread – then pulls the window curtains. Kuznets is talking in broad circles, though, and is in no hurry to get to the point, so first they drink to the future victory over fascism, then to comrade Stalin, to the valorous Red Army, and to the courageous home front ("A good home front, my dear man, is half the victory!").

"So what was it you wanted to talk about, Zin?" says Ignatov, remembering what Kuznets said. His head is already growing heavy, as usual, filling with big, unwieldy thoughts, and his body is lightening, as if it will fly away any minute.

"Ah," smiles Kuznets, placing a powerful brown hand on the nape of Ignatov's neck and pulling him toward himself. "You haven't forgotten."

Their foreheads meet over the table and their front locks of hair touch.

"I look at you, Vanya," says Kuznets, directing a dulled brownish eye at Ignatov, "and I just never tire of it."

Kuznets's face is right beside Ignatov's. Deep pores are distinctly visible on a large nose with dark blue veins.

"Everything's good with you. You're holding eight hundred souls in your fist. Achieving production targets. Fulfilling the plan. The kolkhoz is working and the artels, too. The cucumbers ..." He takes a large, bumpy squiggle of a cucumber from the table. "Even these are the tastiest on the Angara. Believe me, I know!" Kuznets pokes the cucumber into a puddle of salt sprinkled on the table and bites it with a crunch, spraying Ignatov with small drops. "You even stopped drinking. Why'd you stop drinking, Ivan?"

Kuznets isn't shy about showing he's well informed about life in the settlement and its commandant, knowing far more than Ignatov himself has reported.

"I had enough," says Ignatov, wiping the spray from his cheeks.

"And you didn't find a woman." Kuznets smiles sneakily, shaking the bitten cucumber. "You've been living a lonely existence since you banished Glashka."

Kuznets knows about the brief, long-forgotten little couplings with the redheaded Aglaya, though apparently he doesn't know about the love with Zuleikha that has abruptly come to an end.

A heavy hand presses at Ignatov's neck again.

"Is that really what you wanted to talk about?" Ignatov says. "Women?"

"Eh, no!" Kuznets chomps juicily at the cucumber, finishes it, and pokes the end at Ignatov's forehead. "This is about you, a hero! Vanya, it's time for you to be promoted from sergeant to lieutenant, junior lieutenant for starters."

Ignatov swats the cucumber end from his forehead. He looks at Kuznets's bushy black brows, where a heavy drop of sweat is swelling in a deep wrinkle between them. Kuznets has never once raised the topic of promotion with him.

"Here in the woods it's all the damn same if you're a sergeant or a lieutenant."

"What? You've decided to stay here forever or something?" Kuznets smirks slyly and his pupils are sharp and narrow. "You used to want to leave. You took me by the throat."

"I did."

"So it's your choice, and you're still young. But it's not fitting for someone a mere step away from becoming a second lieutenant in state security to stagnate as a settlement commandant. Huh?" Kuznets's palm squeezes the nape of Ignatov's neck. "I've already filled out an appraisal form on you. Years of flawless service, I said, dedication to the motherland's ideals. I just haven't sent it yet."

"I'm not getting this, Zin. You're holding something back."

"What's to understand?" Kuznets licks his lips and his bluish-gray tongue with white bumps flashes for a moment. "War, Vanya. We're living in fast-moving, chaotic times. It even rings in your ears. Heads are rolling. Stars are rolling, too, and they're made of red silk, framed in silver. They're on smart people's uniform cuffs."

"It's only been a couple months since your last ..." Ignatov looks sideways at Kuznets's uniform jacket, which is hanging neatly on the back of a chair. There's a brand-new dark ruby bar in maroon collar tabs with a raspberry-colored edging, a sign of Kuznets's recent promotion.

"That's what I'm telling you, my dear man. It's that kind of time, when anything's possible, do you understand me? Anything! Promoted to first lieutenant in half a year, another year to captain. You and I just need something to happen, something big and loud. Did you hear about the uprising at the Pargibsky commandant's headquarters? About the attempt on the commandant in Staraya Klyukva? They arrested about a hundred, and that's just the plotters. That's what we need, for lots of people to be involved. We'll give the whole affair a clever name ..."

"What kind of uprisings and escapes are there now, you fool? Anybody who escaped a long time ago is coming back to the settlements now, to get away from the war, from the army."

"Exactly, Vanya! They're all afraid of the fascists. But some people are waiting for the enemy. And, like good hosts, they're preparing a welcoming ceremony for the occupiers, with bread and salt. That's who you and I are going to find in the settlement. We'll discover the plot, reveal it, shoot the organizers under wartime law, and send their lousy accomplices to the camps. All Siberia will find out. It'll be a lesson to the settlers, as a precaution! An example to other commandants' headquarters. And you and I" – Kuznets pokes a brownish fingernail at himself, below his Adam's apple – "we'll be fixing new collar tabs onto our uniforms."

He's breathing deeply, hotly. Sweat's flowing from his forehead in two glistening streams, along the sides of his nose and further down, into the stiff brushes of his mustache.

"You're off your head, Zin. You're prattling on here, you're smashed."

"Nobody'll check. I'll take the case myself." His palm on Ignatov's neck is now a sweaty iron pincer. "You'll compile the list of suspects yourself. Everybody you're sick of, who gets in the way, get them out, the dogs. I won't interfere – you can even put Gorelov on it. Your love for him is well known. We'll crack them all, don't worry. It'll be a crystal-clear case. They'll write about you and me in textbooks."

"Hold on. You're proposing that these are, what, my people?"

"Well, who else's?" There's a yellowish tinge in the network of red veins in Kuznets's dark eyes. "I'm no magician here – I can't pull a hundred plotters out of a magic hat for you. But you've got lots of people. This won't ruin you. If you feel sorry for the old ones, pick the new ones, the outsiders. They won't survive here anyway – they'll drop like flies in the winter."

Ignatov lowers his gaze to Kuznets's broad, damp lips.

"Well?" say the lips.

"Take your hand off me, you'll break my neck."

The hot, damp palm releases Ignatov's neck.

"Well?" repeat the lips.

Ignatov takes the flask and splashes the remainder of the alcohol into their empty glasses. He tightens the metal top slowly, with a squeak, and puts the flask back on the table.

"I didn't think," he says, "comrade lieutenant, that you'd test me, a former Red Army man. I thought you trusted me, based on our old friendship."

"Hold on, Ivan! I'm telling you the truth, you hear? I've thought it all through, done the calculations. We'll have the case wrapped up in a month, receive our ranks by summer. Well?"

"Are you acting out this charade for all the commandants or just a chosen few?"

"Stop playing the fool, Ignatov! I'm being human with you, but you –"

"You can report that the political situation in labor settlement Semruk is calm. The commandant turned out to be a morally stable person and did not yield to provocation."

Ignatov slowly raises his glass, tips it down his throat without clinking, then wipes his mouth dry. Kuznets is breathing heavily, wheezing a little. He pours the alcohol from his glass down his gullet and chomps an onion. He stands, continuing to chew, puts on his jacket, fastens its belt, and pulls his peaked cap over his forehead.

"Fine, commandant," he says. "That's what I'll report. But just you remember" – his large, wet red fist moves in front of Ignatov's nose – "that I have you right here if anything happens!"

Kuznets's fist hovers there, his white knuckles big and bumpy. He spits the remainder of the onion on the floor and goes out.

What Kuznets said comes true. The new batch turns out to be in poor health. Their warm southern blood doesn't withstand the frosty Siberian weather well and many take ill with pneumonia during the very first cold spells. The infirmary, which had already been expanded to twenty beds by that time, can't hold even half those in need. Leibe wears himself out and has no strength left but can't save everyone, and the Semruk cemetery increases by fifty graves that winter.

The outsiders bury their kinsmen in varying ways. Greeks knock together thin wooden crosses from stakes and Tatars carve intricate crescents from long logs. Both the crosses and the crescents find places at the cemetery, close to one another in crooked, crowded rows, alternating with other markers.

A large article appears in *Pravda* about a pro-fascist plot that was revealed in the Pit-Gorodok labor settlement on the Angara.

As a result of this fairly notorious case, the core of the plotters, numbering twelve people, faced the firing squad and a band of accomplices was sentenced to twenty-five years in the camps for anti-Soviet activity.

Nonetheless, on April 11, 1942, the State Defense Committee of the USSR approves a resolution on drafting labor deportees for military service. Sixty thousand former kulaks and their children are drafted into the Red Army and permitted to defend the motherland. The brand-new Red Army men and members of their families are removed from the rolls of labor exile and issued passports without limitations. A thin stream of those freed from "kulak exile" begins flowing toward the mainland from the labor settlements.

A bright poster appears on the agitational board during the summer – a half-grayed woman in fiery-red clothing standing before a wall of raised bayonets, beckoning with a hand stretched invitingly behind her. She's summoning to war, summoning the young, the old, even adolescents, everyone who can hold a weapon. She's summoning them to their death.

Each time Zuleikha walks past the poster, she answers the woman with a long, stubborn gaze that says, *I won't give up my son.* The woman resembles Zuleikha – even the gray in her slightly disheveled hair is just the same, in striking strands, and Zuleikha feels awkward because it's as if she's talking to herself.

Zuleikha's ancestors fought the Golden Horde for centuries. It's unclear how long the war with Germany will go on, and Yuzuf will soon turn twelve. Izabella told Zuleikha that men can be taken into the army from age eighteen. She can count the number of years left until then on her fingers. Will the war manage to end?

Yuzuf has grown quickly during the last year and is now taller than Zuleikha. He works at the bakery, selling bread. Hardly anyone bakes their own now and a line forms at the bakery in the evenings. Zuleikha loves observing her son as he stands behind the tall counter and nimbly serves the customers, handling their jingling yellow and gray coins with ease. He always does the sums in his head, without using the abacus. The store opens after lunch, when the first shift of lumbermen returns from the forest, and that's just in time for Yuzuf to run over from school.

Yuzuf is praised as a good student. He was accepted into the Young Pioneers for his achievements and a red Pioneer tie like a dragonfly has blazed on his chest ever since. He works like an adult at household chores, chopping firewood, fixing a fence, or repairing a roof. As before, he tries to find free time whenever possible so he can run off to the clubhouse to see Ikonnikov.

Ikonnikov has let himself go badly and grown flabby in recent years – he drinks a lot. The exiles have learned to distill home brew not just from cloudberries but also from bilberries, stone bramble, and even sour rowan berries. Ikonnikov is a particular devotee. They've allowed him to remain at the clubhouse, in an artistic artel composed solely of himself. With his help, Semruk supplies Krasnoyarsk not only with lumber, fur, and vegetables but also a very specialized form of product: oil paintings, moreover paintings of very decent quality. Rosy-cheeked lumbermen, busty farmer women, and well-fed, round-cheeked Young Pioneers – alone, in pairs, or in groups – jauntily stride or stand, their thoughtful gazes directed into the cloudless distance. Rural and even urban cultural centers eagerly take his pictures.

Yuzuf has been planning to join the artel after turning sixteen, but for now he's working on an unrestricted basis. Zuleikha is afraid her son might develop a passion for home brew under Ikonnikov's unsavory influence. "My example provides the strongest possible deterrent against alcoholism," Ilya Petrovich calms her after noticing her wary glance one day. And he's probably right.

Zuleikha has always been jealous of Yuzuf's attachment to Ikonnikov, but those feelings have subsided over the years. Ilya Petrovich is the only man who looks at Yuzuf with loving, fatherly eyes filled with pride, and for this Zuleikha even forgives the stale smell of alcohol on his breath.

Her son's relationship with the doctor has broken down, or, rather, faded away: Yuzuf and Leibe exist in the same house but on parallel planes that never intersect. One slips through the internal door to the infirmary after barely forcing himself awake and drinking down a mug of herb tea for breakfast, then returns only after midnight, to sleep a little; the other sees nothing and nobody around him as he rushes off to the clubhouse with a handful of homemade paintbrushes, then goes to school and to the bakery after that. They have no time to interact and nothing to talk about.

The reason this distance had grown between them came out later. Leibe told Zuleikha that he'd once had a serious, adult conversation with Yuzuf, proposing that Yuzuf help at the infirmary and study medicine. Leibe had promised to teach him the basics within a couple of years and, in about another five, everything that graduates of medical schools know. Yuzuf heard him out carefully, thanked him, and politely declined. He would like to work as an artist when he grows up. Although he didn't show it, Volf Karlovich suffered painfully over this refusal, in spite of its being completely adult and justified.

One time Zuleikha complained to Izabella that after twelve years of living in the same house, her son had gained nothing from such an intelligent and worthy person as the doctor, neither character traits nor noble gestures and behavior, nor a profession so generously offered. Yuzuf and Leibe were different people, very dissimilar, alien to one another. "How can that be, my dear!" smiled Izabella. "What about their eyes? They have the exact same gaze. It's passionate, even obsessed."

Zuleikha and Yuzuf still sleep in the same bed. They have difficulty fitting on the crowded sleeping ledge, so her son either places his long, skinny legs on his mother or lets them dangle over the edge. He can't sleep by himself and won't drift off unless he takes refuge by her chest, his face stuck in her neck.

Sometimes she seems to dream of someone. She'll wake up in a sweat, her braids mussed from tossing her head on the pillow. There are vague memories of a flame at a distant lighthouse, glowing red as if it's scorching hot; the door curtain in a black tent knocking in the wind; and the warmth of someone's hands on her shoulders. She steadies her breathing and opens her eyes; the hands are her son's.

She hasn't been able to forgive herself for that night when Yuzuf ran off into the snowy taiga searching for her. At first she thought her punishment for that was in her son's illness, in the torments of fever and delirium, and his drawn-out struggle with death in her arms at the infirmary. But she later understood that her true punishment only came after Yuzuf's recovery, in her own distressing, nagging, and endless thoughts. At times her guilt seems so enormous and monstrous that she's prepared to accept retribution; she wishes for any, even the most dreadful. From whom, she doesn't know. There's nobody here on the edge of the universe who can mete out retribution or pardon. The Almighty's gaze doesn't reach the banks of the Angara and there aren't any spirits to be found in the dense thickets of the Siberian *urman*. People here are completely on their own, alone with one another.

Yuzuf wakes up when the door squeaks behind his mother. She always leaves for the taiga early, at dawn, after carefully disentangling herself from his arms and slipping soundlessly through the house, afraid of waking him as she prepares to go. He feigns sleep, as a nice gesture for her. He jumps up when her light footsteps fade outside the door. He doesn't like sleeping by himself.

He tosses off the blanket with his legs and his bare feet slap over to the table, to the breakfast his mother left covered with a coarse cotton towel: a piece of bread and a mug of milk. (Ten bearded goats were recently brought to the settlement and milk remains a treat.) He gulps down the milk and stuffs the bread in his mouth. From a nail on the wall, he grabs the jacket that his mother crafted out of the doctor's old dress uniform, patching and darning the holes. Feet in shoes and he's on his way.

The door slams hard behind him. He suddenly wonders, belatedly, if he's woken the doctor. He forgot to look to see if he was sleeping in his bed or if he'd gone to the infirmary. It doesn't matter anyway. Even if he did wake him up, the doctor won't complain to Yuzuf's mother. He's a good person, despite being unbelievably boring.

His feet speed down the steps. Chewing the bread as he runs, Yuzuf's shoulder pushes the little gate and he races out to the road, past the infirmary and down to the central square, where bright posters gleam on the long agitational board and the fresh golden logs of the newly opened reading hut are shining; he passes small, square one-room houses on Lenin Street and then heads right, along River Street (Semruk's private sector housing has grown in recent years, filling the entire knoll and even spreading to the foot of the hill, biting a large chunk out of the taiga); from there, along fences, past the bakery with its store, past kolkhoz storehouses, past the turn to the fields, where Konstantin Arnoldovich reigns supreme, cultivating his outlandish, giant melons alongside grain; and to the very end of the settlement, where the clubhouse hides under a canopy of firs.

It's summer vacation so he doesn't have to go to school. He can stay here, with Ikonnikov, right up until lunchtime. He just hopes Ikonnikov will be dry today … Yuzuf doesn't like when Ilya Petrovich knocks back the drink early in the morning. Sometimes the knocking back is light, for invigoration, and Ikonnikov greets his pupil with paint-spotted hands joyfully thrown wide open, laughs a lot, and cracks long, intricate jokes that Yuzuf doesn't understand. As the sun rises higher over the Angara, the light knocking back becomes heavier. The scent coming from his teacher turns into an unbearably sharp smell, the bottle standing behind crates and boards in the far corner of the club empties, and Ilya Petrovich himself grows sullen and somber toward lunchtime, and soon drops off in a heavy slumber, right there on the crates.

It's better when he doesn't drink until the evening. On a sober morning, Ikonnikov isn't as cheerful and talkative – he sighs, slouches, and mills around his homemade easel a lot, endlessly scuffing his brushes at the palette – but for all that, something appears in his eyes that Yuzuf is prepared to watch for hours. Once he even wanted to draw his teacher at work, but Ikonnikov wouldn't allow it.

Yuzuf's shoes thud on the floorboards when he bursts into the clubhouse. Oh, he should have knocked, since it's early and Ilya Petrovich could still be sleeping. But Ikonnikov's dressed in a white shirt, a buttoned-up jacket, dark gray in color (maybe from dirt, maybe from time), and polished shoes. He's standing by the wall and pounding at a nail, hammering it evenly.

"Here, help," he says without turning.

Yuzuf runs over and hands him a picture that's on the floor. Ikonnikov hangs it on the pounded nail.

"Like so," he says, examining the room with a fastidious gaze, and repeats, "Just right. Like so!"

The canvases that had previously decorated all four of the walls have been gathered on one. Montmartre and Nevsky Prospect, Prechistenka Street and Semruk's Lenin Street, the beaches of

Viareggio and the Yalta embankments, the Seine, the Yauza, the Angara, and even Pyatiletka, the best kolkhoz goat, are all clustered together, touching each other in places and covering an entire wall. The other three walls are empty; glistening nail heads gawk forlornly.

Yuzuf looks at Ilya Petrovich. Is he drunk? No, he's completely sober.

Ikonnikov takes a fat bundle of homemade brushes from the windowsill – thin are squirrel, thicker are fox, the biggest are badger – winds them with string, and sets them back down with a thud.

"That's for you. I don't need them any longer."

"Are they sending you away?"

"No." Ikonnikov smiles; under his eyes, bulging bags like preserved apples gather in large and small folds. "I'm leaving on my own. Can you imagine? On my own!"

Yuzuf doesn't believe it. A person can't go away anywhere on his own, everybody knows that. Or can he?

"Where to?"

Ilya Petrovich takes a long cotton scarf that's worn to translucence in places and winds it round his thin neck.

"Wherever it turns out."

How can someone leave without knowing where they're going? A cold thought suddenly comes, like a vivid spark:

"To the war?"

Ikonnikov doesn't answer. He slaps at his pockets, takes out the key to the clubhouse, and places it in Yuzuf's palm.

"I won't need this anymore, either," he says, taking Yuzuf by the shoulders and looking him in the eye. "I'm leaving the artel to you."

"But I'm still just a kid." Yuzuf swallows hard. "A minor."

"The commandant's not against it. He needs good sales figures. The artel's a whole production entity! It would be too bad to lose it. So you manage things here, please."

Ilya Petrovich walks along the walls, touching the glistening nail heads with his fingertip.

"There's still a lot of work to be done, isn't there?"

Yuzuf rushes to his teacher and embraces him, burying his face in the smell of paints, turpentine, dusty canvas, coarse tobacco, and yesterday's alcohol.

"Why are you going?"

Ikonnikov pats Yuzuf's back.

"I always dreamt of seeing distant countries. When I was a child I wanted to be a sailor and travel the world." Ilya Petrovich's eyes are slyly narrowed, gleaming right next to Yuzuf. "Tell you what I'll do. I'll write to you from Paris itself. Deal?"

Yuzuf hates when people talk to him as if he were little. He moves away, wipes his eyes, and keeps silent. Ikonnikov picks up a thin knapsack from the floor and slings it over his shoulder. They walk together to the shore.

Despite the early hour, a whole delegation has gathered to see Ikonnikov off. Izabella is there. She has wizened and thinned in recent years, and her facial features show more clearly through withered skin that seems as carefully curried and scraped as leather. Konstantin Arnoldovich is with her. He has changed little over the years, though his frame is wirier, his face darker, and his hair lighter. Doctor Leibe is there, away from the infirmary for a short while. The commandant is drifting around at a distance, leaning on his stick, and half-facing the rest.

The morning is gray and cold. The wind carries slate-colored clouds over the Angara and tears at the exiles' clothing. "So are we going or not, citizens?" a chilly sailor drearily inquires yet again. He's standing in water up to his knees, holding the bow of a small, peeling boat that's rocking on the waves. His bare feet are bluish-gray from the cold and he's wearing a quilted jacket with a dirty mesh singlet peering out from under it. A gloomy Gorelov is sitting in the boat, his red nose turned away from the shore and his ears deeply sunken into his shoulders; he's embracing a bulging duffel bag. Aglaya, who's been living with him for three years now, had tagged along to the shore to see him off ("I'm practically your wife, Vasya, don't you see?") but he chased her away, afraid she'd cry on him.

"I asked Gorelov to keep an eye on you." Izabella winds the unending scarf a little more snugly on Ikonnikov's neck and fondly tucks the ends into the grubby collar of his jacket.

"I'm afraid it's up to me to look after him." Ilya Petrovich is peppy, even cheerful. "He was so scared when he got his draft notice."

"Not everybody's a hero like you." Izabella looks into his eyes and shakes her head in distress. "Do you yourself even understand why you are?"

Ikonnikov smiles in response and narrows his eyes like a child. Ikonnikov is nearly fifty. Unlike Gorelov, who's been called up for army service in accordance with his age and eligibility (absence of violations and punishments during time spent at the settlement, labor success, loyalty to the administration, overall degree of re-education), Ilya Petrovich has called himself up to the front as a volunteer. His application was evaluated for a long time, then evaluated again, and finally, astonished at Ikonnikov's action, the authorities agreed to take him.

"Well ..." Konstantin Arnoldovich extends a very withered hand that's entangled in gnarled, ropy veins. "Well ..."

"Who are you going to argue with now?" Ilya Petrovich shakes Sumlinsky's hand for a moment before suddenly withdrawing it and embracing him.

They slap each other on the back cautiously, as if they're women afraid of causing pain, then quickly back away, averting their flustered faces.

"Take care of yourself," says Leibe, taking Ikonnikov by the elbow.

"Enough of this parting!" says the commandant's harsh, annoyed voice. "You're done."

Ilya Petrovich gives Yuzuf's hair a strong, hurried ruffle and winks. He turns to Ignatov and nods at him. He walks with a hunched and shuffling gait to the boat and gets in awkwardly, nearly dropping his bag into the water. He sits down alongside Gorelov and raises his large hand, and when he waves to those seeing him off, it becomes obvious how much his arms stick out of his too-short sleeves. The scarf around his neck has unwound again and is beating in the wind.

"*Mon Dieu*," says Izabella, pressing her long fingers to her chin. "*Mon Dieu*."

The sailor pushes the boat into deeper water and jumps in. A couple of seconds later, the motor wheezes then roars, musters its voice, and finally lets out a harrowing wail. The little boat turns around and leaves, cutting through foam that pulses on the waves. Konstantin Arnoldovich and Izabella, along with Leibe, watch it go. Yuzuf runs along the shore and waves his arms. Ignatov walks away without looking back.

The triangle of the boat shrinks and dwindles. Something long and light-colored (the scarf?) breaks away from it and flies over the waves like a seagull, before falling into the Angara.

"The first two of us to leave for the mainland," Konstantin Arnoldovich utters quietly, as an aside, as if he's not addressing anyone.

"The first of many?" asks Leibe, also as an aside.

Izabella gathers her narrow mouth into tight folds, throws back her completely white hair, and silently leaves the shore.

Yuzuf and Zuleikha

On a clear May day in 1946, the nimble little dark blue launch that delivers the weekly mail and printed materials to Semruk is carrying three passengers. Nobody greets them at the shore so there's nobody there to be surprised that one of them is a rather dandyish military man wearing a stiffly ironed uniform and lavishly sprayed with cologne. Vasily Gorelov, in the flesh.

He jumps decisively, even jauntily, out of the launch and strides broadly and rapidly along the wooden pier, which moans underneath his ferociously squeaky and shiny boots as if in pain. The smooth sides of the small pigskin suitcase in his hand keeps blazing a fiery orange, as though it's absorbed all the sunlight into itself.

The two other passengers, apparently a grandfather and grandson, climb timidly out of the launch and walk slowly behind him, looking around, confused. They scrutinize the smooth undersides of overturned boats glimmering in the sun, the broad flags of fishing nets lazily fluttering in the wind, the sturdy stairway that runs up steeply from the shore, and houses of various colors sprinkled on the high knoll.

"Comrade," the unnerved grandfather calls to Gorelov, "we want to see the local healer. Know how to find him?"

Gorelov turns around, looks the old man over with a stern gaze, as a policeman looks over a prank-playing little boy, and mumbles, "They've let this place go, you know ..." A juicy tutting comes through his clenched teeth and he walks ashore without answering the question. The old man sighs, takes his grandson by the hand, and trudges after Gorelov.

It's Sunday so it's noisy in the settlement and people are out and about. Fresh curtains breathe with the breeze in wide-open windows and small front-yard gardens are white with jasmine. A group of boisterous lads chase a ball and whack it into a detachment of strutting gray geese whose leader hisses, snakes its long neck along the ground, and flings itself forward. A couple of shaggy dogs quickly fly out from under a gate, barking deafeningly and scaring away the geese. There are smells of smoke, the bathhouse, freshly planed wood, milk, and bliny. A gramophone's cooing somewhere, hoarsely but tenderly, about love that's true, friendship everlasting, and dreams fulfilled.

The old man and the little boy occasionally stop to ask the way – from an old woman leaning out a window and beating pillows, and a guy with an athletic torso who's carrying a couple of little kids on bare shoulders that glisten with sweat. They finally reach a large, unprepossessing structure that stands at a distance. It's made up of three buildings of various colors that have been added onto one another: in the center is the oldest one, already dark from time; the one to the right is a little lighter in color and more spacious; and the one to the left is completely new, honey-yellow, and still smelling tartly of pine. "Infirmary," announces an inscription above in green paint.

The grandfather meekly knocks and enters without waiting for an answer. It's cool and quiet in this spacious building with scrubbed floors, where identical white pillowcases shine softly on empty beds, stern instruments flash metallically on a neatly tidied table, and the breeze rustles at a large ledger that's lying next to the instruments, its browned pages covered in small handwriting.

"Anybody here?"

There's nobody. The grandfather goes outside and slowly circles the building, his grandson following with small steps. And there's the back yard with a tiny gate, a meager woodpile, a broad and utterly dried-out block of wood with a half-rusted axe driven into it, and a couple of faded rags flapping on the clothes lines.

"Good afternoon," the old man says, carefully opening the door a little.

After detecting the sound of motion, he steps inside and peers into the darkness of the room. A small, aging woman is placing things on a large checked headscarf with a long fringe. She has a pale face covered in fine flourishes of wrinkles, tired eyes under steeply arched brows, and broad white streaks in her long, black braids.

"Excuse me, ma'am," says the man. He pulls off his floppy cap and nods low, with dignity. "Does the famous healer live here?"

"He lived here" – Zuleikha is stacking linens and clothes together – "up until yesterday."

"He met his maker?"

"They hired him in town, down in Maklakovo." Her tiny, unexpectedly strong hands tie up the bundle. "Apparently there was nobody to run the regional hospital there."

"Oh no, how 'bout that …" The grandfather shakes his beard in disappointment, places a hand on the boy's head, and clasps him against himself. "It took a week to get here. My grandson needs treatment."

"They promised to send someone new in the next few days. Stay, you can live here for now while you wait."

The flow of callers for the famous healer has grown each year. Zuleikha has gotten used to patients' relatives staying at the infirmary.

"It's him we need to see. We'll go to him. Listen, ma'am …"

The grandfather lowers his voice. "The doctor himself, he's not overly strict? What do you think, will he see us? Won't chase us out? That's the town, after all, a proper hospital."

"He won't chase you out." Zuleikha gazes at him for a long time. "And if you want to run off, he won't let you go until the treatment's done."

"I heard, I heard …" The old man immediately breaks into a smile. He sighs with joy and relief as he hurries to the door, pulling on his cap. "Are you his wife?"

"No," she says, becoming pensive, her fingers tugging at the knots on the headscarf. "I just helped with housekeeping. And now I'm to move out, too."

The grandfather nods understandingly and hurries out after hastily saying goodbye, pushing his grandson before him. They nearly run back through the settlement to rush for the mail boat, which hasn't cast off yet. The drawling, caressing sounds of an accordion drift after them through a wide-open window, along with sweet words about the prime of youth, never-ending joy, and inseparable love.

The grandfather and his grandson reach Maklakovo two days later, find the regional hospital and, in it, a small, lively person with a silvery halo of hair around his smooth skull. Another two days later, he operates on the boy and keeps him in the hospital for a month, for observation.

When the treatment is coming to an end, the grandfather begins pressing the nurse about how best to show gratitude to the famous healer, with money or some sort of gift. "He won't take money," she announces authoritatively, "but that coffee, now there's a safe bet. He's always swilling it down."

Shaking his head distrustfully in a local food shop, the old man exchanges all the yellow coins sewn into the hem of his shirt for a sack of strange, oily beans with a sharp smell. He brings it to the hospital, petrified that he's bought the wrong thing. To the old man's tremendous relief, however, the healer accepts the tribute and smiles gratefully, his nostrils reveling in the bitter aroma coming from the sack. Who doesn't love good coffee?

Gorelov doesn't hurry as he walks through Semruk, right down the middle of Tsentralnaya Street, in his gleaming boots. He carries his puffed-up chest with dignity, and a round yellow medal casts a reflection on his brownish uniform jacket. His right hand holds the little suitcase a short distance away from his body, as if he's exhibiting it for the hens and chicks running past, while his left hand keeps touching his smoothly shaven temple, using a cautious circular motion to smooth the short hair under his dark blue service cap's raspberry-colored band.

Curtains in the windows on Tsentralnaya are trembling as if they're alive and surprised faces flash behind them. People come out of their houses and talk among themselves, their gazes following the new arrival. Acting as if he hasn't noticed the stir his appearance has caused, Gorelov parades leisurely to the main square, where the political information board, once small, sprawls lengthwise. It now looks like a long fence.

He places the little suitcase neatly on the ground. He watches Zaseka's thin, scoliotic back as he pastes up a fresh sheet of *Soviet Siberia*, which flutters in the breeze. The sheet settles over a poster that's faded and brown from rain and snow, where there's a black-browed major leading a buxom white-toothed peasant woman in a dance, straight toward the joyful inscription, "Their happiness was restored!"

"You're putting it up crooked, you clod," Gorelov lazily says through clenched teeth, turning his calm, maybe even slightly sleepy, face toward the Angara.

"It looks perfectly straight to me," says Zaseka, not turning around as his thin fingers carefully smooth the newspaper's upper edge and small drops of white paste come out from under it. "How about that?"

A rough hand grabs him by the nape of the neck and thrusts his face into the sheet, which smells sharply of typographical ink.

"Is that how you talk to a security officer, you scum?" Gorelov whispers softly in Zaseka's ear.

Zaseka's scared, hare-like eyes look to the side.

"Comrade Gorelov ..." he wheezes in surprise.

"What kind of *comrade* am I to you, you louse? Well?"

"Citizen – Citizen Gorelov ..."

The iron grip weakens on Zaseka's neck and releases him.

"As I said, you're putting it up crooked," says Gorelov, painstakingly straightening the newspaper, which is now creased from Zaseka's bony head. "Get outta here, you useless dolt."

Gorelov brushes off his hands and watches Zaseka clumsily smear paste on his cheeks and bolt down the street, where curious people immediately surround him. Then Gorelov places one boot on the suitcase, leans an elbow into his raised knee and freezes, directing his gaze at the Angara stretching below.

A female figure moves away from the crowd. Aglaya slowly walks toward Gorelov, pressing the ends of her faded headscarf to her chin, and stops a few steps away, undecided about approaching closer.

"Vasya, is that you?"

He doesn't answer. He takes a hefty pendant-like gold watch from his right pocket and clicks the cover. A sheaf of fiery sparks falls on his tanned face. The melody of "*Oh du lieber Augustin*" thrums plaintively inside. He anxiously scrutinizes the watch face then slams the cover shut.

"You waiting for someone?" Aglaya takes a timid step forward.

Gorelov finally meets her gaze. She's aged and grown unattractive; her face is pockmarked, her cheeks slightly droopy, as if they've deflated, and her hands are wrinkled, with broken nails. She's not saucy Aglaya now; she's jaded Glashka.

"How come you didn't stop by the house?" Glashka takes another step. "We haven't seen each other in four years."

Gorelov takes a cigarette case (a blue-tinged silver eagle is spreading its wings on snow-white enamel) from his left pocket and slowly lights a long, thin cigarette. He releases spicy, dark gray smoke into her face.

"Listen here, you slut," he says calmly, all businesslike. "What happened, happened. It's over. My home's in another place now. I'll send for you if I want to screw around. Till then, get lost. About face, march!"

Glashka's face twitches and collapses into one big, wrinkled grimace. She shrugs her shoulders, turns around, and trudges away, her gaping eyes brimming with large tears that don't roll away. Even so, she looks back, craning her neck like a chicken.

"On the double!" commands Gorelov. "Faster!"

She quickens the pace of her small steps as she goes down the street.

"Don't try getting too friendly with me, you hussy!"

Gorelov's booming shout behind Glashka urges her on. She trips over her own feet, raising dust on the road as she falls. Gorelov blots his sweaty neck with a white handkerchief and turns around.

"You've become vicious ..." says a quiet voice not too far away. It's the commandant.

He's standing at the slope that descends from the commandant's headquarters, uniform jacket tossed on his shoulders and a fat, knotty stick in his hand. His hair, once thick and fully brown, is now dappled and lightweight, and his eyes seem to have been absorbed into his face, though his cheekbones have leapt outward. Furrowed wrinkles have settled evenly along his forehead, as if a pencil outlined them.

Gorelov looks at the river and doesn't answer.

"Why aren't you talking? You don't recognize me or something?" The commandant walks closer, leaning on his stick and limping heavily, swaying.

"Of course, how could I not recognize you?"

"You've toughened." Ignatov whistles as he circles Gorelov and examines the green shoulder boards with light cornflower-blue edging on his jacket. "Lieutenant? Since when do they accept former convicts into the officer ranks?"

"Don't you shove my past in my face! I was fighting while you were sitting on your backside by the stove."

"I heard how you fought. As a driver for a field kitchen, and a procurement officer in the rear."

"And what of it! My rights have been reinstated and I don't have to do what you say anymore." Gorelov stuffs his paw into an inside pocket and takes out a dark burgundy rectangle with a row of dingy yellow letters on it – a passport – and waves it in the air, then opens it and shoves it under the commandant's nose as if to say, *You seen one of these?*

"Everybody has to do what I say here," says Ignatov, walking right up to Gorelov and placing the knotty end of his stick on the shiny nose of Gorelov's boot. "And since last year we've had a ban on hiring free workers. So you roll on out of here on the very next boat."

Gorelov kicks the stick, which falls to the ground with a thud. The commandant reels and drops his jacket in the dust.

"I'm just as familiar with Order 248, *bis* 3, dated January 8, 1945, as you are, Ignatov." Gorelov's boot steps on Ignatov's jacket. "And so let me ask you: why aren't you following it?"

Ignatov awkwardly places his foot to the side and bends to the ground for his jacket, where he freezes.

"Why is it that free workers are bumming around the settlement in droves," Gorelov whispers damply above Ignatov's ear, "but the inmates are running off to the city? You let people get out of hand, commandant, oh, but you did." Gorelov finally takes his foot off the jacket. "Boat, you say? Fine, I'll go greet it."

He stamps a boot to shake off the dust that floated onto it, slightly dulling its mirror-like shine, takes his fiery orange suitcase off the ground, and waddles back to the pier. People crowded at the edge of the square scatter.

Zuleikha ties everything she can consider her own into bundles: summer and winter clothes, a couple of changes of bed linen, blankets, pillows, dishes, kitchen utensils, and small things dear to her heart, like several napkins she embroidered and Yuzuf's old clay toys, like the doll with irrevocably broken-off limbs and the fish without fins or tail. She leaves the cast-iron pots for boiling bandages (they'll come in handy for the next doctor) as well as the wall clock that ticks loudly and has a slightly crooked inscription burned by a red-hot awl: "To the dear doctor from the residents of Semruk, on your 70th birthday." That wasn't given to her so it's not hers to take.

Leibe hadn't taken it, either. He didn't take anything with him: he just left in the clothes he was wearing and carrying a half-empty, worn traveling bag on which the outline of a once-red cross could just be divined.

They'd parted quietly, silently. She'd stood in the middle of the house, her hands lowered to her apron, not knowing what to do or say. Volf Karlovich had walked over to her, stood alongside her, taken her hand, and bent his dry lips to it. Zuleikha saw that the fluffy silver halo around his bald spot had become much sparser and that the skin on his delicate pink and once-shiny skull was now all speckled with large gray and brown spots.

Yuzuf went to the pier to see Leibe off but Zuleikha stayed at home. She'd begun gathering her things right away. They'd proposed that she live in the infirmary when the new doctor arrived, too, and promised to wall off part of the house and register her as a full-time nurse, but she'd refused, deciding to move back to the barracks.

They aren't barracks at all now. They're called dormitories and they've installed lots of partitions to divide them into small rooms. No more than six or eight people are housed in them, and although the bunks are two-tiered, as before, they now have real mattresses, blankets, and pillows, and some people even have colorful cross-stitched bedspreads. Those living in the dormitories are either new residents (very few have been brought in recently) or people who've been held back from setting up their own homes and households, either by their own ineptitude or laziness. It scares Zuleikha that separation from Yuzuf is imminent – he'll turn sixteen this summer so he's been assigned his own bed and space in the male dormitory.

He's already been working in the art artel for four years. The artel's products have the same subjects: field laborers, lumber industry shockworkers, active workers on the kolkhoz front, Komsomol members and Young Pioneers, and sometimes gymnasts. The buyers had noted that the style of the Semruk artwork had changed rather abruptly several years ago but they attached no significance to that since, as before, the rural people depicted are round-faced, the gymnasts peppy, and the children smiling. The fruits of the artel's labor continue to be in demand.

Yuzuf paints for himself at night, in his free time. Zuleikha struggles to understand these paintings of his, with their sharp lines, mad colors, and hodgepodge of strange, sometimes frightening images. She likes the lumbermen and Young Pioneers much more. He hasn't painted her once.

She doesn't speak much with Yuzuf. Zuleikha senses that he misses talking with Izabella (she died in 1943, right after news that the blockade was lifted in Leningrad) and Konstantin Arnoldovich (who outlived his wife by only a year). She sees that he still pines for Ilya Petrovich, who vanished after leaving for the front. There's been no news from him whatsoever. Yesterday it even seemed that Yuzuf was very upset about Leibe's departure, though their relationship had never gotten back on track.

She can't replace anyone for him but she feels like he needs her even more than before. After losing people dear to him, he's been directing all the ardor of his young heart toward his mother. He wants to talk, ask questions and receive answers, argue, discuss, interrupt, attack, defend himself, and quarrel – and all she can do is keep silent, listen, and pat him on the head. But this makes him angry and he runs off. Then he'll return a while later, downcast, guilty, and affectionate. He'll embrace her, squeezing until her bones crack (he's a head taller and strong for his age) and again she says nothing; she just pats him on the head. That's how they live.

The little flame on the front steps of the commandant's headquarters has stopped summoning her at night. Ignatov probably smokes inside now.

Yuzuf didn't steal the boat – it had been promised to him. When red-haired Lukka was still alive, Yuzuf had often helped him repair it. They'd plugged gaps with bast fiber and old rags, covered it with gooey pitch, soaked and dried it, and applied more pitch. In return, the old man took Yuzuf with him night fishing – he himself angled and Yuzuf sat alongside, watching and learning. The Angara at night was quiet and taciturn, completely different. The firmament, spotted with constellations, was reflected in the water's black mirror, and the boat floated between the two starry domes, along the exact middle of the world, rocked by gently splashing waves. In the morning, Yuzuf would attempt to paint from memory what he had seen at night but he never liked what came out.

Lukka had said, "The boat will be yours when I die, my boy." He died in the spring. While the others were still in Lukka's tiny, empty house on the night of their old comrade's funeral meal, Yuzuf went to the shore, released the boat on the water, and led it beyond the far bend in the river, where he hid it in bushes under the cliff, tightly tied to the fat roots of a gigantic elm. He flooded the boat as Lukka had taught him, so it wouldn't crack.

He needs the boat. He's planning an escape.

Sometimes news items and even entire articles about prisoners' escapes from jails and camps appear in newspapers on the agitational board. They all end the same, with the fugitives being captured and punished harshly.

Yuzuf knows he won't be caught.

Of course it would be best to escape in the summer. Go down the Angara to the Yenisei, and then it's a stone's throw to Maklakovo. From there, hitchhike to Krasnoyarsk, go west by train, through the Urals and through Moscow, to Leningrad. Straight to University Embankment, to the long, severe building with columns the color of dusty ochre and two stern sphinxes of pink granite by the entrance, to the Academy of the Arts, the famous "Repinka," Ikonnikov's alma mater. As it happens, he'll make it in time for entrance exams. He's decided to bring a couple of his paintings with him (some of the ones Ilya Petrovich would have liked) and a folder of pencil sketches.

Yuzuf knows they'll definitely admit him.

He could live at the institute, in any tiny room, even a caretaker's quarters, even a storeroom, even a doghouse. He could earn his lodging as a caretaker. But he has something stored away, in case of emergency. In a hiding place carefully guarded from his mother's gaze there lies a thick, snow-white sheet folded in quarters, where there are several brief lines written in Konstantin Arnoldovich's floating calligraphic hand. Sumlinsky appeals to some "Olenka," sending her distant greetings and requesting in the name of youth to shelter a young lad, bearer of the letter. Above is an address whose magical words take the breath away, beaming like an inviting lighthouse: "Fontanka River Embankment." Unsigned. "She'll understand," Konstantin Arnoldovich had said when he handed Yuzuf the letter. That was a month before his death.

Yuzuf has no money for the trip. They've told him that if he's lucky, he'll be able to make it there by riding a month or a month and a half in freight cars.

Yuzuf knows he'll be lucky.

He doesn't have documents, either: all the birth certificates of the exiles' children are kept in the safe at the commandant's headquarters. Yuzuf will turn sixteen soon, but he won't be issued a passport, since the majority of Semruk residents still live without them. They don't need them. But this doesn't matter. The main thing is to reach Leningrad, race off to the Neva, burst into the building under the approving gaze of the sphinxes' slanting eyes, fly up the stairs to the admission committee's room, and spread his work on the table: "Here I am, all of me: judge for yourself! *Roi ou rien.*" Who needs a passport?

He's been thinking about escape for a long time. A couple of months before, something happened that served like a well-dampened lash, whipping up all his ideas and wishes, subordinating them to this one passion. Freedom.

That day, Mitrich, the old office worker who fulfilled a whole slew of various responsibilities in Semruk – secretary, clerk, and archivist, as well as mailman – called out to Yuzuf on the street.

"Letter for you," he said, smiling with surprise and affection. He rummaged around for an unbearably long time in a large canvas drawstring bag for carrying newspapers, fished out a dirty white paper triangle soiled by fingers and finely frayed on the folds. "Let's see, how long did this take from the front?" he said as his hands twirled the odd-looking letter, which was blotched with round postmarks. "A year, no less."

He finally handed it over. He stood alongside Yuzuf, watching attentively instead of going away; his brows even tensed and bristled. Yuzuf had no desire to open it in front of him, though, so he thanked Mitrich and ran off into the taiga, to the cliff, far away from everybody. He thought his heart would leap out as he was running. The letter was on fire in his hands, burning his fingers.

He flew between the boulders and sat on a pink rock. He swallowed and opened his sweaty hands.

Krasnoyarsk Krai. Northern Yenisei Region. Labor Settlement Semruk on the Angara. Yuzuf Valiev.

Yuzuf unfolded the letter carefully so as not to tear it. There were no words in it but at the center of the sheet was the candle of the Eiffel Tower (pencil, ink) and in the corner was a small inscription: "Field of Mars, ▓▓ June 1945" (the censor had blotted out "Paris" in black but left "Field of Mars" and the date). Nothing else.

He somehow folded it back up, though his fingers had suddenly gone numb and unresponsive, and stuffed the letter inside his jacket. He sat for a long time, gazing at the leadenness of the Angara, which the brownish-gray taiga squeezed at the edges and the skillet-like sky flattened from above.

And that's when he decided he'd definitely run away. He knows he'll do it. And he would run away now, even today, but one thing holds him back: his mother. After leaving the hunting artel, she became somehow tired, broken, and aged quickly, irrevocably. She's been completely lost, like a child, since the doctor left, and her huge eyes look at Yuzuf in fear. He can't leave her like that. But he also can't stay here any longer.

Ikonnikov's letter is hidden in the same secret spot as Konstantin Arnoldovich's. Sometimes it seems like his heart doesn't beat in his chest but in there, in that cold, dark crevice where two letters from two close friends lie tightly pressed against one another.

Yuzuf doesn't know what to do about his mother; she's probably the only obstacle to leaving he can't see a way round.

And so that's that: things are packed, bundles are tied. Zuleikha and Yuzuf are moving into the dormitory in the morning and they'll sleep apart tomorrow. Now, on this clear Sunday afternoon, she can finally sit and say goodbye to this quiet, empty building. Zuleikha walks around the house checking that she hasn't forgotten anything. She peers behind a door, behind the stove, on shelves, benches, and windowsills.

One floorboard squeaks underfoot; it's the far one, by the window. At one time, maybe a hundred years ago or maybe in her sleep, she and Murtaza had hidden food items from the Red Hordesmen under a board like this. Zuleikha steps on it again and the long, high-pitched squeak sounds like someone's voice. She sits down, inserts her fingers in a crevice and pulls, smiling to herself as the wood gives, easily lifting a little. A black rectangle of darkness under the floorboard breathes of the cold, damp earth. She slips her hand in, gropes around, and pulls out a light little parcel wrapped in a rag. She unties the strings and folds back old fabric and pieces of birch bark. Inside are two sheets of paper that don't look alike: one's snow white, the other's dirty yellow, and they're stuck together because they've grown into one another, from lying here so long. Zuleikha unsticks and unfolds them. She can't read the first message and doesn't know what outlandish building is depicted on the second. She understands only that Yuzuf hid them and that it is his secret, something so huge he couldn't share it with his mother, or that he was protecting her for a while from whatever they contained. She stares at beads of small letters with long tails that seem to twist in the wind and the tower's thin skeleton, which vaguely reminds her of a minaret; the words and the drawing scream of something, of summoning somewhere.

She feels it shoving her in the chest: her son has decided to flee.

Zuleikha sits on the floor for a few more minutes, pressing the fist with the crumpled letters to her chest, then she stands and runs to the clubhouse. She doesn't remember running; it seems like she's flown in an instant, in one leap. She tears the door open. Yuzuf is inside, at an easel, as always.

"Mama, why are you barefoot?"

"You! You …" Gasping for breath, she hurls the balled-up letters at him as if they were cannonballs.

He bends, picks them up, slowly smoothes them on his chest, and puts them away in his pocket. He doesn't look up and his face is hardened, white. Zuleikha understands this is how things really are, that her son has decided to flee. To leave her. Abandon her.

She shouts something, throws herself against the walls, and thrashes her arms around; canvas crackles under her fists, frames break, and something falls and rolls along the floor. She herself falls, too. She coils up, huddles, and twists like a snake, burrowing into herself, wailing at something inside her. *Abandoned, abandoned* … She understands she's not wailing at herself but at Yuzuf, who's attached to her from all sides. His body, his hands, and his distorted, wet face are around her. They're lying on the floor in a ball, tightly interlocked.

"Where?" she whimpers into Yuzuf's chest. "Where are you going? Alone, without documents … They'll catch you …"

"They won't catch me, Mama."

"They'll put you in jail …" She clings to him as if she were drowning.

"They won't put me in jail."

"What about me?"

Yuzuf keeps silent and embraces her so it hurts.

"I won't survive." Zuleikha tries to catch his gaze. "I'll die without you, Yuzuf. I'll die as soon as you take the first step."

She feels his damp breath on her neck.

"I'll die," Zuleikha stubbornly repeats. "I'll die, die, die!"

He mumbles, moves away from her, and detaches himself from her. He pushes away her grasping hands and scrambles out of her embrace.

"Yuzuf!" Zuleikha rushes after him.

Her outstretched fingers slide through the dark hair at the back of his head like a comb, down his neck, leaving red scratches, and catches at the collar of his shirt so that Yuzuf runs out of the clubhouse with it torn.

"You're no son to me!" Zuleikha wails after him. "No son!"

Her eyes don't see, her ears don't hear.

Abandoned. Abandoned.

She stands and trudges away, reeling. The wind is in her face, carrying the mewling of seagulls and the sounds of the forest. Underfoot: soil, grass, rocks, and roots.

Abandoned. Abandoned.

The world is flowing, streaming, before her gaze. There are no forms or lines, only colors that float past. And then there's a distinct figure, tall and dark, amidst the flow. A head proudly set on broad masculine shoulders, long arms almost to the knees, a dress beating in the wind. *You're here, too, you old witch.*

Zuleikha wants to push her away. She raises her hand to do so but for some reason she falls on the Vampire Hag's chest instead, embracing a powerful body that smells of either tree bark or fresh earth. She buries her face in something warm, solid, muscular, and alive, feeling strong hands on her spine, the back of her head, around her, everywhere. Tears rise in her throat, winding around her gullet like a rope, and Zuleikha cries long and sweet after burying herself in her mother-in-law's bosom. The tears flow so generously and swiftly that it seems they're not coming from her eyes but from somewhere at the bottom of her heart, urged on by its rapid and resilient beating. Minutes or maybe hours later, after purging herself of every tear she's kept inside over the years, she calms and comes to her senses. Her breathing is still fast and her chest is still heaving convulsively, but a tired, long-awaited relief is already flowing through her body.

"Tell me, Mama," she whispers, either to her mother-in-law's bony shoulder or to the wrinkles at the base of her neck. She doesn't force open her eyes or unclasp her arms; it's as if she's afraid to let go. "Those stories about you going out into the *urman* when you were young – I always wanted to ask, why did you do it?"

"That was a long time ago. I was a stupid girl … I was looking for death, for deliverance from unhappy love." The old woman's broad, firm bosom rises and falls in a long, powerful sigh. "I went into the *urman* but it wasn't there, that death."

Zuleikha backs away in surprise so she can look her mother-in-law in the eye. The old woman's face is dark brown, with large, twisting wrinkles. And it's not a face at all: it's tree bark. Zuleikha has a gnarled old larch in her embrace. The tree trunk is bumpy and immense, with streaks of silvery pitch, roots like knots, and long sprawling branches that look upward, piercing the sky's blueness; the first gleams of spring foliage tremble on its branches with a light emerald radiance. Zuleikha wipes away pieces of bark and needles that have stuck to her cheeks and trudges back to the settlement from the taiga.

Ignatov has known for a long time that he'll be discharged. Kuznets has cooled greatly toward him since the 1942 incident with the plot that never happened. He rarely comes by, sending his fine fellows for inspections instead. He and Ignatov have never again sat for a bit. Kuznets himself is flying high, at colonel altitudes. He thinks it unnecessary to hide his hostility, so Ignatov's personal case file has already been enriched with two official reprimands. A third means inevitable dismissal from his position.

Ignatov, who's now a senior lieutenant, recently turned forty-six. (The promotion wasn't the result of valiant service, just a planned restructuring within the hierarchy of the People's Commissariat for Internal Affairs, shifting the line of ranks.) He's spent sixteen of those years in Semruk. He's not old yet, but he's already half-gray and limping. His face is sad and his disposition is gloomy. He's lonely.

Gorelov's excessively obnoxious appearance on the morning boat can mean only one thing: that Ignatov is being discharged. He couldn't wait, the dog, and had rushed over before everybody else so he could delight in his own power and drink it down leisurely, savoring it. Ignatov's discharge might even come today.

He takes his brown uniform jacket from the chair and starts swishing a brush over the thin wool. *So, you bastards, I might as well be all dressed up to get fired.* Ignatov has often worn civilian clothes in recent years so his uniform looks almost new and cleans easily and quickly. Jacket, breeches, peaked cap – everything is dandyish, bright and fresh, flaunting itself on a nail pounded right into the middle of the wall. Ignatov places his wax-polished boots underneath and the picture takes on an appearance of finality. It's as if someone let the air out of Ignatov himself and hung him up for all to see: *Here he is, our commandant, feast your eyes on him.*

The scariest thing is that he doesn't want to leave. How has he come to be so attached to this harsh and inhospitable land over the years? To this dangerous river, treacherous in its perpetual inconstancy and possessing thousands of shades of color and smell? To this boundless *urman* that flows beyond the horizon? To this cold sky that gives snow in the summer and sun in the winter? Damn it, even to these people, who are often unwelcoming, coarse, ugly, poorly dressed, missing home, and sometimes wretched, strange, and incomprehensible. Highly varied.

Ignatov has imagined going home: being jostled in a third-class railway car, watching as monotonous landscapes change through a dingy little window, and then, dazed from the long journey, stepping out on the Kazan platform and walking along deserted evening streets. But where to? Who will he go see? Mishka Bakiev is no longer in his life; the fleeting crushes of his youth – Ilona and Nastasya – married long ago; and his former subordinates – Prokopenko, Slavutsky, and the rest of the group – have forgotten him. Kazan is no longer in his life. But Semruk is.

Ignatov starts packing his things. What is there to pack, anyway? He's wearing his set of civilian clothing. You can't roll up the view out a window and put it in your suitcase. There's nothing else to take since he has no household equipment, never acquired any. Or even a suitcase – he doesn't have one of those, either. He'll leave here empty-handed, just as he arrived. It's the same in his soul: empty, as if everything has been extracted.

He decides to go through his papers so he has something to do with his hands. Mishka Bakiev was going through papers back then, too, as he prepared his exit. The time has now come for Ignatov to do the same. He opens the large, steel safe. All of

Semruk is stored here, on five high, strong shelves in the deep, cool innards. There are children and adults, old-timers and brand-new residents, the living and the dead, their personal and work lives, hopes, crimes, unhappinesses, successes, punishments, births and deaths, illnesses, production targets, and performance figures. All of that is lying stamped and threaded together, neatly sorted, distributed into piles, folders, and boxes, carefully tied with string, pressed by paperclips, and smelling of absorbed iron and ink. Ignatov looks through the passports (they've been issued to several exiles but there was an order to store the documents at the commandant's headquarters, as a precaution), children's birth certificates (he himself has written them out, every last one), photographs, lists of new arrivals, statements, denunciations, recommendations, petitions, letters seized by the censor and not reaching the addressees, all now buried here for the foreseeable future in personal files …

People, people, people – hundreds of figures stand before him. He's the one who greeted them here, on the edge of the earth. Sent them off into the taiga, exhausted them with excessive work quotas, squeezed the economic plan out of them with an iron hand, scoffed at, frightened, and handed them over for punishment. He built homes for them, fed them, scared up foodstuffs and medicines for them, and protected them from the authorities at the central office. He kept them afloat. As they did him.

Something dark and flat is lying in a corner on the lower shelf. Ignatov kneels, reaches in, and pulls it out. It's the "Case" file. Once gray, it's now brownish and covered in faded stamps. He opens it without rising from his knees. Thin sheets smelling of papery dust have been scribbled on with pencil and coal. Several names are boldly circled. There's a crooked inscription in the corner of one page: "Yuzuf." A couple of dark-reddish spruce needles are stuck to the sheets.

Someone knocks at the door. The thought belatedly flashes into his mind that, oh, he doesn't have time to change his clothes. They've showed up fast. He hastily rises from his knees, flings the folder in the safe, and closes the door. He stands in the middle of the room, hands behind his back.

"Come in," he says clearly.

The door opens. It's Zuleikha.

She slowly walks into the house. She's pale and thinner, and there's a headscarf wound down to her eyebrows. She stops and her teary eyes, the lids puffy and reddened, look up at him, then down again. The sound of the wind and the nearly inaudible drone of spruce trees in the taiga rushes through the open window. They stand silently for a moment.

"Are you here for a specific reason?" he finally asks.

Zuleikha nods. Over time, her skin has become yellowish and waxen instead of white, and thin, fine wrinkles have settled on her cheeks in many places, but her eyelashes have remained just as thick.

"Let my son go, Ivan. He needs to leave."

"Where?"

"He wants to go to school. In the city. This isn't a life for him here, with us."

Ignatov clenches his fingers in a fist behind his back.

"Without a passport? Even if he had one, there'd be a note in the tenth box all the same, so who would take him, the son of a kulak?"

She looks even smaller when she lowers her head more, as if she wants to scrutinize something below her, under her feet.

"Let him go, Ivan. I know you can. I've never asked you for anything."

"Whereas I asked so much!" He turns around and walks off toward the window, positioning his face toward the breeze. "So much I lost count ..."

The bed squeaks plaintively for a long time. Zuleikha has sat down on the edge, with her hands squeezed between her knees. Her head is lowered all the way to her chest and only the top is visible.

"Take what you asked for, Ivan. If you haven't changed your mind."

"That's not what I wanted, Zuleikha." Ignatov is looking at the Angara's gray breadth, covered in fine frothy ripples. "It's not like that."

"Nor for me. But my son, it's not his fault ..."

A familiar brown rectangle emerges from the bend in the river. It's Kuznets's launch. How about that – he's making the visit himself. So it's definitely to discharge him.

"Go, Zuleikha," says Ignatov, observing the boat's rapid approach to the shore.

He buttons his jacket on his chest; he's decided not to change into his uniform since it would infer too much honor. He combs his hand through his thinning hair. Zuleikha is no longer in the room when he turns around.

Kuznets understands everything as soon as he enters and sees the stern Ignatov by the window and his cleaned-up uniform on the nail.

"You were expecting me," he says.

Kuznets isn't wasting his words so he opens his map case, puts the document on the table, and sets a bottle of the white stuff next to it. It's a flat bottle with a bright label, obviously trophy vodka. It's as if Ignatov doesn't see the bottle. He takes the document, though, and scans through it: *Relieved of post occupied ... stripped of title as someone who's discredited himself during his time working in the administrative organs ... become unworthy of said rank of senior lieutenant ... transferred to the reserves for ineptitude ...*

"Where are the glasses here, anyway?" Kuznets is forcefully twisting the screw-top (they do know how to seal a bottle, those imperialists!) as his gaze roves the room.

Ignatov's cold fingers fold the paper and pocket it.

"You're driving me out of the commandant job, fine!" he says. "But from the administration as a whole? What for?"

Giving up on the glasses, Kuznets tosses the cap to the floor and holds the bottle out to Ignatov. Receiving no answer, he tilts it toward his own mouth: the liquid slides out as cleanly as a blade. After drinking up a good third of it, he grunts, mumbles, and shakes his balding head.

"We don't need you, Vanya. Not here, not anywhere else."

The son of a bitch.

Ignatov looks for an instant at Kuznets's flushed and flaccid face, at his gray old-man's mustache drooping over his lip, and the pudgy fold under his square chin that hangs over his collar tabs. Now, if only … using that same bottle to the skull, then his fist to the well-fed mug and the ample paunch … But there's none of the usual cold malice in Ignatov's heart, no rage, no desperation. He's empty.

"I have nowhere to go from here, Zin."

"Then stay," Kuznets simply says. "There's a ban on free workers but we'll find something for you – work can be found in the forest. There are empty houses – settle in one, live there. You'll find yourself a woman for your old age."

"This means Gorelov's taking my place?"

Kuznets swigs from the bottle again, running his hand from his throat, over his gullet, down his powerful chest to his belly, as if it's accompanying the liquid. He exhales loudly and pungently, then nods:

"He's a familiar person here, won't let me down."

"He'll let them all rot the hell away." Ignatov looks pensively out the window.

"He'll improve standards of discipline!" Kuznets raises a fleshy finger and his shining eye looks askance. "He won't touch you, don't worry. I'll keep track of that, for old time's sake." He pours the rest of the vodka into his mouth, places the bottle on the table with a thud, and stands, overturning the chair behind him. "All right, Ignatov, five minutes to pack. You'll turn the commandant's headquarters over to Gorelov." And Kuznets walks to the door without saying goodbye.

Through the window, Ignatov can see Gorelov waiting by the front steps. *Has he been eavesdropping, the dog?* He catches Kuznets, who's unwieldy from vodka, and leads him down along the path, solicitously holding him at his spreading waist.

Ignatov opens the safe and takes a birth certificate out of the packet: "Yuzuf Valiev. Year of birth: 1930." He tosses it into the stove's cold, black hole and strikes a match; a small, hot flame quickly overcomes the paper. After thinking for a second, he tosses in the old "Case" folder, too.

As the smoldering corners of the papers slowly rise and disappear into the orange flame with a crackle, he takes a blank birth certificate form, dips a pen in ink, and traces out: "Iosif Ignatov. Year of birth: 1930. Mother: Zuleikha Valieva, peasant. Father: Ivan Ignatov, Red Army man."

He stamps the birth certificate and puts it in his pocket. He places the key to the commandant's headquarters on the table. And leaves.

The immaculately clean uniform remains hanging on the nail and a sunbeam warms itself on the peaked cap's scarlet band. Long-forgotten names writhe in the stove, blending, bonding, and burning into black cinders. They smolder, turn to light smoke, and float out the chimney pipe.

*

Zuleikha opens her eyes. The sun is beating down, blinding her and cutting her head to pieces. The vague outline of trees all around her are quivering in a sparkling dance of sunbeams.

"Are you feeling unwell?" Yuzuf is leaning toward her, looking at her face. "Do you not want me to go?"

Her son's eyes are enormous and a thick green: they're her eyes. Zuleikha's own eyes are looking at her from her son's face. She shakes her head and pulls him further into the forest.

At first she'd felt lost when Ignatov came, his face hardened as if he were all frozen, to bring Yuzuf's birth certificate, which was still crisp and smelling sharply of new paper and fresh ink.

"He should leave as soon as possible," he said. "Right away. Now."

Zuleikha bustled around, rushing to gather things, some sort of food.

"There's no time." Ignatov placed a hand on her shoulder. "He should go as he is, empty-handed."

In the right breast pocket of a jacket with mismatched buttons and worn to weightlessness, Yuzuf placed the two letters from the hiding place; in the left pocket was the new birth certificate and a fat packet of wrinkled banknotes of various colors, also from Ignatov. Zuleikha had never seen so much money in her life. And that was all Yuzuf took with him.

She didn't even have a chance to say thank you to Ignatov, who left quickly, vanished. So she ran with her son into the taiga, to the cliff where Lukka's old boat was hidden, down roundabout paths along back yards with neat, square garden beds; past the small clubhouse, thickly grown with moss and seeming to have contracted and settled with time; and past the broad swathes of kolkhoz fields already sprinkled with their first timid green shoots.

Nobody noticed them leave. Only the cracked yellow-brown skulls on the leaning poles watched them continuously; gazing through black eyeholes, they understand everything. One of the skulls – the largest, the bear – fell to the ground long ago, rolled off into the tall weeds, and burst in half. A little redheaded bird has woven a nest in it and is now looking around uneasily, sitting on the eggs she laid, her eyes following two people hurrying into the *urman*.

Yuzuf and Zuleikha have now been running for a long time. Old spruce trees extend their boughs, pricking at their shoulders, arms, and cheeks. The Chishme thunders, resounds, and roars under their feet. High grass at Round Clearing whips at their knees.

Zuleikha stops a moment for breath, inhales deeply, gasping for air. It catches in her nose and throat, and that hurts. Bushes, tree trunks, and treetops float past as she runs; bright greenery gleams like an emerald, blazing with flashes of sun and beating at the eyes, and that hurts. Evergreen needles slither treacherously underfoot and bristle with cones like sharp rocks; tree roots lie in knots, catching at their shoes; the clayey rise is steep and harsh, and climbing hurts. It hurts the legs, hurts the back, and it hurts in the chest, in the throat, in the belly, in the eyes. Everywhere.

"Just tell me and I'll stay." Yuzuf stops again and searches for her eyes.

She has no strength to look at him. Without raising her face, Zuleikha pushes her son further. Ahead, up.

Red-trunked pine trees burn with an unbearably bright, scorching color. Mossy boulders roll under the feet, trying hard to throw Zuleikha off. The fine teeth of thorns on a dry spreading bush tear at her dress. And here's the height of the cliff where the Angara's dark blueness is so blinding it pains the eyes horribly. And there's the unprepossessing path, almost for wild animals, down to the river. That's where Yuzuf is going.

"Mama."

He's standing in front of her, tall, ungainly, and guilty. She averts her gaze: *Keep quiet,* ulym, *don't make it more painful.*

"Mama."

Yuzuf extends his hands. He wants to embrace her in parting but she holds her hands out in front of her: *Don't come closer!* He grasps her hands, pressing them in his own, and Zuleikha breaks away, pushing him back. *Go, right away, as soon as possible, now.* She clenches her teeth, holding the pain inside so it doesn't spill over.

He looks at her helplessly, lost, then lowers his eyes and strides toward the bluff. He turns around at the edge; his mother is pressing her hands to her throat and has turned her face away. He exhales hard and descends the cliff down a winding trail of rustling stones between boulders, picking up his feet and flying. The sky withdraws as the Angara nears, opening in a broad, deep-blue embrace.

When he reaches the bushes at the river's edge, Yuzuf stops, scans to find the thin figure at the top, and waves. His mother is standing motionless, like a stone pillar, like a tree, and her long braids are half-unplaited, beating in the wind. She hasn't even looked at him.

He darts under green masses of plants by the water. He unties the boat, pushes it away with his foot, and the current catches him immediately, directing him forward. Yuzuf inserts the oars in the oarlocks and splashes icy water on his flushed face. He turns around, reaching his hand toward the distant cliff again, but still his mother isn't moving; only the wind flutters the light cotton of her old dress.

Zuleikha can't hold in the pain anymore so it spills out, flooding everything around her: the gleaming Angara water, the malachite shores and hills, the cliff top where she stands, and the firmament in a white froth of clouds. Seagull wings cut the air like blades and that hurts; the wind bends shaggy spruce tops and that hurts; Yuzuf's oars rip open the river, carrying him beyond the horizon to the Yenisei and that hurts. Watching it hurts. Even breathing hurts. If she could close her eyes and not see anything, not feel, but …

And is it really Yuzuf there, in the middle of the Angara, in that tiny wooden shell? Zuleikha peers out, straining her sharp hunter's vision. A boy is standing in the boat and desperately waving his arms at her – his dark hair is disheveled, his ears point in different directions, his tanned arms are thin and fragile, and his bare knees are covered in dark scratches; this is the seven-year-old Yuzuf leaving her, floating away, saying goodbye. She cries out, sharply raising her arms with her hands flung wide, "My son!" And she waves, waves with both hands, answering so strongly, broadly, and furiously that it's as if she's about to take flight. The boat recedes and shrinks, but her eyes see the boy all the better, clearer, and more distinctly. She waves until his pale face disappears beyond a huge hill. And much more after that. She waves for a long time.

Finally, she lowers her arms. She pulls hard, tightening the knot of her headscarf very firmly on her neck. She turns her back on the Angara and leaves the cliff.

Zuleikha will plod off, heeding neither the time nor the path, trying not to breathe, so she won't increase the pain. At Round Clearing, she'll notice a person – grayed, limping, with a stick – walking toward her. She and Ignatov will catch sight of one another and stop, he on one edge of the clearing, she on the other.

He will suddenly realize how much he's aged. Eyes that have lost their sharp sight will not be able to discern the wrinkles on Zuleikha's face or the gray in her hair. And she will sense that while the pain that fills the world hasn't gone, it has allowed her to breathe.

ACKNOWLEDGEMENTS

I first heard about *Zuleikha* before the book was even published, thanks to Elkost International Literary Agency, who represent Guzel Yakhina. Yulia Dobrovolskaya and Alexander Klimin of Elkost thought I might be interested in the novel. Of course I was – I love reading contemporary fiction set during the Soviet era – and I ended up enjoying the novel so much that I was more than happy to translate excerpts and, later, agree to translate the entire book for Oneworld. Thank you to Yulia and Alexander for thinking of me.

Guzel Yakhina has been unfailingly helpful, extraordinarily patient, and very warm in answering my numerous questions about details of the novel, its language, and her preferences for the translation. It's been a pleasure to meet with her and talk about the book, and I appreciate her flexibility when making suggestions and her trust in my work.

My colleague Liza Prudovskaya read through a draft of *Zuleikha*, checking for errors, answering hundreds of questions, and offering hundreds of additional suggestions. Liza's help is always an important part of my translation process but her ideas felt particularly important with *Zuleikha*, given the difficulties of decisions for translating Tatar words, historical and political vocabulary, and Guzel's beautiful descriptions of nature.

It's been a pleasure to work on my fifth book for Juliet Mabey and her team at Oneworld. As always, Juliet's edits and queries went a long, long way in transforming my manuscript into a consistent, logical, and readable English-language text and I'm especially thankful for her help on horse-related vocabulary, which always feels as mysterious to me in English as it does in Russian. I also thank Juliet (again!) for her strong interest in Russian contemporary fiction and willingness to bring books like *Zuleikha* to Anglophone readers. Assistant editor Alyson Coombes's cheerful help with a myriad of small issues that nobody ever likes to think about – copyright matters, schedules, and miscellaneous administrative questions that inevitably pop up – is always a welcome antidote to deadlines and the difficult decisions that any translation entails. Focused queries and creative suggestions from copyeditor Helen Szirtes kept me busy for weeks, pushing and inspiring me to reconsider, rewrite, and sharpen chunks of many difficult passages. I can't thank her enough for her many contributions to the text, as well as her sense of humor and dedication. I'm no versifier, so I'm very grateful for poet and translator George Szirtes's quick, slick work on the songs in the novel. I also appreciate Ruth Ahmedzai Kemp's help with vocabulary for prayers and holidays as well as proofreader Charlotte Norman's fantastic eye for spotting inconsistencies and nonsensical phrasing. As always, I'm thankful to production head Paul Nash for his clear schedules and instructions.

Thank you to everyone involved in the translation process and thank you to *Zuleikha*'s readers. I hope you enjoy Guzel's novel and Zuleikha's story as much as I did.

Lisa C. Hayden

Oneworld, Many Voices

Bringing you exceptional writing
from around the world

The Unit by Ninni Holmqvist (Swedish)
Translated by Marlaine Delargy

Twice Born by Margaret Mazzantini (Italian)
Translated by Ann Gagliardi

Things We Left Unsaid by Zoya Pirzad (Persian)
Translated by Franklin Lewis

The Space Between Us by Zoya Pirzad (Persian)
Translated by Amy Motlagh

The Hen Who Dreamed She Could Fly by Sun-mi Hwang
(Korean) Translated by Chi-Young Kim

Morning Sea by Margaret Mazzantini (Italian)
Translated by Ann Gagliardi

A Perfect Crime by A Yi (Chinese)
Translated by Anna Holmwood

The Meursault Investigation by Kamel Daoud (French)
Translated by John Cullen

Laurus by Eugene Vodolazkin (Russian)
Translated by Lisa C. Hayden

Masha Regina by Vadim Levental (Russian)
Translated by Lisa C. Hayden

French Concession by Xiao Bai (Chinese)
Translated by Chenxin Jiang

The Sky Over Lima by Juan Gómez Bárcena (Spanish)
Translated by Andrea Rosenberg

The Baghdad Clock by Shahad Al Rawi (Arabic)
Translated by Luke Leafgren

The Aviator by Eugene Vodolazkin (Russian)
Translated by Lisa C. Hayden

Lala by Jacek Dehnel (Polish)
Translated by Antonia Lloyd-Jones

Bogotá 39: New Voices from Latin America
(Spanish and Portuguese) Short story anthology

Last Instructions by Nir Hezroni (Hebrew)
Translated by Steven Cohen

Solovyov and Larionov by Eugene Vodolazkin (Russian)
Translated by Lisa C. Hayden

In/Half by Jasmin B. Frelih (Slovenian)
Translated by Jason Blake

What Hell Is Not by Alessandro D'Avenia (Italian)
Translated by Jeremy Parzen

Zuleikha by Guzel Yakhina (Russian)
Translated by Lisa C. Hayden

Mouthful of Birds by Samanta Schweblin (Spanish)
Translated by Megan McDowell

City of Jasmine by Olga Grjasnowa (German)
Translated by Katy Derbyshire

Things that Fall from the Sky by Selja Ahava (Finnish)
Translated by Emily Jeremiah and Fleur Jeremiah

Mrs Mohr Goes Missing by Maryla Szymiczkowa (Polish)
Translated by Antonia Lloyd-Jones

In the Shadow of Wolves by Alvydas Šlepikas (Lithuanian)
Translated by Romas Kïnka

Humiliation by Paulina Flores (Spanish)
Translated by Megan McDowell

Guzel Yakhina is a Russian author and filmmaker of Tatar origins. She graduated from the Kazan State Pedagogical University and completed her PhD at the Moscow Filmmaking School. *Zuleikha* is her first novel. In addition to the Big Book Award and the Yasnaya Polyana Award, *Zuleikha* also won the Prose of the Year Prize, the Ticket to the Stars Award and was a finalist for the Russian Booker Prize.

Lisa C. Hayden's translations from the Russian include Eugene Vodolazkin's *Laurus*, which won the Read Russia Award in 2016 and was shortlisted for the Oxford-Weidenfeld Prize. Her blog, Lizok's Bookshelf, examines contemporary Russian fiction. She lives in Maine, USA.